Praise

"I'm someone who devours big, epic books, and Joy Jordan-Lake's *Echoes of Us* takes her readers to the next level. This sweeping dual timeline novel, set in St. Simons Island, Georgia, during WWII and the present day, has all the jewels that historical fiction lovers crave: love, loss, secrets, sacrifices, insurmountable courage, a strong protagonist ahead of her time, and, of course (my fave)—a richly entangled love story that claws at the heartstrings and spans decades. Masterful, daring, and unputdownable, Jordan-Lake's gripping new novel soars."
—Lisa Barr, *New York Times* bestselling author of *Woman on Fire*

"A thrill of a ride . . . heartfelt and lyrical prose."
—Patti Callahan Henry, *New York Times* bestselling author of *The Secret Book of Flora Lea*

"This epic novel spans back and forth through time culminating in an immersive, affecting tale that echoes of Jeffrey Archer's *Kane and Abel* and Kristin Hannah's *The Women*. With compelling characters you can't help but fall for, audacious women braving the skies, and the sacrifices we make for those we love, Jordan-Lake delivers a story that brims with courage and hope. A big, beautiful book I couldn't put down."
—Rochelle B. Weinstein, bestselling author of *What You Do to Me*

"Exquisitely written with characters who linger long after you close the book. Read Joy Jordan-Lake; you will be enthralled."
—Robert Dugoni, *New York Times* and internationally bestselling author of *The Extraordinary Life of Sam Hell* and the Tracy Crosswhite series

"In *Echoes of Us*, author Joy Jordan-Lake illuminates a little-known piece of American history in WWII, bringing the conflict stateside. But the turmoil lies not only on Georgia soil—hearts and friendships are made and broken as unlikely friends come together for common effort even while their personal lives are stacked against each other. Secrets and heroism, loves and losses are woven into a compelling tapestry as characters sweep the reader into the world of this masterful saga."
—Camille Di Maio, bestselling author of *The Memory of Us* and *Come Fly with Me*

"There's a little-known story that my mother-in-law handed down to me: the sighting of German U-Boats off the Georgia Coast during WWII. Brilliant historical fiction novelist Joy Jordan-Lake takes this family tale of war-time heroism and creates a heavily-researched dual timeline page-turner, carving out compelling characters caught in dangerous situations they would never have anticipated. Historical mystery at its very finest from one of the best practitioners of the genre."
—Thelma Adams, bestselling author of *The Last Woman Standing* and *Bittersweet Brooklyn*

"*Echoes of Us* is a deftly woven, heart-tugging tale of courage, bittersweet love, and resilience, set amid the turbulence of world war. Joy Jordan-Lake's remarkable cast of characters will captivate you with their intertwined pasts and hold you in thrall until the poignant, extraordinary end. A moving paean to bravery, empathy, and forgiveness."
—Paulette Kennedy, bestselling author of *The Devil and Mrs. Davenport*

"From the salt-soaked shores of St. Simons Island, Joy Jordan-Lake's *Echoes of Us* is a love letter to a generation shaped by inequality and war, an immersive page-turner where the tragedy of the past holds the key to a future, and love becomes a tie that binds across the years."
—Sharon Cameron, #1 *New York Times* bestselling author of *The Light in Hidden Places* and *Artifice*

"Joy Jordan-Lake takes readers on an immersive historical journey brimming with detail and characters who positively leap off the page. Brilliantly researched and meticulously plotted, *Echoes of Us* runs the emotional gamut from loss to forgiveness, allowing us to step into the shoes of a protagonist, who both breaks our hearts and leaves us cheering."

—Barbara Davis, bestselling author of *The Keeper of Happy Endings* and *The Echo of Old Books*

ECHOES
of
US

Other Titles by Joy Jordan-Lake

A Bend of Light

Under a Gilded Moon

A Crazy-Much Love

A Tangled Mercy

Blue Hole Back Home

All the Little Animals

Sir Drake the Brave

ECHOES

of

US

A Novel

JOY JORDAN-LAKE

LAKE UNION
PUBLISHING

Text copyright © 2024 by Joy Jordan-Lake
All rights reserved.

Published by Lake Union Publishing, Seattle

www.apub.com

Amazon, the Amazon logo, and Lake Union Publishing are trademarks of Amazon.com, Inc., or its affiliates.

ISBN-13: 9781662514760 (hardcover)
ISBN-13: 9781662514753 (paperback)
ISBN-13: 9781662514746 (digital)

Cover design by Kathleen Lynch/Black Kat Design
Cover image: © PaulSG, © SEAN GLADWELL, © Oana Malaeru / Getty;
© Tim Robinson / plainpicture

Printed in the United States of America
First edition

*For all who served in and sacrificed during
World War II in big and small ways
and
for all who work every day for a world
of kindness, equality, and peace*

*Also for my late father, Adiel Moncrief Jordan,
whose favorite place in the world was St. Simons Island,
and for my extended family on his side who either grew
up there or cherished visiting: the Moncriefs, Mayberrys,
Shedds, Jacksons, Boricks, Whites, Mayberry-Whites,
Jordans, Jackson-Jordans, and Jordan-Lakes*

Sonnet 65

Since brass, nor stone, nor earth, nor boundless sea
But sad mortality o'ersways their power,
How with this rage shall beauty hold a plea,
Whose action is no stronger than a flower?
O, how shall summer's honey breath hold out
Against the wrackful siege of batt'ring days,
When rocks impregnable are not so stout,
Nor gates of steel so strong, but Time decays?
O, fearful meditation! Where, alack,
Shall Time's best jewel from Time's chest lie hid?
Or what strong hand can hold his swift foot back?
Or who his spoil of beauty can forbid?
O, none, unless this miracle have might,
That in black ink my love may still shine bright.
—William Shakespeare

Chapter 1

Hans Hessler

April 7, 1942
Off the coast of St. Simons Island, Georgia

At twilight, the U-boat rises to just below the surface, its periscope spearing up through the waves. Its view of the shore is good. Startling, even. A splay of lights from what might be a grand hotel blink cheerily back at the chief engineer.

"*Mein Gott*," he mutters.

The hotel's glow, golden and shimmering on the water, strikes him as what the Americans must be like themselves: bright and shiny and confident, still fresh to this war. Cocky, even, in all their New World, never-tested assumptions. They must be so different from him and this crew, who are bearded now, with boils and blemishes erupting over their boyish faces. They scrabble like rats for decent food. They stink, too, from long weeks without baths.

How untouched by deprivation these Americans still are, how not yet warped by horror. He feels resentment rise like bile in his throat, burning and sour.

Verdammt, Hans thinks, though even a full ocean away from his mother, he does not curse aloud. *Why do they have to be such easy prey, these Americans?*

Peering into the periscope should be the commander's job—and even now he rests one hand on the ocular box like he's laying claim to his territory. As the chief engineer, Hans has been invited—commanded, actually—to look, which could mean the commander is wary. Maybe beneath all his glinting medals, he's reliving his mistake with the Portuguese tanker, a neutral ship he mistook for an Allied vessel and torpedoed to shards.

"You see . . . what, precisely?" the commander demands from behind.

His voice has gone husky. Dehydration, no doubt—they never have enough drinking water inside this cigarette lighter of a ship. But maybe fear too.

"Can the Americans," Hans wonders aloud, "really be this stupid? The lights on the shore, they're blazing."

His voice, too, is hoarse. He's been trapped in this straitjacket of steel himself for weeks now—he does not let himself count how many.

But the commander makes no response. Hans's speech is snarled over with a rough rural Bavarian accent from the south of his country, one that a sophisticated German from the north very well might not understand—or acknowledge if he did. Either way, the commander merely clenches his jaw, his hands clasped behind his back.

Hans takes one last look at the stretch of water and the glowing island beyond.

These ridiculous people, he thinks, *drinking their port, surrounded by palms. Do they not know that in New York City, also blazing with light, this very sub only a few weeks ago hunted prey? Like now, it was the light that allowed the kill. These too-happy, too-shiny people can't possibly know just how close Death is stalking.*

Their ignorance—their innocence too—is about to be shattered. Snuffed out. Ruined. As war does. As war has already done to Hans.

He is homesick. He is frightened. Above all, he must never appear to be either of these.

Closing his eyes, he pictures the farm back home in Bavaria: its green shutters sturdy, its window boxes brimming with red geraniums, the spruces and fir towering above its steeply pitched roof. For a moment, he forgets the commander standing at his elbow and Death coiled around the ocular box, waiting.

Now he forces his eyes open again, presses his forehead to the cold steel.

Before he can stop himself, before he can pretend nothing new is passing the scope, Hans gasps.

Chapter 2

Hadley Jacks

April 7, 2022
Off the coast of St. Simons Island

The word *tragedy*—I'm sure that's what he just said—spins me around at the rail of the yacht, and I suck in my breath. The wind whips my hair into my face. "*Here*, did you say? How long ago?"

Nothing about this place feels tragic—the ocean swelling and sparkling around us at twilight, the island off to our port with its palms and live oaks, its pastel cottages hemming a golden beach, a line of red tiled roofs and blue beach umbrellas suggesting a posh resort.

The captain's face is fixed ahead, his jaw and shoulders squared, rigid even. As if speaking isn't technically allowed in his role.

Patience has never been one of my virtues, but I manage to wait, focusing on the yacht's bow two stories below where we stand on the flybridge. The Atlantic defers to us, parting in shimmering blue fans on each side.

This, I think, *must be what it's like to have power and influence—and apparently, money to burn.*

As if reading my thoughts, the captain swings his head back toward our host, who sits a few yards away—his back almost preternaturally straight, his gray suit impeccably tailored and pressed—above a teak deck no doubt custom crafted for lolling about. I've worked for his type before: the sort of man who's become his own monument to wealth, so much of too much that it's turned him to stone.

Though his face shows no expression, he's listening to my sister, who is laughing and lifting her glass of chardonnay. Because Kitzie could find kinship and connection with an eel.

"Eighty years ago today exactly. That is, from tonight."

The voice jolts me back to attention, though it takes me an instant to realize it's the captain answering my question.

"And yeah. Right here," he adds. But that's all, as if he's now used up his daily quota of words.

With his eyes covered by Ray-Bans, his jaw rigid, his feet planted, with tanned forearms and hands unmoving on the ship's wheel, I'd swear he wasn't real—just some heavily themed restaurant's mannequin of a sea captain—if some of the sun-bleached hair poking out from under his cap didn't lift just a bit in the breeze or the muscles under his polo didn't tense. Now and then, too, his jaw, scruffy with blond stubble, shifts side to side. He's younger than I first thought.

"What sort of tragedy?" I ask, glancing back toward the yacht's owner.

Ernst Hessler is watching me—watching us—his eyes flicking forward and back, even as he gives a sharp nod to something my sister has said.

What I'd like to do is stay here at the rail and wait for the captain to finish his story—his hint of one, at least, with that *tragedy . . . eighty years ago . . . here*. I want to let the big band music streaming from the yacht's sound system—"Begin the Beguine"—buoy me in its swirling currents of horns and progressions and carry me with it.

I want, too, to study this shore in the last of the day's light—the way the pelicans dive and the herons soar, a silver surf washing across the sand.

Instead, though, I slink awkwardly back to my seat, because yachts apparently make me feel as out of place as a washboard at a Sotheby's auction, and because it's clear the captain has said all he plans to for the moment, and because my sister—bless Kitzie's too-friendly, too-trusting heart—ought not be left alone too long with our host.

Easing back into my seat beside Kitz, the canvas warm under my skirt—a little shorter than I remembered when I threw it on before catching our flight and a little shorter than one wants on a boat, but it's the least of my worries. I watch the brass ice bucket sweat as if it's nervous too.

I return the stare from Hessler and try my best smile, the professional one full of warmth, goodwill, and assurance of a positive return on investment. We might be young, Kitzie and I, for high-dollar clients, but we're good, *darn good*, at what we do. Also, in our late twenties now, we're not *terribly* young. In street-smart years, in fact, we're late middle aged.

He responds by, of all things, turning away. "We are nearly arrived," Hessler announces, his German accent pronounced. He pauses, apparently annoyed by something at the rear of the flybridge, toward the boat's stern. A phalanx of teak chairs with flawless white canvas cushions march across the back rail, each chair about three inches apart. Yet Hessler rises, strides to one end—*Agile for his age*, I think—and shifts a chair a quarter inch to the right.

In our business, Kitzie's and mine, we've recently moved up to planning all sorts of grand events for grand big-spending clients, but we've kept to our original rule: we work only for people we like and trust. About our host just now, I already have doubts. Mostly just a gut feeling, but my track record for judging books by their covers and men by first impressions is solid.

The same goes for judging men in my dating life. I can spot the liars, cheaters, and emotional train wrecks from acres away, ones with killer smiles that do *not*, it turns out, correlate with colossally big hearts. Safer, then, just to build my own walls and the walls around our business still higher, particularly since my sister lives life like she's running the world's welcome desk.

Also, Kitzie hasn't read, I'm guessing, the article from *Forbes* I texted her on the long flight here, about the turmoil at Ernst Hessler's international real estate development firm, Boundless: an ugly multifamily battle for determining the firm's future direction. I might not know much about family—Kitzie's and mine mostly missing in action. But corporate family battles strike me as prone to blast out of control—casualties by the Porsche load—so best to stay well away.

"Upon arrival"—Hessler lowers himself into the precise middle of his seat—"I will offer some background. All that I am able. For some questions, I have nothing to offer as answers." Stiffly, he reaches for a black leather briefcase and rifles through whatever it holds.

"An awful lot of murkiness," I murmur to Kitz, "for us to be plunging into."

"Look for the good," she murmurs back. "I'm sure it's there."

Typical. Somewhere in our childhood of hard knocks and loss, while I watched for danger around every bend—where, for the record, it usually lurked—my sister found her own invisible rose-colored glasses that she never, *ever* takes off. Kindness: that's what she exudes with every breath. It makes her everyone's favorite person, especially mine.

But also, between you and me, Kitzie is not someone who sees trouble crouched right in front of her nose—or, quite possibly, across a yacht's teak-and-brass table.

"Look for the good," she says again and squeezes my hand.

But with very few hours of sleep in the last couple of days, wound tight with caffeine and rubbed raw with worry, I might not be capable of it just now. I set my chardonnay down inside the teak table's brass divots—cupholders in Yachtland, I assume—since the last thing I need right now is to relax, topple my drink, or kick loose the whole messy spool of what I'm thinking and let it go rolling around out loud.

Our host here on this floating palazzo turns his profile to me. His features jut out, startlingly craggy and washed of all color.

Like the white cliffs of Dover, I think. *Where bluebirds fly over.*
Although those aren't quite the words of the song.

It's a fair description of the face, though, trust me, and also not too surprising that those lyrics dropped into my head. All during the long flight from LA, my brain lit bright with three lattes, I read up on the background for this World War II lollapalooza of an event our host has envisioned. I crunched some figures on what it might cost—a *freaking bundle* is the answer to that. I also began some research, brushing up on my 1940s history, facts left rusting since college. Turned out to be more rust than facts, to be honest, so I stayed up the whole red-eye reading and taking notes so my sister could sleep.

Ernst Hessler, he of the white-cliffs face, wants us to take over the apparently bungled planning of a reunion set to take place in one month, which will bring together three families descended from three soldiers—the most unlikely of friends, we've been told: one American, one Englishman, and one Axis prisoner of war—who met on St. Simons Island, of all places, during World War II. Why a businessman from Berlin would be the one ensuring this reunion takes place, I haven't a clue. Not yet.

Our host has been less than forthcoming—in the way of crypts and granite cliffs. But he's promised a clearer picture once we reach the site of the three soldiers' meeting, some resort hotel that during the war was requisitioned for training.

I wouldn't be here at all, you understand, if I'd gone with my gut and just said *no* after the first peculiar phone call from Berlin. But in the business we run together, my sister and I agree that we always have to agree, meaning that when she insisted we at least let him fly us out to learn more, I had to come.

"So many red flags already," I say under my breath.

As the captain glances again over his shoulder toward us, his mouth opens like he might say something, then tightens into a line. Those Ray-Bans and the shiny brim of his cap effectively hide his eyes, but you can tell a lot by the set of a guy's jaw. His says he's not loving his job. Anything but happy to be here.

My sister, by contrast, is leaning forward, lifting her wine in a toast to something our host has said.

Me, I feel pushed back, nearly pinned to my seat by our increasing speed. The engine's roar feels as if it's drilling into my inner ear. I wonder for an instant if this angry young captain in shades is piloting the yacht at so many knots above what's surely normal precisely to make chitchat a challenge.

Ridiculous, I decide.

Still . . . there's something not right here that I can almost taste on the breeze.

Ernst Hessler seems to sense I'm the one he'll need to convince to take on this job—that Kitzie is a big *yes* to life and feels no need to look under the hood, ever. Me, I need the hoses flushed, the pistons lubed, and every part checked for soundness before I'll drive a job off the lot.

Watching my face, our host pulls an envelope from the breast pocket of his suit and hands it to me. From inside, I pull out a black-and-white photo, and I bend over it to guard it from the wind. It's been torn down the middle and clumsily put back together with yellowed cellophane tape.

On one side of the tear, a young woman in white shorts, with brown hair tumbling to her shoulders, stands laughing, head thrown back, as a dark-haired man on the other side of the rip tugs her by the hand. Running down the beach, he's in khakis and a white T-shirt, his face turned away from the camera. The shoulder of another man, this one in uniform, appears at the bottom right of the picture.

I run a finger above the figures without touching them, then raise my voice—essentially to a shout—above the engine. "And who might this be?"

The music—"Moonlight Serenade" now—has been turned down a notch, but still swirls dreamily from the speakers. "Some of the key people you will get to know as you work," Hessler replies, his mouth closing into a thin line.

It's evasive at best. And he's assuming we'll take the job.

Maybe people with this much money rarely hear the word no. *To anything, ever. But he hasn't gotten our final answer.*

Flipping to the photograph's back, I squint at the handwriting, smeared and faded.

A date comes first in slanted numbers.

"*May* something, *1945*," I read aloud. The actual day is blurred.

Then, from the line under that, "*Janie*. No, wait. Maybe *Joannie*. That's it. *Joannie and us.*"

Across the whole glossy backside run slashes and blobs forming a single word that takes me a moment to make sense of, which I blurt the moment the letters fall into place.

"*Traitor.*"

My jaw drops at the punch of the word. Looking up, I meet Hessler's eye. He's waiting, squinting to gauge my reaction.

"Oh my," Kitzie says.

"*Traitor?*" I ask. "That's quite a scrapbook caption."

Our host is watching my face. "Indeed."

"Mr. Hessler, you must think I'm one of those people who'd be roped in by a whiff of romantic or, given the wartime era, political intrigue. Or both."

His gaze flicks down to the picture in my hand, then back up to me—a challenge. *You would appear to be* exactly *one of those people,* his look seems to say.

I try for nonchalance as, clutching its slim white edges, I show the photo to Kitzie. "So. This man running down the beach is one of the three friends, I assume?"

A single nod.

"And which person in this picture was the traitor?"

Hessler's gaze drops again to the photo. "As it was told to me, these were three men with a deep friendship. Also, a complicated one."

"But the young woman, Joannie. How does she figure in?"

"Oh *my*," Kitzie breathes as she scans the picture and the scrawl on its back.

"My father," Hessler says, not addressing my question.

"He's the man on the beach with his face turned away?"

"*Nein.* My father was quite fair. Blond, I mean. As I am."

Hessler's hair is iron gray and surely has been for decades, but I don't argue the point. "Your father was one of the three soldiers who became friends?"

Again, that slice of a nod.

I glance down at the image. The uniformed shoulder in the corner could hardly be a German prisoner of war. "Was your father the one holding the camera?"

"This I do not know. The photograph, it was among the items which my father left for me at his death."

"I'm sorry for your loss," Kitz and I offer in unison.

"The death, this was recent. However, he was lost to us for some years. Dementia."

"I'm so sorry," I say again, Kitz echoing me. We've not walked through dementia with a loved one—no loved ones stayed around long enough. But we know, Kitz and I do, the grief of life ripping away goodness and health and love.

It's my turn now to study his face, and I wonder if I've misjudged the man—if his hard, cold exterior is as much the result of the pain of loss as it is the privilege of too much.

Hessler looks away and then back. "I know little more of this photograph than you, only that it was somehow quite important to him. Before his death, I was focused primarily on the running of the corporation."

"Boundless," I say quietly.

"This is correct. Built by these three men, and later, those of us who were in line to . . ." He pauses here, searching for the right words as his eyes drift over his boat and to his captain, where he seems to find the proper imagery. "To take the helm. Stories of the old days"—he jerks his chin toward the photo—"seemed trivial at the time. Obviously, now, when it matters, it is too late to ask."

"If I may, Mr. Hessler," I ask, "why does it matter especially now?"

He meets my gaze, and the flintiness has returned to his tone. "It matters."

He offers no more than that.

Traitor, I hear so clearly it might as well be in the screech of the gulls that dip and glide beside us.

I stare down at the photo clutched in my hand. A whole world at war, a woman and three men, the most unlikely of friends.

I scan the handwriting on its yellowed backside again.

May . . . then the date I can't read . . . *1945.*

Joannie and us.

And then, once more, the word scrawled in large, angry letters across it all.

Traitor.

Chapter 3

Joannie DuBarry

April 7, 1942
Off the coast of St. Simons Island

Joannie has stayed out too long, too close to dusk, the deep blue sea darkening to an impenetrable black. But she has to know if she truly saw what she thought she did.

She holds the tiller steady, despite both arms going numb. Releasing the mainsail to slow the boat, she stares through the mist at what looks for all the world like a periscope.

"Good God," she murmurs. "It can't be."

Because the United States is only officially four months into this war, if you don't count the lend-lease program to try and back up the poor blitzkrieged British and other Allies. The Japanese might have wreaked destruction on American ships and sailors just this past December, but that was Hawaii—not even a state, just a territory floating alone all the way out there in the Pacific. The Nazis are still a whole vast Atlantic away from Georgia.

Aren't they?

Yet there it is, a gray line rising straight above the roll of the waves. At the top of the line, a disk of some sort or a piece of glass reflects the last of the day's light.

"Good *God*," she says again. But there is no one to hear her.

She holds her breath. Breathing might draw attention to her little cockleshell of a sailboat.

The disk appears to turn as Joannie huddles lower down into her hull. For the first time, she regrets the coat upon coat of lacquer she stroked so lovingly onto the boat's unpainted wood. In daylight, the hull glows golden brown beneath its white mainsail and jib. Here at twilight, that same high-polished hull might easily catch the last sputtering beams of the sun sinking low to the west.

Might catch the eye of an attentive periscope operator.

Slowly, carefully, since too quick a movement might draw more attention to her little boat, Joannie hauls the sheet tighter, its tight-braided length comforting under her fingers as the mainsail and jib fill. Sliding the tiller hard to the left, she aims the boat's bow back toward shore. For a moment, the wind lifts her ponytail like a flag.

"Germans," she murmurs. "Dear God."

The sea, swelling and heaving beneath her, does not answer her back as her sailboat heels toward the St. Simons Island Pier.

But neither does the sea contradict her.

That scope, she realizes, could still be trained even now on her back.

She and her boat might be small, but she's spotted something she shouldn't have. She needs to give warning. Once the local authorities hear what she's seen, the Civil Air Patrol will deploy its ragtag fleet of private planes, bombs precariously strapped to their wings, and track down this sub.

Assuming she reaches shore.

Small or not, she has become, she knows, a target worth taking down.

Chapter 4

Hans

He had been just about to let loose the handles of the ocular box and step back from the periscope when something up above billowed past. Like a cloud, though it was too low for that.

A ghost, perhaps.

Now Hans presses his forehead back to the steel.

"You see something?" the commander demands. "A ship is approaching from the harbor, yes?"

"Not a ship." Hans squints. "Much smaller. Nothing but a sailboat. Civilian. Of no significance."

The smallest sailboat, in fact, he has ever seen. He can't be certain, but a lone figure, just a glimpse of a silhouette, appears to sit at the stern. Perhaps even . . . though he cannot be sure . . . perhaps even a swing of a ponytail.

My God, surely not a girl.

"Sir, it is gone," he lies. "Perhaps only a cloud after all."

The commander scowls. "We watch," he says at last. "Then we strike." He pivots in place—no room on this boat for swaggering away to make a point. "Is this understood, Hessler?"

Hans nods. They are too cramped—man upon man upon metal—for him to raise an arm in salute, and the commander is already facing about.

Hans takes one last look in the periscope, then whispers—in English, no less, for reasons he couldn't have said, *"What the hell?"*

The commander spins around. *"Was zur Hölle?"*

It's the same question, only in German—and this time a demand, curt and angry, to know what Hans has spotted.

Their gazes collide. A flash of accusation from the commander. A spark of defensiveness from the chief engineer. But neither speaks.

Hans squints back into the periscope. The little vessel above bobs on the waves, its sails two slim triangles of white backdropped by the lights of those so-cocky, so-unprepared Americans, eating and drinking and supposing so naively that they are safe here in their homeland.

"You have spotted something?" the commander demands again.

There's no help for it. He is elbowing Hans aside and will see for himself.

Reluctantly, fearing for the figure on the tiny boat who's looking furtively back toward the periscope, Hans steps away to let the commander look.

If this lone mariner has noticed the scope jutting out of the water, surely he'll—or, God help us, *she'll*—report it to someone . . . So then, even this skinny, young civilian sailor in this tiny, not-even-seaworthy *Ruine* of a boat will be a threat to the war machine that is the Reich.

No doubt the skinny little civilian sailor, who is perhaps just a slip of a girl, will need to be destroyed.

Why? Hans thinks. *Why must the appetites of whole nations come down to this, a girl on a boat?*

He berates himself, remembering he shouldn't give a damn about one little boat in this whole vast sea of troubles. For two heartbeats, it works: his pulse slows.

Except that billowing sail and that ponytail feel like symbols of what's happened to him: he's no longer fighting for the Fatherland, or for his own family. Not even demonstrating his own courage. No, he's merely one minuscule cog in a vast, merciless machine run by, Hans has come to suspect, a pack of madmen.

Hans turns so the commander can't see his face, no doubt drained of all color. The steel walls of the sub are closing in fast, crushing him, crushing them all. Sweat pours down his back and neck, his vision blurred.

Up so close to the surface, *U-123* rocks with the waves, and his stomach roils, less with the currents than with what is coming. Death has coiled itself here in this capsule of steel, has slithered through every bunk and torpedo shaft. Death is ready again now, poised to strike.

It's not his role, giving the next order: to fire the conning tower's guns. They must eliminate the potential informant, and Hans is now in the way of achieving that.

"Hessler!"

Someone shoves him to one side, slamming him into a wall.

For a moment, only one blissful moment, Hans is simply up there on top of the water, boating, just boating, trolling about on a friendly sea, the American sun warm on his cheeks.

Chapter 5

Hadley

April 7, 2022

"Made it hard to spot the subs, how dark the water is. Sediment from the marshes."

It's several beats before I realize the voice has come from the yacht's captain, his head angled toward me, though I still can't see his eyes behind those sunglasses. My uneasiness about this whole thing has made me pace, and I've returned to the flybridge's rail.

Honestly, I didn't particularly mean to comment on the color of the ocean out loud. This water, with the last of the day's light sifting down on its swells, has some sort of soul-tugging pull in the whorls of deep blue and green and brown. It's darker, though, than what I'd have imagined.

"Wait. *Subs?*" I ask. "As in German subs? But they couldn't have been here on this side of the Atlantic, certainly not so close to shore." I wait a beat. "Could they?"

The captain's head swings around fully to face me. His nonanswer—a little arrogant, if you ask me—tells me that, once again, my supply of World War II information appears more rust than supply.

Still, that doesn't excuse the guy's rudeness.

Leaning on the flybridge's railing, I hold the envelope and its photo carefully as I stare at the sea below. I try to imagine a long cylinder of steel sweeping past under the surface.

Even on this warm April evening, my skin goes clammy and cold. When I look up, Ernst Hessler is staring again at me. Since I've apparently absconded with his photo, I let him see me slip it into its envelope, then carefully into the pocket of my sundress where it can't be whipped away by the wind.

I should hand it back, of course. Of course I should. But it feels like I'm already connected somehow, like these secrets have suddenly, illogically become mine to protect.

Ironic, these feelings of mine, not wanting to betray these people, especially given the word scrawled on the photograph's back.

As the next song spirals out of the yacht's speakers, the trombones of "It's Been a Long, Long Time" sliding, the trumpets and saxes teasing and swelling, I try to imagine the story behind the ripped photograph, what sort of passions or patriotism or loyalties—or betrayals—drove these people.

Hessler must've caught snippets of my conversation with the captain. Marching forward, he pauses to mutter some sort of correction to the captain, a spew of words I can't fully make out—German profanity, for all I know—then turns his attention to me.

"Unterseeboot." Hessler enunciates each syllable like he's nailing down roofing tiles.

I feel a stab of compassion for the captain. Below the stoical mask, the muscles of his shoulders and back contract under his polo, the only indication he heard Hessler's invective.

Grudgingly, I turn back to our host. "You were saying, Mr. Hessler?"

"*U-boat* was, of course, short for *Unterseeboot*. A boat *under the sea*." He says this last slowly, as if he assumes two young American women need time to process big words. "The speed and the endurance of the *Unterseeboot* surpassed the submarines of the Allies."

"We do agree, though, I hope," I say, "about which side we're glad won the war, yes?"

But there's no time for Hessler to answer or for Kitz to jump in, covering for my impertinence to our host. The captain has pushed the throttle and the yacht's speed faster, so suddenly my hair whips my face, and whatever question I might've asked next is blown back into my throat. I'm left to grip the yacht's rail to keep from being knocked off my heels as our host stalks to the wheel.

"Stop this," Hessler hisses to the captain. "Do you not see they are nearly knocked off balance?"

The captain lowers his voice—though not so much that I can't hear. "You hired me to drive your yacht, not to coddle a couple of spoiled Californians who wear pink stilts out on the open ocean."

Livid, I look down at the coral knockoff designer sandals I'm wearing—which pinch and which I cannot stand, granted, but which my sister chose for me. And *coddle? Spoiled Californians?* It's a swipe that could not be more wrong. I'd like to list for him all the meals my sister and I made of Ritz Crackers and RC Cola, the only food left in the house. I'd like to describe our mom, but I have almost no memory of her, except of me begging the form curled into itself on the couch to get up, begging day after day, until that last time, she couldn't.

But these aren't things I share with strangers, *ever*—at the risk of sounding pathetic or weak. Instead, crossing my arms, I stare at the captain so he'll register that I heard, but he's focused solely on the sea.

I turn my back to him and let the wind cool my cheeks, hot with fury.

Plucking the photo back out of its envelope for a moment and careful to hold its corner against the buffeting wind, I squint at the uniformed shoulder and at the man and woman running down the beach together, their moment of unbridled joy captured by a third person's gaze—the man with the uniformed shoulder—and a fourth person's camera.

Traitor, I see again on the back, the sheer vehemence of the word lifting it off the slick back of the print so that it seems to throb.

I stare down into the deep blue of the sea and find I'm looking for flashes of silver, a sub just beginning to surface, its conning tower rising up through the waves, its deck guns ready to fire.

Chapter 6

Joannie

April 7, 1942

Heart pounding so hard it feels as if it might drown out the crash of the waves, Joan shoves the tiller and hauls on the sheet, bringing the mainsail into a broad reach. She will not, she will *not* look behind again to see if the sub has surfaced or if sailors are scrambling up onto the tower to man guns.

All she can do is sail her little craft downwind as fast as she can, jibing the mainsail from one broad reach to the next, aiming for the light at the end of the village pier. All she can do is hope to outrun what she thinks—what she *knows*, by God—she saw.

If a U-boat is lurking here in the waters off her little island, it might be willing to aim its deck guns on some annoyance like her, but it came here looking for bigger targets. For the beach of a hotel like the King and Prince. Or for whole ships it might torpedo to shreds.

This desperation, this urgency makes her jibe the boat again for another broad reach, then yank up the centerboard for greater speed. A plane buzzes low overhead—searching for U-boats, no doubt—but it's flying too fast, its pilot merely going through the motions.

So all-fired sure there can't be any German subs on our quiet coast. Not yet.

The pier is ahead, if she can just reach it in time. If she can just sail fast enough, live long enough to relay what she's seen, ships and men can be saved.

She will not, she will *not* turn again to look behind.

Chapter 7

Hadley

April 7, 2022

Making myself face forward at the rail, I feel sure Ernst Hessler watches my every move and the captain's. He appears to miss no detail. I refuse to give him the satisfaction of my looking rattled.

The sea air sweet, smelling of brine and faintly of fish, I draw a long breath as the yacht arcs suddenly to the left to round the northern tip of the island.

Hessler barks orders behind us while the captain, not turning his head, pulls back steadily on the throttle, slowing the yacht as it enters the intracoastal waterway that runs between the island and the mainland.

"The tragedy I mentioned," the captain begins. "Eighty years ago today."

Still incensed by his *coddled* and *spoiled* comment, I'm in no mood to make nice, so I turn to face him but don't speak.

"You should know about what happened," he adds.

A beat passes in which he flips up his shades—a sunburn across his cheekbones—and I think he'll tell the story. But, lowering his shades, he jerks his head back toward Hessler instead. "Although he'll want to describe it himself."

I bet he will, I think. Hessler, after all, has shown himself to want to control every detail.

Our host has stepped to the rear of the flybridge again—this time to take a cell call, one hand pressed over one ear as he barks into the phone.

"So, Hadley Jacks, you and your sister will be planning this event," the captain says.

It's not a question, the way he says it. But I answer it anyway, if only because I don't like the assumption that Hessler can just throw money at my sister and me and we'll do what he wants, no questions asked.

My arms remain crossed over my chest. "We've not signed a contract yet, on either side." It's as much as he needs to know.

His gaze does a quick sweep, and I get his point: the yacht itself, the wine, the charming island where Hessler will pay for our dinner, our accommodations. The captain's implying Kitz and I are already in deep, and I bristle—partly because he's not wrong.

"Obviously, Mr. Hessler has been generous to fly us out here." *In first class,* I think but don't add aloud. *With what felt like acres of room to spread out. Warmed brie, toasted baguette slices, chilled champagne. And now this lovely boat ride . . .*

A few yards away, Kitzie is smiling as though she's enjoying every moment, gazing at the island downright rapturously. As if she were coming home after a long absence.

I try to recall if I've ever once seen her look so ecstatic at returning to LA after one of our trips.

Never, I decide. *After five years of living in LA, not even close.*

Good God. Clearly it can't be Hessler who's the attraction. So is it this place that's already seduced her?

"Speaking of being seduced . . ." This part I don't realize I've said aloud until Angry Young Captain's head swings slowly toward me.

"By Hessler," I hurry to say, and I flick a hand toward the island. "By that, I mean." And now I'm piling up words to cover the flush that's crept again up my neck and face. "It's always best not to fall in love." One of Angry Young Captain's eyebrows lifts above the Ray-Bans. "With a *destination*, I mean."

Holy Mother of God, I need to quit talking.

I'm about to retreat while I can, clearly needing to exit this conversation and totter on my knockoff sandals back to my seat, but the captain's head twitches my way again.

"So *we* refers to . . . You and your sister are the deciders at your firm?"

"The deciders and the entire staff. We punch way above our weight, you could say. We like it that way, just my sister and me, working pretty much twenty-four seven." *Anything but coddled or spoiled,* I think but don't say. "We run our business together out of Pasadena."

"Storied Events." He offers our business' name with a quirk at one end of his mouth. He's amused, and this annoys me enormously. I fight the urge to smack him right in the smirk.

"That's right. Despite the, okay, admittedly grandiose drama of our name—my sister was a theater major in college, so *grandiose* and *drama* are not to be sneezed at. I take it you're no big fan of the event planning industry."

Eyes focused ahead on the ocean, he glances down once at a dial and once, even more quickly, at me. "Always seems to me like just people with more money than sense paying for champagne fountains, chandeliers hanging from big outdoor tents, and upholstered sofas sitting out on the grass—with lots of string lights thrown in."

"What, and steering a Berliner's yacht is saving the world?"

They're surprisingly mean, these words of mine, and I'm rarely mean. Defensive maybe, protective of my sister and what we've survived and then built all by ourselves, but not mean. Another reason not to like this captain fellow—for the way he's gotten under my skin.

But if he heard me, the captain's face doesn't change.

25

"You know," I add, "if I had the time or patience, I'd tell you all sorts of heartwarming tales of how these sorts of events bring people together. As it is, since your path and mine will never be crossing again, I'll leave it at this: we're proud of what we do, my sister and I. We're no-nonsense businesswomen. In a good cop, bad cop kind of way."

"And you'd be the latter."

"I am ferociously protective, you could say. Of my sister. Of our business."

Kitzie's not coddled but gentle, too gentle, I want to shake him and explain. *Our whole lives it's always been my role to protect. To make up for the family that was never there, to be a buffer in all the stiff winds of life.*

Coddled? *Really? You have no idea.*

He glances back over his shoulder, and I follow the glance: my sister tilts her pale, pretty face—slightly pink today from the sun—and smiles back at the sky.

Angry Young Captain faces straight forward again. "Maybe it's just me, but your sister looks like she's ready to start working on this reunion before dinner."

It's more blunt than I like in a yacht captain—not that I've had one before, but in theory.

Truth is, though, she does look a little transported.

Because she's guileless, I want to say. *The meek might inherit the earth someday, but in this meantime we call Real Life, the meek are just sitting ducks.*

"Kitz and I decide everything together." This next, I add more to myself: "Which is maybe why, to be honest, I'm tense as an overstrung banjo right now."

His eyes leave the waterway, just for a flash, and one eyebrow lifts above the Ray-Bans. *"Banjo?"*

"Not your favorite instrument? Something else in addition to event planning you don't approve of?"

"Doesn't sound much like a California chick with her own glitzy business, that's all."

That word *glitzy.* I like him even less, despite the nice forearms and the curls poking out from under the ridiculous hat.

He guides the boat toward a marina and decreases speed.

"I'm not a Californian, by the way. At all. We're—" But there's no explaining our growing-up years, Kitzie's and mine, in a spate of small South Carolina towns where the people mostly tended hydrangeas under towering pines and roasted brussels sprouts in balsamic reductions at chic new eateries on revitalized Main Streets, while a handful—including, apparently, more than one generation of my family—cooked meth in the basement. No explaining in whatever short splash of this cruise we have left.

Meanwhile, Hessler has put his cell back in his breast pocket, and Kitzie has gone from buoyant to bubbly. Speaking loudly while the yacht is purring along the intercoastal waterway slowly now, she can be heard—all too well—over the engine.

"Hadley and I so appreciate your belief that Storied Events is the right firm to deliver a stellar reunion that not only meets but far exceeds your vision."

"I should mention up front, Mr. Hessler," I interject from the forward railing, "that, as I'm sure you'd anticipate, the sort of event you've described—including, apparently, our research into the major players and their relationships during the war, in addition to the complexity of an event of this size scheduled so soon—comes with *quite* a hefty price tag. Which I'm sure a businessman of your experience would anticipate."

Angry Young Captain's head cocks my way, voice low so only I'll hear. "Although Good Cop sounds excited enough, she'd plan the whole reunion weekend for free."

Jackass, I want to say. *Captain Jackass.*

Instead, I straighten, turn toward the ship's wheel and murmur right back to him. "My sister's the lamb who can usually sweet-talk the lion into lying down, rolling over, and waiting a few hours to eat. Me, on the other hand, I'm the one who stands up with the whip and the chair, ready when the sweet talk wears off with the lion. Either way, we've got it covered."

I make my way back toward the loveseat, with its flawless white canvas.

Kitzie clears her throat, and I know it's my cue to say something polite.

"Your boat is delightful." It's the truth—and has the advantage of having nothing to do with Hessler himself.

"Lürssen," Hessler corrects me.

"Pardon?"

"This *yacht* is a *Lürssen*."

I take that to mean the brand or the builder—and that I should be impressed. Also, that I should avoid the word *boat*—apparently too plebian—at all costs in the future. Like two chicks who grew up in the rural South Carolina foster care system have opinions about brand names of yachts.

Ah, a Lürssen, is it? In that case, we'll come after all. We are so relieved *the soiree isn't just on . . . well, you know, just any old yacht.*

Dahling, do grab my wrap. Our Lürssen's waiting . . .

"Lürssen," I say. "Of course."

When you're this rich, do you pinch millions instead of pennies? Do you pay more than the sticker price just for kicks?

I have questions I'd like to ask. Meanwhile, it's definitely the fanciest taxi I've ever taken from an airport.

We slow to canoeing speed as we enter the outskirts of the marina, where several other yachts and speedboats are docked, though none as elaborate as the Lürssen.

I sit forward and say to Hessler, "I'd love to hear more of the three friends at the heart of this reunion. Of this woman, Joannie, too. Of whatever would have provoked someone to rip the photo and scrawl *Traitor* on the back. And the tragedy that happened out there in the open water eighty years ago tonight."

After a blink of surprise—possibly that I know of the tragedy—Hessler rises. "Yes. Soon. Watch the bow on the starboard side." He motions to the right front of the boat, apparently in case the captain might be foggy on his nautical terms.

The captain turns, his face inscrutable as ever—but his jaw shifts forward and back. I amuse myself for a moment imagining exactly what words he's holding in.

As the captain eases the Lürssen into a slip, an old woman watches us from a bench on the dock. She's wearing white boat shoes, white capris, and a navy-and-white striped top, a navy scarf at her neck. A cane leaning against her leg, she looks somehow both immensely comfortable and immensely cute.

The woman's hair tumbles in short curls all over her head, as starkly white as her capris. Her skin appears nearly transparent, the delicate opacity of a pork dumpling in LA's Chinatown. I lift a hand to her, and her face muscles readjust—not a smile, exactly, but something dreamier, as if her mind is far away and she's only half seeing me.

Leaning back toward the yacht's wheel, I ask the captain, "You come here often?"

I realize too late it sounds like a pickup line in a bar. Sure enough, one of his eyebrows lifts again above the Ray-Bans.

"What I mean is, do you come here to the St. Simons Marina enough to know who that older woman might be?" I gesture with my head toward the bench on the dock below us.

The captain doesn't answer at first, an insolence that doesn't surprise me this time. But then, cutting the engine, he nods. Just a quick swipe of his head.

"She's a fixture." It's all he offers. Looks away, even.

I turn back to the dock to find the woman has risen from her bench. For an instant, I have the strange feeling again that she's looking at me—as if she waited here precisely for our boat—our *Lürssen*—to come in.

But I'm wrong. She's looking far past me, out to the waterway and beyond it, to the ocean. From this distance, I can't tell if the expression on her face is fear or some twinge of pain or the unearthing of a long-buried memory.

As she gazes out at the sea, her chin suddenly rises as if she's desperately mustering courage, meeting some old terror head on.

Chapter 8
Joannie

April 7, 1942

Yanking on the rope, Joan secures her boat with a hasty bowline at the village pier before she scrambles up the piling. Railroad spikes have been hammered every ten inches or so, crude footholds, and the wet, cardboard-patched soles of her Keds slip more than once. Only her hands' precarious grip on a spike above keeps her from dropping into the sea.

She shouldn't be leaving her boat here—but then, she shouldn't have been so far out sailing at all this time in the evening, especially as a young woman alone.

But this is an emergency, and every second counts.

Lives depend on how fast she can relay what she saw to the authorities, how fast they can send up the Civil Air Patrol's planes.

The village pier boasts only two lights, one at the crosspiece of the T and one where it meets land. In between the two lights, there in the shadows, a tall, lanky figure shifts positions.

As the figure turns, the last rays of the sinking sun snag on his jacket's buttons and on a gold emblem on his cap. He's in a uniform of some type. He lifts one hand to his mouth as a red tip of light blinks, then a plume of smoke snakes through the dusk.

As she breaks into a run, Joan tugs down her brother's old blue button-down shirt, tied at her waist, so that no skin will show. Her shorts and shirt both are damp and cling to her skin. Sensing how this must look, her hands round to fists at her sides.

Whether this man lurking in the pier's dark poses a threat, she has no idea. What she does know for certain is there's far greater trouble out there just a few miles offshore, and she needs to report it before the U-boat finds its ultimate target.

She's running from danger to danger, she knows, as she races between lights on the pier.

My Joannie, her father used to say when she was little, *can't you once, even just once, slow down and be careful? Be just a little ladylike, maybe, for the sake of your old dad?*

Joannie draws a sharp breath as she runs.

Pops.

What will they do about him? The familiar worry eats deep in her gut.

As Joan sprints past the tall, lanky man skulking at one side of the pier, a long brown case gripped under his arm, she doesn't turn her head, though he's staring at her.

He gives out no whistle, no catcall, just that white, translucent snake—the smoke from his cigarette crossing her path—and the red flash of the Lucky Strike logo as he slides the pack back into his breast pocket. She plunges through the smoke and through the intensity of his stare and does not break stride.

But now she can hear his footsteps behind her, heavy on the old boards. He's a large man, she can tell with a quick glance behind at the shadow cast from the setting sun—slender but disquietingly tall. Her heart rate doubles, triples, as she hears him begin running, too, drawing closer, the shops of the village's one main street still too far away and most of them closed for the day.

Still closer come the thuds of those footsteps.

Close enough nearly for him to reach out and grab her neck, her arm, the collar of her soaking-wet shirt. She can smell his scent, a whiff of Lucky Strike and man-sweat and engine oil and something else she can't name.

The footsteps hammer directly behind her now. *Thud thud thud thud.*

As fast as she is, she cannot outrun him.

Fists on her hips, Joan whirls to face the man.

Chapter 9

Hadley

April 7, 2022

The Lürssen in its slip, I whip around to confront our host directly. I'm tired of guessing, of tiptoeing around the World War II panzer in the closet.

"So, Mr. Hessler, I feel I should ask before we go on: Why hire a firm run by two young women based in California? We're flattered, of course. But why not hire a local firm here?"

Kitzie squeezes my hand again. "Because we are *that good*."

We *are* good. She's not wrong about that. Our reviews are superb; our social media reels shared gazillions of times.

Still . . .

"Your sister," Hessler answers, though he doesn't meet my eye, "expresses it well."

"You're kind." I stop there—because he's not, of course. Sometimes my Southern upbringing makes me say something nice that's not even spittin' distance from true. "But there must have been a reason you sought us out in particular."

"I will say this, Ms. Jacks. I did not come to run Boundless by jumping blindly into a deal. I do my research."

With that, our host turns away to examine the Lürssen's digital dashboard, then jots notes on his phone.

I catch only a bit of his commentary: "Waste of petrol . . . excessive speed . . ." Even that is more than I want to hear.

The captain says nothing at all in response, though I see his jaw clench. *How much,* I wonder, waving for Kitz to take the stairs down, *can Angry Young Captain take before he wrings that gray, granitelike neck of his boss?*

Hessler himself motions us forward to the stairs that lead from the flybridge down two flights to the lower deck. I can't help but glance across the interior of the yacht as we descend. At the first floor's far end, the galley gleams with white marble counters. In a sitting room closer to us with mahogany wainscotting, books climb up a whole wall, floor to ceiling.

"I am, yes," Hessler snaps as he's about to step onto the wharf, "a great reader."

"I am, yes, impressed," I call back, my smile genuine for the first time today. I still don't much like the man. But I give him bonus points for the floating library.

"Yet we are expected at the King and Prince."

My chain jerked, I fall in line behind my sister, who stumbles just before she reaches the rail—oddly, pitching sideways like one of her legs just gave out. Jumping forward, I catch her by the arm, and she laughs it off.

"Clumsy is as clumsy does," she says merrily—too merrily, if you ask me.

And she won't meet my eye as I ask, "You okay, Kitz?"

"Totally fine. Just klutzing over my own feet."

Letting the captain relay her luggage to the wharf, she takes his hand as she leaps off the boat—Lürssen. Kitz is telling him "Thanks so awfully much, truly," to which the guy not only doesn't answer but also looks away.

It takes several layers of jerk to be rude to someone as kind as my sister.

As he holds out a hand for my luggage, I look him square in the eye. "*Not* coddled. *Not* Californian."

With that, I heave my suitcase to the wharf, the bag's wheels taking it clear to the other side, where the next slip begins, and it teeters there. I have to lunge after it—not so graceful myself. But, balance regained and suitcase saved from the brink, I've managed to ignore the captain's hand.

As I glance back, he's standing exactly in the same position, hand still out for me to grab. Only his eyebrow has moved, arching up above the Ray-Bans yet again.

At least, I think, *I never have to see him again, this Skipper Superior.*

"Samantha!" someone calls from shore.

The old woman swaying—daydreaming, I suspect—on the dock jumps like a person startled out of deep sleep.

The person jogging toward the old woman appears exasperated but also immensely relieved.

"Samantha, dear God, *there* you are!"

"Same place I was last time you lost me."

A young woman, tall and slender, continues to scold this Samantha Gone Missing—not with the deference of an employee but rougher and more familiar, the tone of a close friend or relative. Though the young woman is darker skinned, her mannerisms and those of the elderly, White Samantha are remarkably similar. Both of them tilt back their heads, just a little defiant, then cock their heads to one side. They both open their arms affectionately. They're like synchronized swimmers, these two.

"Yes, well, you'd think I'd learn." The young woman's hands go to her hips. "And also, I'd think *you'd* learn I don't like it when you wander out here alone. Samantha, honey, honestly. We've talked about this. What if you were to trip?"

"Then I'd show you how well I can swim."

I'm chuckling as my sister crosses the dock to lean into me.

"Hadz," she whispers. It's her nickname for me. Long ago she found a way to stick a *Z* into my name to go better with hers—the Jacks sisters, as unlike each other as lightning and lightning bugs and as devoted as we are different. "Hadz, before we jump on this next leg of the Incredible Journey, what do you *really* think of our host? Your most generous assessment."

"Wouldn't trust him to water my garden during a gully washer of a rainstorm."

"Seriously."

"That was me being serious. And generous. Wait till you read that article I sent you about his firm. If you ask me, he's wanting to use this reunion to reframe the firm's whole image, starting with its origin story."

Kitz gives another small shrug. "Everyone's story needs reframing at some point. It's part of what we do best."

"Hold on. I know that look in your eye. The theater major part of your brain has already envisioned the World War Two backdrops you'll design, the ways we'll reveal the story to attendees not all at once but—"

"Throughout the weekend"—she nods—"let it unfold bit by bit. The only way to do it."

"Look, Kitz, we'll discuss it later when we're alone. After you read what *Forbes* has to say about the battle for control of Boundless. If the squabbling of these families leaked into our reunion planning . . . Can you imagine the mess?"

"The fact that these families descended from these three guys who never even should have met, then managed to work together and stay in touch all these years . . . ," she counters. "To me, that's extraordinary."

I sigh. Hessler must've had her at *family*. That faraway look in my sister's eyes tells me she's head-over-strappy-sandals-in-love with the idea of all these interconnections—the romance and mystery of it all. The appeal of that word *family* to people like Kitz and me, who've never known a group of people who felt bound to stay in our lives, even if only to fight, is more than even I can scoff at.

Ahead of us on the wharf, the elderly woman links her arm with the younger woman's and begins, with the help of her cane, climbing the wooden ramp to the footpath. Halfway up, though, she turns back, plants her feet, and says something in the ear of her companion, who checks her own watch and glances, a little more anxiously now, toward the parking lot.

Samantha appears to be in no hurry at all. In fact, she's making no attempt to disguise that she's staring back at us.

Up ahead, Ernst Hessler is strikingly steady on his feet for his age as he strides toward the parking lot.

"'Only the good die young,'" I sing softly to myself as I stroll beside Kitzie, who swats me.

We're nearing the wooden ramp, and Samantha Gone Rogue is still standing there at the top, feet still planted, her companion looking friendly—but in that way of someone about to run late.

Samantha's gaze rests first on the captain. To my surprise, he slows, holds out his hand, and shakes hers—or maybe less a shake, since her hand looks as if it might break with too forceful a clasp, but rather he cradles hers an instant. They trade nods but no words before he strides away. It's a peculiar exchange, to say the least.

Now her gaze swings from Kitzie to me. I step up to say hello, but she's already speaking.

"The older gentleman you're with, dears, appears to be in quite a hurry." She rolls her head slowly to bob in the direction of Hessler's well-tailored back.

"It appears to be his one speed," I agree. "My name is Hadley Jacks, and this is my sister, Kitzie."

"Oh my goodness. How lovely."

Her mind appears to have drifted away once more, and the abject fear I thought I saw on her face a moment ago flickers across it again. For an instant, lips parting, she looks like she might cry out. A pat on the arm from her companion seems to pull her back to the present.

Blinking, the old woman draws a breath that seems to steady her—though the fear hasn't quite left her eyes. "Forgive me, won't you? I'm Samantha Mitchell, and this is my dear friend and neighbor, the Reverend Doctor Felicia."

The neighbor, Felicia, pats the old woman's white stick of an arm. "You don't have to give my résumé every blessed time you say my name, you know."

"I do, though, and I will, so help me God. It's precisely the truth, and precision is important, you know. In my day, women got half the credit for twice the work. Also . . ."

"You'll say whatever the hell you like," the Reverend Doctor finishes for her.

"*Precisely.* Here's what I say to folks trying to patronize me, expecting me to wear old-lady white gloves and carry a bouquet of violets and whine how the world's changing too fast, just going to seed. *Rubbish.* That's what I say—when I want to keep my speech tame, which I don't always."

"Rarely, in fact," Felicia agrees.

"And here's what else I'll add, if you're asking: I've got some crazy-ass stories I could tell from that era."

I let go a big bleat of a laugh that I try to cover with a polite cough.

Samantha angles her head at me. "I like a term that gives a nice jolt in the midst of all the old-people talk I've got to endure: *More fiber's the key to life, hon* and *At your age, that would be too great a risk . . .* makes me want to throw things."

"Good thing," I pipe in, "the world's changed so that's no longer the case, women working twice as hard for half the credit." I wink, and the Reverend Doctor winks back at me.

Now both women hold out their hands to Kitzie and me. Felicia's hand is firm and warm, but Samantha's is like a baby bird. I let go almost immediately for fear my exuberance alone might bruise it.

The old woman's eyes follow mine to the head of her cane, an elaborate cartoon character of some sort, it looks like, carved in wood.

"Felicia here makes me bring it when I'm out with her," Samantha tells me, eyes twinkling. "Good thing the Reverend Doctor's not there to force the blasted thing on me when I'm shaking a wicked leg on the dance floor."

"Miss Samantha," Kitzie says, reverting to our South Carolina manners, "how nice to meet you."

Samantha stares back at Kitzie, and for a moment, I'm sure the poor old woman's mind has skipped off its track again. "What brings you to our island, dear?"

"As it happens, we may be arranging a reunion of three families brought together by events here during World War Two."

I'm shaking my head at Kitz, and I know she sees—sisters don't miss a flicker of an eyelash on each other—but she ignores me.

"Honestly," the Reverend Doctor offers, "Samantha could probably share some stories from those days. She has a better memory than I do. Now if you all will forgive our rushing off, I really do need to get back to work."

Leaning into the arm of her friend as they turn to leave, Samantha lifts her cane to gesture goodbye. "Enjoy the island, Hadley and Kitzie."

Waving, I fall into step beside my sister. "She remembered our names after just one introduction."

"Her neighbor said she had a sharp memory."

"*Nobody* remembers our names after just one introduction. They're too strange."

Kitzie opens her mouth for what, no doubt, is one of her stock responses to one of my perceived suspicions, but a black SUV slides up directly in front of us, and Hessler steps forward. Its windows appear darkened past the legal limit of tinting.

"Drug-runner windows," I whisper to Kitz. "Windows for illicit dealings."

Kitzie widens her eyes in her way that tells me to hush.

A hand reaches to open the front passenger door for Hessler and the back for my sister and me. I recognize the deeply tanned, weathered knuckles and wrist before I look up to see our captain, who has traded his skipper's cap for a chauffeur's and is now holding the door.

"You're killing it on the millinery front," I tell him.

I swear I can feel the resentment coming off him like June heat from asphalt. Circling the nose of the SUV, he folds long legs under the wheel and, spine stiff, looks straight ahead.

It hits me suddenly—too late—that he's wearing the chauffeur's hat now and wore the skipper's cap before only because his boss must have insisted—one of those Rich People Power Moves I've seen up close for myself, and it's never pretty.

Again, I've been snarky, which I'd like to blame on jet lag or concern over Kitz or the captain-driver's arrogance . . . something—anyone—else, but I'm the one blurting these things. I shift in my seat under a sharp stab of guilt.

"Thank you"—I try catching his eye—"for getting the door."

Without looking at our driver, Hessler says, "To the King and Prince side entrance, back toward the restaurant."

"Echo."

"Yes, of course Echo. I should know its name well enough. The restaurant there"—Hessler cranes his head back toward Kitzie and me—"Echo, it is called."

"The King and Prince," I offer, "was turned into a training facility for the new technology radar. Thus, the restaurant's name?" I smile at our host. My brain might be powered solely by artificial stimulant at the moment, but at least I've pulled something useful from all that reading on the red-eye.

Hessler lifts a shaggy white eyebrow at me. "Indeed."

"Echo," I repeat. I try to ignore that little frisson up my spine I get when my curiosity is piqued. I don't need it piqued for a project we're not taking on. "I really know very little about how radar works, except that maybe radio waves bounce back—*echo*, I suppose—from . . . okay, let me rephrase that. I know *nothing* about how radar works."

"I will assume, Ms. Jacks, that you are capable of learning, yes? Since a working knowledge of radar will be important for this gathering."

I wait for a twinkle in the dull of his eyes, but he's not kidding.

"If radar is important," I assure him, "radar we will learn. *If . . .*" Kitzie nudges me in the ribs, so the end of that sentence—if *we take your job, Mr. Hessler*—I don't finish aloud.

I'm aware of the driver's gaze darting to the rearview mirror, though I can read nothing of his expression.

Kitzie, our diplomat, offers nothing of radar or echoes. Instead, she props her head against the Escalade's window, her cheeks pale.

"Are you sure you're feeling okay?" I whisper.

"Just that same cold I can't get rid of. Low iron, the doc said—like I told you. All good."

She doesn't look me in the eye, which for anyone else would mean she's lying. But Kitz and I don't lie to each other. Ever.

We all stare out the windows, and I reach for my sister's hand as a gibbous moon and our headlights reveal glimpses of live oaks and Spanish moss and azaleas in bloom as the Escalade skirts the edge of the island.

"That sweet older woman, Samantha," Kitz tilts in toward me to murmur. "We need to hear some of her stories—for research."

"Right. Her crazy-ass stories from World War Two days. Honestly, Kitz, I wouldn't mind seeing this place decades ago through her eyes."

The last of the sun easing into the sea, I watch the water wash crimson.

Chapter 10
Joannie

April 7, 1942

The ocean is turning bloodred, the sun collapsing behind the edge of the world, and Joannie tries to think not of blood but only of what she must do. And fast. This man on the pier will *not* stop her.

Despite the clench in her chest, she turns toward him. "*Periscope.* Okay? I saw a *periscope* out there." She says it with force, like the vicious slap she'll deliver next if he moves an inch closer.

"*Lordy.*" The man cocks his head. "A . . . *what the holy heck* did you say?"

The tilt of the head. The *Lordy* in a deep country accent. The voice, a low, gentle bass. Even the milquetoast expletive *what the holy heck*. None of it seems terribly menacing. None of *him* seems terribly menacing now that she can see his face.

He is a large man, yes, and his head is set a little askew on his frame, like a scarecrow with a wild thatch of dark hair. His eyes are round, almost too round and too large for his face, giving him a look so innocent, so sweetly pleading, so at odds with the stiffness of his uniform jacket, Joan nearly chuckles aloud.

Except she's too panicked to laugh. "A periscope. I've got to report it. *Now.*"

"Didn't mean to spook you back there, by the way. Just fixing to say hey, but then you took off like a stung colt. Would a merchant marine do, ma'am? I mean, as someone to report it to?"

She resets both fists on her hips. "Only if you're the commander of a fleet. Are you?"

He scratches his chin. "Not hardly. Not even a rooster hop from that. But I reckon I could report it on up the chain, if you'd like, Miss . . ."

She pauses. Then decides the Germans would never choose a spy with such an accent. Or find one with such big, innocent eyes. She walks fast toward Gray's Drugs and flings the name back over her shoulder. "DuBarry."

"Miss DuBarry. When I get back to the ship—mine's the SS *Oklahoma*, docked over to Brunswick, if you know where . . . well, now, 'course you'd know Brunswick." He trots to catch up again and walk alongside her.

"We do leave our pretty little island now and then, Mr. . . . ."

"Dobbins. William—"

"You don't believe me, do you, Mr. Dobbins? About what I saw."

"Well, now. My mama taught me to always believe a lady."

"So, you know how to be diplomatic. But you don't really believe what I saw was a German sub."

He's matched his steps with hers, and she can see he's searching for something gentlemanly to say.

But she doesn't stay to hear more. Turning on one heel, she breaks again into a jog for the last few yards down Mallery Street to the drugstore before tossing back over her shoulder, "Mr. Gray, our druggist, has a telephone. He'll help me call the people who'll send up the patrol planes. But do report it, Merchant Marine Dobbins. Do tell your commander that there was a credible sighting of a U-boat."

~

Careening up to the entrance of Gray's Drugs, Joan screeches to a halt at the threshold, the door open to the evening breeze off the ocean. The warm air inside the shop smells of vanilla ice cream and rosewater, the kind Joannie's mother used to wear before she got ill.

"Just about to close up," the druggist calls from behind the soda fountain, his back to the door. But peering over his shoulder, he brightens. "Oh, it's you, Joannie girl. If a lonely old druggist can't stay open a little longer for his next-door neighbor, I don't know what the world's come to."

Joan's breath is still short from running—and caught for a moment on the rosewater. But she gets out the one needful word: "U-boat."

"How's that?"

Joan covers the distance to the counter in four running strides. "I was out sailing just now . . ."

"Young lady, your daddy would have your hide, you out there on the open water so late. Why, if one of our boys in uniform who hadn't got the right raising—"

"Mr. Gray, if you could just listen. I was out there on my boat—"

"Your brother Sammy too. He wouldn't be any too pleased, I don't reckon."

"U-boat," she announces again, louder this time.

The druggist blinks back at her. "If'n I didn't know better, I'd thought you said . . ."

"Just a few miles offshore. I saw its periscope. Which means it's just floating out there, waiting. Mr. Gray, we have to let the right people know!"

Hands flat on the counter, Mr. Gray nods. His eyes, though, settle on her with paternal concern. "Joannie, hon. I know with all these servicemen in town, the demon liquor has got to be an awful temptation."

"Mr. Gray, I am *not* intoxicated. Please, if you'll just let me use your phone."

"Now, now, Joannie. No need to get all worked up. We just can't be bothering folks who've already got so much responsibility filling their plates, what with the big war and all."

From the threshold, the bell that hangs over the door tinkles, making both Joan and the druggist turn. The man from the pier stands there, the top of his head having knocked the bell. With his dark haystack of hair brushing the top of the frame, he looks taller—and more awkward—than ever. The long brown case is still tucked under one arm.

"Well, now," he muses, sauntering forward, "I had myself just about the same reaction as you, Mr. Gray. But now that I cogitate on it, I reckon this young lady here's got to know what she saw. Back home, there's the kinds of folks when they tell a tale, you know it's just them flapping their jaws for the breeze of it. But then there's the folks who, if they say there's a fox, even maybe eyeing the henhouse from three fields away, you best snatch the shotgun right now from over the door. I'd reckon Miss DuBarry here's the second type, wouldn't you?"

Joan tries not to mind that this little speech—by a stranger from outside St. Simons at that—is what spurs the druggist to lift his telephone from its cradle. She does mind, but she can't afford to dwell on it, since this is the only way she's likely to get the news to the right people—the right *men*—who will know what to do.

With a quarter smile that's more indulgent than convinced, Mr. Gray makes all the right calls, including to a navy commander and several leaders in the Civil Air Patrol.

"That's right, Harold," he assures one. "Joannie DuBarry swears that's what she saw, sure enough. What's that? I reckon she does work out at the Ritz Theatre over to Brunswick, yep, and they got all the latest in newsreels, sure do. But s'pose she's *not* just imagining this from her watching too many of those? Reckon it *could* be Hitler's got his subs over this far . . ."

And so it goes, call after call, as Joan paces near the cash register. William Dobbins doesn't budge from his spot near the root beer.

Standing guard, Joan thinks, chewing on her bottom lip. *Hitler's navy has shown up at our doorstep, and we've got one oversized scarecrow of a merchant marine standing guard.*

At last, Mr. Gray lowers the black, shiny receiver. "That leaves only your own brother. He still got hisself that hunk-of-scrap-metal Gee Bee to take up and have a look? Need me to give him a call so's he knows even before this merchant marine fellow walks you home?" The druggist winks.

"Yes. That is, Sam does still take the Gee Bee up as part of the coastal patrol. But, no, there's no reason to call."

"No trouble, really."

"No. Thank you. No need."

"Let me just give him a quick ring, so's—"

"Because"—this next comes out in a rush—"they just this week shut off our phone." Joan has to turn her face away from Mr. Gray's sorrowful eyes.

Just one more bill we couldn't pay, she nearly adds, but won't humiliate her family further.

"I'm awful sorry your daddy's doing poorly, Joannie." He says it softly, and she knows he means well, but she can't bear his pity.

She's desperate to change the subject. Desperate to leave.

Again, the merchant marine steps forward. "Well, now. Seeing as how the calls have got made, let me congratulate you, Miss DuBarry, on doing your duty for the war effort."

He salutes smartly and, despite herself, she laughs. The fellow's arms are so long, it's like having a stick figure salute you, only with the widest, most winsome grin and that dark tumble of hair.

The druggist extends his hand from behind the soda counter. "You got a name, son?"

"Private First Class William Shakespeare Dobbins, sir, US merchant marine of the SS *Oklahoma* at your service. That's the full wagonload of the thing, but everyone calls me just Will."

"William Shakespeare, is it?"

"With a Dobbins hooked to the axle."

"Who in heaven's name chose that for you, son?"

"Well, now, that'd be Mama. Loved the sonnets even before her official book learning, she always says. Came to visit Walden—our little town on the backside of Signal Mountain, prettiest place known to man—with a friend one summer. Used to be called Hog Wallow, our little town, so you can see where there's been some progress."

"I can see that, sure."

"Came up visiting from Chattanooga to stay on our mountain, out in what we call Summertown, seeing's how it's the home of the summer people. That's where she met my daddy, him hired by her friend's parents to sweep off their tennis court."

"Let me guess, your daddy's a poet."

"Furtherest thing from it. But he had the thickest black hair—like mine, she says—falling just so into his face, and the most poetical eyes. He could tell stories that'd melt the trousers off your backside. It was the eyes and the stories, she says, that made it so she never went back. To her own world, I mean."

Mr. Gray pries up the red lid of the metal cooler that sits, big and wide, along the side wall. "Tell you what, son, seeing as how you're serving your country—"

"Merchant marine," Will clarifies, and he stands tall, though he already towers above the druggist and Joan. "Not military officially. Had to buy my own uniform, matter of fact. But I reckon we're under a fair piece of fire—more, even, than most."

"Young man like you in the merchant marine, then. Still and all, those supplies on your ships won't reach our boys overseas without you. Also, you've told me more of a story than I typically get for one bottle of cold Co'-Cola." Mr. Gray hands a bottle to him and one to Joan.

"I thank you. I got a bad habit of rattling on. Me being the youngest of seven, so long as I wasn't sticking my toes in the churn, they all just let me yammer. I got mates on the ship now, though, who say I keep up the jawing straight on through sleep."

"Well, now, Will Dobbins, a young man like you, a guest on St. Simons, ought to be introduced proper to some of our local girls. Joannie DuBarry here, she's smart as she is pretty," the druggist offers—like she's not standing right here. "Though not much known for a quiet temperament. This young lady, she's a bit on the restless side—had to go and learn to fly one of them old biplane contraptions like her brother. But a good heart, for all her restless—been fine neighbors to me, her and her family."

"Truth to tell, sir, a boy from East Tennessee can't often wander into a drugstore and find a girl who'd be a mighty dead ringer for Miss Rita Hayworth."

Joan can't help feeling drawn in by the merchant marine's warmth, his rough, funny farm-boy magnetism. But she also wants to dash outside to see when the navy will send up surveillance and when the coastal patrol will send up a plane in the dark—if word gets to Sam, he and his Gee Bee could be the first. She takes a step back toward the door.

"Thank you, Mr. Gray, for the use of your phone."

He winks. "In service of a good cause, little lady. Tell your daddy I'll poke my head in on him soon."

Blinking, standing stock still, Joannie realizes suddenly, a punch to her gut, the reality of it. In that wink, that sweet, fatherly smile of Mr. Gray's, she sees the truth: that he doesn't believe what she saw out there in the ocean—and neither must a single man he spoke with tonight.

She's overcome with the need to get out of this shop, as if somehow being outdoors, out there where she can hear the tide, where she can see the moon, might somehow, irrationally, help keep the shore safe from that sub. Stumbling, she backs out the door and turns to stare out beyond the pier.

Behind her, she hears the shop door closing, the deadbolt sliding into place as the druggist locks up.

"Reckon I'd like to say I'm awful sorry." Behind her, the merchant marine speaks gently, a voice soft enough you could wrap it around you like fleece. "That maybe they didn't all rightly believe what you saw."

She doesn't turn to look at him. "Let's be honest. None of them did."

He waits several moments—she's glad of the silence—before saying, "If it helps even a piece, I believe you."

Crossing her arms, her gaze drops down, back to the case under his arm. "What is that, exactly?"

Will pops an instrument out of the case and up to his chest so fast he nearly smacks her with it. His face flushes crimson. "Back home, I take this here mandolin with me 'bout everywhere. Helps ease just this here kind of day."

Joan looks from his instrument up to his face. "Do you play the mandolin well, Merchant Marine William Shakespeare Dobbins?"

"Folks generally circle up like hogs to a puddle." His flush goes still deeper. "If it's not too prideful to say."

"That depends on just how good you actually are. Although I'd rather be sitting on the beach to judge for myself, if you don't mind." Not waiting for him to agree, she walks on ahead while he scurries to catch up. As they reach the sand and she slides off her shoes, she scans the dark sky for patrol planes.

Nothing.

Still, maybe one of those men Mr. Gray called believed the periscope sighting. Maybe the patrol pilots are just now being informed.

She has to tilt her head far back to meet Will Dobbins's eye. "You're awfully tall."

"Awful," he agrees, ducking his head like he's apologizing. "All the girls back home bellyached how they got cricks in their necks at the school dances. All except Ruby Ann Sloan. She'd grew tall as most of us boys by the seventh grade and never let up, bless her heart. Ruby can 'bout hook a rope on a barn rafter without standing on her tiptoes."

"Well. That is impressive. About you, though, Mr. Dobbins, I still say whether or not you're awful prideful depends"—Joan crosses her arms over her chest—"on how well you play."

Will apparently doesn't need more invitation than that. As Joan sits down on the sand, knees tucked under her chin, he begins plucking the strings. First "Cotton-Eyed Joe," then he transitions to the ballad "Barbara Allen." If he sees the bright, sharp challenge in Joan's eyes, he's not cowed by it. Instead, his lean body sways from the waist as he croons.

> 'Twas in the merry month of May
> When green buds all were swellin'
> Sweet William on his death bed lay
> For love of Barbara Allen . . .

> So slowly, slowly, she got up
> And slowly she drew nigh him
> And the only words to him did say,
> "Young man I think you're dyin'."

> He turned his face unto the wall
> And death was in him wellin'
> "Goodbye, goodbye to my friends all,
> Be good to Barbara Allen" . . .

Joan crosses her arms tighter over her chest. She rarely cries—almost never—and here just after her rage over no one believing what she saw, she's on the verge for the second time tonight. That damn mandolin, or maybe the ache of the ballad's tale as it unfolds or Will's low, longing voice makes her eyes hurt with the pressure of tears she won't let loose. He *is* extraordinary on this instrument.

"That is an awful sad song, Merchant Marine Dobbins."

Will lowers the instrument, then lowers himself beside her. "It is. Mighty sad."

She leans closer to him and smells again the scents of salt, sea, and motor oil, a musky whiff of perspiration and a stronger one of something like just-mowed clover and pine and moss. *Maybe,* she thinks, *that's the Tennessee mountains in him.*

Something about Will Dobbins makes her want to cuddle up for hours—maybe days, maybe years—on the beach and watch him play that mandolin and listen to that accent of his telling stories of Tennessee and think about anything except this damn war, that U-boat out there in the dark.

"Are you a sad person, Merchant Marine Dobbins?" She stretches her leg alongside his, and she feels his whole body stiffen.

"I don't believe I am, no, Miss DuBarry. Reckon I could love a woman, the right woman, all my life long like the poor fella in the ballad, but I tilt hard toward happy—can't much help it. Not sure I could store up the melancholy long enough for it to kill me."

Joan stares at him an instant, then tumbles into a laugh.

She holds out her hand. "I ought to get on home, Private First Class Dobbins."

"Tomorrow," he blurts, taking it. "Tomorrow well before dawn."

"What's tomorrow well before dawn?"

"We're shipping out."

"That right? Darn shame. Because I like your"—she meets his eye—"mandolin."

Bless him, he opens his mouth to respond, but no sound comes out at first try. "I'm afraid," he says on second try—only it comes out more like *afeard*—"I might launch clear into a song again."

Now he looks as if he might faint, all six foot five of him keeling straight over like a sawed tree. Will Dobbins rakes a hand back through his hair so it stands on end. He looks as goofy as a schoolboy, and also all sorts of adorable.

"You got awful pretty green eyes," he says. "Like a summer's day."

Joan has a vague feeling this last might be a reference to some old sonnet of Shakespeare, but she didn't pay much attention in school her senior year, not what with the war on in Europe and things collapsing at home. Refusing to play the part of the ignorant Georgia girl, ever, she doesn't ask.

Instead, she laughs. Something about his sweet schoolboy shifting of weight, that whole skinny tree of him with a mandolin caught in its branches, that ridiculous grin on his face—all that makes a chuckle bubble up.

"Well, Will Dobbins, in one night in port, you managed to chase a girl down a pier, talk the town druggist into making a heap of calls he didn't figure on making, snag yourself a free Coke, then walk a girl down the beach and make her forget how hopping mad she was just a few minutes ago. That's one silver-smooth voice you got."

"'Smooth runs the water where the brook is deep,'" he intones—then grins. "Not sure that pack of words fits here, but thought it'd sound mighty nice."

"Shakespeare," she says, guessing, but figuring her odds are good.

"Now see if you recognize this one." He shifts to his knees in the sand to look deep in her eyes. "'A thousand kisses buy my heart from me.'"

"Shakespeare again?"

"But also me. Just letting you know." This he accompanies with an earnest, searching look.

"A thousand, is it, to buy your heart?" She leans closer to him, aware how alone they are on this beach.

Regardless, she's sure of this: the world as they knew it has ended. The world is now a precarious one, full of dangers and unknowns and vast oceans, where the SS *Oklahoma* will be nothing but a floating straw. This gregarious, funny, big-hearted young man might not live to come back.

How is it, she wants to demand of someone, *we live in a world where we send the most vibrant, most alive out to die for their countries?*

A sense of foreboding swelling in her chest like a wave, she makes herself look at him. Sweet, kind, funny Will Dobbins.

"I don't think," she says, running one finger down his nose, "we got time for a thousand kisses. So maybe we'd better not start."

He brings her hand to his cheek. "Reckon we can't know if we'll ever see each other again. I say we risk it and start counting now. See how far we can get."

All those boats being sunk far out at sea. All those boys who will never come back.

Joan shakes the hair back from her face and lifts it to him, his fingers just grazing her waist. A few yards away, the sea crashes and purrs, crashes and purrs.

"Kiss me, Will Dobbins," she says.

He does not need to be invited twice.

It is only one kiss, though a long one.

When Joan pulls away and lets him walk her to her own sandy lane just down the beach, he makes her laugh again at something he's said—she's not even sure what, two moments after he's said it. Her mind is swirling.

From someone's open window, a record player spins out the song "I'll Be Seeing You," Vera Lyn's voice sorrowful and seductive at the same time.

"This may sound strange, Will Dobbins, but I feel like we've been friends forever."

Stopping there in the lane, he turns to her. "Not to scare you—us just meeting today and me shipping out—but I feel like I got to say: I've always reckoned I'd like to marry a girl I could just talk to. I mean"—he flushes—"not *just* talk to, but love the talking to every day our whole lives. Don't let this spook you now, but I'd be grateful for the chance to come home from this war and talk with you more. For however much of forever as you care to give."

The foreboding swells in her chest again, so full she can't speak. She pulls his head down, kisses him slowly, tenderly on the forehead and both cheeks.

"I'll be seeing you, William Shakespeare Dobbins," she whispers.

Chapter 11
Will Dobbins

Evening, April 7, 1942

The sound Will hears is menacing, like a rattler snaking through grass that is flat-out desiccated, nothing but dry blades. Like something fast and sleek—*bent nigh on trouble*—shooting right out there through water, a whoosh that makes Will's hair stand on end.

Could be a tin fish shooting past—what the old salts call "torpedoes." Except now the night's gone still.

Probably just in his head, things all catawampus, his being so tired. It's felt like a long watch already tonight, and it's just begun.

In his daze, he's forgotten to report what Joannie spotted out here in the sea. But that nice pharmacist Mr. Gray made all those calls, and now the *Oklahoma* is about to clear the St. Simons Sound anyhow, out to open sea. No help to report it at this point.

"Right glad that's over," Will says of the swishing sound. He turns to the first mate, who'd been beside him just a minute ago here on deck, but the mate's gone.

Will isn't one to panic. It's why his daddy relied on him to keep things rolling on the farm. Will's capacity for calm is enormous.

He's just now realizing that any guy with even a slosh bucket of sense would've gotten sleep last night in one of the Ritz Theatre seats—two of his buddies bought tickets for the feature, then slept for six hours straight—instead of getting himself all cockeyed over a girl.

Any guy with sense, he muses. *So not me.*

Because he's not one lick sorry that he spent his free hours with Joannie DuBarry.

Will leans against the starboard rail and feels the wind whip at his hair. It's not the same as her fingers ruffling through it, but it helps to pretend for a moment. He's so tall, the railing hits him lower on his body than most, so low he feels a little top heavy leaning on it, like the slightest jolt might send him headfirst into the drink.

Like somebody's reading his mind, a hand grabs a fistful of his shirt and yanks him back.

"Watch it, bud. We don't need a man overboard before we've even cleared the barrier islands."

Will turns, intending only to nod and go back to coiling the rope in his hands.

"What the hell's wrong with you anyhow, Dobbins? You got the goofiest damn smile on your face I ever seen."

"Reckon I do."

"How much you have to pay some poor dame to waste time with you, Tennessee?"

Will's too happy to slug anyone, and he feels, even if he can't see, the spread of the grin that must look silly as heck. In fact, the grin feels like it's stretched across his whole body, shoulder to shoulder and head to toe.

"Well, now, you make a mighty fine point. Poor girl couldn't have got a good look at this mug of mine."

"Blind," another crew member pronounces. "Poor broad was blind."

Will knocks his forehead with the heel of his hand. "I wondered why she thought I was such a handsome young rooster."

Several of the fellows want details. In genuine Technicolor.

But Will describes only Joan's smile. Her quick wit. Her fine intelligence.

This earns him a volley of abuse, and he laughs along with them. They're missing home, these guys, just like him. Like him, too, they know they're headed into the open ocean, unprotected, where merchant ships just like theirs are being sunk every day, maybe bunches of them a day—Who knows anymore? Information like that isn't exactly broadcast to the American public. Or to the sailors themselves.

Word has spread among the guys that as many as half of the merchant ships trying to cross the Atlantic have been hit this year, their crews lost. That the chances of ever seeing home again are more than slim.

So Will lets them go at it.

He coils up his rope and grins his goofy grin and feels the breeze like her fingers again in his hair. He thinks about her lips on his.

And, by God, he'll write to his mother back on the farm about this girl he just met, the girl he'll marry if he ever comes back and if she'll have him.

Will stares out over the water, the stars reflecting like sequins on the black surface. Maybe the hefty Bofors forty-millimeter guns that line the deck should give him comfort. He reaches out to one, its gray metal cold and wet under his skin, then withdraws his hand.

It's the sea, he decides, more than the guns that gives him comfort. So peaceful, it looks.

A peace, Will knows, that could explode any moment. Any moment at all.

Chapter 12
Joannie

"I'm telling you, Sam, the whole world could be about to explode, but if a *girl* reports she sees the stick of dynamite with the fuse lit, nobody's going to so much as duck."

Leaning against the live oak closest to their porch steps, Joannie's brother at least has the good grace to nod, though a half grin betrays what he thinks. He's wearing his aviation goggles on top of his head, and it makes him look even more skeptical, as if he could roll two sets of eyes. "A periscope. As in a German U-boat. Off the coast of St. Simons Island."

"Sam, seriously. All of you Civil Air Patrol guys buzzing around in your pasted-together planes—"

"I thought you loved the Gee Bee!"

"You and I both know she's held together with baling wire, some cast-off parts, and hope. Subs are exactly what all of you CAP guys are looking for."

"Except there *aren't* any. Not here. Not yet."

"There was that Japanese sub off the coast of California a few weeks ago that fired on Santa Barbara."

"Not saying it can't happen eventually. Just not here. Not yet. We're keeping watch for when the time comes."

"I'm telling you, *what I saw was a periscope.*"

"Because of all the periscopes you've seen in your nearly twenty long years of life."

Joannie shoves her hands deep in her pockets, her tone hardening to defiant. "It's what I saw, whether you believe me or not. I've been looking for the past hour for some sort of surveillance someone should've sent up. The sub was in shallow enough water, whatever the new thing is the military uses for detection, it could find the sub and drop a depth charge itself or put out the call for you guys in the coastal patrol. Somebody could still do *something.*"

"So, you being out there on the beach was all looking for surveillance craft and bombers? Nothing to do with you sitting out there necking with some fellow?"

"My God, can you not *listen* to me?"

Sam's friend Marshall steps from behind him. Dressed in coveralls, grease stained from his work and a contrast to Sam's khaki uniform of patrol number 6, he cocks his head before speaking—in the way he's done since they were small: his way of saying he's weighing two sides of a conflict. In their little community of three, Marshall is the living scale of justice.

A born judge, Joannie thinks. *Ironic, since he's the one of us who for sure can't ever become one.*

All three of them grew up with money always tight, both families living on crabbing, fishing, and vegetables from the backyard—so one strike already. But Marshall, he's starting out with at least two other strikes.

"You get a good look?" Marshall asks. "Even though it was getting fast on to dark?"

"That's just it. I thought I was seeing things at first—the light just playing tricks. But I'm telling you . . ." Her gaze swings back to her brother, the skeptic.

Sam nods toward their friend. "Can't see how she'd know for sure with the sun already so low. Can't hardly even make out Marshall from here."

As if to demonstrate, Marshall holds his arm directly overhead, hand cupped and rotating in imitation of a periscope.

His skin, darker by several shades than Joan's, blends almost seamlessly with the dusk.

Marshall drops his arm and addresses Sam. "Still and all, I got to say I believe her."

"Typical." Sam shrugs good naturedly.

"Marshall knows," Joannie says, "which sibling's the smart one to side with."

"Swell. You're both off your rockers. You know, too many newsreels can make the brain see things."

Too many newsreels.

It's what those men on the phone with Mr. Gray said about her. *What if they're right?*

In her job at the Ritz Theatre on the mainland in Brunswick, Joannie takes tickets, works the popcorn machine, and slips in to watch the newsreels before every feature. Which means that when she gets home from work long after dark, her dreams explode with naval and aerial battles, planes spinning and banking and shooting, ships heaving, fire and spumes of water everywhere in the sea and sky, all of it cavalcading together, surreal and all too true.

But Sam isn't finished. "With all Hitler's had going recently on the Soviet front, the two of you lug heads figure the Nazis got time on their hands to send subs over here to the Georgia coast? Where Hitler could capture, let's see, some wild ponies, a few shrimp boats, and a hell of a lot of marshland. Sounds to me like a key target for sure. Skip worrying about taking London and keeping Paris. Yep, Hitler's clearly moved his big push for taking the St. Simons Pier."

"Jekyll," Marshall offers. Just that one word. He points to the south.

Again, typical. Marshall uses fewer words than the average person—maybe because he thinks faster.

It's all Joannie needs. Throwing her hands in the air, she, too, points toward the island to their south. "He's right. Jekyll Island. So maybe not so much the wild ponies. Instead, a whole herd of the richest people in the country have mansions on Jekyll Island, right? Vanderbilts, Rockefellers, Morgans, Pulitzers. *There's* a target for you."

Marshall gives Sam a conciliatory smack on the shoulder. He's that rare personality that can bend between the tension of two sides without ever appearing spineless himself.

Sighing, Joan leans against the rail leading up to their cottage porch. It gives under her weight—a reminder of all the work yet to do since their father quit knowing there was work to be done. "What were the two of you doing out here anyhow?"

For a moment, stiff and crowded with unuttered words, neither of the boys looks at each other.

Straightening, Marshall speaks first. "Walking."

I don't need to ask where, their feet caked in sand.

Sam gazes out into the tangle of live oaks as he does. "Saw the recruiter over to Brunswick. Got them to give me the physical all over again. Still came up with the damaged-heart nonsense and the same old 4-F."

He says this last like it's an obscenity, the vilest and most vulgar kind, and they all look away from each other. As if contracting the rheumatic fever years ago, which weakened his heart and led to his 4-F classification, is a personal moral failing.

She waits till Sam meets her eye. "I know you're determined to join up, but I'm glad for the 4-F. Pops and me, we need you here. Look, you know I don't scare too easy."

"That's putting it mild."

"Sammy"—she hears herself use his boyhood name, and it makes the lump swell still bigger in her throat—"I'm scared for you to go."

They hold each other's eyes for several beats. There's pleading in hers.

"I'm not the same delicate, sickly guy I was as a kid, you know, *Little* Sis." He draws himself up, a stubborn set to his jaw that she knows well—because it matches her own.

"*Little* Sis by two minutes," she says. "Doesn't even count. Right, Marshall?"

"When have I ever been fool enough to take sides with you two?"

"Marshall here, he's got his own news from the recruiter. Or, like mine, a hell of a replay of an old broadcast we already heard too many times."

Marshall looks out at the ocean. "Still got my mind set on driving a tank. Told them—again—I aim on fighting for my country, not mopping floors for it."

There it is. A handful of words that peel back the reality on all the recruiting posters slapped all over the island and mainland, a world of Uncle Sams and men in army fatigues and marine dress uniforms pointing their fingers to say, "I want YOU."

By which, it turns out, they didn't actually mean every *YOU*. Certainly—if your skin happened to be darker than the St. Simons sand—not in combat roles, or in mixed-race units, or up in the sky behind the controls of an airplane.

Marshall speaks out toward the trees. "Meanwhile, I got me a job at the shipyard, where they're fixing to build those Liberty ships we read up on in the papers. I'll do me some construction there, just until the army's ready to hand me a tank."

Which could be never, Joan wants to warn him. Wants to shield him from how much that could hurt, waiting for the country you're willing to die for to decide whether it even wants you.

As if reading her mind, he turns, gazes steadily at her. "Stubborn, you know—stubborn can sometimes move mountains."

The eyes, Joannie thinks, *of an eighty-year-old man in the face of a teenager.*

They let several heartbeats go by. The three of them stare off into the dark shadows of the jungle of oaks and palmettos. There's nothing to say—and also too much. Silence feels empty and powerless—yet better than a jumble of vacuous words piled up to pretend things aren't what they are.

"You've always been the steady one of the three of us," she says at last. "You know how volatile this knucklehead brother of mine'd be."

Sam reaches to give her head a shove. "If I'm dynamite, you're a payload of bombs."

She dodges his hand, then swats at him.

"Y'all," Marshall observes, "still fight like you're four."

Sam bends for a blade of grass to chew on. "Civil Air Patrol."

Typical of him, Sam has answered her question of what he and Marshall were doing outside at night not when she asked it, but when he felt like responding.

"So, hold on, you were up in the Gee Bee just a little while ago? Looking, no doubt, for enemy subs. Like—let's be honest here, buster—*the one I just saw.*"

Sam shrugs—one of his most maddening habits: shrugging when things are at their most urgent. "Only the difference is, I don't buy all the propaganda that Hitler's got boats over here already. We got plenty of other worries. This just ain't one of them yet."

Livid, she plants her feet, fists to her hips.

"I'd duck," Marshall offers to Sam, "if I was you."

"You know what, Samuel DuBarry? You are an absolute . . ." She stomps away instead of supplying whatever slur would've been insufficient. Spinning back, she pauses to snap, "We better get in. He'll be worried."

Sam's eyes go soft. "If he recollects we're missing. Poor Pops. Him not even knowing how you and me worry more every day about him."

And just like that, her fury at Sam dissipates. Which is always the challenge of being his twin: he's tough to stay truly irate at for very long. That alone makes her mad.

By the light of the moon, Joannie can make out the moss and old palm fronds that cover the roof of their bungalow, a good fourth of its shingles missing. Its siding, too, needs paint. By moonlight, at least, the cottage looks more storybook cozy than badly run down.

Joannie draws in a long breath.

Her brother nods grimly, agreeing with what she's thinking. Then, turning to Marshall, he gives a second nod to say good night to his friend, who holds up a hand in return, then disappears into the night.

"Maybe," Sam whispers, as they mount the porch stairs, "you shouldn't start with whatever you spotted out there. Might get him to thinking it's the Huns from the last war."

Joannie pauses, her hand on the knob. "*Periscope,*" she insists. "I *know* what it was."

~

At the table, Terrence DuBarry sits slumped over an empty plate, right hand gripping a photograph in a silver frame as if it's his last handhold on the cliff above a chasm.

Pausing to kiss him on top of the head, Joannie walks to open the window over the kitchen sink. Gripping the sink's ceramic edge, she lets the rhythmic roll and rumble of the sea steady her. Without speaking, Sam enters behind her to make their father a cup of weak Maxwell House coffee—the rations down to just a brown dusting at the tin's bottom—while Joan fries him the last egg in the Frigidaire. She planned to add a strip of bacon, but the icebox is all but empty, the ration book on the counter used up. Instead, she fries a slice of Spam. As she and Sam set the food and coffee in front of their father, Terrence lifts his head.

"You need to eat something, Pops."

"Oh, I will, sugar. Thank you. I'd just like to wait till your mama gets home. You know we always wait for each other."

Joan's eyes lift to Sam's.

Crouching by their father's chair, Sam lays a hand on top of Terrence's, which clutches the photo of a young woman in a straw hat, brown curls tumbling from beneath it. "We know, Dad. But she may be a while this time, so she'd want you to eat without her, just this once."

Terrence tears his gaze from the photograph long enough to blink up at his children. "Reckon I'll wait a spell yet. Your mama's worth waiting a lifetime for."

Joan reaches a hand to grasp Sam's. "She is, Pops. She is."

No point, they've learned, in telling him once again that she's not coming back, that she lost her battle with a wasting disease that didn't fight fair.

That she's the one now waiting for him.

Without speaking, Sam rises, opens a cabinet near the sink, and turns with three hats in his hands.

"Remember these, Dad? They got left by patrons at the old Hotel St. Simons, and someone gave them to Mom. She always loved it when we wore these for dress-up tea parties."

Setting a top hat, its felt moth eaten, gently on her father's head, Joan dons the straw hat with flowers, while Sam adjusts the straw boater he's wearing. Joan brews a pot of weak tea in their mother's chipped Wedgwood pot and slices the last apple. Sam fries the last slice of Spam for the two of them to share.

Together, they flank their father, cut their Spam and their apple into yet-more-minuscule pieces to make the meal stretch, and lift their teacups, holding their pinkies out. They make themselves chatter—about the weather, about the new jobs at the shipyard . . . anything but war or disease—as their father slowly begins to smile, then to eat.

Terrence lifts two fingers to the brim of his tatty top hat. "Well, now. Aren't we four just grand?"

We four, Joan mouths to Sam. They both have to blink back the press of tears.

With the dishes and teacups washed up and Sam right behind her as she drags herself up the stairs, Joan tips her head toward the brown-spotted mirror that hangs on the wall at the upper landing. The glass shows hair windblown into a rat's nest of brown curls.

Sam's mouth twitches. "You do look like her, you know."

"If she'd lost her brush for three weeks, maybe. You're the one who looks most like her."

There is, in fact, something delicate about Sam's features—the small nose and chin, the sharply defined cheekbones—that captures their mother's smile, her gentle loveliness.

"I still miss her so much it hurts," Joan whispers.

"Me too." Bending slightly, Sam rests his chin on his sister's shoulder, and they both stare at their reflections. "I got to get up extra early for the milk delivery run."

From below, they can hear their father half humming, half singing "Let Me Call You Sweetheart." He thumps up the stairs behind them, kisses them both on the back of the head, and limps into his bedroom.

"You children sleep good and say your prayers. Remember now: your mama and I thank God for you every day."

They listen to the thud as he falls into bed, fully dressed. Later, once he's asleep, they will creep in to take off his shoes and change him into a nightshirt.

"I don't want to ever marry," Joan says to their reflection, "unless someone loves me like that. Like they loved each other."

Squeezing Joan's shoulder, Sam's eyes drop to the floor.

"Also, I don't want to ever marry unless the man I love believes me when I say I saw a U-boat just off the coast. In maybe just thirty feet of water. Maybe less."

Sam scrubs his knuckles on the top of her head like they're kids again. "Too many newsreels for you, Joannie Lou."

Swatting him away, she reconsiders her image in the mirror, now raising her chin—unbowed, apparently, in the face of all doubt. Behind her, Sam rolls his eyes.

"Just wait," she says. "Just you wait till we're all blown to bits."

Chapter 13
Hans

It is, Hans knows, almost time, Death coiled at every steel threshold of this stinking cylinder.

He has ceased to think about peace, or even about the next moment.

The patriotic frenzy that brought the crew here—or in his case, the draft—kept them churning at first, flailing about to prove their loyalty and mettle and masculine prowess. But all that fizzled long ago. Most of them now are floundering, fighting more for each other's lives, for their mothers and lovers and siblings back home, for their own survival, than for their country.

Several hours have passed now since Hans's sighting of the civilian sailboat. *U-123*'s delay in using its deck guns was thanks in part to his lie, though the others don't know this.

"Let us hope," the commander said, "for your sake, Hessler, the civilian vessel has failed to spot us."

Now the commander's hand falls to his side as if by reflex, reaching for his Luger.

Hans tries not to let himself think about why he'd reach for his Luger while standing in a steel tube with only his own crew pressed around him. Sometimes it does not pay to think. Sometimes one can only remind oneself, *This is war. In war, men are turned half to beasts.*

The commander runs a hand over the contours of the Luger in his pocket, then steps forward. Perhaps he is imagining climbing up to the conning tower, disposing of the problematic civilian himself—although the little *Ruine* of a skiff disappeared hours ago.

Rolling his shoulders, Hans feels the leaden weight of his duty—so heavy just now, it's crushing. All the engines, all the mechanical systems, the lives of fifty men rest on his shoulders as if a thousand tons of steel—the entire weight of *U-123* itself—are docked there.

Everything that keeps this iron coffin from letting the seawater in and drowning them all is up to him. Should anything go awry with any of the engines or motors or batteries, should *U-123* need to be scuttled, as the chief engineer, he will be the one to set the demolition charges. He will be the one, not the commander or crew, who will likely go down with the boat.

Maybe, Hans thinks, remembering the splay of golden glow from the shore, the people behind those bright lights know nothing of the Kriegsmarine's Operation Drumbeat, how German U-boats have begun hunting in lethal packs close to the American shore. Maybe what they call their democracy—their naive New World government—has made the undemocratic decision to keep quiet the destruction the U-boats are wreaking in order to stave off public panic. Because panic would surely ensue if civilians knew the truth of the U-boats' killing spree. Panic and mayhem and despair if they knew how doomed they are.

Doomed and damned.

Now, though, *now*, *U-123* has spotted a target worthy of pursuit.

The chief engineer understands his role. It is, like for all fifty other men on this boat, to follow orders: the commander's. It is *not*, Hans knows, to think his own thoughts.

He stands now at his post, awaiting the word he knows will come, this attack, and he knows he will do nothing to stop it, even as the merchant ship makes its way out of the harbor, slipping quietly past these barrier islands and assuming it's still well within safe waters.

Hans's stomach churns, as it has each time before an attack, and like every other time, he pictures the sailors on deck, the faces that are about to be obliterated or burned beyond recognition or blown into the sea. This must be a sign of weakness, a clear indication he is not yet the sort of man he must become to fight well and bravely, without hesitation.

But all Hans wants is to be home in Bavaria, sitting before a roaring fire and playing his father's zither as the scent of his mother's freshly baked *Semmelschmarrn* wafts from the kitchen—not, dear God, here in the reek of old sausage and canned fish and body odor, listening to another speech of the Führer's piped through the sound system. He would gladly even go back to shoveling crap out in the barn or milking old Helga in the frigid predawn hours until his hands and her teats are both about to break off.

Anywhere but here, where he's grown daily more claustrophobic and pale and anemic. Call him a weak link in Germany's mighty military chain of invincibility, but his sleep is tortured these days—these nights—by disembodied arms and legs of men floating past little portholes that do not exist in this boat. In Hans's dreams, though, the portholes grow bigger and bigger, improbably swinging inward so that some of the arms and legs float inside to bob among stacks of bunks.

His knees lock and his breath stops as he waits for the order. He horrifies himself by thinking not of the honor of yet another kill, another ship sunk, but instead of the men on board the enemy deck even now, eyes scanning the waters as they exchange playful banter. Nothing but farm boys, he guesses, who'd like to be home milking the cows and mucking the barn, just like him.

Barn, he thinks in English. His vocabulary in the language is limited, but this word he knows. Also *cow* and *crap*. Is that word *crap* a vulgar term for defecation in English or one of the more polite ones? He doesn't know, his few words coming only from Father Bernhard in Hans's town, the priest especially fond of several curse words in German, so there is no telling.

Hans is so deep in his thoughts of *barn* and *cow* and *crap* and his farm back home that he's startled when he hears the commander shouting.

"*Rohr eins . . .*"

But of course.

The number one shaft is ready, the torpedo about to be loosed. Of course the next word will unleash Death into the water, and Hans's nights will be filled with yet more ghosts.

Of course some young man just like him, maybe one who's just fallen in love or just sent his mother a letter assuring her of his safety, of course this young man is about to die.

The commander bellows the last word.

"*Los!*"

The torpedo rockets out of its shaft. The crew braces, all fifty men staring east at walls of steel as if they can see the torpedo's path through the black waters of night toward its target.

Hans closes his eyes.

Chapter 14
Hadley

As we glide down the road in the Escalade, I google the question I haven't yet been able to get anyone to answer: what tragedy happened here eighty years ago exactly.

The night of, the captain had said. So I include both *April 7* and *8, 1942* in the search bar, along with the words *tragedy* and *St. Simons Island.* Then hold my breath.

Black-and-white images fill my phone's screen: an oil tanker, the SS *Oklahoma*, being consumed by fire. Gaping holes the size of a bus in the hull of a ship, torpedoed. Sunk. Two more ships hit that same night, the *Esso Baton Rouge*, also sunk in the waters just off St. Simons, and a bit farther south off Florida, the SS *Esparta*.

"Dear *Jesus*," I breathe. "You weren't kidding about tragedy." I address this to our driver. "Eighty years ago exactly. Looks like no one could've survived."

Showing the images to Kitzie, I feel my stomach twist as I try to imagine the horror of that night. The Escalade swings through a roundabout, not helping my rising nausea. Ahead stands a sign pointing drivers toward the pier and the village.

Glancing behind from the passenger seat, Hessler's gaze locks on the images on my phone, which I've left lying flat on my knees.

He faces forward to say, "More people were killed off the East Coast of the United States during World War Two by German U-boats than in Pearl Harbor. A fact little known to you Americans."

"More than . . . surely not." I find this hard to believe.

Hessler fixes me with those steely eyes as if to say *case in point.*

"Truly," Kitzie jumps in, "I'm guessing most people in general have no idea." She gestures out the window toward those live oaks, those billowing clouds of azaleas that glow a hazy-filtered fuchsia and purple and white in the moonlight, like a faded Polaroid. "It's breathtaking here. Don't you think so, Hadley?"

I nod once—it *is* breathtaking, she's right. But I'm scrolling through the images on my phone again, more pictures of the SS *Oklahoma* on fire, the black thunderheads of smoke dominating the sky, then pictures of its wreckage, not much but the top of a smokestack and a piece of hull sticking out of the water.

"I'd read about the Spanish moss," Kitzie goes on to fill the fissures of silence. "It's even more lovely to see it in person."

Kitz having covered diplomacy, I cut to the chase. "I'd love to hear, Mr. Hessler, more of the torpedoing eighty years ago—and what it has to do with this reunion."

"Also," Kitzie adds, "it would be helpful to hear more of your vision for the reunion itself. I believe you mentioned the save-the-dates were sent out months ago and some preliminary plans were made, but that you'd dismissed the original event planner."

Hessler swivels back toward us briefly but does not meet my eye. "The event planners at the first, the initial planners, these were removed."

His use of the passive voice strikes me as odd, a strange sort of distancing himself from responsibility.

Kitzie looks genuinely sad, as only she could. "We're so sorry to hear that. Aren't we, Hadley?"

"Devastated," I say, sounding, even I can hear, not devastated.

"As I have said, the reunion is for the three families descending from the three young men who served in the Second World War."

"On different sides," I interject. "You mentioned one"—*your father*—"served on the Axis side."

Hessler acknowledges this only with a pause before going on. "They were linked, these three, not only by an unusual friendship. Later, they formed Boundless. Successful, of course. Multinational. They met as they were able in person. In those early years, they also gathered their families. They vowed they would stay close."

"Boundless," I offer. "A firm much in the news. And did they stay close?"

"For the first decade, they gathered back here on this island every three years or so, then less often as the families became more busy. As the technology improved, they could run the business with fewer dealings in person. One of the men died in his seventies of the heart attack. One died not long ago of Alzheimer's—my father."

Kitz leans forward to lay a hand on his arm. "It must have been a painful journey for the whole family."

Hessler surprises me by not jerking back from her touch. He does, though, gaze out the window rather than meeting her eye.

"And the third of the friends?" I prompt him.

"Is celebrating his one hundredth birthday this summer. This is another reason behind our gathering. A number of family members expressed interest in renewing the ties that . . ." He pauses here. "That bind us."

Something about the way he pronounces that word *bind* sends chills up my spine. Nothing warm and fuzzy in it—more the feel of coercion and conflict. Like the Boundless struggles I'd read about.

"That *bind* you," I repeat.

Stiffening, he shifts topic. "My father was transported here as a prisoner of war. His job was to serve meals to the officers at the radar training school."

"Housed at the King and Prince," I supply, then stop to consider. "Wait, so they trusted Nazi POWs to serve American naval officers? How was that even safe?"

"*German* POWs. These were not all Nazis."

"But Germans fighting *for Hitler*."

Hessler is actively scowling now, and I'm intrigued to see those dull eyes blaze.

Pausing, he seems to be sorting his words with care. "There is one more thing the three men had in common. They shared a friendship with one another, yes, and also with a young woman."

"A friendship?" Kitzie asks. "Wait, the woman in the photograph. On the beach."

"*Friendship* is not exactly the word. Let us simply say for now that each of the three men may have been in love with the woman. Of her feelings toward each of them, I could not say."

I take this in, my eyes following his out the Escalade's windows. We're stopped at a light in what I assume is the island's village, a cluster of small restaurants and shops, including a hardware store that looks as if it could have been here during the war. The whole village looks like it could have been frozen in time for the past eighty years, with its ice cream shops, its awnings fluttering in the sea breeze, and its gray-boarded pier at the far end of the street.

"Why," Kitz whispers to me, "are we stopping at a green light?"

Glancing back at the stoplight, I squeeze her hand. "You really are tired. It's red."

Her eyes narrow on it. "Of course it is." She leans up toward our host. "About this friendship. Please do tell us more, Mr. Hessler."

"How interesting," I offer, "that this young woman somehow drew them together and not apart. I mean, it's not hard to believe, if three men were in love with the same woman, they might not have ended up friends, right?"

He grunts in agreement.

"Also, there's that tear in your photo like someone ripped it intentionally between two of the people, and that word on the back." I pluck the envelope from my sundress pocket. I ought to hand it back to him now.

Instead, I pull the photograph out and hold it up by its white rim so we can all see. "*Traitor.* Not exactly the stuff of lifelong friendship and growing a business together."

Gazing out the window once again, he says nothing.

As we roll away from the village, we pass recently built three-story beach homes on each side, but a number of last century's bungalows remain—homes with shutters and wide porches and wide-girthed live oaks, their branches reaching over and around the cottages like an embrace. These would've been here when the U-boat fired its torpedoes, sinking those ships and, I'd just read in several of the images' captions, shattering windows of the local homes and wreaking terror.

Something suddenly occurs to me. It creates as many questions as it could answer. But I still have to ask, particularly since our captain-driver made a point of mentioning the tragedy of eighty years ago—something our host hasn't seemed eager to address.

"I wonder, Mr. Hessler, is there any chance the torpedoed ships here were somehow part of what brought these very different people together? That maybe your father was even on that U-boat that attacked?"

Hessler meets my eye, then looks away. It's as clear an answer as if he'd spoken.

"Not," Kitzie murmurs beside me, "your typical beginning of a beautiful friendship."

So Hessler's father was part of the crew that sank ships just offshore and took who knows how many lives, some possibly connected with the other two friends or with this "Joannie" in the picture. But that doesn't explain the word *Traitor* scrawled on the back of the photograph. A prisoner of war would be assumed still politically loyal to his home country—that's hardly the stuff of traitors. Just as baffling is how an

American, a Brit, and a German POW came to fall in love with the same woman.

If anything, this connection of Ernst Hessler's father with the U-boat attack complicates more of the story than it clears up. It does explain, though, our host's pretending not to hear the captain's allusion to the tragedy eight decades ago tonight.

Staring through the dark at the yellow lights flickering from the old bungalows, everything goes sepia again. I can almost hear their windows shattering from the killing blast just offshore.

Chapter 15

Joannie

Just after midnight, April 8, 1942

Joan is sound asleep and dreaming of flying with Sam in his Gee Bee, the two of them looping and gliding, when the world explodes.

Fighting her way out of sleep, she's sure at first that the Gee Bee's single engine has blown apart, and she braces for a downward spiral.

But her body is not spinning. She is, in fact, still, very still, her legs swaddled in sheets. Her eyes spring open. The dark space around is quiet, eerily so.

She's in her own bed, the only indication of turmoil the fact that she's snatched the pillow from under her head and is clutching it for dear life.

Sitting up, she hears what she's heard every night of her whole nineteen years: The crickets outside her open screened window. Her twin tossing in his own bed across the room. The sound of the surf, the steady crash and fizz of the waves that have been the rhythm of all her days.

Yet some hollowed pit in her stomach is telling her the explosion was not only in her dream. That whatever woke her wasn't merely a particularly vivid nightmare or a flock of seagulls battling over a slice of Sunbeam bread dropped on the beach.

Joannie slips from under her sheets and pads through the darkened house to the front porch, sliding carefully through the screened door so that its hinges don't squawk. Turning, she gasps.

The horizon glows a lurid orange red, flames dancing against a charcoal sky and reflected in the ocean, the edge of the world on fire. The boards of the front porch glitter, the shattered glass of the kitchen and living room blown inside, but a scattering of shards here.

"So you heard it too," Sam says from behind her, just inches away.

"I thought I was dreaming."

He stands next to her. Joannie can see in the faint light he's in the white T-shirt and dungarees he wore yesterday, as if he fell asleep in his clothes. For several beats, she tries to make sense of what she's seeing.

Tomorrow well before dawn . . . We're shipping out, Will Dobbins had said.

Oh, God. Will Dobbins.

On the SS Oklahoma.

Don't let that horror be the SS Oklahoma.

"Will." Joannie whispers, reaching for her brother.

"You will . . . what?" Sam's head twitches toward her. His eyes, though, stay on the fire.

Not a verb, Joannie wants to explain. A person. A man . . . hardly more than a boy. With a drawl from the Tennessee hills and a smile as big as a crescent moon.

And a wariness, just a little, of launching back out to sea.

"That boy on the beach," she finally gets out. "The one you saw me kiss . . ."

"Oh, *God.* You don't think . . ."

Whipping around, she jerks Sam's arm. "Let's go."

"*I'll* go, Joannie. Things could get awful gruesome."

Joan steps in front of her brother, the fire on the horizon reflected still in his eyes—and no doubt burning in hers. "So are you driving us both or should I take my bike?"

She can only make out the basic contours of his face in the dark, but she sees his mouth quirk.

"I'll warm up the truck."

She's already thrown the screened door open when she calls back over her shoulder, "Give me thirty seconds so I'm not on rescue detail in a nightgown."

With Sam behind the wheel, neither of them utters a sound as he floors the truck along Ocean Boulevard. After screeching onto Mallery Street, he kills the engine near the hardware store. Leaping out of the truck's cab, they sprint toward the pier, where a handful of silhouettes shift about.

On the horizon the flames have grown larger. Hungrier.

Sam looks from her out to the tongues of red and orange licking the heavens.

Joannie stares straight ahead, out toward the flames and the stench of oil and the cries of terrified men. Then she begins running toward the left end of the pier, where she'd left her boat.

Because Will Dobbins. He's out there in the fire.

Chapter 16
Will

He was thinking of her, in fact, when it hit: lightning that seemed to ignite right by his head, thunder crashing right by his ear, the whole ship lurching.

He'd just dropped below deck when the whole world seemed to explode. For several seconds or several days—he has no idea—he can see nothing but black.

Water pools at his feet. This he can feel, and now, his vision beginning to clear, he can see it.

Water.

Inside the *Oklahoma.*

Will's not one to panic. But this, the explosion and the lurching and now the water swirling around his shoes, this cannot be good.

"*Lordy,*" he says.

It's the worst obscenity he uses. But he delivers it now in a way that empties out his lungs. They feel, in fact, as if they might collapse.

Another deafening sound, the entire ship lurching again.

"Jack!" he calls for the first mate. "*Jack!*"

Battle sirens wail all over the ship.

Will knows he should scramble fast, no turning back, up the metal ladder through the hatch to the deck above. Getting trapped down here would be every nightmare he's had.

But what if there are men who can't get out?

A torpedo. He knows they've been struck by a torpedo. But he refuses to give the other side credit for a kill.

Joannie's U-boat, he thinks as he runs. *The one she tried to warn people about. But nobody listened. Not even him. He'd climbed on board the* Oklahoma *last night, his head full up of her, of her lips and her warm leg against his. He never reported what she'd seen to the officers.*

So now he's running, sloshing through rising water. The ship must be going down fast, smoke everywhere. The steel walls amplify the men's screams.

Will wants to stop himself, wants to reverse his own gangly limbs, even as he plunges deeper into the bowels of the ship.

Down the hall, the water is nearly at his knees. A boy no older than sixteen lies sprawled at the door to the galley, his head only above the water because of how he crumpled against the door, but his nose is about to go under.

Will starts by shaking the boy's shoulder, but he's out cold. Scooping him up, Will hoists him above the water.

Battling against the current of the seawater pouring in, Will holds the boy, his own shoulders taking the brunt of being knocked into the walls on either side of the metal corridor.

Will's heart hammering inside his rib cage, he does what he always does in a crisis: he talks—even though his own voice is nothing but a broken cattail of a reed.

"You got to have gone and lied about your age, kid. Wait till your mama gives you a piece of her mind . . ."

The water nearly knocks him off his feet, and he has to stand still to regain his balance. The words keep coming from him—which words no longer matters. He's vaguely aware of screams all around.

He does the one thing his brain can focus to do. He takes a step against the surge of the water. And another.

He holds the boy up higher, shoulder height now, above the rising flood.

They're back near the engine room, the shrieks for help growing louder. A charred body topples into his path.

"I'm coming back!" Will shouts. "Hang on! I'm coming back!"

But he's spoken too soon. He's reached the metal ladder leading from the engine room up to the next deck, and he's climbed the first two rungs, his left hand gripping the boy and his right hand clutching the ladder. The hatch door above them, though, is blocked by something.

Will lets go of the ladder long enough to shove the door, but it doesn't budge. He has to grab the ladder again to keep from falling backward into the flood.

He could let go of the dead weight of the boy and use both his hands to push on what's blocking the way overhead. It would save at least one life, his own, rather than lose two.

The math assures him the action makes sense.

But Will cannot do it.

He can't.

"Help!" he adds his voice to the screams.

Every ounce of his remaining strength he exerts against the hatch door.

Still, it does not move.

The boy's eyes flicker open, two brown orbs of terror. Instinctively, the boy wraps his arms around Will's neck, cutting off his air.

The voice Will hears himself use sounds like another man's, someone who's out fishing, maybe, not within moments of drowning.

"I need you," the voice says, "not to choke me. I need you to stay calm."

The boy's grip on Will's throat tightens, fear blazing in his eyes. But then the grip loosens, if only a fraction.

"I need you," Will goes on, "to hold tight to my shoulders. Can you do that?"

Will has pressed himself up another rung of the ladder, the boy coiled against his shoulders and back. The water has risen now to Will's lips. All out of strength, he says what he knows may be his last words: "I need you, kid, to take a deep breath."

Feeling the boy respond, the skinny chest shifting behind him, Will himself draws the breath he knows must be his final one. The water is above their noses now.

Picturing himself on a summer's afternoon at the top of the hayloft, aching all over and sweating clear through his overalls as he pushes his arms to shovel one more load, and another, Will uses both arms to heave on the object blocking their path.

Still, the way up stays blocked, the water washing above their heads.

Chapter 17
Hadley

Feeling suddenly as if I can't breathe, still imagining the shatter of windows from the U-boat's torpedo, I've rolled down the Escalade's tinted window to hear the ocean, its beat keeping time in the silence.

I'm struck again by the sheer, haunting beauty of the place—so different from our grade school years, the bare, treeless yard of that first foster family, whose only flowers were dandelions and clover. Different, too, from what I've grown accustomed to in LA.

In Southern California, beauty bursts all around, even in the bougainvillea and oleander spilling along interstates. But like the surgically enhanced, too-perfect bodies of its people, LA is frenetically pretty. As if all the blooms and faces are aware they're just one broken sprinkler system or Botox treatment away from reverting to desert and deep lines again.

This place, though, has a beauty that's almost painful. As if a brutal, tangled past has been woven into the natural beauty. Spanish moss drips from the live oaks in silvery spills, with palmettos in clusters beneath them.

I'm content right now just to lean toward my window and breathe. The air smells of salt and pine straw and spring, of decay but also new life.

The driver swings us into a tree-covered lane, toward a collection of Spanish-style buildings, their red tile roofs and white stucco arresting. Even in the dark, I can see the grounds of the resort are meticulously trimmed, flowers spilling not only from planters but even from crevices in the palms.

"This," Ernst Hessler announces, gesturing, "is the King and Prince."

Kitzie makes all the properly gushing comments: *How splendid! The view!*

I'm drawn in by the architecture. "Which of these wings and turrets were part of the original 1935 structure—the dance club?"

Hessler's eyes spark, as if my research—knowing when the resort was first built—is evidence that we'll accept the job.

"I research *everything*," I add. "Regardless."

The main building of the resort sits near the water, its entrance grand and genteel but not imposing. A valet and two bellboys scurry to greet us.

Hessler gives instructions in his clipped, overly enunciated English, then waves us forward. "The driver will see to the rest."

The captain-driver stiffens again but doesn't acknowledge our leaving. I wonder if it bothers him that Hessler never uses his name, never offers a single word of gratitude.

"Thank you," Kitz—of course—calls back to the driver just as I'm thinking this about Hessler, and I add my own "Thanks!" over my shoulder as we walk away.

I'll say this for being raised how we were, Kitzie and I: you notice the servers and drivers and haulers of life, the folks people like Ernst Hessler expect to melt into his gilded background.

"I still don't have a good feeling," I say close to my sister's ear, "about this job." That's the extent of our conversation as we follow Hessler into a lobby with a grand high-vaulted ceiling, its wooden beams oiled to a sheen.

Kitz and I stop walking at the same moment, both of us staring up at the ceiling, then over at a massive fireplace. Straight ahead, the ocean swells blue beyond a patio with café umbrellas, and to the right, just beyond a line of outdoor fire pits and couches, a massive round pool sparkles.

We both exhale, shoulders already relaxing.

"So maybe," I say in a low tone, "you and I agree we'll be declining this job, but we take our time getting to an out-loud kind of no."

Kitz turns fully around to me now, her oval face pinched and guilty. "Hadz, I thought sure you'd come around by now. Look, the truth is—"

"You already told Hessler yes."

Her little bow of a mouth opens like she'd like to deny it, make herself form that word even now. "Well . . . kind of. Yes."

"Kind of?"

"Maybe more like a full yes."

"Kitz, how could you? We always agree on—"

Fuming, I've only begun to say what I need to say. But Ernst Hessler is gesturing for us from the far end of the lobby.

Kitzie squeezes my arm. "We'll talk about it later. I'm sorry, Hadley."

Dazed, I follow her to where Hessler points up to a wall on the left, where black-and-white photos hang. "Pictures from the Naval Radar Training School days." He looks at me: a kind of challenge.

Angry at Kitz and annoyed by Hessler, I pluck a fact from the back of my jet-lagged brain. My voice sounds wooden, like the sixth-grade nerd I used to be and maybe sometimes revert to under stress: "The development of radar made perhaps *the* crucial difference in the outcome of the war. Because in 1942, the U-boats ruled the Atlantic. More than any other one thing, it was the U-boats that made Winston Churchill think the Allies might actually lose. Until radar offered some hope."

Hessler takes my measure. "It is possible you know more of this radar technology than I might have imagined."

"It's possible, Mr. Hessler"—I meet his eye—"my sister and I know more of a great many things than you might imagine." I'm smiling, but my gaze doesn't flinch from his.

Do not, I hope he reads in my look, *underestimate Kitzie or me.*

A hostess leads the way through the restaurant to the patio bordered by ocean.

"Welcome to Echo," she trills, waving us to the table closest to the water, strands of lights swaying overhead in the breeze.

"A bottle of your best cabernet sauvignon," Hessler calls over his shoulder to a waiter standing nearby.

"Right away, sir."

Hessler doesn't bother asking if we prefer red or white. Which is just as well. I'm a white-wine-only chick, and this will save me the strain of self-discipline. I need my wits sharp around this man.

I watch Kitzie settling herself, and I register that something's not right. It's as if she's in slow motion, every movement oddly drawn out, unsteady. Even lifting a glass of water, her hand doesn't seem to operate right, nearly knocking the tumbler sideways.

It's fine. She's tired from traveling, run down, low on iron, short on sleep, I tell myself calmly. But my pulse speeds up in response—like my heart is already rejecting the lie.

We sit in a semicircle facing the ocean, the servers appearing with platters of lobster nachos, bowls of ceviche and shrimp cocktail.

"Now," Hessler says suddenly, lifting his wine as if in a toast. "I will tell you about the three men. The first, my father, Hans, was a prisoner of war, as I have said. The German officers of course were not forced to work."

"Because of Geneva Convention guidelines," I say, my red-eye-flight reading coming in handy again. "And enlisted men had to be paid for their work." Once again I sound like the grade-grubbing, book-worming me of elementary school—and it's cringeworthy. Men like Hessler, though, can stand being reminded they're not the only ones in the room.

His eyebrow flicks up. A recognition, at least.

Ridiculously, I feel gratified by Ernst Hessler's notice.

"Indeed. The enlisted men like my own father were paid like the day laborers on farms. In this case, to serve the meals to the Americans in this radar training school."

"That must've caused incredible tensions, surely," I say.

He frowns but continues. "The second of the three friends, Dov Silverberg, was an officer. Great Britain exchanged him for an American instructor because of Silverberg's knowledge of radar. He was trained in the south of England, his home. A recent graduate from Cambridge. Set collegiate records there in the hundred meters. Took a first in physics. He was also, perhaps I should mention"—he clears his throat—"a Jew."

I set down the lobster nacho I've just picked up. "Seriously? A Jewish British officer became friends with a German POW? In the middle of the war?"

"The third of the three men was—"

"Pardon me, sir," our waiter interrupts. "Will the gentleman at the far end of the terrace be joining you?"

Kitzie and I turn. Hessler's captain-driver, hatless now, leans against a wall several yards away, arms crossed and facing out toward the sea.

"I hope you'll join us," Kitzie calls to him. Because Kitz never met a closed door she didn't want to open to let someone in.

But the driver doesn't so much as glance our way.

"I take it he's also high-level-clearance security?" I joke, just trying to break the silence.

But Hessler frowns. "Perhaps then he would make himself useful."

The harshness of the comment seems to hang on the breeze a moment, the surf the only sound for several beats.

The captain-driver may not have been listening.

But, no, a muscle in his lower jaw flexes.

He heard the comment, all right.

Ernst Hessler, you bastard, I think—and very much need to say.

"Ernst Hessler, you—" I begin.

"Must tell us more," Kitzie says over me, because she knows me well. "About your own connection with the island. We'd love to hear. Wouldn't we, Hadz?"

I pull my gaze from the captain-driver to look out over the nighttime ocean, edged in meringue where dark water meets milk chocolate sand. My feet now out of my heels, I manage a grudging "We would, yes."

Hessler gestures to the north of us. "I purchased significant property here in the 1970s. This property and high-yield stocks—as well, of course, as the company founded by my father and his two friends— these have made me what is called in your press an ultra."

I look blankly back at him. "Ultra?"

"U-H-N-W-I. You know this term, yes?"

Kitzie and I both shake our heads.

"*He* knows." Hessler gestures toward his captain-driver, still standing, arms crossed, against the wall. Still staring out at the sea.

The driver speaks without turning his head, and with no inflection at all. "Ultra-high-net-worth individual. Those whose assets amount to or exceed fifty million."

As if Hessler had pressed Play on a prerecorded response.

Looking pleased with himself—*Like a dog trainer,* I think, *who's finally taught a vicious mutt to sit*—Hessler looks to my sister and me.

"An *ultra,*" Kitz says with an admiration I know she's faking, but it passes for real.

"U-H-N-W-I," I murmur and manage to get through all five letters without snickering. Kitz, though, must hear the dangerously high register of my voice. She gives me a warning look.

"It seemed fitting to acquire portions of the island where my father once served as a prisoner of war."

"So . . . wait." He has my full attention again now. "I'd love to hear more about how your father ever even got to know the other two men during the war, what happened to bond them so they'd want to stay connected through the years and, Lord knows, start a business together."

Hessler lifts his cabernet sauvignon for a contemplative sip. "There is much you need to understand in order to execute the work properly."

"Execute," I echo. *Interesting choice of words from He of the Ghoulish Face.*

Hessler's head swivels to meet my gaze. "The wider publicity, of course, will be crucial—the media presence for a reunion that tells the true story of Boundless from its beginnings."

There. Right there is the truth, I think. *His motive for all this.*

"Mr. Hessler, if I may ask with all candor: Would part of our purpose actually be a kind of facelift for the Boundless international image? Perhaps a marketing extravaganza that's also massive family reunion?"

Kitzie turns wide eyes on me, but Hessler, to his credit, meets my gaze and does not blink. "It is, yes, both of these things. The story of the three friends remains crucial either way, yes?"

Including, I think, *exactly who the woman in the photo was and who that man was with her. And what* Traitor *scrawled on the back had to do with the three friends.*

Hessler holds up a hand. "Perhaps we start with the . . . *tragedy,* I believe was the word used." His eyes flick to his driver, still staring, cross-armed, out to sea. "Yes, we begin with the tragedy."

Kitzie stands suddenly, nearly knocking over her chair. "Perfect. Do please start there. I'll only be a moment in the powder room."

Our diplomat gone, I hesitate to say much, and I'm mesmerized by the sea—the calm, reassuring steadiness of its surf.

The conversation lulls, until Hessler says, "I see, Ms. Jacks, that you have something on your mind."

Turning, I find his eyes boring into mine.

Maybe I'm just one margarita short of a smile, I nearly say. But the truth is, he's read my face well.

"The thing is, Mr. Hessler, you've certainly been generous in bringing us here, but—"

My sister is just emerging from the lobby. Instead of taking the shortest route back to our table, though, she's detoured by the pool and bends to swish one hand through the water. Straightening, she takes a step in our direction, but now she's wobbling a little. In fact, she looks particularly small just now, balancing on her yellow wedges beside that huge blue orb of a pool.

And particularly pale. Fragile even.

When she popped into the doctor last week for her lingering cold, they cleared her of anything worse. Just a little deficient in some things easily fixed, they said. She assured me of that. Supplements and rest, and she'll be good as new.

Yet, her wobbly gait. The expression on her face. The confusion.

I bolt up from my seat and reach her side just as she crumples to the ground. I catch her head before it hits, but just barely.

"Kitz, what's wrong?" My fear has gone full wind sock on me.

Her eyes flutter open.

"This cold's got me so weak," she whispers. "Nothing to worry about."

"Kitz. Please. Really, what's wrong? We're taking you to a doc—"

"*Really*, that's it. Just give me a minute here before I get up."

You're lying, I want to scream at my sister. *Kitzie Jacks, you know something, and you're lying to me!*

But I can't. Kitz and I do not lie to each other. Ever.

I can't say those words.

Instead, I hold her head on my lap and whisper words I've said to my sister so many times over our frayed string of years.

"Don't be scared. I've got you."

Chapter 18

Will

April 8, 1942

He can't do it.

Having finally burst through the hatch door, heaved his way out to the top deck, and reached the metal promontory that remains poking out at a precarious angle above water, the body of the boy still in his arms, Will knows he should listen to the shouts of his mates already on the life rafts.

Get the hell in the raft, Dobbins!

You and the kid. In here, NOW!

Flames devouring the *Oklahoma* yard by crackling yard, Will uses the rope someone has tied to a piece of remaining railing to climb down partway to the raft and hand off the boy. He'd like to climb in himself, but he can't.

Because he has no choice about going back.

A person can't hear voices of trapped souls screaming for help and just paddle away. Or if you can, something inside you would die as surely as your physical form might survive.

He's on the point of dropping below deck when a shout to the ship's port side stops him. By the light of the flames, he can make out the silhouette of a surfaced submarine.

"Halt! We offer help," a voice calls in heavily accented English. "This is Commander Hardegen speaking. You will be hurt if you go below." A man, maybe two—nothing but just shadows in the flickering dark—are standing several feet above the water. Part of Will's mind registers that there must be a logical explanation, but in this instant, it feels like a monstrous reverse of the biblical story of walking on water—holding out a hand not of reassurance or grace, but of threat and capture.

I am delusional, Will thinks. *The smoke, the flames, the oil.*

I am not seeing the conning tower of a surfaced German sub.

I am not hearing its commander speaking to me.

Also, the irony is too much. Even in dreams, a U-boat commander who has just blown up your ship doesn't warn you that you might harm yourself.

"Come! Surrender!" the voice that must be a dream insists. "We offer to help."

Will ignores the mirage and plunges into a hole that once was a passageway. He and the *Oklahoma*'s captain behind him, the two of them covering their noses from the smoke with the collars of their soaked shirts, fight their way forward to where the screams continue.

It takes both of them yanking to pry open the door. The man that spills out into their arms has been gashed in the gut and is losing blood fast.

Will rips off his shirt and wads it against the wound. But he knows it's probably no good. They'll lose their lives in saving a man who cannot be saved.

Together, they carry the man through melted steel and smoldering paper—*The map room,* Will realizes vaguely. *Of a ship that hardly sailed beyond Brunswick Harbor.*

A wall of fire falls across their only exit.

The man they carry shrieks again, perhaps in pain and perhaps in fear of the fire encircling them.

The captain meets Will's eye. "German bastards gave us a way out, didn't they, Shakespeare? Wish we'd taken it?"

With bile in his throat, Will realizes the delusion was real. The U-boat commander was actually offering an opportunity for them to surrender—and be saved.

"I do not, sir."

"A noble lie, Dobbins."

Praying the wet of his hair and clothing will protect them at least for the first instant, Will plunges with the dying man into the flames.

Chapter 19
Joannie

Joannie holds in the scream that's growing inside her throat, nearly choking her now. Letting the sailboat's sheet, the rope that controls its mainsail, slide to limp between her fingers, she lets the little craft slow as she and Sam move closer to the spill of oil, the burning ship, the char-blackened, bloody men clinging to rubble and lifeboats.

By the light of the flames, she can make out parts of the ship's name just beside a rupture in its hull at least the size of a semitruck.

She tries not to hear Will Dobbins's words again from yesterday in the drugstore.

SS Oklahoma. *At your service. Shipping out early tomorrow morning.*

O-k-l-a, she can read near the smoldering bow.

Men beg for help from the water, from rafts, from she doesn't even know where in the fire-licked dark all around.

Too many, her mind shrieks. *Too many to save.*

A yacht Joan recognizes as belonging to a Candler family member of the Coca-Cola empire has arrived first, its captain, Olaf Olsen, hauling yet another load of men from the water. Several smaller crafts, too, navigate through the bodies and wreckage, though none as small as hers and Sam's.

She makes herself focus on the form, not much more than a shadow, closest to the starboard as Sam steers the little boat through the wreckage.

"Take my hand," she says to one sailor, whose arms embrace a beam like a lover, his cheek to the wood, his eyes closed.

The man's eyes blink open but take a moment to focus on her face.

"Daisy?" he asks, his voice sandpaper, all hope, all despair.

Joannie doesn't disabuse him of possibly being his Daisy. She and Sam lift him from under the armpits and haul him onto the hull. His uniform, his skin, his hair are all coated in oil.

Sam lowers his head to her ear. "We'll only be able to fish out a couple of men at a time. The boat's too small for more."

"Maybe three." She finds herself scanning the inky waves looking for one face in particular, a mop of dark hair, impossibly long limbs.

The mandolin, she thinks. *He's lost his mandolin.*

She will not let herself think that the owner of the mandolin himself might also be lost.

"Look at me," Sam suddenly commands. "Do not look down."

Sam never commands her, his gentleness a signature of his nature.

She can't help it: she looks down.

A leg, severed at the hip, is floating by on a piece of steel spiraled into a jagged S.

"Dear Jesus," she chokes, reaching for Sam's hand.

In the dark, she can only see the flash of a sailor's arms as he flails toward them. She prays it is Will, even as she realizes it can't be. The arms aren't long enough.

Are they?

Raising his face from the water, the man sputters for help, and for an awful instant, Joan wants to push him away in case Will Dobbins is struggling nearby.

Instead, she has Sam hold on to her legs as she reaches far out into the water for this man, who's run out of strength. Together, she and Sam haul him up onto the tiny sailboat.

Ahead of them, the ship is still on fire, lighting the sea around them. Another lifeboat full of drenched, moaning men is pulling away. But she sees two men rowing back toward the wreckage.

Fragments of their words carry across the water.

Hearing voices . . .

Inside . . .

For a moment, Sam and Joan both stop moving. Above the groaning of their own passengers, they can hear men calling from inside the ship.

Will Dobbins, she thinks, *is inside the ship as it burns. Trapped.*

But now a towering beam comes crashing down and falls into the sea. Its fire sheds light on the *Oklahoma*'s deck as one man scrambles across it. He's unusually tall, and he moves as if he's still getting used to the length of his own legs. He turns his head to say something to the man following him.

Joan sucks in air.

So Will Dobbins is not dead—not yet.

He's climbing across a deck tilted now at a nearly forty-five-degree angle, a deck that's on fire. With a final shout, he ducks below.

Stop! Joan wants to scream. *Come back! You can't possibly save anyone now!*

"Daisy," one of the wounded sailors on her own hull murmurs. "Daisy."

Still staring at the *Oklahoma*, Joannie bends to rest a hand on the man's back, his body trembling under her palm.

"I'm here," she whispers. Because what else is there to say to a dying man?

"Joannie," Sam might've just said. She's hearing as if she's deep underwater. "We got to get these men to shore."

She wants to argue, but Sam is right. These two men they've plucked from the water may not survive, but they certainly won't if they aren't seen by a doctor soon. Forcing herself down to take the tiller, she steers them back toward shore as Sam adjusts the mainsail and jib.

I'm leaving Will Dobbins here in the ocean to die, she thinks.

For the sake of the wounded men in the boat and to block out her own frantic thoughts, she fills the silence with whatever words come to mind. She's vaguely aware that she's reeling off chunks of the Declaration of Independence—*We hold these truths to be self-evident, that all men are created equal*—and singing bits of "Boogie Woogie Bugle Boy." Anything to keep the dying man from calling out for Daisy again, which makes Joan want to weep when she needs to see straight to steer.

Sam turns his head once to raise an eyebrow at her, at her word-swirl of Enlightenment eloquence and dance floor swing that shouldn't be served up together. But she finds she can grip the tiller against the slam of the waves, finds she can keep singing and talking, talking and singing, as the wounded men lie still and listen.

Even as the mainsail fills and she steers them into another broad reach toward shore, she glances back toward the ship. The SS *Oklahoma* is sinking lower into the sea, its upper decks a frenzy of orange and red.

Chapter 20
Hadley

From the balcony of our hotel suite, I'm watching the sunrise over the ocean, an explosion of color, when I hear Kitz stir from her bed.

"So, Hadz, it makes sense, right?" she calls out to me, vaulting straight over *good morning*.

Before I can ask how she's feeling, she launches herself out from under the sheets and raises her arms over her head.

For an instant, I see us both in footie pajamas again, listening to the crashes outside our door—our first and most volatile foster home— the two of us stretching our arms overhead and pretending we could latch onto a star and ride together on it, far away. A shard of memory pierces through: that first foster mother screeching at us through the door after I'd, once again, kicked her dead in the shins—confusion and grief raging in my nine-year-old brain with nowhere to go. That early foster mother's words ran in my head on endless replay, and all these years later I can still call them up, verbatim.

Just what I should've seen coming from your kind. Everybody 'round here knows y'all's whole family way back is trash, nothin' but addicts and trash . . .

Closing my eyes, I focus on the sound of the waves until the last fizz of the words, *your kind . . . y'all's whole family way back . . . nothin' but addicts and trash . . .* has ebbed away, leaving only the surf.

"Kitz, you seem better, but—"

"I am *so* much better today, see? Just a dizzy spell yesterday. Feeling fine now. Also, it's going to be great, this job."

"Let me take you to a doctor. Just to be sure."

"Just went. Nothing some iron supplements and rest won't fix. Case closed. About this reunion . . ."

Sighing, I give up forcing the doctor visit. "Well, let's see. Ernst Hessler has shown himself to be impossible to please. Though he's got a good tailor."

"There you go again, being histrionic."

It's my sister's favorite word for me at these times—*these times* being when she's focused on the butterflies and roses of the world while it falls to me to lay out its dark alleys and dangers, along with making us laugh whenever either of us sinks too low in the old bone-deep sorrow of all that the addictions of our parents stole from us: Stability. Trust. Home.

For a moment, I close my eyes and see Kitzie and me holding hands, our mother curled up again on the pilled brown couch—this time not budging as we pulled on her and begged—our mother's arm growing cold, then her whole body stiff, Kitz soiling her pants in fear, me pummeling the couch in my own panic. Because who do two little girls call when their mama's tried to do this parenting thing—this whole life thing—all by herself without help, and now she won't wake up again, ever?

With effort—but then, I'm practiced at this—I shake the image away.

"Okay, let's say I am being histrionic. Still, it's a tall order even with a reasonable client: planning a reunion for the descendants of three war buddies who have some crazy-complicated past and who now, if you google the firm, seem to be at each other's throats over the business?"

"First, I can tell you're as intrigued as I am how these guys got connected during the war and what the deal is with that woman laughing on the beach in the photo."

"Joannie," I fill in before I can stop myself.

"See? I knew you'd been paying attention, despite all your efforts not to. Second, we're spending this next month in a charming resort, fully funded. Even if this . . . cold . . . of mine—"

I catch the infinitesimal pause before that vague designation, *cold*—like she's not sold on the diagnosis herself—but she's rushing on, fairly bubbling over with plans.

"Even if I'm slowed down a little, I can design all the backdrops and price compare the caterers from my laptop, while you do the running around. At night we can dine seaside. You can't tell me the ocean isn't good for the soul."

"Sure, but—"

"Thirdly, the money is . . . let's just say it's worth our while."

"We've been doing well, though. If anything, we've been working too hard. Clearly, we need to go easier on you—as your passing out poolside demonstrated. It really was Broadway worthy, by the way—very graceful, complete with well-lit backdrop." I watch her face. "Of course, since you already agreed to this job on behalf of us both, you already agreed on a figure."

Again, she looks embarrassed. "I know we never keep things from each other. I could just tell from talking with him you'd dislike the guy right away."

"You weren't wrong there."

"But when he called, sounding like an . . . okay, a stuck-up billionaire sort—"

"Finally, we agree."

"Then when he laid out the basic reunion he wanted, and that he'd like us to be on site for nearly a month, and what he was offering to pay . . ."

"You couldn't help saying yes."

"Are you angry?" she asks, the same eyes that looked up at me at ages four and eight and twelve, wanting to be sure my rage at the world wasn't directed at her.

Never, I used to tell her while the two of us shared a single sucker. *A whole cannon blast at the world but never at you.*

"Wait," she says, "before you answer if you're mad—"

"You're assuming my loyalty can be bought, Ms. Jacks."

"Wait till you hear the figure, Ms. Jacks—then you tell me." She yanks me down to whisper a number in my ear. Then, beaming, she lets out a squeal. "Right?"

I gape at her. "Apparently, I *can* be bought. Who knew?"

She squeals again. "So you agree?"

"Wasn't aware I had much of a choice since my *beloved* business partner and *most trusted friend* already signed on before we'd consulted. But that figure certainly increases the likelihood I could just smile and chew through any future dinner speeches on Ultra-High-Net-Worth Individuals." To demonstrate, I give her my best vapid smile and pretend to lift a glass in a toast.

"Oh, Hadz, I'm so relieved. Especially since . . ."

"Since what?"

"Never mind about that. So look. Last night when I couldn't sleep, I pulled up the website for a museum on the island that we need to visit right off."

Reaching for her laptop, Kitzie shows me the screen.

World War II Home Front Museum, the banner reads.

At the bottom of the page is a link to an interview in which a St. Simons resident and US Navy veteran describes a later attack in the Caribbean, where his own ship was torpedoed.

"Hadz, can you imagine?"

I scoot next to her on the love seat out on the balcony and take comfort that however skinny her frame, she's assured me again the doctors were clear: it's just a cold.

Together, we listen to the veteran struggle for words to paint that world he faced.

I'm imagining the *Oklahoma* now: the explosions, the fires, the bodies floating in the ocean, the loved ones desperately waiting for word . . .

Together, we stare, stupefied, at the screen.

Chapter 21

Hans

April 9, 1942

Fire encircles him, licking at his legs, his arms, crackling with what sounds like glee.

Hans wakes in the night with a jolt, sitting upright so fast in his bunk he slams his head on the steel pole supporting the man above.

It was a dream. Only a dream.

Yet it wasn't just that, he knows.

U-123 has sunk three boats in the span of two days, the third earlier today. The commander will be commended by the Führer himself, no doubt, if they survive the passage back to occupied France. More kills. More medals.

Hans should feel elated, of course, should join in the toasts and back slaps of his fellow crew members.

Perhaps this nightmare he's still shaking off—and his sour stomach—is partly the fault of the letter from home he received before launching on this latest mission. His mother had chosen her words carefully to avoid the black swaths of the censors.

Father Bernhard's sermons continue to interest us, yet he may be obliged to travel.

Her verb is the key: *zur Reise verpflichtet*. In this case, not just *traveling* but *obliged* to travel—and travel, Hans gathers, not to anywhere of the priest's wishing.

Hans understands she means that their priest must still be calling his parishioners to compassion for the oppressed, that he must still be quoting verses—too often—that insist they lay down their lives for neighbors and friends, that God's definition of neighbor is broader, so much broader, than they might imagine.

From the pulpit, Father Bernhard never mentioned Jews or Gypsies or homosexuals or anyone else by category, particularly. But in private homes, he has been known to comment on the roundups of certain sorts of people.

He has been known, even, to weep.

More than once, his voice during the *Confiteor* had shredded on *mea culpa, mea culpa, mea maxima culpa*—my fault, my fault, my grievous fault.

The SS has been watching, his mother means Hans to understand. Should the old priest's heart keep breaking in public, should he continue to speak but not speak, his conscience stretching him on its rack every day, their beloved Father Bernhard might not be with them much longer.

Perhaps Father Bernhard is one cause of Hans's struggle with his own role, this duty he must perform. Even before Hans was drafted, the old priest showed weakness this way. The Third Reich is all about strength—and Hans should be, as well.

In the dark of the sub, while his shift is supposed to be sleeping, Hans tears the letter to pieces so small he can't possibly read it again.

Hans returns to sleep, but this time his nightmares are of Father Bernhard, sometimes in the pulpit weeping, sometimes on the ground, unmoving, the villagers gathered around.

Chapter 22

Joannie

Joannie pushes past the rows of pine boxes in stacks that reach above her head on either side of the funeral home's passageway.

Coffins.

Even the sound of the word has its haunting resonance, sounding of cobwebs and final goodbyes. Of lilies and holes in the earth and holes in the heart.

So many coffins.

The funeral home director, Edo Miller, bustles from one end of the passageway to the next, with a notebook in one hand. His own face has gone ashen as he scribbles another name on the pad, scrambles back to the front entrance to usher another stretcher in with another corpse.

It's only April, but the air outside is hotter than a typical St. Simons spring, and inside the funeral home, with crowds of people swarming in, driven by the need to help somehow—and maybe, too, by morbid curiosity—it's stifling. The soles of Joan's oxfords are sticking to the floor, when she realizes with horror the viscous substance is blood, some of it congealed into dark Rorschach blots and some still a bright garish red, with dozens of footprints through.

Gagging, Joan presses her way back toward the front door. Under a live oak, she doubles over.

"Twenty-two," a voice says from just a few feet away.

Straightening, Joannie keeps four fingers over her mouth—she doesn't trust herself yet not to be sick.

The voice comes from a man with a fedora angled on his head and a camera around his neck, a cigarette in one hand. He's leaning on the trunk of the tree, one foot propped on its toe against the opposite ankle. As his right hands swoops to his mouth, he inhales the smoke and exhales back out in a calm, rhythmic motion. From a few more feet away, he would appear relaxed.

This close, though, Joannie can see that his right hand is trembling.

She's in no mood for a reporter. What is there to say when the world turns on its head and blood runs in the ocean?

This sort of thing never happens in our little village on our little island. We just expected it to stay an ocean away.

"Twenty-two," he says again. "Souls lost. On the two ships together, the SS *Oklahoma* and the *Esso Baton Rouge*."

"*Esso Baton Rouge*," she repeats. So that was the name of the boat that suffered the second explosion an hour or so after the first. Or perhaps it was ten minutes. Or ten days. Time is all bent and misshapen like that painting by Salvador Dalí, the one with the melted clock faces.

Like horror and loss have torched time, Joannie thinks. *Made reality collapse.*

"You okay, miss?"

"Other than being out in the water surrounded with burned men and floating body parts, the water gone to oil and blood? Other than that?"

She doesn't realize she's said it out loud until the reporter's eyes go wide and he reaches for the notepad and pen in his shirt pocket.

She holds up her hand. "That wasn't meant to be a quote. I'm just here to see if I . . . can help." A lie, mostly. She'd help if they needed it, but it's not why she's come here.

She's come because at the hospital the nurses blocked all visitors. No one there would answer questions about which men had been admitted or how any patient was faring—and which ones had already been sent to the morgue.

"I'm also looking for someone."

The reporter wipes sweat from under his fedora. "Don't blame you for being worried." He puts a hand to his stomach, and Joannie realizes hers is pressed over her own. "You had a fella on one of those ships, little lady?"

"Would you happen to have any sort of . . . list?"

"Of the dead, you mean? Sorry, bluntness is part of my profession." He shakes his head. "I don't think anybody does at this point. Even that number *twenty-two*'s just a guess. Too early to tell who'll make it and who won't." He gestures with this head toward the Edo Miller Funeral Home entrance. "You tried in there already, I take it?"

"It's chaos."

He studies the building as if he can see inside its walls. Another pair of men stumbles from the back of a pickup, holding what appears to be a door pulled off its hinges. On the door rides a form in the shape of a body—or part of one—covered over with a floral sheet, blood soaked through the cotton.

"It's the part of the job that's the hardest these days," the reporter mutters. "We're not supposed to let folks know there's a threat right in their own backyards. Not supposed to breed panic. Meanwhile, I stand here talking to some pretty little dame about how she spent the night fishing bodies out of the sea, and I'm watching fellows trek inside with homemade stretchers, and all I can think of is synonyms for the word *hell*."

"Hospital," she says.

"Pardon?" The cigarette droops in his mouth. "Sister, if you've got it into your head they're gonna let you into the hospital just 'cause you got a fella you want to check on, I can save you the time. I'm a pushy guy, and they wouldn't even let me through the door. No way are they letting you in unless you got a stethoscope or you're FDR—and even then, I'm not sure."

"Thanks for the warning," she tells him. Then tosses back over her shoulder, "I'll find a way."

∼

Perhaps Joannie intended to lie all along.

She's not admitted this consciously to herself, but she's flung a scarf over her hair, tying it at the neck. She's donned large sunglasses. She's traded the pencil skirt and white blouse she'll wear tonight for her ticket-tearing job at the Ritz for a lilac dress she's only ever worn to church, and she's not been to Christ Church Frederica in months, since she works Sundays helping out at McKinnon Airfield. She doesn't know many medical sorts—most of the doctors and nurses commute from the mainland—but St. Simons is a small place. Precautions are necessary.

As is, she realizes now, lying.

The delivery-bay doors of the hospital have been left open, which Joannie considers an invitation. She knows she's not technically allowed in. Too many victims of the torpedoed ships are suffering here, the hospital beyond capacity.

Some of the relatives of the dead, dying, or suffering men still haven't been found and notified.

Their boys dead, nailed in pine boxes, Joannie thinks, throat swelling, *or dying in the corridors of this hospital while their parents are still pulling the milk bottles in from the back door, still reading the evening paper in the favorite overstuffed armchair, still gathering around the radio for the fireside chat—all with no glimmer of an idea how their lives have already capsized.*

Joannie scurries up the ramp and waves to the loading dock worker, who straightens, startled, and turns from opening boxes of what appear to be huge rolls of gauze.

She waves again. "Sorry to intrude. I parked in the wrong place, clearly, back here, and thought this was quicker than going all the way around to the front. I need to hurry. My brother's in here, you see, and . . ." Her voice catches, a gloved hand traveling to her eye.

She doesn't need to finish. The worker puts a hand over his heart in respect and asks nothing. It's his role to unpack the trucks, not question frantic sisters.

Besides, the tragedy is still so fresh.

Five sailors have been burned so badly they couldn't be identified. They've been buried in a shared grave, marked as merchant marines whose names are known only to God. Joannie is still trying to shake a lingering, festering fear that perhaps one of the five might be Will.

How many mothers and sisters and lovers, Joannie wonders, *will lie awake every night wondering why the post hasn't brought any word? How long will they have to live in the heaviness, the moment-by-moment suffocation of not knowing?*

From the top of the ramp, she hurries through a stock room and down a long corridor, nurses looking up to see her pass, but saying nothing. Her urgency, the gloved hands she's wringing, deter questions.

"William Shakespeare Dobbins," she says when she stops at the nurse's station. "I'm looking for my brother."

An older nurse, the skin of her cheeks sagging and dull, glances up from a file. She looks Joannie up and down. "You're his sister?"

"He's . . ." Joannie's hand goes to her mouth, and it's no act, her recalling all too vividly the charred flesh, the severed leg . . . "He's here? He's still alive, then?"

The nurse drags herself to her feet. Joannie feels a brief stab of conscience in lying to a woman who's clearly in the midst of a long, draining shift.

"Mr. Dobbins has had a rough time of it. Hasn't mentioned a sister."

Joannie holds her breath. Tries to recall what he told her about his family. "There are several of us. Siblings, I mean."

"Poor soul's been mumbling lines from Lord only knows where."

"Shakespeare."

"What's that?"

"His—*our*—mother loves Shakespeare. That's what Will's been quoting, no doubt."

The nurse's white saddle shoes squeak a few steps around the nurse's station. "So, you've just come into town?"

"From Tennessee, yes. It's quite a long drive."

"Feel lucky you had something to drive. Most of us don't." The nurse stops, pivots, and eyes her skeptically. "What with all the gas rations and tire rations and people doing their part, most people just plain couldn't come all that way, no matter how hard up a brother was."

"Forgive me, but I'm so anxious to see him. You understand, I'm sure."

Grunting, the nurse waves for Joannie to follow her down the corridor to a large room with six beds, three on each side. "He's a nice kid, I'll say that for him."

Joannie's voice comes out tight and fractured as she sees the bed the nurse points toward, the body on it nearly mummified, bandages covering both arms, both legs, and part of his face, which is staring straight up at the ceiling. "Yes. He is."

"Been in terrible pain, that much I know, but always says thank you."

"Always tells the nurses they look nice in white," Joannie suggests, "or their hair is fixed 'specially well?"

The nurse snorts. "Even us old crones. The kid's a charmer, I'll give him that."

"That's our Will."

At the sound of his name, Will lifts his head off the pillow an inch or so and focuses on the two women—then on just Joan.

"Lord have mercy, if it ain't Joannie D—"

She rushes toward him, arms out. "Yes, it's your Joannie Dearest. Dear, *dear* brother Will, all of us back home are so worried about you!"

Will has struggled to a half-sitting position by the time Joannie reaches him, and he holds out both bandaged arms, latching onto her with his free fingers. The action must surely hurt his wounded skin, but he still manages to pull her to him. His kiss is not a brotherly peck on the cheek but directly on the lips. Lingering, even, before she can pull away.

His eyes, when she pulls back, twinkle.

Joannie can't help glancing back to find the nurse standing stock still, a cringe crumpling her face.

"Tennessee," Joannie says.

It's not much of a way to explain the kiss, and the nurse is already shirking away.

Will is laughing, enjoying himself.

Joannie touches a finger to a bandage that runs along the left side of his face. "It looks like it would hurt to laugh."

"It does, dadgummit. But hurts more not to. Let me look at you now. I'm one big horror flick of a sight, I'd be guessing."

She touches his dark hair poking up straight from behind the bandages. "Will, you *survived*. Is the pain too awful?"

He wraps her free hand in both his bandaged ones. "I'm just so god-awful glad you've come. Seeing you, that's the stuff as dreams are made on."

"*Midsummer Night's Dream*?"

He grins—with effort, it looks like. "A mighty fine guess. *The Tempest*, though. Also happens to be true."

"I've had nightmares, panicked about you."

A hand to his heart, he feigns hurt. "Was our time together that bad?"

"You know exactly what I mean." She perches on the edge of his bed. "It's been hard getting the information on which men survived—and which didn't. They want the families to hear first, of course. But still."

"I hope you've not suffered too awful much, worrying."

"My word, I've never known anyone quite like you, Will Dobbins. You look actually concerned that I might've suffered worrying over you."

"Is that odd, really? As odd as my looks?"

She tries to laugh, since he clearly means for her to, but the bandages, some of which are putrid shades of pink and yellow and green with leaking fluids, are not easy to see. Or to smell. "I did worry, yes, if that helps your ego. Quite a lot, if you must know."

"Ah. My ego thanks you."

"Truly, are you in very much pain?"

He doesn't answer for a moment, and Joannie flinches. A stupid question to ask someone with burns all over his body. She can see from the strain of his smile that he's trying hard not to tell her the truth—or not to cry out right now.

"The pain, to be honest, is a mite worse on the inside. Hearing my mates calling for help. Seeing those bodies all covered in oil. The U-boat circling our ship, firing the deck guns."

"At the men on the lifeboats? That's horrific!"

"Not at the lifeboats, no. They were bent on wrecking the ship good so it couldn't much be repaired. Jerrys acted happy enough to let the lifeboats alone, just us and the dolphins and sharks. Even called to us once to come aboard the sub and be saved." He blows out disgust. "Reckon I'd rather swim those miles to shore or sink trying than be a dang prisoner of war in a steel box underwater."

"You don't cuss, do you, Will Dobbins?"

He grins back at her. "Our mama was real strict on that, as you'll recall, *dearest sister*. Had to cut our own switches off the forsythia bush for a whipping if we let out certain words in Mama's hearing. You remember that, right? Nurse is approaching again, by the way."

"Visitation time's over," the nurse announces from the doorway. "Time to bathe the patients and change the sheets."

Earnestly, Will clasps Joannie's hand with his few free fingers. He winces again but covers it quickly. "Nurse, my sister might want to stay and help with my bath. She's by far the strongest one back home on the farm for this sort of thing. Do please now, let her stay."

Joan does not blink. "Oh, Will. I don't reckon I could bear to see your wounds." Bending over him, she whispers into his ear, "It'd serve you right if I stayed."

Turning his face quickly to hers before she can straighten, he kisses her again on the lips. "Dear sister. Parting is such sweet sorrow."

"From *Romeo and Juliet*," she whispers. "Meanwhile, your nurse is appalled."

Releasing her hand, he waves a bandaged clump at her. "You sure are a sweet little heifer, as Daddy would say back home on the mountain. Come see me tomorrow, sis. I need a reason to live."

Joannie hurries by the nurse without looking at her but hears what the nurse mutters under her breath.

Lord help us. Tennessee.

Joan's heart has lifted so far it feels as if it's fluttered up through her throat, as if it might lift off the top of her head.

Will Dobbins.

Bless him. Goofy, sweet, handsome Will Dobbins is alive—in terrible pain and maybe maimed, but alive—and for all the defeats and aerial dogfights the newsreels might show tonight at the Ritz, this dark, ugly world at war has a sliver of light in it still.

Chapter 23
Hadley

The sun is just chinning up above the ocean, the water and sky striated with pink and orange, and I'm trying to focus on that, the blaze of sunrise, its colors jolting in their beauty. Electric.

What I'm trying to ignore is the car trailing behind Kitzie and me on our bikes, lurking there. I press harder on my pedals, my quads burning, reminding me I haven't been on a bike in years.

But the car neither tries to pass me nor turns onto one of streets where old beach cottages huddle in stands of palmettos and pines.

Finally, I stomp on the brake, yank down the skirt of my sundress, drop one leg down, and turn to face the driver. Our wearing sundresses to ride bikes is Kitzie's fault, and I remind myself to tell her that later.

The Escalade eases to a stop behind us, the driver's shades covering what little of his face I can see through the windshield.

My left hand goes to my hip. "You have a strange way of getting someone's attention."

I cannot read his expression—beyond the perpetual frown.

"I got stuck behind some slow-moving traffic is all."

"Meaning us?"

He tilts his head.

Circling my bike to face the open driver's side window, I intend to give him a piece of my mind. But he's pulled off the sunglasses now, and his face has lost some of its arrogance from yesterday.

As usual, though, his mouth is set in a hard, straight line.

Kitzie smiles at him. "Oh, it's you, Nick."

Nick.

So the captain has a name. Leave it to Kitzie to have asked at some point, even in the midst of a cold so rough she'd pass out in public.

The captain-driver—*Nick Adams,* Kitz whispers to me, because names are important to her—slides out from behind the steering wheel. There's no baseball cap, no skipper's cap, no chauffeur's cap, just the hair. The very nice hair. "My boss asked me to pass on the message that he was compelled to return to Berlin today but that he'll be checking in daily through email and phone. He should be back a week or two before the reunion to oversee final details in person."

"I bet he will," I say—to which Kitz shoots me a look. "That is, thank you, Nick, for passing that on."

"So you two are taking the job?"

"We are, yes," Kitz chirps.

He looks to me—*blandly,* I think, *maybe even a little smugly. He knew the answer.*

"I feel better about it now." Not meaning to, I bite my lip.

Nick examines me a moment, and I watch him weighing my lie, flimsy and hollow as a tinfoil tube, against whatever he sees on my face. Running a thumb and forefinger across a stubbled jaw, he opens his mouth, then shuts it again. "The two of you are close, I take it."

"Very." Kitz nods. "Tends to happen when the two of you are the only family you both have. The two of us and, of course, Lindy. She was the best foster mama we had—and last. But she's like family now. She came almost too late."

It's true, of course, our sad little growing-up saga. But the vulnerability Kitz just exposed makes me look away. Past the sand dunes of East

Beach, red-orange waves sparkle in the early morning sun as if glitter were scattered across the water.

Not coddled. Not Californian, I want to shout at him. *You have no idea about our story.*

"If you don't mind," I say instead, "we need to get to the museum before it opens, since the director offered an interview."

Nick straightens suddenly, as if I've yanked on a rope attached to his spine. "It can wait. What I was going to say."

"If there was something else . . ."

"Nothing pressing." Giving me a nod, curt and peremptory, he slides back behind the SUV's wheel. Spinning it around, sand fanning out from the tires, he lifts a hand as he drives away.

Kitz shakes her head at me. "Every. Single. One."

"*Every single one* what?"

"Every man who crosses your path you send away before he can so much as sneeze."

"Untrue."

Kitz quirks her mouth to one side, then holds up one finger after another, murmuring names of men I've dated in the past few years as she ticks them off on one hand. Then starts on the other. Like it's evidence.

In my defense, some of the guys were players, or the sort who walk out when you have the flu and haven't brushed your hair for five days. The rest of the list, some of them seemingly sweet, would surely walk out eventually, too, since that's what men do. So safer to send them away before they sneak in too close.

"Okay, maybe that was an old pattern of mine, but—"

"*Was?*"

"*Is* a fairly clear and perhaps-a-little-disturbing pattern. But you don't get to include Hessler's driver—*Nick*. He just had something he wanted to say. That's all. No arguing."

"Before," Kitz mutters under her breath, "you sent him away. And who's arguing?"

I'd rather laugh off Kitzie's point, but she's not wrong—though I'm in no mood right now to admit it.

For all the confidence I might seem to exude, the truth is I'm mostly just trying to keep the walls in place around my sister and me, trying desperately to avoid the hurt I know will come if I let anyone get too close or stay too long.

We've watched so many people disappear, either because of death (our mom, by overdose) or because they walked out (our dad—we have no memory of him) or because they don't give a damn we're alive (relatives, apparently, on both sides, more invested in their next hit than two scared, stringy little girls, the older one prone to lashing out). A royal flush of rejection.

Seriously, I think, not meeting my sister's eyes, *why keep showing up for more rejection or grief?*

Locking our bikes to the rack outside the museum, I readjust my sandals and sundress.

"Appearances matter," Kitz had insisted when she tossed me a green linen sheath and motioned for me to change out of the Nike shorts I had on. "If you'd like the director at the museum to treat us with even a modicum of seriousness."

"This little modicum of dress will be seriously wrinkled by the time I bike to the museum."

I stomped around muttering, but Kitz heard my tone shift from Belligerent Grumble to Surrender Grumble and knew that she'd won.

Checking my watch now, we trot up the steps to the door of the World War II Home Front Museum, an attractive Cape Cod–like structure freshly painted a dazzling white with a red tile roof. The building once served, I read last night, as the boathouse of the Coast Guard headquarters. The director, who graciously agreed to meet outside of business hours, sounds abnormally cheerful for this early in the morning—also eager and well versed. She reels off what the museum offers and where we might find different exhibits on the island's role in World War II.

"We'd especially like to learn more," I tell her, "of the radar training school, the fighter pilot training, and the torpedoing of a couple of ships that happened here."

"Well, now, that should only take you a couple of years to learn all you'll need to know."

She's teasing, but I hear the truth beneath her quip, the clock inside my head ticking louder now.

"The U-boats," I suggest. "Let's begin there."

The director beams at me. "Marvelous. An excellent choice."

"We're grateful for your time," I say as she bounces ahead into a tiny room with interactive video and audio recordings.

"The hole in that hull!" Kitz exclaims, gaping at a huge photograph of the SS *Oklahoma*. "Incredible that anybody at all survived."

"The local funeral home was swamped," I summarize from another display's caption. "What a shock to think you're an ocean away from the war, then realize the Germans are right there on your doorstep."

Kitzie lowers her voice. "So here's the truth. I never realized the Germans sank ships this close to our shores. Maybe I was too busy passing notes to cute boys."

"I honestly hadn't remembered it either—if I ever learned. Too busy delivering notes back to you from cute boys."

I let Kitz lean heavily into me as we head into the smallest room. This one features a video recounting the Third Reich's Operation Drumbeat, the U-boats' offensive to sink as many merchant vessels as possible.

"Good God," I breathe as the screen lights up with spots of red, representing the 132 American ships destroyed by German subs just in the first four months of 1942—ships sinking faster than they could be built.

After rattling off facts about Allied ship convoys and the wolf packs of U-boats that hunted them, the director concludes with a sweep of her hand toward the screen. She leaves us to the exhibit's video and headphones.

Whipping the small spiral notebook from my pocket, I scribble notes as fast as my fingers will move.

More images of merchant ships headed from the East Coast of the United States across the Atlantic dot the screen. Silhouettes of submarines appear. One by one, the ships explode in a flash of light, our headphones resounding with the noise.

The date April 8, 1942, blinks, and two ship silhouettes appear just off the coast of Georgia. They, too, explode in orange flames. It's as if the four walls of this little room have dropped away and I'm in the midst of it all.

My imaginings far too vivid and real, I reach to steady myself, to make the room return to nothing but a charming museum in a former Coast Guard station.

Kitzie sits slumped on the stool. "How terrifying . . . I mean, if the Germans could do this in American waters, it must have been horrific for people to wonder what else they could do."

Kitzie lifts her hair up and twists it into a knot, an old habit when she's worked up. Today, though, it exposes how thin her blonde curls have become.

She's still staring at the screen, eyes rounded to pale saucers. "They were watching Hitler's panzers roll across Europe and his subs attack every tanker, every ship full of soldiers or supplies, anything that moved in the ocean."

The soundtrack of the museum's video intensifies, the red lights on the screen flashing as one merchant ship after another explodes and disappears.

"All those supplies," Kitzie whispers. "All those *lives*."

The director clears her throat from the little room's entrance and smiles at us.

"Would you like to see our rooms on the naval aviation training here on the island and the training for fighter directors housed at the King and Prince? We have the most wonderful interactive exhibits to help you experience how it must have felt."

We make our way to the next rooms.

I pass old posters urging citizens to ration—even department stores suggesting customers buy less, only what they need—and to donate scrap metal and rubber. On a far wall of one room are the old *Tally-Ho* newspapers from the naval aviation training period. I'm drawn to several pictures of the Civil Air Patrol that preceded the US Navy's taking over the airfield.

"Private planes," I summarize for Kitz, "lots of them just old jalopies, sounds like, were outfitted with—*oh my God*—with bombs just strapped onto their wings. Are you seeing this? Just private citizens, not even trained, putzing around in their own planes, looking for where to drop the bomb they'd just belted on."

She points to an enlarged black-and-white photograph. "Look at this, Hadz. All the coastal patrol together. Maybe, what, fifty or so guys. But also—"

"*Women*," we say together. Five, maybe six of them.

"Support staff," comes the perky voice of the director. "As far as we know. Just support staff."

I turn. "Is it possible, given the Golden Age of Aviation with Amelia Earhart's and Bessie Coleman's popularity, that some of these women could've been pilots too?"

She inclines her head. "Possible, I s'pose. We just don't have any evidence of it."

Kitzie, still facing the picture, grips my arm. "Look. Smack in the middle."

There, in the photograph's center, is a young woman with dark wavy hair that just brushes her shoulders. Her head is slightly thrown back, as if she's about to erupt into a laugh at something someone's just said.

I inhale a long breath and swear I can make out the scent of marsh and pine and salt air as if I'm standing right there in the picture. As if I'm standing in front of this face that's become strangely familiar.

Kitzie is beaming even before I say the name out loud.

"Oh my God. *Joannie*."

Chapter 24
Joannie

July 1942

Hoisting herself up onto the lower wing, Joannie lowers her goggles into place. She has to maneuver around the Gee Bee's upper wing and its supports.

"It's a wonder," Joan says, "the old girl still gets off the ground."

"I'm gonna pretend not to hear that. Lady Bracknell's still in her prime."

"You do realize, darling brother, if your plane were human, you'd be in love with a corpse."

Her brother is already seated in the open cockpit of his Gee Bee, a biplane Model A from the late twenties—already more museum piece than modern airship. The Gee Bee crashed three years ago in the waters just off Sea Island. Its owner, a guest at Sea Island's posh Cloister who'd bought the old biplane to entertain beachgoers—managed to limp away from the wreckage, but his femur, his pride, and his love affair with aviation became casualties. Swearing off flying forever, he'd not even bothered to salvage the flight log or his own suitcase from the wreck-age. Sam, together with Joan, had pieced the plane back together with cast-off parts, more mismatched bits than Frankenstein's monster—and more wire, Joan suspects, than she wants to know.

It was Sam, though, not the champagne-swilling Cloister guest, who'd named the plane Lady Bracknell—which, Joan pointed out once, was not the norm.

"All planes," Sam had contended, "are female. As everyone knows."

"Not all planes are named for a character in an Oscar Wilde play."

Sam had lifted a bottle of Coke in a toast. "So much the worse for other planes."

Sam watches now as she scrambles into the cockpit of Lady Bracknell. "So, what do you hear from everyone's favorite merchant marine?"

Joan settles herself into the pilot's seat, merely the left side of a cushioned bench, the right of which is the passenger seat. They do, though, have separate headrests. "Still healing. Still charming as ever. They've got him up walking now. I'll see him tonight. So, Sammy . . . you sure you trust a broad today with your precious plane?"

Sam angles his head at her. "Only this one broad, and only because she shares my own brain."

"Surprisingly sweet, coming from you."

"Not, of course, the part of my brain that handles complex tasks and higher-level reasoning."

Joannie lifts the end of her scarf—she always, *always* flies with her lucky aviator scarf—and whips him in the face. "If you, dear brother, are the example of higher reasoning, we are in very deep trouble. You realize what they're calling you guys in the Civil Air Patrol."

"The Sandwich and Suicide Club, you mean? Not like I'd *choose* to eat a sandwich if I could get my hands on steak, or even choose to fly my sweet little tin can with her double-the-fun wings if somebody offered me a P-51 Mustang."

"Don't tell me you begrudge your country's need for the metal parts." Joan adjusts a backpack behind her, pushing herself closer to the foot pedals that control the rudder since her legs are shorter than Sam's.

"What I *do* begrudge . . ." But he stops there.

"What?"

"Forget it."

Joannie turns and waits for him to finish. When he averts his face, she finishes for him, more quietly. "What you *do* begrudge is being stuck here at home when you're dying"—she pauses there, cringing at her choice of words—"to serve your country as a pilot." She reaches for her brother's arm. "Sam. You're just as valuable here on the home front as any—"

"As any hero aviator? As those guys in the RAF who saved London— maybe saved all of us in the free world? Valuable as those guys taking off from aircraft carriers in the South Pacific every day? I kept trying to tell myself that."

Kept, she hears. Past tense.

Thankful for something to look at besides her brother's face, Joan checks the instrument panel: the airspeed, the altimeter, the fuel gauge, the manifold pressure, the directional gyro, the compass . . . going through the checklist for takeoff keeps her occupied for several precious moments during which she doesn't have to ask the next question, doesn't even have to let the words take shape in her head—since that will make them real.

Sam, though, leans forward as if he's poised to stand and walk on the wing once they're airborne.

Ignoring all that eagerness—maybe some fear too—she glimpses at his face, Joan points the plane into the wind, grips the throttle harder, and accelerates as they race down the runway. The wind whips the curls hanging loose beneath her pilot's helmet, snaps the ends of her scarf. As usual, she finds something freeing in this speed, this defiance against gravity.

It's not the time for this conversation, not when her full attention should be on takeoff, but she asks anyway, because it's got to be asked. "You gone and done it yet?"

She knows he won't answer, not yet. And she's grateful for that.

Eyes straight ahead, she feels the lift under the Gee Bee's tail, even as her heart, her stomach, everything inside her feel as if they're sinking into the marsh all around. She feels that instant when the plane's body and hers are no longer connected to Earth, the release of being a creature only of the air.

Every other time, she's gasped with delight at this moment, this freedom. But not today.

Pulling up the landing gear, she checks the plane's manifold pressure and wonders what her own intake of air would measure right now—probably unsafe levels. She's dizzied already with what she knows Sam will say next.

He waits, just as she knew he would, until they've cleared the pines just beyond the edge of the field, banks out over the beach, then rises higher, still higher over the sea. When the altimeter reaches a thousand feet, he raises his voice over the roar of the engine, but his tone is quiet. Calm. Assured.

"I told the folks at the dairy you might could take on my milk run in the mornings for however long I'm gone."

She says nothing. She can't.

"They accepted me, Joannie. Finally. Today. I passed the physical."

Joan does not shift her gaze from the sky in front of her. She's grateful to be facing off with fluffy cumulous clouds and not her brother's blue eyes. "Sam, you *can't*."

"Let's just say my issues didn't show up in the exam this time."

"Sam, it's not your fault the rheumatic fever damaged your heart. You're contributing to this war in other ways—without having to get shot down over an ocean somewhere. Sam, *think*. Your heart might not survive the kind of strain—"

"As your older brother—"

"Older by *two minutes!*"

"Two all-important minutes for gathering superior wisdom. You of all people should understand, Joan. I'm a damn good pilot. It's what I've got to offer in this fight—it's *all* I've got to offer."

"That's *not true*. Sam, there's so much else you—"

He holds up a hand to stop her. "I want you to be glad for me. I'll be sent to basic training, then I'm hoping to get sent back to the naval air station here, since the navy's taking over the airfield soon, and do flight training here. Then ship out whenever, wherever they send me."

Joannie feels the words bore deep, a corkscrew that keeps twisting. She's not sure if she can bear this much emotion, and she tips Lady Bracknell sideways into a barrel roll.

"I can't be glad," she shouts as they turn upside down. "Don't ask me to."

Waiting until the plane is upright again, Sam looks straight ahead. "You've got to help Pops understand. Also, don't take your fury at me out on Lady Bracknell. She won't stand for it. Won't hold together for it, either, is my guess. Go ahead. Say what you got to say, and spare the plane."

"You stubborn idiot." The words fire-hose out from her. "You had a ticket, an ethical one, to stay here and do good, valuable work on the home front. To stay safe."

The Gee Bee's engine noise fills the air between them for several more moments: a mercy.

"You done?"

"No. Not hardly." She banks left and decreases altitude, flying low over the Sea Island beach.

Sam watches the palms tick by beneath them. "I think you'd tell me, if the tables were turned, that staying safe isn't . . . safe. Not when human beings are being herded into ghettos, treated like animals—and worse. God only knows what else."

She agrees with him, of course. She would have said it herself, probably with more colorful language, if it'd been her who signed up. But she can't agree with him right now. Not as irate as she's feeling. Or as scared for him.

Finally, she settles for the only words she can get out—and still she refuses to shift her eyes from the beach below. "I'm so afraid for you, Sammy. And I'm so angry with you."

He waits, sensing there's more.

"And, damn it, I might also be proud of you."

He lays a hand on her shoulder a moment, and it's that touch that makes her want to weep, that connection that reminds her she has no idea what it will mean to be separated from this other half of herself.

"I wish, Sam . . . I so wish I could go with you. If they'd just let me help too. Let me fly . . ." He squeezes her shoulder, a brotherly grip that's part comfort, part pinch, as if he wants her to remember his unique role as tormentor, protector, and friend, as only a brother can be.

"I know, Joannie. I know. Tell you what: I'll fly extra hard, extra good for the two of us."

~

She's not stayed in the air nearly as long as she meant to, but she doesn't have the stomach for flying today. Right hand gripping the throttle, like she might keep hold of her brother if she hangs on a bit tighter, Joannie makes herself breathe as she eases the landing gear down.

"Down left," she says.

Sam's neck cranes out of the cockpit. "Down right."

She taps at her brakes. Working. There's comfort in this, at least: the protocol Sam taught her, the same taught to him by a World War I vet here on the island.

Leveling out with the runway, she lowers Lady Bracknell to tease just over the ground. Then she lets the wheels ease down onto pavement.

"Smooth as butter in June," she says.

Head flopped back, relaxed, against his headrest, Sam grunts. "All in the caliber of the instruction."

Joannie slowly unfolds herself from the cockpit. She might've appeared cool and unflappable landing the plane, but her palms went clammy, her heart pounding in her throat. She can land a plane with grace and precision each time—at least in good weather—and with a cool-blooded confidence. But today, the looming date of Sam's leaving makes every movement feel momentous—as if she were headed into aerial combat with him.

He is, after all, half my brain, half my heart.

As she climbs onto the lower wing and swings herself off, Sam is already speaking with a uniformed man on the ground.

Turning, the officer surveys Joan up and down, then works his jaw like a cow chewing cud.

When he focuses in on Joannie's face, his left eyebrow quirks. She meets his eye but doesn't like the leering glint she finds there, the way her skin crawls in response. She looks just past his left ear to the marsh beyond the airfield. A heron lifts off, soars above the pines.

The officer stops his cud chewing for a moment. "So, this'd be some sort of publicity stunt, that it? Get some good-looking broads up in the air, pretending they can operate the controls? What I don't get is how the hell that's supposed to boost the morale of the men who damn well fly these planes into combat, land on aircraft carriers or in muddy, hand-dug strips in jungles, and sure as *hell* deserve respect for it."

Sam leans closer, drops his tone to a conspiratorial bass. "When has a good-looking broad ever *not* helped any effort?"

The officer's face cracks into something between smile and sneer. "You got a damn good point there . . ."

"DuBarry. Samuel DuBarry. Recent recruit. Soon-to-be navy pilot, sir."

"That right?" The officer extends his hand to Sam. "Lieutenant Rex Brock. Son, you strike me as damn sure on the skinny side for the job, but if you were the one that just landed that hunk of junkyard with wings, you sure as hell got a gift."

Sam slings an arm over Joannie's shoulders. "That was actually my sister, sir. I swear, this little woman here can handle a plane as well as she bakes a pecan pie."

Turning away into Sam's shoulder, Joan mutters, "Never baked a pecan pie in my life." Turning back, though, she smooths her face to pleasant. Sam is trying to help, and playing the game is part of that.

Sam has to play his own games too, she reminds herself.

"That right?" The officer rears back, then spits to one side. "If you want to take those kind of risks with your own damn bird, that's up to you. Don't suppose I got to tell you to never let this dame or any other so much as touch a pretty little finger to one of the United States Navy's planes. *Ever.* In fact—"

A voice from behind them inserts itself. "Ho there, what's this?" A man wearing a V-necked white sweater, despite the summer heat, saunters toward them, with his hands thrust into the pockets of white flannel trousers. The jet-black of his hair against his pale skin is like ink on newsprint, so pale is his complexion—*Like someone who's been indoors too much of the summer,* Joan thinks. This fellow's movements are all long strides and grace: an athlete's.

"Good God, Silverberg. You look like you're headed for a cricket match and bloody crumpets with the king. Where the hell's your uniform?"

"Actually, Brock, I would fancy a good cup of tea and some crumpets about now. *Real* tea, I mean, not the brown dust we're all keeping calm and carrying on with these days." Without waiting for a response, the newcomer nods first to Joan and then Sam. "Lieutenant Dov Silverberg, Fleet Air Arm, His Majesty's Royal Navy. A humble visitor here to the American colonies, and grateful for your warm hospitality."

Dov, Joan thinks. *An odd name. Pronounced with a long o, like the past tense of* dive. *He looks both the dashing intellectual and a man who'd dive headlong into life. Disconcerting to see both together.*

Before anyone else can speak, the Brit has rounded on his colleague. "By the way, Brock, what was this nonsense I overheard just now? So you'd not fancy your own countrywoman Amelia Earhart, God rest her soul, flying one of your planes? Or Louise McPhetridge Thaden? Or Bessie Coleman?"

The fact that he knows not just the most famous of the female American aviators but three of them makes Joan stare, open mouthed, at the man. A shank of dark wavy hair falls onto his forehead and, smiling, he rakes it back with one hand.

"Or Jacqueline Cochran," Joan adds.

The Brit hits his forehead with the heel of one hand. "By Jove, of course. Ferrying planes for the Royal Air Force this very moment back in the mother country, in fact, along with a score of other American women, because you Yanks won't let them help you here."

He turns his smile on her.

It's startling, the intensity of it, as if a lighthouse's beam landed directly on her. There's something sad, though, in the smile—perhaps tragic, even—as if he's seen pain in the world, his eyes more serious, more intense, than the playfulness of his tone.

His gaze tangles a moment with Joan's before he drags it back to Brock, who's stomped closer, khaki chest puffed out.

"Go piss yourself, Silverberg. You made your damn point: you're a fan of girl pilots."

"Forgive me, but I'm a fan of aviation. Of anyone who's at the top of their game—*our* game. Anyone who's won the Bendix Trophy, for example, as Mrs. Cochran has."

His gaze swings out toward the airfield, and the smile slides from his face. "I'm also a fan of anyone who flies against the Wehrmacht or the Imperial Japanese Navy—anyone who has to land their planes on a ship whose runway is half the size of these here." He nods toward the airfield, then toward Sam. "I overheard—do forgive the eavesdropping, won't you—that you've signed up with us, yes? Godspeed to you."

Sam holds out his hand. "Samuel DuBarry. A naval aviator hopeful."

"*If*," Brock grouses, "you survive basic training. DuBarry, Silverberg here's an instructor out of Cambridge University and whatever training His Majesty's Fleet Air Arm involves." Curling his lip, Brock pronounces *Fleet Air Arm* as if it's a latrine cleaning product. "We exchanged one of our own instructors for him. Why the hell, I got no idea."

Dov Silverberg turns from Sam to Joan and holds out his hand. "Honored to make your acquaintance."

His eyes, merry and teasing when dealing with Lieutenant Brock, grow serious.

"Joannie DuBarry." The hand she raises to shake his feels unsteady, or maybe it's her whole body that's gone out of balance as he holds her gaze. She's not the type to go all weak kneed over a man, any man. So she straightens her spine and lifts her chin.

She knows she should drop her eyes from his—or he should from hers—but they're suspended there for a moment.

Swallowing suddenly, Dov Silverberg takes a step back, thrusts his hands into his pockets, and, clearing his throat, turns back to the men as he takes a light tone once again. "The original model of Gee Bee, as I recall, wasn't a particularly safe bet in its racing heyday a good decade ago, yes? 'Widow Maker' I believe was only one of the friendlier monikers for it, yes? Yet Miss DuBarry here appears to have rolled it with great aplomb and landed it with evidence of . . . what was it you were saying there, Brock? Evidence of someone who's *sure as hell got a gift*, was it?"

"If I were your commanding officer, Silverberg, I'd tell you to go to hell."

Turning to Sam, Brock adds, "Let's just hope you fly as good as your *sister* here, DuBarry."

"I do, sir. Almost as well, that is."

The insolence of that last—or the mischievousness, at least—hangs in the hot, humid air, beating there like a pelican's wings.

Almost as well, that is.

It's not true, not really. Sam is the more experienced pilot by far. He's only being generous.

But she does have a gift.

Brock steps nose to nose with Sam. "That the way you want it, DuBarry? Fine. I'll be watching you. Let's hope you don't make any mistakes in training. Not a single damn one."

With that, Brock stalks off in the direction of a cluster of tents just erected this week.

"Thank you," Joan says to Dov, finding her voice. "For speaking up as you did."

"Forgive me if I stole any of your thunder." His eyes rest on hers again, and the smile returns, twitching at the edge of his mouth. "Although, I suspect, Miss DuBarry, you have rather plenty to spare."

Sam raises an eyebrow at her, but she ignores him. She's not one to blush, but she can feel heat creep up from her thighs, her chest, her neck. "I can usually hold my own. But the backup shelling was still welcome."

Dov waves this away. "I confess, I'm not as adept with women as I am with radio detection. But I think I can detect an unwelcome harangue against the fairer sex when I see it."

He extends his hand again, first to Sam. "I do wish you all the best, DuBarry. I suspect you'll make us proud, your country and mine. I hope to see you again after your basic training, once you're back for pilot school, the Wildcats and all that. Well, then. Splendid."

His gaze swings back to Joan again. For all his outward sunniness, the seeming happy-go-lucky good cheer, there's that intensity in his eyes again—a keen intelligence that burns there. The molten core, perhaps, that drives him. And that sadness under it all.

She's both drawn to and wary of the intensity of him.

"I do hope, Miss DuBarry, aviatrix extraordinaire, to see you again too. I must say, I salute your skill. As well as, might I add, your courage. Well, then, an excellent day to you both."

With that, he strides away.

Chapter 25

Hans

July 1942
On the Brittany coast of France

It isn't courage that drives Hans to commit the crime, not initially. Or the crime that follows.

Initially, it is more his own mother who causes him to do this thing. Her, and the look in the young woman's eyes as she lies sobbing on the ground.

Hans and the rest of the crew of *U-123* returned to the French seaport Lorient in early May, in time for their *Kommandant* Hardegen to be called to Berlin to be decorated by the Führer himself, the number of *U-123*'s kills having risen to the level of notice. Hans tried repeatedly to picture this, the commander holding out his hand to shake Hitler's—this same commander who turns away each time the Führer's name is mentioned. Not that he ever speaks a word against the Reich—that would mean death. Still . . .

The crew will launch out again soon for the ninth patrol, but meanwhile there are repairs to be done on the sub. They eat their first fresh apples and bread without mold or vermin for weeks. Hans has once more shaken and sweated and clawed his way out from under the influence of Pervitin, the drug the Wehrmacht dispenses to ensure its soldiers and sailors and aviators stay awake and alert for days on end, when there's no time to sleep and when they need to function like machines. No inhibitions. No moral qualms to get in the way of raw duty to their supreme leader and their devotion to the Fatherland.

Cogs, Hans is thinking as he strolls to the outskirts of Lorient this evening. *Nothing but unthinking cogs in the vast, crushing panzer of the Third Reich.*

Hans's first mistake is to stroll so far out of town, into the farmland along the Brittany coast. Its rocky shorelines, its whitewashed farmhouses, the way the light turns its boulders a deep rose at sunset—all this has its dangerous, deleterious effects.

Because all this makes him see beauty again.

He's stayed to watch the sun sink bloodred into the ocean, the lighthouse's rotating beam sweeping over a darkening sea. The last of the fishing boats troll back into harbor. In the silence, and in the turmoil of his own meditations, he hears her cries. But the cries come muffled, drained of all strength, and the tumult in his own head tells him perhaps they're not real.

Does he hear the German commands—*Bleib still und schweig!*—to be still and shut up? Is that what makes him circle to the other side of the lighthouse's base so slowly?

Is he that much of a coward?

Or perhaps he still isn't sure what he's hearing. Surely, *dear God, surely* that is it.

He sees the baby first, just an infant lying swaddled beside the woman right there on the pebbled path.

The baby's arms are free, he thinks. Perhaps because his own arms hang there weighted and stiff by his side.

God help me. His arms will not move. Or his legs, either one.

He slouches there, paralyzed, for . . . how long? He has no idea.

Longer than anyone with a beating heart should—this much he knows for sure.

The soldier on top of her had removed only his gun for the act, and it lies a few feet away, beside an unmoving man in faded, frayed civilian garb, a thick red ooze over the back of his head. A fisherman, perhaps, in his rubber boots. A brother or a father or lover or neighbor who must have tried to defend her.

It is the look in her eye—desperate, agonized, enraged—that finally unlocks the weight from Hans's arms and legs.

In one stride, he reaches the soldier's Luger on the path. He has no idea if another bullet sits in the chamber. He has no plan beyond this moment.

Hans focuses only on the young mother's eyes, her baby beside her, waving its little arms and beginning to whimper, her own voice choked off as she spots this German sailor standing there holding the Luger.

The soldier rolls aside long enough to let Hans scan his face—the brutality, the remorselessness, the vicious sneer of it.

"Here to have a go?" the soldier asks, panting. "The rumor is she's half-Jewish, so . . ."

So not even really a crime hangs in the air, unspoken.

For a moment, there is only the splash of the waves below, the whimper of the infant on the path, the whoosh of a gull angling past.

In that way the brain registers some details even as it shuts out others in crisis, Hans notes the clean-shaven jaw of the soldier's face, the ice-blue eyes, the breadth of powerful shoulders, the brass over his heart polished to a high sheen—the adherence to the Wehrmacht's ideal.

"What the hell—" Hans's voice sounds gummed in his throat, like the ooze of the fisherman's head has coated his vocal cords. "What the *hell* have we become?"

It's all he says before he shoots.

The young woman does not scream, though blood spurts onto her dress, filthy and torn at the neck. She looks at Hans once more, and her lips part, but her eyes travel over his uniform of the Kriegsmarine, and her mouth closes again, as if she cannot give words of any kind to anyone wearing that.

Leveraging herself out from under the soldier's limp form, she yanks at what Hans realizes must be her underclothes before he turns quickly away. Scrambling to her feet, choked sobs escaping from her, she sweeps up the infant and, holding the child tight to her chest, runs without looking back.

"*Es tut mir sehr leid!*" Hans wants to call after her. *I'm so sorry,* so very sorry. *For this monster in the skin of a man. For this war. For the long moments before I acted. For . . .*

But there is too much to be sorry for. No logical place even to start, when the world is beyond reason.

Hans is sorry, too, to strip the fisherman of his clothes, but he at least does not defile the man by dressing him in Hans's own clothes, the uniform of Hitler's navy. When the young woman returns to bury the fisherman, she at least will not have to face that.

"*Es tut mir leid,*" Hans whispers to the fisherman, for leaving him in only his undershirt and pants.

Hans at least spares the young woman having to see the body of the soldier again by hefting it over his shoulder—the man thick with muscle and heavy—and hurling it over the cliff to the beach below. High tide might wash the body out to sea, or it might not.

Someone will still find him, of course. The soldier's unit, and Hans's, will notice them each missing this very night and begin searching.

Hans has never killed a man before, beyond being part of the crew of a U-boat that sends ships to the floor of the sea. Seeing this man's face before he died, no matter how vile the man, has done something corrosive to Hans's soul—he can feel the lead in his gut, as if he'll bear the weight of the bullet there, and the body that no longer breathes, for the rest of his life.

So he's committed this first crime, taking not only a life but that of a brother in arms. Now Hans commits another. Because he can no longer fight for a lunatic, no longer pretend it's enough to protect his crew, his family, the Fatherland.

Still, this next is also a crime.

A soldier may *be killed*. Hans has heard all his commanders quote Hitler. *But a deserter* will *be killed*.

He watches the last red fingernail of sun sink into the sea and wonders how such beauty can still exist in a world that has gone mad.

He makes himself speak aloud what he has become now, a kind of counterweight to that beauty.

"Deserter."

One who will be hunted down. Executed.

A traitor—despicable—to his fellow soldiers.

Still, his mind shifts back to beauty, to this lighthouse here on the Brittany coast and to another one, the one whose silhouette he made out in the blazing light on that beach off the Southern coast of the United States, and to the windows of the houses there glowing with warmth.

He will think of that as he walks—as he *runs*—for hiding.

Chapter 26
Hadley

In the middle of sifting through the background notes we've accumulated so far, I stop to call up the "Our Founders" page of the Boundless International Real Estate Development LLC website. Curiously, given the three men's extraordinary story, this page is strikingly spare—just pictures of the three men, each in a dark suit and tie, each with his hair slicked back with a front wave in the style of the 1950s. The only biographical information mentions their places of birth but makes no reference to education or family—and no reference to their having met during a war in which they served on opposite sides.

In his photo, Hans Hessler as a young businessman is, as Ernst described, markedly fair, his eyes startlingly pale in the black-and-white image. I can see his resemblance to Ernst, including a heaviness in the expression. But the sadness that appears in the eyes of both father and son must have fallen two different ways: for Ernst, a demanding exactitude and focus on wealth that apparently hasn't brought him much joy; for Hans, a look of guilt, I think, but also, not predictably, kindness.

Though maybe I'm reading too much into one photo.

I trot my laptop out to Kitz on the balcony of our hotel suite.

She's already got files of information printed out and stacked on the desk we moved out here so she'd have a covered outdoor office with a sea view. On her laptop screen, I see two men in uniform, one in the dress whites of the Fleet Air Arm of the British Royal Navy and one in the US Navy uniform. Though their faces look nothing alike, both men have dark hair and broad shoulders so that from behind, either could be the man on the beach in the ripped photo.

Kitz's fingers slow on her keyboard as she glances back at my screen. "So which of our three Casanovas ended up with our Joannie?"

"You'd think there'd be a straightforward answer, right? But so far it's weirdly murky. What I've been able to find online so far would suggest none of the three did—but then there's this."

I hold up a photo, one of a thick stack that's just arrived from one of the families. This particular faded black-and-white snapshot features the same young woman from Hessler's beach photo. She's wearing a simple party dress with a full skirt that must've dated to before the war, when material could be spared. Walking toward the camera, her face is in profile as she gazes out at the water—a river or marsh, it appears, trimmed in palmettos and live oaks and dripping moss.

Joan, the writing at the photo's bottom says, *on her wedding day, Lovely Lane, May 1945.*

The handwriting, I note, isn't the same as that on the back of the ripped photo.

"So, Kitz, this one was sent by the Dobbins family. The picture's taken right as the war in the European theater is ending. I looked up Lovely Lane. It's a beautiful little chapel here on the island. But no explanation as to who the groom was. Odd how this Joan keeps popping up, like whatever happened to all of them, her story's somehow interwoven with theirs. How you feeling today, by the way?"

"Better'n I deserve."

Her answer is residue from one of our South Carolina foster homes and means nothing coming from Kitz except that she's engrossed in her work. Watching her bending intently over her laptop, fingers tapping, I feel that contraction, familiar now, of my heart that tells me something's not right.

"So, Hadz, I've made a spreadsheet of the contact information for all the relatives we can call for interviews. Hessler obviously gave us several, but I've found a few more. The magic of white pages and social media."

She nods toward the paper scrolling up through the portable printer. "I've already emailed everyone whose addresses I have, asking for any photographs, letters, any memorabilia from the war years that they could overnight mail us—and the account number to charge it to."

Plucking the spreadsheet from the tray, I begin scanning it. "Remind me why you're not in charge of the world?"

"So, you'll be making the phone calls—just asking family members to tell stories about the three men."

"That sounds like a gross misuse of resources, since everyone knows you're much sweeter."

"But you're the one who's never minded asking nosy questions." She picks up my cell from the desk and thrusts it at me.

I take it obediently.

"I'll make the calls. What question should I start with: *So, which one of your ancestors was the despicable traitor?* Or maybe *How did you people let things move from three devoted friends building a successful business to an international crapfest?*"

Kitz doesn't even look up from her screen. "Baffling—why anyone would think you're not the sweeter of the two of us."

～

"Rabbi Silverberg!"

He's the first on the list to pick up the phone, so my euphoria at hearing a live, human voice probably sounds a bit outsize.

But this grandson of Dov Silverberg listens attentively while I explain why I'm calling.

"Extraordinary, don't you think, Ms. Jacks?" The rabbi's effusiveness cartwheels through the phone lines. "Rather splendid, really, that three men whose backgrounds could not have been more different became close and then went on to do much good in the world?"

"Good in the world?"

He chuckles, warm and avuncular. "You sound surprised."

"Forgive me, Rabbi. It's not that creating a multinational real estate firm can't potentially be a form of doing good in the world—job creation and all that—but—"

"But all you know of Boundless is, of course, what everyone knows. That it's currently a sort of real-life version of *Succession*—with, perhaps, one or two more likable characters and no monthly subscription fee."

"Pretty much, yes. And I'm so sorry if I was rude just now to question—"

"Ah, but questioning is how we show devotion, I firmly believe—to care enough to probe further. By all means, continue."

"You're suggesting there's more to Boundless's vision than the usual interest in the bottom line?"

"Once upon a time, there was, I can tell you, quite the humanitarian focus on affordable housing globally, as well as a number of other worthy causes. Do, Hadley, see if you can find old shareholder reports that show partner organizations. Quite the inspiration."

"The current state of Boundless, from what I've read, is . . ."

"A bloody battle for power, ruthless and raw—is that what you're too polite to say, Ms. Jacks?"

"You, Rabbi Silverberg, are the first person ever to accuse me of being too polite."

"Well, then, hurrah for me. Please call me Benedick or Ben, if you prefer."

"Benedick," I repeat, trying to recall what the name reminds me of.

"I am delighted, by the way, that you and your sister are researching this remarkable story. What a great gift to all three families, to the memories of three fine men, to all of us. When Ernst became aware of your firm and decided to replace the original event planners, I agreed you were quite the ones to capture their stories, their vision."

"So the original firm didn't botch the job so much as he decided for some other reason to switch?"

I can almost hear Rabbi Silverberg's gears grind backward, as if he's trying to decide how much to say—or how much to cover for what he's already said.

"Fancy that Cousin Ernst, of all people, is the one to sponsor so sentimental a project. I say, though, bravo for him. He appears to have hired a crackerjack team."

"Did you say *Cousin* Ernst? I thought the descendants of the three men—Dov Silverberg, Hans Hessler, and Will Dobbins—weren't related."

"No blood relation, of course, but the long-standing tradition among the three families has been to address one another in familial terms. Aunt Juliet. Cousin Richard. Aunt Beatrice, Cousin Cordelia . . ."

"Wait . . . Your names—Benedick, Juliet, Richard, Beatrice, Cordelia. They're all characters from Shakespeare's plays."

"Jolly good observation, yes. It was, I believe, originally Hans Hessler's idea. Fancied naming his first child Viola to honor the spirit of his army pal Will Shakespeare Dobbins, who, at least as a younger man, often quoted the plays and sonnets—with great self-effacing humor, as I recall."

"All of you have these names?"

"Every last John, Dick, and Harry, quite literally, I'm afraid. Not to mention Claudia and Portia and the whole bloody lot of us. No Goneril, for obvious reasons. Can you imagine prep school with that one?"

"No Dogberry?" I can't help but ask. "No Yorick?"

"'Alas, poor Yorick,' no. No Yorick either. It started out, I believe, as a sort of inside joke among them. Then became, as these things do, a kind of mark of loyalty. Boundless, as I'm sure you've learned, is quite"—he slows here, feeling his way word to word like tree trunk to tree trunk in a dark forest—"concerned with loyalty, Hadley."

"Loyalty," I echo. "Of course. Did you say all three families honored Will Shakespeare Dobbins this way?"

"Including nieces and nephews, yes—important to establish fealty, you know. Much like the British aristocracy here sometimes hyphenates family names."

"For inheritance reasons," I offer. Then wish I hadn't.

He's silent a beat. Then the laughter again, deeper this time. "I see you catch on rather quickly."

"I try."

"For inheritance reasons, wouldn't *you*, too, choose a name that might pull your family closer to the inner circle of influence? Especially, let's say, if your child wasn't technically legitimate?" He sighs. "Forgive me, I'm saying more than I should. At any rate, succession battles and the vision for Boundless appear to be our challenges at the moment. Quite honestly, Ms. Jacks—"

"Hadley. Please."

"I'm hopeful, Hadley, that this event could remind us of the original spirit of these three men—despite all the current jockeying for power and position. All while the world needs the brightest minds and deepest pockets working for environmental and affordable housing solutions in global property markets." He sighs. "But I fear I've already taken too much of your time."

"Rabbi—*Ben*, I'm the one taking yours."

"Before we ring off, I wonder if I might tell you a story about one of the three men that's been handed down through all three families. Told as often as it was, I like to think the founders saw it as rather the sort of spirit all three of them embodied. This particular story has to do with Will Dobbins and a young woman, I believe, he was courting . . ."

I listen, taking notes, my imagination filling out the scene as he speaks. As he spins his story, I can picture Will Dobbins clearly. Even more so, though, the young woman in the story is becoming so real to me I blink into the sun, half expecting her to appear beside me, bending back her fingers where they've become stiff and sore.

Chapter 27
Joannie

August 1942

Having torn off tickets all afternoon, her fingers are going raw.

But never mind. Just sitting under the neon lights of the Ritz is worth crossing the causeway for—a sense of normalcy, that there's still a world outside scrap-metal drives, and gold stars in windows marking each armed forces death in that home, and grim newspaper headlines. So far just in August, the Germans are successfully marching toward Stalingrad, while the Luftwaffe and U-boats have decimated a convoy near Malta. Between March and July, more than two hundred American ships were sunk, more than one a day.

Perhaps most telling of all, the swastika flies now over most of the capitols of Europe.

Joan sympathizes with those who despair of ever again seeing a less barbaric world. Despair, in fact, feels like the only sane response. Some days she envies her father's blur of unknowing.

Scents of buttered popcorn and caramel waft from behind her, along with cool currents from the theater's air-conditioning. A long line has formed for the six o'clock show, just as a summer shower blows in from the west. Customers pop open umbrellas, black mushrooms springing up and down the line. The men lacking umbrellas adjust their fedoras, as if their hat brims can fend off the deluge. The mood of the crowd feels as dark as the storm whipping at the women's skirts.

Joannie works faster, jerking bills out of hands and hurling back coins, but no one is happy at the speed with which she's getting patrons inside, where it's dry. She's keeping an eye out for Will Dobbins—and also trying to shake the image of that Brit from her head, the one with the easy air on the surface and eyes with the glow of burnished brass.

It's shameful, she knows, waiting on one fellow to show up while your mind slips repeatedly back to another you don't even know, not really. But her mind's gone a bit mutinous today.

Regardless, she can't leave her post—and maybe it's what she deserves.

The strains of a stringed instrument reach her well before she spots the musician off to one side, leaning against a lamppost so he can devote both hands wholly to the mandolin. Will's instrument, it turns out, wasn't technically his but was only borrowed from a shopkeeper in Brunswick, so it hadn't gone down with the ship. "The White Cliffs of Dover"—its mournful words and its notes—floats through the drizzle, the images of bluebirds swooping past bright granite cliffs of a free, peaceful England making the crowd go silent.

She's struck all over again at that deep velvety bass coming from a dark cornstalk of a man, wild hair sprouting from his top like a cob's silk. The line bends into a sort of huddle, circling close to this man and his mandolin under the awning for the tear-wrenching end of the song, when love and laughter and peace ever after finally win and a little child goes to sleep in his own bed again.

Rain drips down collars and from fedoras and umbrellas, but nobody seems to care now. They're weeping openly and singing along. Swaying, even, some of them. By the time they get to Joan and her little tan paper tickets, their eyes are lit bright with hope and tears, and some turn to kiss their dates or hug an acquaintance. One old man kisses her fingers as they reach through the hole in the glass.

From the corner of her eye, Joan watches Will play and sing for the crowd—his voice, the notes flowing from his mandolin soft and light as silk, spinning slowly over and then settling onto the crowd, tucking them in, making them feel safe. Seen. Their most secret fears of this war, this day, this life, heard.

For the span of his songs, at least, it's okay to weep, okay to love without loss lurking in the corners. Okay to hope.

Joan doesn't know if she's in love with Will Dobbins or, like the rest of this crowd, with his songs and his mandolin. But right now, she doesn't care. She wants only for him to stay close, both him and the calm he brings to the crowd.

It is nearly nine by the time a coworker arrives to relieve Joan of her shift. Will's merchant marine jacket is soaked through, so Joan helps him peel it off.

She tries to make her small frame sturdier as, hobbling, he leans into her.

"Lordy, I'm using you too much as my right crutch."

"Not a bit," she says, even as she grunts with the effort of holding him up. They both laugh.

"I should be a gentleman and use both crutches they've given me. I reckon they're not near so appealing as our Joannie here, though a mite less likely to be crushed by me."

"I'll let you know if I can't hold you up any longer."

"I wouldn't reckon there's a single thing you can't do."

"I'm a horrid cook, for one thing. Catch-things-on-fire horrid. For another, I don't fit well into groups of women, like they're all swans floating past, so pretty and serene. Here I come, the odd duck, flapping by in an old boat or an old Gee Bee, me wanting to know how it all works and never sitting much still. Like there's something wrong with me, truly."

"I reckon all that hearth and home, that'll come someday when you're good and ready."

Not for me, she wants to tell him. *I don't think it will for me. Ever.*

The theater, packed, has gone quiet. She leads him to the back row—the newsreel for the late show has started—and helps him lurch with his crutches into a seat.

Up on the screen, German panzers charge forward, their rolling tread massive, unstoppable, as the voice from the newsreel pronounces the latest advancements. The voice assures its audience that Germany has underestimated the Soviet Union's strength, despite its catastrophic casualties—but the images of the German tanks crushing forward into the very theater here suggest a different story. Japan, the voice concedes, still occupies Sumatra, since its invasion a few months ago.

The newsreel shifts to a merchant ship far out at sea, the conning tower of a submarine emerging in the background. Guns from the merchant ship aim at the half-surfaced sub, and bullets strafe the water around it. The U-boat submerges.

The camera cuts away then, letting the viewer imagine the merchant ship possibly sails on unharmed. But Will's hand has gone limp beside hers.

All rules of courtship aside, Joan takes his hand, as she might lift the wounded paw of a pet.

Will's face is washed of all color.

She waits as his breathing gradually steadies.

"They could win, couldn't they?" Joan whispers. It's the first time since Hitler invaded Poland nearly three years ago, and the first time since the United States entered the war last December, that she's let herself think this.

Right now, it feels not only possible but inevitable.

Hitler will soon roll over the rest of the world.

She watches Will's profile, his eyes fixed on the screen, and she knows he's thinking the same thing. He puts an arm around her shoulders, like she's the one shipping out soon into bullets and bombs and storms at sea.

Joan moves closer to him as they watch the bright white of the bold ten-foot-tall letters roll up on the screen.

REMEMBER,

LOOSE LIPS SINK SHIPS!

She sees the bright white reflected in his eyes and the pale of his cheeks. He won't even be able to tell her where he's going. Just *shipping out* is all she'll be left with. Only the vast waters of the world to picture him in.

The feature film flickers on, *To the Shores of Tripoli* with Maureen O'Hara, but Joan knows she'll remember little of the story. When Will leans close and asks if she wants to leave, she's on her feet before he is.

~

On the causeway back to the island, Joan takes a breath, then pushes out a voice that sounds worlds brighter than she feels. "So, Will Dobbins, I meant to ask earlier: How'd you sweet-talk your way into borrowing this car?"

"The nurses at the hospital were some kind of swell. One of them offered."

"Some kind of sweet on you to loan out a yellow Studebaker convertible. I will say, you know how to put the farm-boy-poet charm to use."

"I try to be extra judicious in using the charm." He winks at her. "Wouldn't want to just overpower some unwary soul, you know?"

"Real thoughtful of you, Mr. Dobbins."

Back on St. Simons, they walk side by side through the village, past the pier and toward the lighthouse. She can tell by the way his eyes keep darting out to the ocean that Will has something pressing to say. But like a pitcher warming his shoulder with tosses on the side of the field, Will appears to be winding up.

"On a farm, you step up to whatever's got to be done. *Age don't make no never mind,* my daddy used to say—right before he asked one of us kids to dig post holes near deep as we were tall. You learn to steer whatever's got wheels. You best learn balance real good: one foot on each rafter of the tobacco barn when you hang up the plants to dry."

"Your mama let you do all that?"

"Man's got to do what a man's got to do." He grins as she bristles. "Truth is, I had to compete with my sister Biscuit for the place at the top. Lordy, that girl could climb like a monkey with pigtails."

"*Biscuit* is your sister's name?"

"Not the real on-paper official of the thing. Mama named all of us for characters in her favorite plays, all but me, who got the whole hog of it. Biscuit's real name is Bianca Sue—the Bianca from *The Taming of the Shrew*. So you can see how it was Biscuit stuck."

"Of course. Anyone could see that."

They walk together—Will hobbling and Joannie supporting—a few more paces. He stops and rears back to view the top of the light-house. "She's awful good looking."

"This is our second one. The first was completed in 1810, but that was blown up during the Civil War. The lightkeeper's house is my favorite part. The stairs to the second floor were added on the outside when the lightkeeper and his assistant had a squabble and the assistant wasn't welcome to pass through the head lightkeeper's quarters on the first floor anymore."

"Is it really that all-fired hard to get along with folks?"

"Not for a temperament like yours, apparently."

"Always seemed to me a good piece of the squabbling in the world could get itself smoothed with a little more music—mandolin 'specially, but also fiddle and guitar." Adjusting his left crutch to face her, he's still grinning, but she feels the tectonic shift in his tone toward something she might not be ready for. "I just want to say that these past several weeks, you coming to see me at the hospital, they've been some of the best days of my life."

"Outside of some truly unbearable pain."

"Don't reckon I'd have mucked through without you."

"You've been incredibly brave. All your pain. Your going back for those men trapped inside your ship."

He blinks. "Didn't know anyone else knew about that."

"Secrets have a way of leaking out here like seawater gets in."

Head dropping, he flushes. "I best get a running start on what I got to say or I won't likely clear the fence. I won't ask you to say more than you're ready to. Heck, I wouldn't even speak now if it weren't for what I got to say next."

His words seem to float for a moment on a current of hot summer breeze. Will's gaze shifts from her face out over the ocean, as if he's heard something in the gull's cries.

"Joannie, your talk of being up in the sky with your brother Sam, it got me thinking. The navy's let me know they'll have me—be training me to fly."

Joannie feels her chest contract. "But you're not even fully healed!"

"In wartime, I reckon they'll take a half-wrecked carcass like me and teach him how to ride a big metal bird."

"To . . . fly." Her echo is faint.

"Let's just hope an addle-headed mountain boy like me can be taught something useful. Our side needs pilots something fierce. Too many shot down every blessed day."

Shot down, she thinks in a jumble of too much at once. *Sam. Now Will.*

Too many shot down.

"I think," she manages, "I might be ill."

Gently, he slips an arm onto her shoulders and raises one side of his mouth into an almost grin. "I reckon I see how it is. A man professes undying love to a woman, or is fixing to, and she says she's feeling sick. Don't mean to spook the filly away from the tit."

She laughs along with him—how can she not? "I see why your mama thought a little Shakespeare might help you with your lines."

He gazes again out over the ocean. "I wouldn't be speaking out now if it wasn't . . ."

"Dangerous," she says softly. "The whole world feels dangerous now."

"I could've stayed with the merchant marine and been right proud to be sailing supplies to where they're needed. But I listened to you talk about flying . . ."

"No. Don't say you've enlisted as an aviator because of me. I couldn't bear it."

His words feel like another pack of sea boulders strapped to her back, all the dangers he'll face in the air laid upon her.

"Not just you, Joannie. From the hospital, I been catching wind of the navy taking over the airfield here."

She makes herself quote President Roosevelt just to make herself form the words and to hear them out loud: "'Never in the memory of man has there been a war in which the courage, the endurance, and the loyalty of civilians has played so vital a part.'"

"From one of the fireside chats back in April. I recollect you read it to me from the paper when I was still laid out flat in the hospital."

"Right now I need to remind myself not to beg you or Sam or anyone else to stay where it's safe. Remind myself there've got to be more ways I can sacrifice too."

As they walk from the lighthouse down the path, along where the sea splashes up onto a wall of boulders, they wind back to where they parked in the village. Sliding into the Studebaker, they ride in silence a moment. As Joan points to the next street, Will pulls into the sandy lane that leads to her cottage. The kitchen light glows gold, her father slumped at the table.

"That's my dad in there."

"Well, now. You got to respect a man who wears a top hat that well."

"It's his favorite. He's just . . . waiting for my mom."

Bless him, Will, who appears to remember every fact she's told him about her life, doesn't speak but reaches to squeeze her hand. She's grateful for the silence before she goes on.

"I told you about how he can't remember anymore that she's died. But some days now, he can't remember who my brother and I . . ." Even as she says this, Sam, wearing the straw boater, walks into view, holding a steaming pan.

Fried apples, Joannie guesses Sam must've made. *Or apple cobbler.* Not much else for ingredients until she gets the new coupon book tomorrow.

Another figure walks into view. On his head, this third person has fashioned what must be a pillowcase into a makeshift chef's hat, its top puffed up like a white mushroom.

As the third figure turns to face the window, he catches sight of the car outside and, apparently, Joannie in it. It's Marshall, holding up two fingers on each hand in two *V*s for Double Victory—on the home front for civil rights and abroad with the war—before turning back to the table. Behind him, an older woman turns toward the window, spots Joan, waves, then turns back to set down a plate.

Will cocks his head. "They y'all's help?"

"Friends," Joannie shoots back, hearing an edge to her voice she'd not planned. "And neighbors. Marshall's my brother's best friend. The woman is his mom. Kindest person I know."

Except maybe Marshall. And Sam.

Will's head remains cocked, but he says nothing.

The rain has stopped, the gulls silent. The waves of East Beach's high tide crash a few yards down the shore.

Pulling the mandolin from its case in the back seat, Will plays "If I Had You." By the third verse, Joan has to put a hand on his long arm to stop him. She can't bear it, the longing there in each line.

"I swear, Will Dobbins. Just look what you did tonight at the Ritz. You make folks forget about war for a few marvelous minutes and think only of bluebirds and laughter and peace."

He begins playing again, those huge brown eyes of his fixed on her face. She realizes with surprise that with Sam leaving soon—the knowledge like a giant's foot on her chest—Will leaving soon, her father's memory that's mostly already left him, and a whole world gone mad, she's been barely breathing for days, maybe months now.

This young man, with his gentle humor and the loveliness of his music, has somehow given her a great gift. She's breathing again without feeling that the air is rasping through a clogged straw in her chest.

Yet, like Sam, this young man at her side will soon ship out and might never come back.

Will shifts into another song, "All the Things You Are," the thrum of his mandolin and the deep bass of his voice mixing now with the sea.

Chapter 28

Hadley

The phone is running through a Spotify playlist of World War II–era music we're tweaking for the reunion. The lyrics are haunting. The tunes, sensual. Seductive.

"Dear God," I mumble to myself, "how on earth did anyone keep their clothes on, ever, with that playing?"

From behind me, a hand reaches to pick up the phone sitting next to me: Nick Adams's hand. Nick Adams's phone.

Although maybe he didn't hear.

Cringing, I open one eye to find his usual stony demeanor has shifted to merely unreadable—with one eyebrow raised.

I'd forgotten he and Kitz were discussing 1940s music earlier this morning. She's fallen asleep in a shaded chaise longue here by the pool, and he must've returned for his left-behind phone.

"Don't let me disturb the . . . mood," he says, meeting my eye, and then he walks back the way he came.

Dropping my forehead to bang it twice on the table, I drown my mortification in the rest of a large Diet Coke with lime.

"Why? Why do I have to think out loud?" I ask my laptop.

With another long swig of my drink, I dial the next number on my list.

"Richard Silverberg here." The voice is smooth as port wine, the British accent upper crust.

In his late forties, he's another one of Dov's grandsons and head of the British Silverberg branch of Boundless. Educated at Oxford and the London School of Economics, according to *Forbes*, Richard instigated the attempted boardroom coup at Boundless last January. The board ultimately voted to keep Ernst Hessler in place, but the attempted ouster resurfaced ongoing feuds over who would eventually take Hessler's spot.

Richard Silverberg's vision for Boundless is, I've gathered, even more focused on the bottom line and more ruthless than Hessler's. Another contender to replace Hessler is a great-niece of Will Dobbins and is a proponent of returning the company to its earlier ideal of doing good on a humanitarian level while still doing well for shareholders' interests. She is younger, though, and less battle tested. *Forbes* also alluded to a couple of wild card future leaders of Boundless, including one hellion descendant who'd faced recent legal troubles, but the article didn't bother to name them, referring to them only as "unlikely heirs to the Boundless throne."

"Yes, thank you. My name is Hadley Jacks of Storied Events, the firm handling the upcoming reunion of the Boundless founding families. I wonder if I might have just a moment of your time."

"A very brief moment. I am, *Hadley*, an extraordinarily busy man."

Richard Silverberg is one of those people, apparently, who wields the first names of his inferiors—waiters, Uber drivers, event planners—like leashes, snapped.

"I'll try to be brief. Our firm has a reputation for telling captivating stories about our clients at our events. In this case, we want to celebrate the remarkable friendship formed among the three men who founded Boundless."

"Yes, rather. Of course, dear old Uncle Ernst is behind this, so the grand *story* you're telling would already be stamped with certain biased viewpoints, yes? Beastly thought, that."

This renders me speechless for a moment, a state I'm not accustomed to often, so I ask the next thing that pops into my mind: "You're Rabbi Benedick's brother, is that right?"

His tone of voice buckles here into a laugh, brittle and short. "Indeed, yes. Although one of the apples appears to have fallen quite far from the grandfather's tree."

"One grandson a spiritual leader and one grandson an executive of a world-renowned real estate development firm," I agree, but manage not to add aloud, *who staged a coup.* "It would appear you took different paths."

His voice is smooth, sinewy, but I sense something else, too, the sharp bits and hooks. "Although, not so different as it might first appear. My brother Ben has his own vaulting ambitions."

Again, I'm flummoxed. "His ambitions, Mr. Silverberg?"

I'm trying to form a mental picture of Richard Silverberg just from what I've heard of his voice over the phone: aggressively fit, the kind of body sculpted by a private trainer, and with closely cropped hair, the color and sheen of mink. As I call up images of him on my laptop, I see I'm dead on.

The silence on the other end of the line tells me he has no intention of answering my last question.

"Mr. Silverberg, I wonder if I might ask you just one or two more things."

"I haven't much time, but anything for a project Ernst has thought up *for the benefit of the whole group.*" His emphasis on those last words hangs heavy with sarcasm, like a great weight swinging on a fraying rope.

"I wonder what you recall in family stories about your own grandfather Dov—or, for that matter, about Hans Hessler or Will Dobbins."

"Well, Hadley, brava for your diplomatic little turn away from family . . . *politics,* shall we say." He manages to slide so much condescension into a handful of words, I nearly have to set down my cell for the heaviness of it.

Barefoot, the brick pavers warm on the pads of my feet, I rise to pace the King and Prince path running above the beach.

"One of the stories your brother Ben told me was of Will Dobbins playing his mandolin in the rain for a crowd of people, how he moved them to tears—and hope."

"Yes, yes. Part of the legend, you could say, around Uncle Shakes, as we call him. Always the model of charity and goodwill."

There's an aftertaste to his tone, like a skinny margarita—salt and sour together in a jolt of lime.

"He's celebrating his hundredth birthday at the reunion, I understand."

"Yes, rather. Though in no shape, of course, to have any say in the running of our little ship."

That "little ship" has an estimated worth in the billions.

"You don't personally care for your 'Uncle Shakes' much yourself, though?"

There's a pause on the other end of the line, and I realize I've overstepped. "Sorry. Absolutely none of my business."

"*Everyone,*" he assures me, "loves Uncle Shakes. *God,* did I imply otherwise?"

"No, not at all," I lie. "Perhaps it's simply more the softer side of the corporation's original vision that you feel no longer serves Boundless well now."

Another pause fills up the miles of ocean between St. Simons Island and London.

"It would appear someone has been reading *Forbes.* It's no secret, Hadley, that Boundless has been admired, at times, for its . . . softer, humanitarian side, to which you allude. Uncle Shakes was—is—nothing if not *universally* likable."

His tone implies he might be an exception to the category *universally.*

"There are, however, other considerations to running one of the largest and most influential real estate development firms in the world, one that is prepared to step aggressively into the future."

There, I think, *right there is the rift.*

Though apparently the rift goes even deeper than the age-old generational divide of needing to adapt to the modern era.

"Mr. Silverberg, I do hope you'll make the reunion."

"Oh, I am *devoted* to the idea. Believe *me,* I wouldn't miss this *production* for the world."

Train wreck, I think. *He says the word* production *like he's relishing getting to see a train wreck.*

"Wouldn't miss it because . . . you're close to the other families, or . . . ?"

Again, this is none of my business, but something in the glister of his voice makes me want to push back against it.

"Let's go with answer D: all the above. I do remember our gathering every three years or so when I was young. Always at the King and Prince, of course. Bonfires on the beach. Clambakes. Horseback riding. Dancing on Sea Island."

"Sea Island? Why the next island over?"

"Why indeed? That was Grandfather Dov's idea. Not that *anyone* is keeping track." He almost snorts now, the sarcasm thick, a sound not in keeping with the silvery, sleek persona. "Apparently, Grandfather Dov had some especially important memories from the war that were made on Sea Island. At the Cloister there. 'Under the stars,' Grandfather always said. The Cloister hosted dances outdoors by the pool for officers and their dates during the war, it seems."

"Although not for Hans Hessler, since he was a POW, and probably not Will Dobbins, since he was apparently shipped out sometime in 1943."

"More questions for your *inimitable* research, Hadley. Just as well you're the one being paid from the Boundless coffers—handsomely, I would presume—to do the research. Perhaps it was simply some sweet memories of Grandfather Dov's from events out on Sea

Island—interestingly, when Grandmother Deborah was still just his fiancée and an entire ocean away. Do by all means uncover a salacious scandal with some scullery maid to add to our current deluge of unfavorable press."

I lower my cell phone so I can stare open mouthed at the screen.

"I say, though, Hadley, let me suggest keeping your distance, lest you become embroiled in our intimate family drama. By the way, have you contacted Uncle Shakes for an interview?"

"Because of his age, I wasn't sure . . ."

"By all means, don't. Poor bloke, early-stage dementia. Quite the confusion, and then gets upset, rather pitiful really, when he realizes how much he's impaired. Painful, that. Now, one final question?"

Still processing what he's just said, I fumble my words. "The three families are still close, would you say?"

"Close? Oh, *rather*, yes. Loyal too. Dear God, *such* loyalty and closeness. The family feeling among us, Hadley, is simply to *die* for."

Chapter 29
Joannie

August 1942

They're going to kill him, Joan thinks, whirling the pony around.

It's Saturday morning, and she's just finished delivering extra cases of milk to the King and Prince. She's taken on Sam's delivery shift, since he's in basic training, and now she's covering his shift with the horseback shore patrol. The group had first brought in fine gaited horses—Sam had been keen on the Tennessee Walkers—for shore patrol at first but found the animals clumsy and skittish in the wet sand—some even frightened of the surf. Now they've taken to lightly training some of the Marsh Tackies that run wild on the island. Sturdy, sure footed, and smart, these little horses trot easily along the beaches, giving their riders plenty of time to look for trouble in the form of spies, subs, enemy planes, or invaders of any sort.

Most days, Joan feels sure it's more an exercise in making citizens feel useful, rather than actually helping the war effort. Today, though, she's afraid she's about to witness a murder.

She has no business telling American guards how to handle their prisoners, but they're standing off to one side, rifles slung over their shoulders and deep in conversation, while three men with *PW* stamped in black on the backs of their shirts stumble, shouting, out of the King and Prince kitchen, two of them punching a third in the stomach and face.

"Aren't you going to *do* something?" she demands.

One shrugs. "Happens at least once a week."

"Are you not going to *stop* them?"

"*Ordnung halten*," another guard offers tentatively. "I think that means 'stop.'"

The prisoners ignore him.

Yawning, one of the guards lumbers toward the skirmish. "You Jerrys quit beating the holy crap out of each other."

"I think," Joan calls from her horse, "you'll need to be more convincing. *Do* something!"

A few yards away up the beach, three men in white T-shirts and shorts appear to be finishing a run with a final sprint to the finish, sand flying.

"Go piss yourself, Silverberg," the stockiest one of them pants, pulling up last.

At the approach of the officers, the two guards use the butts of their rifles as battering rams to beat into the fray of the prisoners.

Behind them, a deep voice barks orders, the two American guards pinioning the two aggressors' arms behind their backs. Staggering back, the third collapses onto the grass and wipes blood from his mouth.

Joan turns in time to recognize the stocky officer, the rude one—*Brock, was it?*—from the airfield. Just behind him stands an officer Joan's never seen and also the exchange instructor, the striking Englishman, whose name she does remember.

"Well, well." Brock shakes his head. "If it isn't the lovely little Miss DuBarry. Commander Flint, you wouldn't have had the privilege of knowing, but Miss DuBarry's brother taught her to fly."

"A splendid aviatrix, if there ever was one," Dov Silverberg puts in.

Flint takes her measure, his left hand stroking his chin. He wears a silver band on the fourth finger of that hand, Joan notices, a recent trend in the last world war and this one, a mark of commitment to wives back home. "Damn shame we can't give you a uniform, Miss DuBarry. Women like you would be a great help. If you all will excuse me, I'll see to the commotion we have here." He steps to one side to question the guards.

Beside them, one of the three POWs stands at attention, arm snapping up. "Heil Hitler!"

The second imitates the first.

The third, though, crosses his arms and turns away. *"Fahr zur Hölle."*

"'Go to hell,' sir," one of the guards offers, adding hurriedly, "but not you, sir. His words, I mean. For the other two, sir."

"Damn shame," Brock echoes Flint from a moment ago, but with a sneer now. "If our country comes to that, so desperate we're turning to *girls* to save us. Think what the Krauts and Japs will make of *that* news."

"The Soviets," Dov Silverberg says, "deploy women in aviation combat quite effectively."

"They're the *damn Soviets.* Enough said."

"We Brits have enlisted women to help ferry military planes, which frees up more men for combat. The US will need to be more open minded—and quite soon."

"The day we quit honoring American womanhood," Brock spits back, "that's the day this country's gone straight to your bloody hell."

Dov Silverberg casts a look, amused, toward Joan. *"My* bloody hell being the very worst kind, it would seem."

As Brock stalks away, the Englishman rakes a hand through his hair and steps toward her horse. "What mighty steed might this be?"

"One of our coastal wild ponies. Nothing flashy, but just right for patrolling a beach."

"May I?" Dov Silverberg looks up at her for permission to touch the horse.

"He's new to all this, but see if he'll let you."

The horse stands, unfazed, as Dov runs a hand down his neck, flecked in white.

"Apparently equitation and lifesaving diplomacy should be listed among your skills, Miss DuBarry."

"I'm actually not a good rider, Lieutenant Silverberg, but I can stay on. Riding a horse isn't so very different from flying."

He looks up at her, his breathing still slowing from the run. His lips part as if he might reply, but he doesn't. Just looks at her with those eyes the color of St. Simons sand when it's wet: brown mixed with gold.

He smells of sweat and sea air, but also somehow of damp earth and meadows, she thinks, though she has no idea how a meadow in England might smell. His scent is all the aromas she imagined while reading those hefty nineteenth-century English novels her mother kept in the house.

A few yards away, the two belligerent Germans stand straining again, guards holding their wrists.

"*Ein Selbstmord. Das war alles!*" one of them snarls.

"A suicide," Dov translates. "That's all it was, he claims. The death of another prisoner."

The assaulted prisoner shakes his head. "The *hell* it was," he says in English.

Dov lowers his voice to Joan. "There are serious tensions among the prisoners: those who, for example, remain loyal to the Führer versus those who fought because they had—or believed they had—no choice. This won't be our last bout of violence, I suspect."

Flint motions the guards holding the two prisoners to follow him toward Dov.

"Remind me, Silverberg, why it is I'm expected to keep two Krauts alive while, just an ocean away, we're shooting them to damn bits?"

Dov stands at attention. "Geneva Convention, sir. And the mercy of God."

"To hell with that last." Flint turns to look one of the prisoners in the face. "You realize this man here suggesting I don't knock all you

Krauts six ways to Stalingrad is one of my officers." He leans still closer. "And a Jew."

"*Jude*," the shorter German says, and spits on the ground.

"You," Flint asks Dov, "still want to keep these men alive?"

Dov stares straight ahead.

For his part, Flint runs a hand across his crew cut. "Ought to let the whole pack of them kill each other off. Mercy of God, my ass."

Without another word to the guards, Flint strides away.

Dov Silverberg takes a step to follow his commanding officer before he turns, that strangely intense look of his making Joan shift on the mare's short back.

"I confess I'd hoped our paths would cross again."

She has no time to respond before he's gone, leaving her to finish patrolling the shore and watch the morning sun brush its bright fingers across the swells.

Chapter 30

Hans

August 1942
St.-Malo, Brittany coast, France

At sunrise, Hans feels almost human again as he watches the fishermen launching their boats and the gulls squabbling over a fish—he welcomes any sound or movement at all so he doesn't feel as alone as he does during the long, unfathomably dark nights. He's still not used to going without Pervitin, still craving that drive and absence of all inhibitions he felt with the drug coursing in his blood.

But perhaps he deserves to feel fear and sorrow now. Perhaps that's the price of no longer being a cog in a ruthlessly crushing machine.

There are no city lights here on the Brittany coast, and he's conscious of being completely, utterly alone.

He misses his mother. He misses the farm, even the cranky cow, Helga. Misses them all so much he could weep. He's terrified of every step he hears on the path when he travels by night, every owl that flaps into a barn where he's taken cover.

Yet he regrets nothing.

His first sight of the next town on the coast comes just as the sky turns from pink to a pearlescent gray. It will rain today, again, the earth spongy with mud. Hans is grateful for no good reason, except perhaps that the rain feels like a washing away—though of just what, he's not sure.

Perhaps Father Bernhard was right about the human need for a spiritual cleansing.

Or maybe Hans just loves the smell of summer rain.

Now, as he rounds a turn in the path, he begins to look for a place to hide for the day. He's rolled himself in dead fish and seaweed he found eddied in one harbor so he might smell more like the fisherman he's supposed to be. He speaks some French—*s'il vous plaît* and *merci beaucoup*—but he knows his accent will give him away if he speaks more than a few words.

The villages are small here, the farms and harbors set well apart. Still, people must know their neighbors. Some might be willing to harbor a deserting German mariner disguised as a Breton fisherman; some might turn him in for the reward of meat or eggs to feed their children for the first time in months. He won't know which is which. He cannot risk human interaction of any sort.

A walled city appears down below him—very nearly an island unto itself, connected to the mainland with only a whisp of land. He'd have no idea what the town was called if it weren't for the sign, the first he's seen in many miles. St.-Malo, with an arrow posted on the road that runs along the coast. The locals must've pulled down the others to prevent the Germans from finding their way. This sign, though, remains, as if this particular town is too lovely, too extraordinary not to label.

The fear drains from his body. He knows it will return—perhaps in waves for the rest of his life. But for now, he gazes down at the town, its steepled skyline and its city walls bulwarked against a blue sea. For a single moment, the beauty of the scene is enough.

But now running steps, heavy and fast, thud on the path behind him.

The city walls looked so storybook-appealing just seconds ago. Now, with someone charging toward him up the path, Hans imagines those walls collapsing like his moment of calm.

Without stopping to look behind, he breaks into a sprint.

Chapter 31
Hadley

I drop my head into my hands, the archive walls seeming to close in around me.

"Should've had more caffeine at lunch," I mutter. "I'm having a kind of 'Yellow Wallpaper' episode."

Kitzie shoots me a glance. "You're supposed to be the strong one."

"Though not necessarily the sane one."

"True. So just reach out and push the walls back into place."

I drop my head onto the table. Kitz and I are at the archives of the Coastal Georgia Historical Society to get more background on St. Simons Island during the war while we wait for more photos and letters from the families to pour in, but my head is pounding now. "I've read so many soldiers' letters home my eyes have permanently crossed. Dear God, all that homesickness, all that fear."

"All those mamas who read all those letters from so far away. How'd they keep getting out of bed in the morning?"

Both our gazes move back to the stack of letters smelling of mustiness and old dreams. The pages, brittle and creased, are spidered with black ink. Many of the lines have been blacked out by the censors.

I roll my head to the side, cheek flat to the table, to manage a smile for my sister. "Your phone's lighting up." I straighten. "Kitz, Lindy's calling you." Our last foster mom, the best of the bunch times ten, calls often to chat with "her girls."

Oddly, Kitz waves this away. "We can get back to her later."

"We haven't talked to her in ages. Let's just step out and catch her up on our lives." I reach for her phone to answer it.

"No."

"What's gotten into you? It's just Lindy."

My sister doesn't look me in the eye. "Let's just finish up here and call her back later, how 'bout?" She holds out her hand for the phone.

Slowly, I offer it back, just as a text pops up on the screen.

> Sorry I missed you. What's the latest from the doc?
>
> Will catch up with you and H soon.

"So Lindy knows you're sick? I thought the last time we talked with her was together before we got here."

Kitz waves me away. "What is this, interrogation time? I just texted her when the cold was still bad. Hey, did you see this one to somebody DuBarry?"

I know she's trying to change subjects, but also, maybe she's right: maybe I'm being weirdly suspicious. Lindy still checks in with us lots— almost always together, but there's no reason she shouldn't check on one of us who was sick. "Joannie DuBarry?"

"No, it's . . . hard to make out."

Leaning over, I examine the page. "Dear . . . yeah, maybe Sandy. Or Sammy? You're right, the envelope's addressed to a DuBarry. I'm going with Sammy."

I examine the postmark. "Mailed from St. Simons Island and signed by . . . looks like the name's Marsha, with a kind of flourish at the end. Maybe she was his girlfriend? You suppose this Sam was related to Joan? Kitz, look at the second paragraph. This Marsha person, if we've got the name right—talks about delivering produce to the King and Prince kitchen for the men in radar training. Having slurs muttered at her from a German POW sent to help unload the produce. An American standing by just smoking." I run a gloved finger down the page. "She talks here about working another job across the causeway on the mainland. Building Liberty ships."

"Well, bully for you, Marsha."

"Kitz, check this out." I scoot closer to show her the page.

I wish you could see it. The shipyard these days hires anybody who can turn a screw. Got all sorts—hillbillies from Arkansas can't read a line, tenant farmers from Mississippi never pissed indoors, one disinherited white boy from some filthy rich family in Philly—us working together. I'm paid less than the white workers and get the worst shifts, but it's a step up for all that.

We look up from the page at the same time. "She's Black," we say together.

I stand and pace the room. "I haven't found any DuBarrys still living on the island. But if we can make out Marsha's last name on the return address, maybe we can find some descendant in her family."

"Maybe." Kitzie cocks her head. "Although we're getting a teeny bit far afield from planning the reunion, don't you think?"

"You think a World War Two wild-goose chase after the maybe-girlfriend of the maybe-relative of the girl that these three men were all maybe in love with eighty years ago is a bit much?" Sighing, I deposit myself in the closest chair.

"You just want to know, don't you, Hadz?"

"Is that totally nuts?"

"Totally. So, what we tell ourselves is that any of this more . . . *far-reaching* research will simply enrich the whole event."

"So it doesn't make sense. But I can't help it. It's like anything even remotely related to Joannie DuBarry sends me chasing after it. It's like if I can understand her, I'll figure out what connected all three of these friends."

Kitz checks her watch. "We're meeting with one of the archivists in thirty minutes. Let's finish the catering calls, and then afterwards, we go wild goosing."

~

An hour later, we burst from the archives into the noonday sunshine, the lighthouse just a few yards away. Tilting my head all the way back to admire its circular balcony at the top, I lift my hand to shield my eyes from the sun, only to see I'm still wearing the white archival gloves.

"Be right back, Kitz."

Flinging the door back open to return the gloves, I find the archivist we just met standing there, holding one palm out.

"I'm so sor—" I begin.

Her face, framed by silver-blonde hair pulled into a french twist, relaxes into a smile. "I do it all the time myself." The only faint lines on her face crinkle out from her eyes, as if from squinting at old manuscripts. "I hope you understood why I couldn't just give out information—without permission—about the families who trust us with their loved ones' letters."

"I do. My sister tells me I can go a bit golden retriever when I'm into a project. I don't always hear the first *Down, girl* when I get excited."

"We archivists are much the same. Quite wild with pleasure when we're hot on a trail."

Everything about her speaks of elegance and steadiness—no hints of *wild with pleasure.*

But maybe archivists let down their hair like nobody else?

"What I *can* hint towards, Hadley, is that you might want to visit Christ Church Frederica."

Startled, I blink at her. Aside from our one fabulous foster mother, Lindy, a flannel-shirts-and-Birkenstocks-wearing Methodist with cropped brown hair who lured us to evening gatherings with the promise of hand-churned peach ice cream—not a bad connection with the transcendent—no one's checked on my church attendance for years.

"I'm afraid I'm not—"

"I didn't mean attending services. Although that would certainly be a way you'd be sure to connect with one of the ministers there."

"I need to connect with one of the ministers?"

The archivist's eyes narrow—not unkindly, but searchingly—and I wonder if she's analyzing me as she would an old letter. "Given what you were reading this morning, yes."

I wait for her to tell me more.

Instead, she gives a flap to the white gloves I've just returned. "Well, then. I suppose I've said as much as I ought."

But she's said nothing at all, really. Has she?

I take a step—maybe more of a lunge—toward the archives door as she turns to close it behind her. "So, then, Christ Church Frederica. Here on the island?"

"An important historical landmark. Regardless of one's spiritual sensibilities"—*or lack thereof,* her pause seems to add for my sake—"it's important to visit. Its oaks and azaleas are some of the loveliest on the island. It's Episcopalian, you know."

Is she hinting I ought to bike out there in linen and pearls? I wonder. *Do I need to bring wine?*

As I put out my hand to slow the door's closing, she pauses, only a rectangle of her face still visible. "I believe I'm also within the bounds of confidentiality to point you toward what every guidebook on this island mentions."

"Yes, please. Whatever you suggest."

"Do *not* miss that church's graveyard." She stares at me meaningfully. Then closes the door.

Stumbling back outside, I find Kitz leaning against the lighthouse, and we stand together in silence.

We watch thunderclouds roll in, dark and menacing from the southwest. A fog has settled in over the island, swirls of white mixing with the silver of Spanish moss that drips from the live oaks. It's like entering a fairy tale. And like every good fairy tale, all is not as well as it seems in the castle or cottage.

Watching the mist braid itself through the live oaks, I think of the three men who founded Boundless, their complicated relationships with each other and with Joannie DuBarry. I think of Richard and Ben Silverberg's suspicions of each other, of *Forbes*'s reference to some hellion family member, of Ernst Hessler's granite exterior and also, perhaps, his loneliness inside the walls that his wealth and power have built.

I think of Kitzie and myself, polished enough to pass for "spoiled Californians," but beneath a very thin, glossy veneer, we're both still riddled with unhealed bullet holes from our past.

How many of the most confident-looking people, I wonder, *maybe like me, only appear so because we've had to build buttresses, had to stand taller and stiffer, not so much out of confidence as to keep from collapsing when the wrecking ball of the past swings at us again?*

I think, too, of Kitzie's health. Of her assurance to me that she's feeling better, her beaming as we plan this reunion.

But what if all is not really well there either? What would I do without the Good Cop to my Bad, the perky to my wary, the sweet to my strong? How exactly would I go on without my sister, who is my whole family?

Simple. I wouldn't.

The fog sets in even thicker, and although it's not cold, I shiver.

～

Kitzie is nearly yelling to me over the phone, my cell precariously balanced in my bike's basket, her voice on speaker. "By the way, Mr.

Hessler emailed twice today already to check on our progress—with just a few hundred details to check on. But all fair."

"Of course."

"Also, Hadz, it's all here in the letters the Dobbins family FedExed to us today. There's a crazy story Will tells in one letter home to his sister—named, *oh my God*, Biscuit, if you can believe it—about a crash . . ."

These moments hit me like waves I didn't see coming, smacking me in the face: these realizations that the letters were from nineteen- and twenty-year-olds, young adults expected to save the world in planes and boats, by sabotage and heroics and by just staying alive.

The bellow of a delivery truck's horn makes Kitzie fall silent.

"My fault, Kitz. I'm not strictly paying attention to details like . . . oncoming traffic. Just nearing that spot on Dunbar Creek. You know, what we read about—where they're putting in the historical marker to the Igbo people. The ones who drowned themselves rather than allowing themselves to be sold into slavery. It's so hard to think of them walking, shackled together, into the water."

"Oh dear God. So much tragic history here."

Neither of us speaks for several beats as I pedal on, my mind on the creek and the heartbreak still flowing through it, on all the stories woven through the live oaks and moss here.

"Hadz, no wonder you're steering like Mr. Toad."

"Mr. Toad at least had four wheels and no roundabouts."

"Listen, you get to the graveyard safely, and call me once you've found whatever it is we're supposed to care about there."

I should have made an appointment, of course, before biking all the way out to Christ Church Frederica, but I suppose some part of me hoped I could simply wander the cemetery and some key clue would rise up to greet me, bright neon arrows pointing to it so I wouldn't have to go into the church itself.

The Methodist church Kitzie and I attended with Lindy was a place of kindness, lots of soft-armed older folks who wrapped us in hugs at every turn, the air smelling of Murphy Oil Soap and welcome. The pastor, too, an older spherical fellow with round wire spectacles and an open, round face, meant well, I've no doubt. His low, concerned questions—*How are you feeling,* really *feeling lately, girls?*—seemed to comfort Kitzie but made me feel like I'd stripped off my hand-me-down sundress and was doing laps in my skivvies around the sanctuary. These people knew our family's dirty laundry and loved us, despite it all, but it was more stains and stink—people missing and overdosed and dead-beat—than I'd have chosen to hang out in public.

As I wheel to a stop in front of Christ Church, I gawk at its charm—steep gables under ancient oaks, all draped in Spanish moss. The graveyard goes on for acres, and while I appreciate it's also an azalea garden, I don't have the time to just wander hundreds of headstones and wonder which of them might possibly be relevant.

I've learned, thanks to the internet and family letters, that Dov Silverberg was buried in the Golders Green section of London, and Hans Hessler in Bamberg, Germany. Will Dobbins lives outside Nashville, Tennessee, where he has a second home in addition to a place in New York.

I wander among the camellias and azaleas, Spanish moss from the low-hanging branches occasionally brushing my shoulders like the fingers of a wraith.

Two people emerge from the back of the church, both with their heads down, nodding, deep in conversation. From behind, I trot closer. Both are wearing dark suits and clerical collars. One is an older White man; the other a much younger Black woman.

"His basic problem," the man intones, "would be simply that he's stuck on theodicy, his need to explain how bad things can happen to good people."

"This is where," the woman says, "I've found Kierkegaard helpful in—"

"Excuse me," I begin, drawing alongside them. I feel rude inserting myself, but I'm not sure I can wait for two Episcopalians to solve the problem of evil. "I'm so sorry to interrupt."

The man blinks at me over half-moon glasses.

The woman, though, lights up. "Well now, you're the young woman from the yacht."

I laugh. "Definitely the first time I've been tagged that way. And you're the Reverend Doctor Felicia."

"I'd hoped our paths would cross again, Hadley."

I'm a little startled by her warmth—a bit thrown off my game, to tell the truth. Angelenos are friendly enough, but conversations between virtual strangers generally center on silver screen résumé pitching and traffic.

"How can we help you?"

"Actually, I'm not sure. I was sent here by one of the archivists at the Coastal Georgia Historical Society. I'm researching some men who were stationed here during World War Two, and whose families are coming back in May for a reunion. The archivist seemed to think I might find something relevant out here in your lovely cemetery. Although, to be honest, I haven't a clue what I'm looking for, and she seemed, well, reticent to say more."

"I don't know about my esteemed colleague here, but I'm afraid I don't have all sixteen hundred or more—"

"More," her colleague says.

"—grave markers memorized. Though as much as I walk on these grounds, I probably should. You've seen our online search site, I suppose."

Of course I should've checked online first. Except I already know none of the three friends will be here. Something about this whole island makes it feel a bit Brigadoon, as if time got spun backward into the mist. I don't regret, though, seeing this place with its unreal beauty.

On my iPhone, I find a connecting link to search for who's been baptized or married in the church. Trying the names of the men, in case one of them was married here, I come up with nothing.

"I'm taking your time," I apologize. "I don't mean for you to stand here while I try to solve a mystery, especially when I don't even know the questions to ask."

"I like mysteries," the woman assures me. "We value them in my profession."

Maybe, it occurs to me, *Sam DuBarry, not one of the three Boundless founders, was the reason the archivist sent me here, since we mentioned finding his letters to Marsha.* I type in the last name.

No Samuel, but up come the names Terrence DuBarry, died 1944, Lilian DuBarry, died 1941, and also a Joan DuBarry—with no birth or death dates. My heart beats faster.

Beside a color picture of Joan's marker, though, is a digitized black-and-white photo of a dark-haired young woman, waves falling to her shoulders—and she's a stunner.

"It's you again," I murmur under my breath.

The clergywoman tilts her head. "Mystery solved, then?"

"I'm not sure if this was what the archivist meant for me to find. She was . . . more than a little vague."

The man slides his glasses lower on his nose to consider me. "There was a time when, at the very least, we knew all the family names on this island. All of us did. Those days are past, I fear."

"And that sort of change," the clergywoman adds, patting her older colleague's arm, "can be a *good* thing. Now, Hadley, make yourself at home here as long as you like." Plucking a business card from the pocket of her slacks, she hands it to me. "Seriously, do let me know if I can help."

"Thank you. Very kind."

The man bobs his head, then walks on ahead. "Actually, I find James Cone to be more instructive on this."

The woman, raising her hand to me in goodbye, falls into step with him. "I *know* you are *not* quoting James Cone to me."

"Just because I'm a tired old White coot doesn't mean I haven't read . . ."

The two stroll away companionably.

I stand under the sprawling oaks and stare at my phone's screen. I have no idea which ghosts I'm chasing, or why. Holding my phone in front of me like a map, I follow the website's information to the right section of the cemetery.

And there it is, toward a back corner and covered in lichen and moss, but the engraving legible—barely.

JOAN DUBARRY

There's a second line on the stone, though, a date of death that doesn't show in the website's photograph—although maybe the way the shadows fall in the image obscures it? I squint from one to the other. Then it hits me: the date of death on the stone.

"Oh my God," I say into the silence. "She died."

A ridiculous thing to say in a cemetery, I'll grant you, with all those spectral curtains of moss and legions of tombstones.

But her date of death, November 22, 1945, means this Joan DuBarry, allegedly the love of all three of the friends, died just after the end of the war.

Staring at the date, I'm stung by disappointment—by loss, even. Like I'd counted on the stories of these four people, all navigating a world on the brink of destruction, having ended differently somehow. Having ended, I suppose, happily—and together.

Even though I, of all people, should know that real life rarely works that way.

But how, I wonder as I find my way through the graveyard back to my bike, *did Joan DuBarry's life, cut so short, become some sort of connecting thread weaving through all three men's stories?*

~

After pedaling from the cemetery back to the King and Prince, I arrive sweaty and panting. I trot through the lobby, and at the double doors of the hotel's historic dining room, I skid to a stop.

I'm not alone in the room that ought to be locked—all these priceless photographs and letters the families have entrusted us with splayed out on the circle of tables.

Nick Adams's back is to me, and he's sorting through photos. He's opened the double doors that face the ocean, and a light breeze riffles not only his hair but also some of the loose papers.

"What . . . ?"

Without turning, he holds up a key, heavy and brass, from an earlier era. "Hope you don't mind. I was given the key when I said I was helping you out."

I was given? Such a passive-voice way of speaking. Like a child insisting *the cookies were eaten.*

I round to the other side of the tables so that I'm standing in his sight line. "Don't you think you should've checked with us?"

He doesn't look up from whatever he's sorting. "Occurred to me."

"And?"

"Your sister gave me full access."

Of course she did. Not only would Kitz usher the chicken thief into the henhouse, she'd also offer him breakfast and the Wi-Fi password.

I scan the room for signs of plunder.

"Not much to be gained," he says, as if he's overhearing my thoughts, "for the lowly chauffeur. No social security numbers so far, or Swiss bank account numbers."

"Still." I wait until he raises his face to mine. "The families sent their pictures and letters, trusting that only we would handle them. Kitzie and I."

Angling his head, Nick doesn't speak for a moment. Oddly, he appears more amused than offended. "The chauffeur wouldn't count as part of the *we*, I take it?"

I've moved closer to get his attention—we're standing just inches apart now. His lopsided grin does not help me feel less irked.

From the inner door, Kitzie's voice rings out. "Well, hey there, friends! What's up, and can I play?"

Typical Kitzie, emerging from the midday nap she must've been taking when I tried to call her again, but sounding now as if she's arriving at a party. And dressed, of course, impeccably.

"Good to see you up and around," Nick utters gruffly, and his gaze doesn't leave mine. "I was planning to sort pictures, but it seems I may be gum in the gears rather than help."

Kitzie beams. "It's quite the soap opera, right? I swear I'd have driven from California just to figure out how they all ended up. That and to get some decent fried okra."

"Kitz, you should rest more."

"If I rest any longer, I'll climb the drapes, then make a ball gown out of them." She plucks her phone from her shorts pocket. "I got a call from you while I was sleeping—that you were in the cemetery and something about Joannie DuBarry's date of death?"

This nudges me out of my staring contest with Nick Adams. "Right . . ." I shoot him one last wary glance, a sort of I'll-be-watching-you look, to which he gives me a two-fingered salute and that maddening twitch of a grin in response.

"Somewhere in here is the picture Ernst Hessler showed us when we were out there on his yacht—his Lürssen."

Head ducked, Nick reaches to his right on top of a stack. "This one?"

Sheepish, I think. *He looks sheepish because he was just looking at it before I walked in.*

Kitzie and I press in on either side of him as he holds the photograph up.

Nick flips to its back. The words strike me again like a slap as Kitzie reads it aloud: "*May* something, *1945. Joannie and us. Traitor.*"

"What," I ask, "would you guess the date in May is?"

"Hard to tell with the smudges. Maybe ten or sixteen or nineteen. Definitely has a one and another digit."

I open my phone and bring up the photo from the cemetery. "Here's the date of death on her tombstone."

I hold it up so they can both see.

"November 22, 1945," Kitz reads. "Wait. So after surviving the war years, she . . ." Kitz trails off.

"Died. Yep. Yet all three men preserved either pictures or stories or telegrams about her, cherished enough for some reason that all three families have saved them. But why? Feels like instead of answering our questions, we're stumbling across more." I glance out through the double doors toward the sea, where twilight is settling, a cooler front moving in. "The fog just seems to thicken."

Chapter 32
Joannie

Any other day at dawn, fluffy blankets of clouds might look cozy, but today they say only danger to Joannie. The mist swaddling the island has not burned off yet, last night's storm slow to move along.

Absently, she brings the milk delivery truck to a stop on the road's sandy shoulder, but her eyes stay on the plane accelerating on the airfield's runway closest to her. The Wildcat's pilot is still green, she judges, the plane's nose lifting abruptly. He's not bringing the tail up quickly enough. In flying, every detail can mean life or death.

Steady there. You're not piloting a rocket.

Clearing the tops of the live oaks and pines at the far end of the runway, he ascends—too rapidly—then executes a turn, but not gracefully. His left wing dips dangerously close to the water, and she holds her breath. Last week, a pilot just this inexperienced was banking into a turn just this sloppily, and his wing did indeed dip into a wave. That Wildcat turned into a silver pinwheel and crashed. They sent the chase boat to the rescue, its workhorse of a Packard engine getting it there in record time, but it was too late. The navy was short another pilot now, and another shattered mother had the tragic honor of hanging a gold star in her window.

Joan understands why all the armed services have shortened the number of hours required in training before being deployed—men so desperately needed at every front. But fewer hours of training will mean these sorts of accidents—these deaths—happen more.

"And meanwhile," she says aloud to no one but the wind, "Uncle Sam does not want me. Not in the air, at least."

This bit, the resentment, feels good for a moment, a welcome distraction, a relief from the constant pulse of worry that beats through the whole country these days: every call to purchase war bonds, every newsreel at the Ritz, and every thud of the morning paper on the porch at dawn.

Part of her feeling of near panic, she knows, is a constant thrum of fear for Sam.

On their front porch, their father had stood in his bathrobe and slapped Sam on the back. "Off to fight the kaiser now, are you, young fella? Lilian will be so sorry to miss saying goodbye."

Joan leaned in toward Sam. "He thinks it's the last war."

Face pinched, Sam threw his arms around their father and held him so tight and so long, Terrence finally slapped Sam on both shoulders and stepped back.

"When you get done beating those Huns, you come on back to visit the island, hear? Lilian and me, we'd love to have you."

Sam straightened. Seemed to wait until he could speak without his voice cracking. "I'll do my best, Pops."

When they reached the truck, Joannie rounded on her brother. "Not near good enough."

"What?"

"*Promise.* You got to *promise* to come back."

He pulled her head down to scrub on her scalp with his knuckles, but she reached up and grabbed him by the hair.

"*Promise!*" she demanded, twisting the hair.

Laughing, he pushed her away. "Good Lord, maybe you *should* be the one sent to fight. Look, I promise. How's that?" But he did not meet her eye.

A few minutes later, when she dropped him off for his bus to basic training, she held on to him just as he'd held on to Pops. "Remember," she'd whispered, "you promised."

His latest letter sits in her coveralls pocket—*his* coveralls, actually, for the job she's covering in his absence. The letter and the coveralls both feel like a rope connecting the two of them across the oceans and continents.

No doubt you'll whip the home front into fighting form with all that DuBarry impatience.

But he'd closed with a line of affection:

Don't ever doubt how proud I am of you.

This as much as anything tells Joannie how much danger he must be facing daily.

Tucking the letter back into her pocket, she makes herself watch the Wildcat flying patterns overhead, its stubby wings looking still stubbier while being flown without grace. Painted a nonreflective blue-gray, it is hard to make out once it's in the air—particularly through today's fog.

She's always been a person of action, unsure what prayer to an unseen God might do, if anything. But right now she prays for the trainee pilot and his wobbling wings headed out over the open ocean through the dense fog.

An egret lifts off from the swamp. As if demonstrating how flight should be done, the bird soars, then banks left in a gliding, graceful arc.

The Wildcat's wings wobble again. One of its engines appears to emit a tendril of smoke. But it's hard to tell in the mist.

From across the runway, an officer cranes his neck around to look at her. "Interested in the safety of that one in particular, are we?"

Joannie flushes. "Interested in the safety of all our boys."

She can no longer see the Wildcat through the fog, but she remains a few moments watching the flight of the egret as it circles the field.

She hears the trouble before she sees it.

Bursting from the flight control tower at the other end of the field, a young man waves down a group of aviators who've gathered to watch the takeoff.

"Right engine's out!" the young man shouts. "In the drink. Dobbins is down!"

Abandoning the milk truck—driver's side door wide open—there on the sandy shoulder of Ocean Boulevard, Joan races toward East Beach.

Dobbins is down.

~

The rescue boat roars up to the St. Simons Island Pier and cuts its engine. Hair dripping into his face, Will is shaking the hand of every man on the boat. "Right neighborly of you boys to fish me out like that."

It's as if he's just stumbled ankle deep into the marsh, rather than having gone down with a Wildcat into the Atlantic.

"Duck Club," one of the local members of the Civil Air Patrol tells him. "'At's what we call it here. Crashing into the drink, that's the only way you can join. That and surviving to tell about it, I guess I oughta add."

They all laugh, and Joan wants to backhand the lot of them, making light of Will's nearly dying just now.

"Lookee here," the old colleague of Sam's calls, "you got yourself a fan club of one, Dobbins. Joan DuBarry here don't come out for just any old pilot can't keep his bird in the air."

As they all turn to look down the pier to where's she's standing, she recognizes one of the officers.

Dov Silverberg. She's heard rumors around the village that the Brit, this exchange instructor from Cambridge, is brilliant. A confirmation of what she caught in his eyes—swirls of algorithms, perhaps, or kaleidoscopes of equations. Until he smiles, at which point he's simply charming.

You're being ridiculous, she scolds herself.

Also, up until ten minutes ago, when she came careening here in the milk truck and saw Will's tall gangly form pulled from the rescue boat, she thought he might've been killed. She was willing to bargain with the Almighty for Will Dobbins's life.

Will's eyes are on her—on her alone, and her heart swells with that—as he disembarks. Striding down the pier, shoes squishing and soaked uniform leaving a trail of seawater, he salutes Lieutenant Silverberg as he passes, but he's headed toward Joan.

"I'm so grateful," she says with a full heart, "you're okay."

He chucks her lightly under the chin. "Falling out of the sky like that gets a man to thinking, I got to say. It was your face I—"

Heavy footsteps on the planks behind them stop him from saying whatever he might've said next.

"Dobbins."

Dov Silverberg strides forward, hand out.

Will salutes smartly, water running from his sleeve onto the gray planks. "Yes, sir."

The lieutenant's head dips to acknowledge Joan. "Dobbins, it's come to our attention that you're at the top of your class."

Will's salute buckles right there. "Didn't rightly show that too much today, me losing Uncle Sam a plane."

"Through no fault of your own, I'm told by our men on the beach observing that your right engine failed—something only a seasoned veteran is prepared well to handle. Also, you should know I refer less to your skills behind the controls as to your . . . intellectual acuity."

Joan notes the pause before the word *intellectual*. A man with Will Dobbins's Tennessee accent, thick as apple butter, might be hard for this Cambridge man to think of as smart.

As if reminding himself, Dov adds, "Your superiors absolutely assure me of this. Your written test scores are indisputable on this fact, as are, I'm told, your reactions to incoming information under duress. Not just everyone, for example, would have set down that Wildcat in the water in a way that wouldn't have killed him on impact."

Looking as if he doesn't know what to do with his flopping, sopping appendages, Will salutes again. "I thank you, sir."

"Dobbins, the US Navy is shifting focus here on St. Simons from fighter pilot training to an area of equal or possibly greater urgency. We need men aboard our aircraft carriers and on land trained in . . ." His gaze flits to Joannie, as if registering she's not authorized personnel, but then swings back to Will, deciding to forgo protocol. "In radar—'radio detection and ranging.' The name's been declassified. We need men to direct the pilots and planes taking off and landing, letting them know if they're facing friend or foe up in the air—and making split-second decisions that can save or cost thousands of lives. I'd ask, Dobbins, if this—'fighter direction,' it's called—sounds like a role you'd like to fill, but we're at war—not much point in pretending it's a real question. I'll expect you to have your gear transferred and to report to duty at the Naval Radar Training School"—Dov nods up the beach toward where the red tile roof of the King and Prince is just visible through the fog—"by oh six hundred tomorrow."

"Well, sir," Will says, saluting, "knock me clean over and call me stuffed."

As he returns Will's salute, the lieutenant's gaze snags on Joan's briefly. "Miss DuBarry."

"Lieutenant Silverberg."

"As always, Miss DuBarry, my hat is off to you." With that, he walks away.

Chapter 33
Hadley

Though I'm keeping a wary eye on him across the old dining room, Nick has remained here with Kitzie and me, sorting pictures. I hold up one of Dov Silverberg looking dapper in a white Fleet Air Arm uniform. Nick stops what he's doing to look over my shoulder but makes no comment.

"For as many roles as you fill, Nick," I say, "I'm surprised you have time to pitch in to help us."

Sensing the tension—Kitzie does not do tension—my sister excuses herself to fetch us sweet tea.

Pausing in the task we gave him—carefully labeling the photos on the back with the name of the person who sent them—Nick crosses his arms.

"I don't rattle easily, you know," I tell him.

"Am I bothering you, me and my menacing presence?"

"*Byronic* more than *menacing*, I'd say."

"Meaning?"

"He was an early nineteenth-century—"

"Poet who had affairs with pretty much everything that breathed and possibly fathered an illegitimate kid, one of his many, by his step-sister. That the one you're comparing me to?"

I turn, cross my arms to match his, and face off. I refuse to find it attractive that he knows so much about Byron. Though it's not *un*attractive, I'll admit. "I was thinking less about his many sexual adventures as the brooding silences he was apparently famous for."

"Thank you for the clarification."

"Happy to. It is a little disquieting, though, I have to tell you."

"My presence, you mean again?"

"Your habit of appearing silently and just . . . observing."

He stands there, arms crossed, unspeaking, for several beats. "In my experience, most people prattle."

"*Prattle?* There's a good old-fashioned word."

"Prattle. Yeah. I'll stand by my choice of verbs. They prattle without thinking. Just to fill up dead air."

"And you're never one of those people, Nick Adams?"

"Not if I can help it."

"So, you just stand there, feet apart, shoulders back, face expressionless, watching and intimidating others?"

He blinks, looking genuinely startled. "Intimidating?"

"Absolutely."

"No one uses that word for me."

"Maybe not to your face."

This he doesn't answer. He just returns my gaze. I plant my own feet and refuse to look away.

He's the first to move, dropping his arms from his chest and strolling toward one of the stained glass windows that ring the room. "Don't let me interrupt your work."

I try to go back to sorting. But it's distracting having him make a slow lap of the room as he inspects each scene.

"This used to be the dining room of the original hotel," I say at last. "Each one's from a landmark or an event on the island."

"Nice."

He uses the voice I've heard often enough, the low grunt. But his face is lifted to the colored panes in a way that looks genuinely curious.

Gazing up at the window portraying the St. Simons Lighthouse, he takes a sip of his coffee.

I tell myself to work in silence and pretend he's not there, but I hear my own voice fill in the quiet. "You know, it's odd: I'm not sure Ernst Hessler's got my vote for Mr. Congeniality or the swimsuit competition, but at least he's gone to the trouble to make sure this reunion happens when no one else did."

Nick's tone is tinged with sarcasm, his face inscrutable again. "Always driven by his desire to make others happy, that's him." His arms flexed, Nick raises his coffee in a silent mock toast.

"You don't seem to much like your boss."

His head jerks back as if I've surprised—maybe even offended—him, and it's several beats, his eyes locked on mine, before he answers. "It's not a matter of liking or not liking. Also, I do believe he's your boss too."

"Your boss before mine."

But this draws not a grin or a grunt from him. Lifting the captain's hat, he Frisbees it onto the table beside the remaining stacks of old photos. "I wasn't always playing the role of skipper, you know. If that counts for anything."

"Look, it's my turn to apologize. There's not a single thing wrong with being somebody's driver. Of someone's yacht or their SUV or both. I sounded like a snob the other day, and I'm not, truly—especially not with my background. It was really more . . ."

About why you'd let your boss treat you that way. I don't finish the sentence.

I wait for absolution—or even just a sign that he's heard, but Nick only looks out the double doors facing the ocean. "Let's just say my life took a turn a few months back. I lost my situation. My self-respect. My cockiness."

The corner of my mouth ticks upward.

Nick recrosses his arms over his chest. "What?"

"Good news. You haven't entirely lost that last, the cockiness."

Slowly, one side of his mouth lifts. "Well. Thank God for small blessings."

"What happened?" I ask. "That is, if you want to tell me."

He considers for a moment. "It's probably a longer story than you have time for right now."

Try me, I nearly say. But he's already turned away.

"For now," he adds with his back to me, "let's just say I grew up in . . . strange circumstances—without money, always scrambling to make ends meet, me and my single mom. But me with an oversized sense of my own role in the universe. And a hell of a lot of anger. I sort of made a habit of smashing things up, always walking away unscathed. People who go around causing hurt really ought to get hurt some themselves, you know. Otherwise . . ."

I wait until he lifts his head to turn and look at me. "Otherwise?" I ask it softly.

One side of his mouth twitches but falls short of a smile. "The result is a royal jackass. But listen, enough about that. I'm keeping you from your work."

Turning, he steps in closer to look at the photo I'm holding. "I should offer now to leave so you can make progress here. Unless . . ."

"What?"

"Unless you'll let me do penance by helping however you need. More sorting and labeling pictures, maybe?"

"It's hard to turn away a true penitent—particularly one who takes on the title of *jackass*."

"So long as you're owning your inner snob, I'll own my inner jackass, how's that?"

To his credit, Nick works efficiently, rarely stopping to interrupt me with a question. He's not bad at sorting, catching on quickly to recognizing each of the three friends.

He scrolls to his Spotify app, and big band music spirals out from the portable speaker I brought.

"'String of Pearls'?" I guess.

"'Take the "A" Train.' Close."

"So it was your music on the yacht—"

"The *Lürssen*." A dimple appears at one corner of his mouth.

"The Lürssen, *of course*. That was your playlist?"

"Just trying to set the mood for the era. Also—true confession—I love this music. Little-known fact about me."

"You strike me more as an Island Country, Zac Brown Band, Jimmy Buffett kind of guy."

"Sorry to disappoint."

I'm losing focus, our gazes twined up too long. Clearing my throat, I turn back to my own sorting.

By the time I glance back over my shoulder again, he's bending over a photo—but this time not summarily tossing it onto a pile. Instead, he's lifting it level with his face. Studying it.

As Nick comes alongside me—that smell of salt and seagrass again—I point to the man in the picture he holds. "Something I never learned in school was how many German and Italian prisoners were sent to POW camps around the US. Hans served in the kitchen of the radar training station here. Looks eerily like one of Hitler's posters promoting the Aryan ideal, doesn't he?"

Leaning in toward the photo across my shoulder, Nick studies it. "Eerie."

"Apparently, there were serious clashes among the German POWs, between those who remained blindly loyal to the Third Reich and those who distanced themselves. The German POW officers had to be treated according to the code of the Geneva Convention. So they had access to meat and cigarettes that the average American didn't. They could eat at restaurants that Black Americans weren't even allowed into."

"Damn. That can't have gone over well. That's awful."

Nick lifts the photo of Hans Hessler again. "So how does a POW end up getting to know a local girl well enough to fall in love with her—if that's what happened?"

I step closer to him, suddenly conscious of his skin and how easy it would be to brush against it. How I can feel the warmth, the scent of the sea coming off him.

Clearing my throat, I nod at the photo. "Exactly how she connected with Hans, I'm not sure yet. I'm trying to put the pieces together from the letters Ernst Hessler has from his father."

Nick continues studying the photo of Hans. Looking up, he meets my eye. "Look. Hadley. I should probably—"

Holding three sweet teas, Kitz breezes into the room. "Who knew Nick Adams would have already made the world's best 1940s playlist for the reunion weekend? We have the live band for the two evenings, but for all other times . . ."

Accepting Nick's phone from him, Kitzie scrolls through his playlist and taps on "It's Been a Long, Long Time." Sighing, she spreads her arms. "I got to say, these people in the 1940s were just plain more romantic than we are."

Nick, though, shakes his head. "I can't imagine their time was really more romantic than ours. People still fell in love with the wrong people, or at the wrong time. Webs still got tangled. Romance still got turned into the most rancid, most rank betrayal."

Kitz and I both stare at him.

"Maybe," I say quietly, "the one doing the hurting was also hurt after all?"

But his eyes swing away, then drop to the table. "My mother," he murmurs, "was not treated well." But he offers no more than that, lifting a picture instead, head bent low as he studies it.

I can't see Nick's expression, but I can see the subject of the picture and the *PW* stenciled on the man's back. In the photo, several lines of men are marching past a clump of palmettos. One man glances sideways at the camera, the fellow's face striking in that it's contorted with fear.

"That's Hans Hessler," I say aloud. "And he looks . . ."

"Terrified," we say together.

Nick grunts. But it's not dismissive this time. His eyes have both brightened and narrowed, studying the photo.

I step away to another pile, several Priority Mail envelopes from the Dobbins family, then hold up the magazine in its plastic sleeve for Kitzie and Nick to see. "*Look* at this. Someone from the Dobbins family sent this yesterday. A copy of *Life* from the war years, with a female pilot literally in pigtails."

"Sent from the Dobbins family, you're sure?" Kitz asks.

"Got the FedEx envelope right here."

"Where's that one of Joannie DuBarry on the wing of the plane we decided—or Google Lens identified for us—was a B-25 bomber?"

"Twin engine," I say, only to remind myself to look for two propellers, since we have a number of photos of the three friends in front of various planes.

Traversing slowly, my sister tries to hide her unsteadiness by brushing the tables with her fingertips.

"Kitz, you have to tell me when you need to sit down. You're still recovering."

My sister waves this away. "Now where is that lovely B-25?"

I pull the photo she means from the middle of a stack to my right.

The three of us stare at the picture.

"So, weirdly," I say, "this one was sent by one of the Silverberg family in London. From that sweet Rabbi Ben."

"She's a little in love with Rabbi Ben," Kitz stage-whispers to Nick.

"Probably talks about him a lot," he whispers back.

"Probably true," I agree. "Although also he's probably sixty-five, a couple of years outside my ideal range. It's like the man is kind right down to the bone marrow, and with that Oxbridge kind of accent . . . oh my."

"She likes her men kind, *very* kind." Kitz stage-whispers again to Nick.

She means it to be funny, partially, but also as a warning, those cornflower blue eyes of hers narrowing on him.

It's not true, of course, what Kitz said. Only in theory am I drawn to kind men. In practice, I'm drawn to the lethally handsome sort who turn every head in the room, including their own.

I'm embarrassed to see Nick's face go red, like Kitzie's comment was intended for him. Which it was.

"My question," I interject—*anything to change the subject*—"is why all three families have sent us pictures of or mementos about Joannie DuBarry, but none of them have explained why they kept stuff about someone who wasn't a family member. It makes no sense."

I hold up her picture, posed there, smiling, on the wing of that B-25. "So, you flew bombers somehow during the war. And died far too young. What else don't we know about you?"

Nick lifts a telegram.

It's dated December 1945, though the date has been blurred by moisture. Sent after the end of the war but before, I've learned, all the POWs had been returned to their home countries. The recipient is clear: Hans Hessler at Camp Stewart, Georgia, and the delivery source Western Union. But someone has torn off the name of the sender.

Kitz reads it aloud:

KEEP MY SECRET. NOT YOURS TO DECIDE. THANK YOU FOREVER FOR ALL OF IT.

We stand staring at the yellowed page, the three of us silent.

Nick's phone vibrates in his pocket, and he steps away without looking at it—or us. "My signal to go."

He reaches the doors before I catch up. I intend to be candid with him, to ask him why he really came here to help sift through someone else's memories, but he suddenly turns, the gruffness back in his voice.

"Drink?" he asks before I can speak.

"What?"

He looks away, out to the sea. "Can I buy you a drink? Tonight. I know a place at the edge of the marsh close to where"—he jerks his head toward the tables—"they trained."

"Well"—I'm taken off guard—"sure."

Rather than speak, he meets my eye. Gives a single nod. And disappears out the door.

Kitzie has overhead, of course. A sister's hearing on sensitive matters surpasses all innovations of radio detection.

"*Drinks*, Hadz?"

"Drink. Singular. You know me. I'll find a way to send him packing before the first glass is empty."

She's watching my face, but there can't be much to see on it except confusion. Turning away, I wander back to the table and pick up the telegram.

"I asked Mr. Hessler about it already," Kitz says behind me. "Told me he had no idea. Whatever secret his father was keeping for someone, maybe he kept it till the end."

"Or," I suggest, "just didn't share it with Ernst."

Chapter 34
Hans

August 1942
The Normandy coast, near Dieppe, France

Hans understands that his life is over, that he will never again see the green shutters his great-grandfather carved for the family farmhouse. He is a young man of calculations, and he can do the math of his situation.

If any branch of the Wehrmacht—the Kriegsmarine or the Heer or the Luftwaffe, it doesn't matter which—finds him, he will be shot for desertion. Of this he has no doubt. If the French Resistance discovers him, after his first few phrases in French they'll know he's no fisherman from Brittany, despite the rubber boots and his stinking of fish, and he'll be shot as a spy.

So far he's managed to hide in barn lofts and narrowly escaped being seen, but it's only a matter of time until his luck runs out.

A child of two or three spots him now beside a little stream that runs behind a stone cottage. Any older, and the child would know to call out the presence of a stranger helping himself to milk left to cool in the stream. As it is, the child, her little body hardly more than a bundle of sticks, runs a tongue meditatively in a circle around her mouth to lick off the last of a smear of dark jam.

"Bonjour," says the child.

"Bonjour," whispers Hans, a finger over his lips.

"J'ai faim."

Hans isn't positive he recalls what this means, but with that longing look in the child's eyes fixed on what Hans holds in his hand, it likely has to do with her empty tummy.

Hans holds out the apple to the child, who takes it greedily, juice running unchecked down her chin as she gnaws on the fruit with the few little teeth she possesses. Hans's stomach is so hollow it no longer matters. He is going to die anyhow, one way or the other. Also, he stole the apple from a tree on this land. Technically, it is the little girl's apple.

"Au revoir," says the child.

"Au revoir," whispers Hans as he hears the little stone cottage's door slam, a woman calling desperately for her child and the child toddling away.

For the first time in days, maybe weeks or months, Hans smiles as he slips back into the dark.

There are worse final words to hear than *goodbye* from the mouth of a child. Worse final meals than one bite of a truly good apple, shared. Worse final sights than the stars over the ocean, their reflection on the swells so bright, so lustrous, Hans limps to the path at the edge of the cliffs and marvels.

How unlikely there could still be loveliness in this world of armies and torpedoes and starving babies.

If a man has to die, the Normandy coast at night under the stars is not a bad place to do it, and with no uniform on his back.

Chapter 35

Dov Silverberg

August 1942
St. Simons Island, Georgia

They stand smoking together on the beach, Dov and his trainee do, the stars as bright against the black sky as gashed coals. The ocean, its dark, undulating surface reflecting the scatter of light, takes Dov's breath.

He's a man of science who understands the gravitational pull of the moon creating the tides, understands life cycles of stars, the way the nuclei of their hydrogen atoms squeeze together and form helium as they burn, luminous and hot. But none of Dov's equations can explain the pull of the stars and the sea on the human spirit. His own feels less heavy than it's felt since the start of this bloody war—though, God knows, there's no rational reason for hope.

"Sweet Jesus," murmurs Ensign Will Dobbins in that nearly incomprehensible accent of his, "I'll miss this something fierce when I'm shipped out."

Dov shoots him a look. "By which you mean, I think, more than the quite-nice St. Simons Lighthouse just down there and the rather bland mess served to us by surly Germans each day."

"Miss *her* something fierce, that's the whole-barn truth of it, Lieutenant Silverberg, sir."

Dov inhales slowly on his Lucky Strike, the tip sparking red—no doubt as red as the veins in his eyes. None of the men, instructors and trainees both, have gotten much sleep lately, between fifteen-hour workdays and dreams interrupted by news of the day.

"If I may ask, Ensign Dobbins, are you engaged to the young lady?"

"World's too shaky a place these days to be asking two straws of a promise from her. I could come back with only half of this mighty fetching physique, and where'd that leave her?"

Dov takes another long drag on his cigarette. "Thankful you'd be back, I'd imagine."

But Dobbins isn't swayed. "No tomorrow guaranteed, not for any of us. This knobby-kneed farm boy might not be what she wants by the time I come back—*if* I come back. Reckon I can't much reconcile doing that to her."

Dov doesn't speak for some time. "You're a good man, Dobbins. An absolute brick, really."

"Tell the truth now—you whipping my butt ever' day to calculate IFF faster. Did you—?"

"The Identification Friend or Foe calculations cannot bloody well be done fast enough. You know that. Record incorrectly an altitude or speed, make a decision too slowly about an incoming bogey, neglect to factor in weather, any of that, and three thousand lives could be lost in seconds."

"Oh, you got that instilled in us real good. What I'm wondering about is if, at the kick start of the training, you thought I didn't have the smarts."

Dov is startled to hear his own chuckle—Dobbins has caught him with the truth.

"At the *kick start of the thing*, as you say, Dobbins, I did have my doubts. Forgive me. Initially, I thought your flight instructors were thoroughly boffo—we'd all had quite a bit to drink that night—when they suggested you for the radio detection and ranging school here."

Blowing out a long stream of white, Dov turns fully to Will. "I want you to know, I was quite thoroughly wrong. You process incoming data as fast as any man I've ever seen. You'll save thousands of lives on whatever carrier you're assigned, Dobbins. I've no doubt of it."

"That'd be all thanks to you, Lieutenant. That's the God's honest truth." Dobbins pulls his own long drag on his cigarette. "I got one favor to ask. For when the time comes I leave."

"Anything, Dobbins."

"Keep an eye on my girl. Even if I can't rightly call her mine."

The request lands like a punch to his gut, and Dov can't raise his eyes to meet his trainee's, not yet. Slowly, Dov shakes his head. "Don't ask me that, Dobbins. You have my complete respect. You've earned that. But a man can't bloody ask another man to keep an eye on his girl."

"All I mean is make sure she's okay. You with this girl in London you're planning to marry, everything set . . . What'd you say her name was, if you don't mind me asking, Lieutenant?"

Dov exhales a pale trickle of smoke. "Deborah."

"Even her name sounds real fine."

"She is, Dobbins. She is much admired."

"So I figure you'd understand nose to tail what I'm feeling. What with Joan's daddy being bad off and her brother flying in the Pacific, she'll be awful alone."

"On an island overrun with navy men, her being alone is quite possibly safer than the alternative." Dov hears the edge to his own voice, though Dobbins takes no notice.

"Still and all, I'd like you to promise. It'd ease my mind considerable, me knowing you were keeping watch for her once they ship me out."

Hand thrust out, Dobbins stands there, eyes full of all the fear of a man headed to battle—and also full of trust.

There's no help for it. Dov offers his hand. "I'll see that the pirates and blackguards keep away from her, how's that?"

"I thank you kindly."

Dear God, Dov thinks. *What have I done?*

The two men stand together, smoking, not speaking, picturing the battles, the carnage, the pressures, the wreckage to come, as the stars blink—and burn—back at them.

Chapter 36
Hadley

We're both gazing up at the stars, Nick Adams and I, sprawled in Adirondack chairs near the Fiddlers restaurant firepit, and I'm not inclined to break the silence. Nearby in the dark, some marsh creature splashes into the water and a sea bird I can't see lifts off, the flap of its wings a reminder of the life teeming around us.

I didn't let myself do more than run a brush through my hair, since primping might've made it feel like more than just a drink. I insisted on meeting him here, just a walk from the King and Prince, and showed up ten minutes late—again, so I didn't appear eager. At the front entrance before he spotted me, I stopped to balance myself against a palm and put shoes on my bare feet—strappy lime-green sandals borrowed, of course, from Kitz—giving me a moment to view Nick from behind.

With his shoulders a little hunched forward, arms bent at the elbow and feet spread apart, he looked like a wrestler braced for the start of a match. An interesting beginning for drinks.

Turning, he spotted me and thrust his hand out. "Hullo." The voice was a little gruff—his usual tone—but he glanced at the sundress—lime green, too, because, you know, the sandals. "You look . . . lovely."

Lovely. Which itself sounded like it came from a different era. And definitely a different guy.

I was, and still am, completely thrown off my game, like being braced for a half nelson and getting instead a tentative hug. There was something almost shy in the way he greeted me, throwing a long arm around my shoulder from the side but not pulling too close. Something a little sweet, even, in how he stepped quickly away.

Even now, I tilt my head to be sure I have the right guy.

To my right, Nick's hand brushes mine as he leans forward in his chair. His hand pauses—I see it suspended there by the light of the firepit—and turns palm up, like an invitation.

But I'm slow to decide whether it's that, in fact, or just a rotation of the tanned wrist. Not about to make a fool of myself, I settle for lifting my glass of sauvignon blanc to him.

"A toast?" he asks. "To what?"

"You decide."

"To at least a détente. Possibly even friendship."

"Fair enough. Cheers, then."

He doesn't smile, but there's something in his face that seems warmer, more settled than I've seen in him. "You have beautiful eyes," he says—again gruffly.

Which makes me laugh.

"What? What did I say?"

"Your tone of voice. Like you're accusing me of something."

He shrugs. "Maybe I am." A beat of quiet. More flapping of a heron's or egret's wings nearby in the dark marsh. "Listen, Hadley. There's something I should—"

A flash of white hair above us catches my eye. Two women stand on the deck one story up, with their backs mostly to us.

Nick's head turns to follow my gaze.

"Sorry. I'm being rude. It's just that I think that's the elderly woman from the St. Simons Marina the first day."

The older woman turns then: the same nearly translucent skin, the white waves around her face. Her companion, meanwhile, stands with her face turned away, but I recognize the ramrod posture, the glossy black hair: it's the Reverend Doctor.

Before I can answer, she turns and catches me staring, her face breaking into a broad smile.

"Well, hello! From cemetery to Fiddlers firepit. I see we frequent the same haunts."

"Hello!" I stand with the intention only of waving, but Nick, touching my arm, has brushed past me to mount the stairs up to the main level. I'm a few steps behind him as he leans in to shake hands with both women.

Felicia turns to put an arm around the older woman, who is leaning on her cane, the one with the curious cartoon character.

"Hadley, I'm sure you remember my old family friend and neighbor Samantha Mitchell."

I'm about to remind her we met on the dock, but Samantha's head has snapped up. "*Old*, did you say?"

"An expression indicating we've been friends for quite a while, and neighbors. Not, *Lord knows*, a comment on anyone's age."

Samantha winks at us. She's wearing another snappy ensemble, this time a flowing yellow skirt and a top with butterflies on it, a yellow scarf at her neck. "I've got the Reverend Doctor here running scared."

"Honestly, Samantha, when are you going to start calling me just Felicia again?"

"When girl clergy are as common as boys, and when Black Episcopalians aren't scarce as white crows." Samantha rears back as if she's ready to take on dissenters. "Until then, I'm addressing you so people know. It's precisely the truth, and precision isn't important enough to most people."

Laughing, Felicia bends to hug Samantha—but lightly, as if wary of breaking bones. "If I could clone you two hundred times, I'd do it and think about ethics later."

"Can't be easy," I offer, then wish I'd kept my mouth shut. It's not exactly my place to comment on her being Black on a mostly White island in the South, with not only the deep, still-festering scars of slavery but also more recent tragedies, as well as a woman in a profession some people still think is only for men.

But she meets my gaze, all sorts of warmth there in hers.

"Yes, but what would be interesting about easy?" she asks me.

I hold out my hand to Samantha. "We met not long ago at the St. Simons Marina."

"I recall vividly, yes." Samantha has already turned her attention to Nick. "Heavens. You, young man, get better looking each time I see you. In that handsome-as-hell but rugged, rarely smiling way. That look was popular in my day."

That cynical, aloof expression of his relaxes into a laugh as he extends his hand. "If you're coming on to me, Ms. Mitchell, I'm honored."

"You realize, I'm sure, that you're a character in Hemingway."

"I have, in fact, been told that—but I'm not named for him. I did, though, take a class on Papa Hemingway in college, just to see if I liked myself—Nick Adams."

"And did you?"

"Not much, I'm afraid. Didn't spend nearly enough time listening to people's feelings."

This draws a chuckle from Samantha and a pat on his cheek. "I do believe I ran into one or two of those types in my own journeys."

"No doubt," Felicia adds, "you could still recall every detail of every journey."

"Oh, I do forget things sometimes, like the whole crazy-ass line of prescriptions the doctors say someone my age 'must take'"—she air quotes these words with a fluttering lift of both hands—"to live long. They have the nerve to say this to *me*, who's already lived longer than my cardiologist, pulmonologist, and dermatologist put the hell together. Think about *that* for a piece, why don't you? That's what I tell my doctors when they get to assuming they know more than I do. About lungs and livers, maybe. Not about hearts, though. Not about life."

"May I ask," I say, "what the cartoon character is on your cane, Miss Samantha? I'm intrigued." I'm trying to think if I've ever seen the little blonde gremlin with boots before.

Fixing me with a look, she doesn't answer for so long I'm sure she didn't hear me. I'm about to repeat my question, louder this time.

"Sometimes," she says at last, "a cartoon is simply a cartoon. Don't you think?"

I do not. That's what I want to say, and I'm quite sure she can see this in my eyes.

But she's made her face a perfect oval of rice paper placidity. Nothing around her mouth so much as twitches. Only her eyes, something defiant in them, and her chin tilted a little too high tip me off.

She adjusts her weight so I can see the full body of the character, its impish face.

If I were alone with the cane, I'd snap a picture of it with my phone. As it is, I try to fix it in my mind, keywords for googling later.

"Well then." It's all she says. But Samantha's mouth quirks, her left brow arching up again. I'm sure, quite sure, this is a challenge.

Find out for yourself what it is.

Taking her younger friend's arm, Samantha straightens her spine, throws back her head, and moves away, yellow skirt catching the breeze, one hand gripping the cane and its cartoon character firmly.

"So good to see you both," the Reverend Doctor calls over her shoulder.

Samantha turns back only once, and only to blow a kiss our way.

Though the kiss, I suspect, is meant for Nick.

Exchanging impressions about the island—its sea birds and palmettos and oaks—we begin dipping lightly into our personal pasts, both of us kids without material goods and sometimes even without enough food. I'm feeling a connection with him I've not felt for a long time for a guy—maybe haven't felt ever. Which is my cue to keep my guard up. The other shoe's sure to drop soon.

Sitting close enough to each other that our arms brush, Nick and I finish our drinks by the firepit, then walk together back to the King and Prince and settle into seats at the pool bar. The squeals of the children playing Marco Polo nicely fill in the hammocks of quiet between us.

The bartender swivels his head toward Nick. "Sure I can't you get you something a little more interesting than this?" He slides a coupe of cranberry juice across the bar. At Fiddlers, Nick already held a drink, whatever it was, when I arrived.

Nick flushes, shaking his head. "This'll be all for me, but whatever she'd like will also go on my room tab."

His eyes run over the amber bottles—Captain Morgan and Jack Daniel's, varieties of tequilas and triple sec. Then he glances away, like he has to make himself focus on the moon, lovely as it is.

Ordering a peach mocktail named Detection—I assume for the hotel's radar training past, I try to make my voice sound perky, like someone who truly wants a mocktail.

Nick's gaze rests on me a moment. "Thanks" is all he offers on the subject.

"Good for you," I say back. And I mean it. If any family is an example of what happens when no one ever says "This'll be all," it's mine.

Touching my arm, he nods to the bartender and walks with me toward the beach.

We've not discussed taking a walk, but the moonlight on the wet shore and the low thrum of the surf pull on us. We stroll past an embankment of boulders before reaching the sand and, without speaking, shed our shoes to stroll along the shallows.

I close my eyes for a moment and let the tension in my shoulders relax.

"So. Hadley Jacks. You didn't grow up at the beach?"

I open one eye, then two to find him looking at me, bemused.

"What was the tip off?"

"Let's just say you don't have the jaded look."

I stare out at the sea for several crashes of several waves and consider how much more—or not—of my story I feel like telling. "It wasn't just the beach Kitz and I didn't get to. Vacations weren't a thing in our world." I sound more pitiful than I want to. "But we're making up for lost time. Like last fall: we were in Jamaica for an event we ran there."

"Attorneys?" he guesses.

"Proctologists. Not your most chatty bunch. But the event before that was a gathering of sweet horn-rimmed-glasses-wearing podiatrists going footloose, appropriately, in Grand Cayman. I'm guessing they weren't the cool kids in high school—I'm assuming mathletes, science fair—but you should see them rumba after a piña colada or three."

I've made him laugh, and I'm unreasonably pleased about that.

"I meant it as a compliment, you know, your not being jaded. It's . . ." He narrows his eyes at me, brows furrowing, like he's waiting for me to choose my own adjective.

"Odd?" I try. "Unsettling?"

"Refreshing."

"Ah."

"Authenticity. It's important. Crucial, even. So, you and your sister didn't grow up in Southern California?"

I laugh, which seems to startle him, his eyes earnest on me. "About as far from that as we possibly could, unless we'd been Inuits in Quebec." I tell him about our lives growing up in rural South Carolina, about the foster homes, the good, bad, and truly ugly—more than I mean to, in fact. I allude to the addictions that took down our mother and apparently everyone else—the dad and those older generations we never knew—who might've stepped in for us. I'm grateful for his eyes going soft, and grateful for his not asking for details.

I've always been a sucker for a good listener, and he surprises me by being one—the kind who leans forward, head tilting at all the right angles, the well-timed nod.

"It was middle school when things finally changed for us. Thanks to Lindy."

"The final foster mom."

I blink at him in surprise. "How did you . . ?"

For an instant, he looks a little muddled himself, then his face clears. "Your sister mentioned her that day you were headed in to interview the museum director. The only other person who stuck around in your lives."

"Right. Of course. Back when Kitz and I were in the foster care system, Lindy was the one who came through for us, gave us the first real stability we'd known. Didn't blow up every time I rebelled—I was part whirling dervish back then. Helped make college scholarships happen. She . . ." I grope for a verb less dramatic than what I'm thinking, but it's the only word that fits. "Saved us. Lindy saved my sister and me."

Nick takes this in. "So you're the fighter. Of the two of you, I mean."

"I prefer the word *feisty*, if you don't mind."

His gaze drifts out to the ocean, then back. "That's quite a gift, you know."

"My being difficult?"

"Your fighting for someone you care that much about. Growing the thick skin so someone else doesn't have to."

"Not everyone appreciates the attributes of a crocodile."

He chuckles, and again I feel a frisson along my spine as I kick at the surf.

"Your turn, Mr. Adams. It occurs to me I know virtually nothing about you—except that you grew up struggling financially and angry at the world, while you know the name of my imaginary dog when I was six."

"Churchill," he says, holding up a finger as if giving himself a point for remembering our earlier conversation. "Rather prophetic for a woman digging through World War Two archives."

"Wasn't it, though? So now your turn. How did you come to expect everyone to be bored by life in general and jaded by looking at the ocean in particular?"

He opens his mouth, and I can see him assessing, just as I did earlier. How much to tell. How much to trust someone else with your story. Standing beside him in the surf, I step closer so my arm's pressed against his but we can both look out at the sea as he talks—I know how hard a messy past can be to lay out, all stark and bleak, for new eyes to see.

"It's not a pretty tale," he begins—and seems ready to flesh out why. "You asked how I knew about the jaded of the world. Now's probably as good a time as any for me to mention . . . what makes my story complicated. For example, I went to high school at Phillips Exeter."

"Wait. The boarding school in New Hampshire? Isn't that like . . . for the elite of the one percent?"

"It was . . ."

Which is when his cell rings.

"The very definition of bad timing," he jokes, before he pulls it out of his pocket and the contours of his face go slack as he reads its screen.

I don't mean to be nosy, but I'm standing so close. I catch the name Cordelia on his screen. Clearly, a woman's name. And no last name, so a woman he knows well.

Cordelia. An unusual name, and one straight out of Shakespeare's plays. So a member of one of the Boundless families? In fact, hadn't Ben Silverberg mentioned a Cordelia?

Why on earth would Ernst Hessler's driver be talking with a female member of one of the Boundless families? So is this a *Lady Chatterley's Lover* kind of thing, the rich woman in a relationship with today's version of the stable groom?

His face has gone back to hard angles, but he offers no explanation. "I'm sorry. I need to take this. I was waiting to hear back from her, and it's . . . I'm sorry, Hadley."

He's already out of the water before his screen goes dark.

"Of course," I say, slogging a few feet behind. "I understand."

I do *not* understand, actually, standing there in a green sundress, soaked at the hem, shedding salt water onto the sand like a first-class sort of fool. *Pathetic.*

He turns back as he bends for his shoes. "Forgive me."

I mutter the usual things you say at these times—*of course, not a problem at all.*

But my whole body's gone stiff.

I watch him run, the muscles of his back flexing, up the sand toward the hotel, glowing gold.

The moment is over, and maybe it's best, the evening ending so unceremoniously like this—a bit humiliatingly too. I commend myself for doing no more than brushing my hair before meeting him at Fiddlers.

Nothing left now but to salvage what I can of the night for myself, I drop down on the sand.

Glum and determined not to think of Nick Adams a single second more, I rest my chin on my knees and replay the part of the evening that did not feature him: bumping into Samantha Mitchell and Felicia Hammond again—and of the odd little character on Samantha's cane.

Lifting my phone, I type *female cartoon figure WW2* into a search bar. My screen pulls up versions of Rosie the Riveter and those old stylized women with hourglass figures in military uniforms, all with skirts—nothing that looks even remotely like the little creature.

Something—my annoyance with Nick, probably, with his strange, hurried departure to chat with a certain Cordelia, and even more annoyance with myself for having felt so stupidly drawn to the guy—makes me lift my phone again and google the words *Nick Adams* along with *Phillips Exeter* and *chauffeur for Ernst Hessler.*

To my bewilderment, my screen fills with a long line of articles containing those words. Articles from *Forbes* and the *Wall Street Journal*, even one from the *Economist.*

I read one after the other, my mouth hanging open until I'm so enraged, I flop back on the wet sand—the green sundress soaked and gritty, but I don't give a flip.

"*Nick*," I say out loud and hear the bitterness—the betrayal—curdling my voice. I'm so mad I could spit. "Of course. Even the name."

I hear my own words to Ben Silverberg like a taunt: *Your names— Benedick, Juliet, Richard, Beatrice, Cordelia. They're all characters from Shakespeare's plays.*

But I'd missed that Nick, too, fit the pattern: Nick Bottom from *A Midsummer Night's Dream.*

I'd missed other clues too. What was it the *Forbes* article said about wild card future leaders of Boundless? Some reference to *one hellion descendant who'd faced recent legal troubles.* He was not named in that report, but now that I've plugged in the words, plenty of sites have popped up speculating on the DUIs, the playboy behavior, the utter disregard for the Boundless legacy that the youngest child of Ernst Hessler had displayed.

Ernst Hessler's son.

As I picture Nick sorting pictures alongside Kitzie and me of *his own family*, my cheeks burn. I even held up a photo of Hans Hessler to him in a moment I thought we were both noticing the resemblance to a Nazi propaganda poster, when, in fact, the guy standing beside me even more closely resembled the man in the photo.

But I missed seeing it.

Missed seeing, too, what Ernst Hessler on his Lürssen meant, speaking of Boundless and glancing toward Nick as he steered the yacht: *Those of us who were in line to . . . take the helm.*

There Nick was, posing as a pitiful, impoverished son of a single mom, a struggling kid just like me. When all along, he was one of them. Product of boarding school and privilege. Playboy. Hellion.

"So, *Nick*," I say aloud, and promise myself I'll say this next to his face. "What a first-rate liar you are."

Above me, the moon pulls on the earth's oceans, and I watch the tide rise.

Chapter 37

Hans

August 19, 1942
Dieppe, France

He has lived every moment alone now—*How many days or weeks has it been?*—walking by night, sleeping by day, and eating almost never. So Hans is startled to see movement out on the silver-black ocean.

More than just a passing school of dolphins, surely. More even than a fishing vessel out early.

"*Mein Gott,*" he breathes as he realizes what he's seeing: a gathering storm of boats approaching on a choppy sea.

He is only a few kilometers west of the next town, this one called Dieppe, if the road sign he's passed isn't a trick of the Resistance. His routine each day has been to look for food he knows he won't find—even the garbage of these French villages has already been picked through by dogs and mothers of starving children—then find a place on the outskirts of town to sleep through daylight.

He is tired of walking, so tired. So tired he's considered finding a church in the prettiest of these French coastal villages, admitting to its priest in whatever French he might patch together that he's a deserter, and throwing himself on the mercy of God. Today—whatever day or month this might be—is the day Hans has picked to hurl himself onto mercy as if it were a grenade and not care what the explosion might mean. He's too hungry, too exhausted, too despairing to care.

This, though, this gathering storm of a battle was not in his plan.

It is just before daybreak, black waves silvering at their tips, as ferries bearing hordes of men slide onto the beach below. From the cliff where Hans stands, he can see straight across the broad stretch of water where the early light catches on cliffs in the distance.

This must be, then, the English Channel. At the stern of one of the battleships, he can make out three flags, the Union Jack, and beneath it a Canadian flag and an American flag.

Dark figures swarm from the ferries onto the beach, a group of them charging toward the cliff where he stands. Scrambling behind a stone wall, Hans crouches to watch. Not but a few yards away, as early morning rays spill out above the horizon, he sees a concrete pillbox where German gunners are just waking up.

Overhead, the sky suddenly erupts in flashes of yellow, fighter planes swooping down from the clouds, strafing the pillboxes, the cliffs, and what must be arsenals nearby. On every side, bombs scream.

It's too late to take cover, a sea of soldiers flooding the beach, the cliffs. To his east in the town of Dieppe, gunfire echoes, bodies collapsing onto the sand.

It looks, he thinks numbly, *like a whole shore of dead fish a tide brought in back at one of Kiel's U-boat ports months ago. Or was it years?* The bodies of those fish blanketed the whole beach, just like the bodies of these Allied soldiers, and they lay there to rot. Just like, perhaps, these will.

Germany will win this war, it is clear. Even with the RAF planes overhead diving and spinning and firing, even with the dark forms climbing the cliffs, even with the mortar bomb that has just taken out the guns a few yards away, Hans can see what this beach of dead bodies means: another victory for the Germans. Another toehold on the Continent not yet achieved by the Allies.

The Führer will win this war.

Hans hears the howls of the wounded, the staccato of the machine guns, the blasts of the mortar shells. Only the commandos on this western flank of the town seem to have escaped decimation.

"*Mein Gott*," he says again, adding, this time, "*so viel verdammtes Blut*," because, Holy Mother of God, there is just so much, so much damn blood on that beach.

The metal shoved between his shoulder blades sends Hans lurching forward. A hand jerks him by his collar up to his feet.

"Hands up, Kraut," shouts a voice from behind in English. "What the hell we got here? A damn German spy?"

Hans does not need to understand the words. He is plenty sure of the metal drilling into his back, a gun's muzzle.

Slowly, he raises both hands over his head.

Chapter 38

Will

November 1942
St. Simons Island

As the prisoners of war file off their transport this morning, Will watches one of the guards, a mite-too-macho tough kid from New York, prod them along with a muzzle between their shoulder blades. It's mostly for show, of course, that prodding, the prisoners being right docile by now and having nowhere to run. None, in fact, have tried to escape. Will wonders this morning what these fellows' stories were before they were captured—wondering, maybe, because he's about to be shipped out himself, and who knows if he won't end up like them, in enemy hands, a gun jammed into his back.

Knowing he's no good with words—except to make people laugh—Will has scrawled out a sonnet, number sixty-five, one of his own favorites since it cogitates on how nothing much lasts, no matter how strong or fine looking, except for love—and maybe art, Will's mama would add. But for today, Will is just focused on love.

He told Joannie goodbye last night, but he walks toward her once more today as he heads for the transport, his green seabag slung over one shoulder. He hugs her hard but lets himself kiss her just once. More than that would only hurt more. Fresh out of words, he hands her the sonnet.

He's got it by heart, but he won't quote it in front of the other guys and the officers gathered nearby. Instead, he just presses the page into her hand and feels the callouses on her palms. Part of what he loves about Joan: she's a girl unafraid of hard work. Unafraid of anything much.

"I'll miss you, Will Dobbins," she tells him and rises to her tiptoes to kiss him, this time on the cheek.

"I'd be much obliged if you'd read that"—he nods at the page in her hand—"and know my love for you's like it says. Way out beyond even the boundless sea."

"The 'boundless sea'?" a man behind Will echoes. "Lord, Dobbins, I got to get you to write my girl for me."

"The 'boundless sea,'" Joan whispers, and Will hears—if he's not kidding himself—a whole world of affection in her quoting even those two little words.

But now Will's pushed ahead by the line, the officers sticking out their hands to shake the latest class of fighter directors being sent overseas.

At the end, Dov Silverberg's shake is the firmest, and he looks Will straight in the eye. "You're a gifted man, and a bloody good one. I wish you Godspeed. Win this war for us, Dobbins."

Will raises his head dramatically, the way he does, his mama used to point out, when he's about to deliver a quote. "'Once more, unto the breach, my friends. Once more.'"

Before Silverberg can name it or not—he was a Cambridge man, after all—Will does the honors himself. "*Henry V*. Before he goes back into battle.'"

"'Unto the breach, my friends,'" comes a soft echo from the lieutenant. "Indeed."

My friends.

Will knows this is true. They were instructor and trainee. Somewhere along the way, they did become friends.

This posh Brit, so all-fired refined, this physicist who thinks all the day long in calculations, this upper-crust London fellow—a Jew, at that, when Will's only ever known three Jews in his whole life—has somehow become also a real friend, a word Will does not use lightly.

Will's chest swells with the riches of all he's leaving behind and may someday come back to: the big family that sorely misses him in Tennessee, and now here, on this island, two people—the girl Will knows he'll love till he dies and also a friend.

Chapter 39

Joannie

February 1943

At the foot of the lighthouse, Joannie stands still and listens to the smash and suck of the sea, the stars blinking above.

She wills herself to forget the name of the man who's just bought her dinner and drinks. He'd seemed nice enough when he bought a ticket from her at the Ritz. No, that wasn't quite true. She detected bluster and a hint of a leer in him from the first, but at the offer of dinner out, she'd been bought, plain and simple, into ignoring her own instincts.

Lesson learned.

It had been weeks since she'd eaten meat, unless fried Spam counted, and it crossed her mind once—but just once—to let his hand stay where it had traveled so fast under her skirt and up her whole thigh, while she finished her spaghetti with meatballs—two of them, very large.

Instead, though, she whipped her fork under the table and poked its tines where she knew he could feel. He would find red sauce on his crotch later this evening.

"Sailor"—she did not use his name even then—"listen here."

"Lieutenant commander. I'm a lieutenant commander." It came out more squeak than protest.

"Who's drunk and out of line. I appreciate that you're scared, far from home, and about to be farther away. But buy a teddy bear, Lieutenant Commander, and leave me alone."

"Hold on there, doll. A guy's bound to get fresh with a dame pretty as you. Not even my fault. Aw, hell, come on back . . ."

She walked out of the restaurant alone, not letting herself smell the aroma of steak or look at the faces that turned to stare as she marched away. It was a shame, Joan's having no money to come back alone.

But there it was, the price she paid for freedom. Well worth it too. What a shame freedom didn't always come served with meatballs.

A figure has followed her out the front door of the restaurant, but the figure's not nearly as short or stocky as the lieutenant commander she left inside. The figure doesn't move from the shadow just outside the squares of yellow cast from the restaurant windows.

She knows who it is. He's appeared in the corners of her days here and there: at the edge of a line at the Ritz, at the far end of the sidewalk from Gray's, many yards away on East Beach . . .

But this is how they perform this dance: his staying at a safe, watch-keeping distance, her pretending she doesn't see him.

Palm fronds rattle softly in the breeze. From the far end of the pier comes the laughter of children fishing.

Joannie checks behind her, the figure still there in the shadows but, like always, not moving closer.

The lighthouse has gone dark now along with the blackouts for the war, and no lightning bugs prick holes in the dusk this time of year. But Joan can picture how this all once looked in the summers before the war: fireflies blinking on and off through the twilight, nearly synchronized with the lighthouse's beam sweeping over the water.

The male fireflies doing the opposite of the lighthouse, Joannie thinks. *They call forward, not warn away. Each male with his own timing, his own flight, they put on a show for the females waiting, waiting for just the right pattern—then lighting up.*

Even in the absence of those little lights, even here in later winter, the night air pulses with warmth and desire.

Joannie adjusts the waistband of her dress and passes a hand across the back of her neck, then gives a sharp shake to her skirt, as if that might settle all the unruliness underneath.

I won't ask you to wait for me, Will had said before he shipped out, *or to stay home like some nanny goat put to the shed. I'll just be glad if you pine sometimes for your old Will.*

She smiles now, thinking of him—how can you *not* smile thinking of Will Dobbins? She does think of him every day. Every day, she pictures Sam and him separately on whatever missions they might be flying, pictures vividly the guns trained on them, the flashes of yellow and red and white. Every day, she prays for ways she can work harder, risk more, help bring them home.

"Joannie!"

The voice comes from the far side of the restaurant nearest the lighthouse, not the front, where the figure still stands in the shadows.

Joan squints toward the live oaks. She can't make out his face yet in the shadows, but she knows that form nearly as well as she knows her brother's.

He's jogging toward her now, with only a quick glance back at the truck he's parked beside the restaurant.

She meets him in the middle. "Marshall!"

If they weren't in the center of the village, they would hug. Instead, stiffening, he halts, hands in his pockets.

"Marshall, I'm so glad to see you. I've seen your mama nearly every day these past weeks, but you and me, we've been coming and going different times. Miz Rose says you're doing well with the Liberty ships." She doesn't mention what they both know, what she can see in the way he crosses his arms over his chest at the mention of his work: that he works long and hard every day, that he's proud of his work, and that he receives a fraction of the White men's pay. "So, what do you hear from Sam?"

"Just commencing to ask you the same thing."

"Just the usual. A bit of brotherly abuse. Some tips on flying—things he thinks he'd not taught me yet. Nothing about what he's doing, or where."

"To me, mostly the same. Minus the abuse." He chuckles for the first time. Then lowers his voice. "Also, that he misses us both."

Joannie hears the tenderness in his voice, so vulnerable that she flushes.

Marshall jerks his head toward the restaurant. "You meeting somebody there?"

"Just did. The guy needed castrating and sending way out to sea."

From inside the restaurant, laughter explodes, the merriment blasting, incongruous, into the softness of their silence.

"You notice there'd be Nazi officer prisoners with their American guards inside there right now?" Marshall asks.

"Got put in a separate room, but I could hear them."

"Color of my skin keeps me out of a restaurant where a bunch of German officer bastards'd be in there dining and laughing and getting drunk as hell."

Slowly, Joannie nods—there's no arguing it. "And you, an American, not allowed in."

Her gaze shifts to the restaurant's broad windows facing the sea. Inside, in the yellow glow of electric light, the closest table to the window is ringed by German officers.

Joan forces herself to see it. That is, Marshall has forced her to see it.

Their heads are thrown back, raucous and loud, one of them shouting something in a guttural German, the group roaring in laughter again.

Marshall's words come low and so bitter Joan flinches. "Here I am enlisted for a tank battalion, fixing to go risk my life for a country that won't even let me in to a restaurant where a damn pack of Nazi brass are having their damn dinner."

"Tank battalion?" she asks quietly. "Marshall, you're in?"

"The Seven Sixty-First. Formed last spring. Just got word they'll have me. Be headed to training soon."

"The Seven Sixty-First," Joan echoes, all she can think to say. It's as if someone poked holes, one after the other, in the big airship balloon of her world, and now it's shriveled to a limp little ball.

"Mama swears she'll be all right, that she's got you next door. Reckon I'm starting a whole new chapter of life, of history, too, me and the Seven Sixty-First. First one of its kind. A beginning."

Or is this the end? Joan thinks. *What if this is the end—of Marshall's life, or Sam's or Will's? What if none of them ever come back? What if it's the end of any world free from roundups and violence and swastikas draped at every turn?*

The front door flies open again, a cluster of American servicemen in uniform and their dates strolling out. Behind them, the hostess, wearing a strapless black dress, steps to the threshold.

"A Lieutenant Silverberg?" she calls into the dark. "If you're out there, Lieutenant Silverberg, there's a call for you."

Joan hears, but her attention is fixed on her old friend, her hand going back to his arm.

"To beginnings," she says—with gusto, as if she believes it.

Because sometimes it's the job of a friend to say not what she thinks—the hard, ugly truth—but instead, what she doesn't. The flimsy, unlikely whisp of hope.

Chapter 40
Hadley

Riffling through the photocopied pages from the letters Kitz and I have been reading, I can't help but wonder if any of us sees the drama of our own stories as they unfold: the unlikely beginnings, the crises and triumphs and sorrows, however small or stage worthy. They were so young, these boys sent out to fly planes off carriers in the middle of oceans and drive tanks across fields littered with land mines.

I'm still livid with Nick for lying to me—the truth he misrepresented and the truth he withheld, and angrier still with myself for trusting too easily. For trusting at all.

But I know how to channel disappointment with people into hard work and focus. A lifetime of doing just that has made me good at it. My phone's screen shows a voicemail from Nick and three texts, all of which I delete without listening to or reading. What I have to say to him, I'll say to his face.

Meanwhile, I will *not* wallow, and I will not let him back in. For me, trust once broken is broken for good.

Spreading out several pages across my outdoor table at Mullet Bay, careful not to spill my sweet tea, I flip to the copy of the letter from Sam DuBarry to his girlfriend Marsha—at the back of my folder, since it's less directly relevant to the reunion planning. Still, though, I keep returning to it for its tender tone, and for Marsha's having apparently been Black, dealing with Jim Crow at home in addition to war. Its mention of the construction of Liberty ships, too, helps set the story stage that Kitzie is building.

Big, existential, culture-shifting issues and a whole world at war, that's what I'll focus on today, not my humiliation at having been lied to and left standing alone on the beach: small in the scope of things.

Still, I hear it in the way I smack papers onto the table, and other diners on Mullet Bay's porch must wonder what's ticked off the crazy brunette and how far away they can sit from her.

I've slipped Sam DuBarry's letter to Marsha back out from the folder, when the final sentence catches my eye:

Give everyone in the Hammond household my love, remind my sister she is doing good work for the war effort even at home, and know how much I miss you every day.

The Hammond household. Where else have I seen that name recently? Not that it's so uncommon, but still . . .

Then it hits me. Reaching to the back of my Nike shorts, I pull the business card out of the zippered pocket.

The Reverend Doctor Felicia Hammond.

My iced tea arm frozen midlift, I let out a low whistle.

Now I'm hearing the archivist's words again, urging me to make contact with the clergy at Christ Church Frederica.

I didn't mean attending services. Although that would certainly be a way you'd be sure to connect with one of the ministers there.

I need to connect with one of the ministers?

Given what you were reading this morning, yes.

The archivist made clear families who donated letters often wanted to maintain privacy, yet she also tried to point me in a certain direction—which I let go right over my head.

Tapping in the numbers of Felicia Hammond's cell, I begin sorting out what I'll say, but she picks up on the second ring.

"Felicia, this is Hadley Jacks. We met—"

"Of course, Hadley. How can I help you?"

"This is an odd question to hit you with from out of the blue, but the other day, my sister and I read through a cache of very sweet World War Two love letters to someone with the last name Hammond. Forgive me if your family donated the letters to the archives privately and don't wish to be asked questions but—"

"No need for apologies or secrecy, either one. I was the person who donated the letters. I was cleaning out my great-grandparent's house just last year and found them. I confess I didn't read through more than a few—I was a bit overwhelmed at the time—but they seemed historically significant. I've gotten more involved just lately with helping preserve the Gullah Geechee culture on the island, but I keep promising myself I'll get by and read those letters soon. Good for you for beating me to it."

"Honestly, you should. Great snapshots of life at the time. And the kind of love expressed between . . . it looks like Marsha—would that be your great-grandmother Hammond?—and Sammy DuBarry is just beautiful. Incredibly touching."

A long pause follows.

"Felicia?"

"I'm here. The DuBarrys lived for many years next door to my great-grandparents' home."

"Sam DuBarry had a sister, Joan, who keeps popping up in our research for this reunion. These love letters are between Marsha and Sam. Do I have your great-grandmother's name right? I'm looking right now at some of these copies and trying to make out the writing."

Another pause, this one longer than the first. "I wonder, Hadley, if you're somewhere I could join you and see the copies of the letters you have?"

"Of course. Actually, I'm just at a table on the front porch of Mullet Bay in the village."

Felicia has whipped a black Jeep into a parking spot and joined me before I've had a chance to ask for a refill on my sweet tea. She envelops me in a hug before sliding into a seat.

"I should tell you, Hadley, I've actually had a long-standing interest in Joannie DuBarry as a woman before her time. I have a shoebox of clippings—also dug out from my grandparents' attic—that you're going to want to see."

"I'd love to. I have the same fascination with her. Her spunk. The difficulties she faced." *Her losing her mother*, I don't add aloud, but I'm aware that's part of my feeling drawn to Joannie.

"Listen, Hadley. About these letters you mention . . . May I see the photocopies you made?"

"Of course. Please. They were your family's letters, after all."

I spread out the pages as she begins scanning over the lines. More than once, she draws a sharp breath. "Oh my. Their long walks on the beach."

When she finally looks up, her eyes have filled, a tear trickling down one cheek. "I have to tell you, this comes as quite a surprise."

"I'm sorry . . . I don't understand. These beautiful love letters to your great-grandmother—"

"My great-grandmother's name was Felicia—I'm named after her. As far as I know, she never met Sam DuBarry. My great-grandfather's name, though, Hadley, was Marshall. These lines from Sam filled with so much love and devotion—they were to Marshall."

Chapter 41

Joannie

May 1943

She's just leaping off her cottage porch as Rose Hammond waves her over. Apparently just home from her work at Hazel's Café, flour still dusting one cheek—likely from the biscuits or deviled crab she's known for—Rose has a letter gripped in one hand.

Must be from Marshall in his tank battalion training, Joannie thinks, skidding to a halt. If it weren't for the Plymouth packed full of girls waiting on her to pile in, Joan would run next door and hear the latest. But the driver lays on her horn.

"I'll come by tomorrow," Joan calls as she ducks inside the car.

One of the girls, a redhead, eyes Joan up and down—her hand-me-down dress, her windblown hair. "*Please* tell me those people don't live right smack next door to you. How is that even *allowed?*"

Joan returns the girl's look, eyeing her in turn up and down. "You got a nice sense of fashion."

"Why . . . thank you."

"Your attitude, though: that's got some real ugly to it." She waits a beat for that to sink in. "Also, the Hammonds let my family live on their land when we lost ours. Whether or not that's *allowed.*"

The car ride the rest of the way out to Sea Island is silent, shot through with sharp glares and uneasy shifting. Aware the driver would deposit her on the side of the road if it wouldn't cause such a stir, Joan is happy enough just to look out the Plymouth windows as the marsh and then the shore rush by.

She'll need, she realizes, to find another ride home.

~

Saxophones and trumpets chase each other through "In the Mood" as Joannie steps from the car. In a dizzying swirl of skirts and high heels, whispering to each other as they go, the other girls spin—*like colorful tops,* Joan thinks—toward the Cloister's main entrance, Joan lagging behind.

A line has formed to get in. All guests are greeted by a matronly woman wearing an orchid corsage too low on her bosom. She leans forward at her welcome table.

"The event is for officers, their dates, and a few local girls to fill out the numbers. Your name"—the woman checks the bars on the shoulders and cuffs of the next man in line—"Lieutenant?"

"Silverberg. Dov Silverberg."

Joan recognizes the voice and turns. In the crush of people, she'd not seen him there up front until now.

The smile on the woman's face and the pen she wields both freeze in place.

"Silverberg," the woman repeats. "Which sounds . . ."

Dov's voice goes steely. "Jewish, yes. Exactly. Perhaps I missed the sign here that says *Restricted.*"

He's become, Joannie realizes, almost unearthly calm, jaw set, whole body gone still.

He's lived this moment before.

Joan ignores the stares of the other girls as she swishes to the front of the line. "Lieutenant Silverberg trains fighter directors to be deployed on aircraft carriers." Bent down toward the matron, Joan's face nears her orchid corsage.

Which smells of funerals. Of old things.

"I suppose under the circumstances, standards must be relaxed." The matron flicks one finger for them to proceed.

Gaze fixed directly ahead, Dov holds out his elbow to Joan.

"Restricted?" she asks when they're a few paces away. "I've never heard that term before."

He doesn't look at her when he says, voice still cold, "Designating no Jews, among other groups. So. Now you know."

On the pool terrace, she lets the band fill the silence between them through the rest of "Somewhere in France with You." Then finally she steps into the silence. "I hope you've enjoyed your time on the island. As much, I mean, as one can in the midst of war."

"As much as one can, yes. Thank you." His steeliness is slow leaving him, as if the confrontation has put him on guard against the world.

"Odd our paths haven't crossed. It's not a big island, the populated end of it. And lots of the navy men come see movies at the Ritz. Where I work."

"I've been there," he answers. Then flushes. "That is, I've seen you from time to time."

She turns to look at him. "I thought that was you I keep seeing from the corner of my eye. Couldn't break your British reserve to say hello?"

"I didn't . . ." He angles his head, meeting her eye for the first time now. "Right, then. I may as well confess, as it's good for the soul— whether or not the woman back there"—he gestures with his head back toward the entrance—"believes I have one. Ensign . . . that is, Senior Fighter Director William Dobbins asked me to keep a bit of an eye out for you."

"I admit I've wondered, your lurking about in the shadows and all. I wasn't sure whether to be thoroughly annoyed or flattered."

He chuckles. "So much for my future in spy craft with MI5 after the war."

"Yes, perhaps leave the clandestine trailing work to someone else."

"Still, honorable bloke that I am, I have kept my word to watch out for you from a distance. Quite clumsily, it appears, but faithfully done."

"Ah. So I should thank you, then, you're implying."

"He made clear, I should add, he had no claim on you. Just care for your well-being. Which"—he bows slightly here—"even as his envoy, I share."

She tips her face up to him. "So, Will handpicked you for the job. Why you, Lieutenant? Clearly not for your spy craft, we've established."

"Handpicked, perhaps, because I am absolutely no threat. I do, as it happens, have a sort of understanding with an admirable young woman back home in London. You see, Miss DuBarry, we are doubly ensured of our joint good behavior."

"Your girl back home knows you go out dancing, then?"

He bows slightly from the waist. "She has encouraged it, in fact, though I'll admit this is my first time out to do so. *Stick-in-the-mud* is the phrase most often thrown at me. She attends the USO dances on that side of the pond—has rather a lovely time, I believe."

"So she encourages your going out, so long as you don't fail to come back to her at the end of the war."

"That is her hope," he says quietly.

"And your hope?" It's none of her business, of course, a man she met only months ago and only briefly, at that. But the spring night is warm, and the Cloister's pool sparkles, and the saxophones are bending the air.

"Our families have been friends for three generations. We belong to the same synagogue. Our houses are on the same street." A shock of black hair falls onto his forehead. "She and I both have brothers fighting in France, both have relatives in Salzburg and Vienna and Berlin, people we've not heard from for some time. It's a harrowing time, to say the least."

"Of course," Joan says, more quietly.

"Now I see I've quite destroyed the mood. Forgive me."

"You've not destroyed a thing."

"Yet not the topic for a party. My point simply, my dear Miss DuBarry, is that Dobbins perceived me, rightly, as quite safe." He lays a palm over his chest. "*Not* normally a word a man fancies hearing about himself, *safe*. But if you'll allow me, I'll attempt to show you a *safe* and a cracking good time—on behalf of my friend Dobbins."

Joannie offers her hand to shake. "I accept your offer, Lieutenant, to play Lancelot."

"To your Guinevere?" He asks this with a glint in his eye.

She remembers, too late, how that story ends. "Bad choice on my part. Their relationship was supposed to be strictly platonic."

"But became something else entirely, as I recall." He's laughing at her discomfort and his own. "Became lovers and destroyed Camelot—quite the cock-up, rather. We shall behave better, you and I, the Fabulous Flying Miss DuBarry and the Humble Physicist." He gestures toward the dance floor. "May I have this dance?"

She wobbles on her high heels, old ones of her mother's and a size too small. "Just to be clear, if I throw myself against you, it's the fault of my balance, nothing more."

He squeezes her hand. "Thank you for the clarification, lest a fellow assume he's being seduced. A proper tricky time balancing in those things, I'd expect."

"I'd rather be barefoot. Which is something you can report in your letter home tomorrow—how girls over here in the American South *can't hardly stand to wear shoes*."

"Honestly, any proper mention of you might sound rather too glamorous—Amelia Earhart by day, Ginger Rogers by night. I'm not sure that would be received with enthusiasm in Golders Green."

"You left out 'Mildred the Milkmaid by dawn.' Very glamorous, yes. Also, clearly, you've not seen me dance more than a slow box step,

Lieutenant Silverberg. I hope you didn't shine your shoes tonight, because I'm likely to stomp them to a dull mess."

"Stomp away, Guinevere." He sweeps a hand toward the bandstand, the pool, the red tile buildings behind the outdoor dance area. "You've probably been here any number of times before."

"Actually, the Cloister isn't a place somebody like me gets invited in normal life." She lowers her voice. "Which is fine, since it clearly means wearing shoes."

"Ah. Well. We're in the same boat then, you and I. Here's to wearing out the dance floor in a place that isn't entirely sure either of us should be here."

The saxophones swinging out the last phrases of "Take the 'A' Train," Dov Silverberg spins her out and back in. He moves with easy grace.

She remarks on it as he sends her twirling under one arm. "You're quite the dancer—for a humble physicist."

"It's the running track I did back at uni. We sprinters, you know, have feet of quicksilver."

The next song, "When Fools Rush In," is slower, and Joannie feels a little tremor down her spine as his right arm slips behind her waist and she steps in close again. His body gone stiff, she can feel the tautness of muscle on his shoulder.

"Tell me," she asks, "about your life. What you love."

He makes her laugh with stories of punting on the River Cam and losing the quant pole to mud, of cricket games lasting three days, of the release he felt as a sprinter. He tells her of becoming a pilot for the Royal Navy's Fleet Air Arm but then being pulled from that to become an instructor because of his course of study at Cambridge.

He becomes even more animated speaking of physics, about this new radar technology—only recently declassified, he explains with a schoolboy's wide-eyed excitement. "It's all about echoes and radio waves, distance and velocity, how sound bounces back . . . good God, I'm showing you a proper head beating of a boring time."

She shakes her head, laughing. "I'm enthralled, truly. I know nothing, *nothing* about radar except the bits they'll print in the papers—the new instruments 'helping our boys.' You've no idea how nice it is to talk about things other than ticket tearing and whether the milk truck is late and the cream's curdled. Honestly, go on. Please."

He does, for quite some time, through "If I Had You" and "Stardust," their feet keeping time and their heads close together to talk.

"Tell me," Dov asks now, "more about you. What makes your heart beat faster, Joannie DuBarry?"

Joannie begins with sailing and the leaky little wooden skiff she and Sammy—mostly she—refurbished. Then she moves on to flying and the cracked-up Gee Bee she and Sammy—mostly he—rebuilt. How she loves the meticulous, unmysterious nature of airplane engines and sail rigging and math. How in the air or out on the sea, she feels a freedom she experiences nowhere else—not in school, not at work at the Ritz— certainly not in groups of other women.

"The first time I flew upside down—"

Dov holds up a hand. "I beg your pardon. Here's a phrase no woman I've danced with has ever used: *the first time I flew upside down.* I say, you are an original, aren't you?"

"A posh British way of telling me I'm peculiar."

"Indeed, yes."

She laughs, head tipped back.

"By which I mean you're quite the delightful surprise. You learned to fly here at McKinnon, did you?"

"Sam, my twin, saved up his pennies and worked extra hours for lessons first. I s'pose I caught the bug from him. Started saving my pennies, too, letting him teach me what all he knew."

"Sam is where, currently?"

"A navy flier, in fact—4-F at first, so I thought I'd keep him here with me. But he kept going for the physical until he found a doctor—a *quack*—who missed that his heart is damaged, by rheumatic fever when we were small." Joan wonders if Dov Silverberg can hear the shift in the pitch of her voice, the fear thinning it out. "Stationed somewhere in the Pacific."

Through a few more rotations, Dov continues to move them smoothly across the floor. His tone is soft. "Do you hear from him often?"

"Not often enough. His best friend and I share—*shared*—whatever letters we get—*got*." She pauses, struck by the past tense—its loneliness— and by the memory of Marshall's tenderness in speaking of the letters: *he misses us both.*

"I love my brother," she says aloud—a little defensively, even. "Every single thing about my brother."

Another two rotations.

"I hope," Dov says, "I'm privileged to meet him one day."

The band has shifted to "We'll Meet Again," and a singer in a green satin dress who sounds remarkably like Vera Lyn belts it out.

Don't know where, don't know when . . .

"Yes," Joannie whispers back. "I hope you do."

Dov has lowered his head to listen closely to her, and before she can decide whether it's a good idea to step closer to a man with a girl back home in England, she lets her forehead tip forward, just barely. The trumpets and trombones swell and slide as the song grows, pulling them into another turn and another. Closer. Then closer still. Now their foreheads touch.

Just that.

Only that, two foreheads touching as they rotate slowly, slowly.

The trombones ease into "I'll Be Seeing You," which always makes Joan's breath snag in her throat. Playfully at first, Dov croons a few lines in a theatrical tenor. Looking down into her face, though, his voice softens. Then falters. Feet moving more slowly, he manages only two lines more.

I'll be looking at the moon, but I'll be seeing . . . you.

His voice trails off.

Their palms have gone clammy, and they can't look at each other as the song ends.

"Maybe," Dov says, his voice husky, "we should get some air?"

Yes, she thinks. *Away from the heady spell of the music. Out in the sea breeze. Not standing so close I don't know my own name—or care. Yes, we should get some air.*

Chapter 42

Dov

The froth of the waves iridescent in the moonlight, he and Joan walk side by side along the edge of the water. He can't think of her as Joannie—perhaps in part because that's what Ensign Dobbins called her, but more so because she strikes Dov as far too grown up, far too full of courage and a fiery intelligence for a name that evokes a girl in pigtails, or a teenager mooning over boys.

He and Joan hold their shoes, which keeps their hands occupied—a good thing. But their arms brush each other as they walk.

Like two dry sticks rubbed together, he thinks, *until they spark and start a fire.* Not *a good thing.*

They've waded deeper than he's realized, the sand dropping off sharply, so the rogue wave that rolls in next splashes high, soaking them both up to their hips.

"Your dress," he says. "I'm so sorry. It's—"

"Soaked." She's laughing.

He laughs, too, loving that she's not in the least concerned over the state of her dress, loving that here on this beach on this island in this country so far from home, it feels like only the two of them exist in the world.

He reaches to touch the drenched satin of the skirt. "My commanding officer will want to know what sort of trouble that bloody Englishman has been causing this time."

"Bloody Englishman," she repeats softly.

They stand there in the wet sand, the surf licking their ankles, their calves.

Dov runs a finger up her arm and feels a tremor go through her. Slowly, he closes the distance between them, bending his head down to hers so that their foreheads are touching again.

They stand like this, foreheads together, his hands moving gently around her waist, as the waves swell and surge and then fizz at their feet. When she lifts her face, her eyes latched on his, he steps in closer still and kisses her.

He shouldn't. He mustn't.

He knows this, right down to his core.

He should step back now.

Right now.

But she answers his kiss by twining her arms around the back of his neck.

"Joan," he groans, pulling away. "Don't do that. Don't kiss me back."

He can't look at her. Can't let himself see her eyes.

"Will Dobbins," she says into the dark, "didn't propose. He sensed, I think, I didn't want him to yet. And now . . . now I hope he comes home safe and sound and sweet as ever . . ."

Dov hears her next words in his head before she says them.

"But I'm not sure he'll ever come home . . . to me."

Turning from him, she crosses her arms over her chest and stares out at the sea. He stands behind her, not touching her at first.

How does he explain the pulling apart inside him, so real his chest aches? How does he tell her that feeling so perfectly alone with her in this moment, so perfectly in sync with her thoughts, her humor, her way of charging into the world, doesn't make the rest of the world—this war, his family, the people depending on him, the horror they all have to fight—go away?

But then Joan shivers in the breeze off the ocean. Before he can decide not to, he wraps his arms around her from behind, and when she relaxes back against him, he rests his chin on top of her head. He can feel the pounding of her heart in his own chest.

"Joan," he whispers into her hair. "I don't . . . I don't know what to do."

Perhaps he says it aloud. Perhaps not.

The only sound in return, though, is the swell and crash of the sea.

Turning in his arms, Joan holds his face in her hands as she kisses him lightly. Tenderly.

Like she's saying goodbye, Dov thinks as she pulls out of his arms.

She takes a full step away, as if she's afraid to touch him again. "I should go."

"Wait. Joan . . . ," he says.

Because something about the set of her face in this light refracted off the water tells him she means more than just leaving the beach.

Chapter 43

Hans

June 1943
Norfolk, Virginia

Hans has been merely standing at the rail of the ship looking out over the ocean and marveling that he is the same man who gazed over this sea from the opposite shore just a few months and a lifetime ago. He's hatched no plans for his future—*what future does a prisoner have?*—but he's just now heard a word that sounds familiar. A place, maybe. *Georgia.*

"Beautiful," he calls out to the front of the line, in English.

This becomes the word that seals his fate.

With so little room to house prisoners of war in England, the Allies had agreed, he learned, to ship hundreds of thousands of men like him to the United States.

"God help you Krauts," one Welshman had said, and then translated his thoughts to German, "if the ship you're on gets sunk in the Atlantic by your own bloody subs. I'll call that poetic justice, I will."

It was quite possible, Hans realized at the time. Which would have been, even he could admit, justice—though more violent and crude than poetic.

The crossing was beset by storms, and he wished at points in the worst throes of seasickness that he might die. But they arrived, each of them in one nauseous piece, at this place called Norfolk, Virginia, where prisoners are being processed.

He has no right to request which place they send him, of course. No hope that anyone would care to listen to him.

But he is tired, so tired, of being cold. Even in spring he'd been cold in England in the holding facility. He was cold on the ship, the Atlantic spitting as if it were laughing at him, a submariner above water, a deserter, a prisoner.

So when he hears one of the Americans, bored and reeling off names and places of POW camps—scores and scores of them, all of which mean nothing to Hans in English—the word *Georgia* stands out.

Georgia he remembers from *U-123*'s map room, and from the three ships they sank in two days. Off the coast of Georgia, he climbed up on the conning tower in April and felt warm. He remembers the glow of the lights he saw through the periscope. The sounds of the word *Georgia* he associated even at the time with that glow and that warmth, before Death—with the help of the fifty-man crew on the U-boat—blew that glow into fire and burned flesh and screams.

The American behind the desk here on the deck of the ship is yawning and stamping a page of the next prisoner in line.

But everyone stops and looks up when Hans shouts again, "Beautiful!"

In the following silence, Hans plays the best hand he has, one vaguely remembered, badly pronounced English word at a time. "Georgia. Is. Beautiful."

The Americans assigning the prisoners to camps chuckle. They're looking for something, anything, to laugh about, it seems.

"Well, hell," one says. "It's as good a place as any to send that one. Mac, see if there's room at Camp Stewart."

"Beautiful," Hans says again—for gratitude this time. He's too exhausted to remember the word *thanks*, which Father Bernhard taught him in English.

"Yeah, yeah, knock it off, Fritz. You got what you wanted. Enjoy the mosquitoes in Georgia."

Chapter 44

Hadley

I'm bounding out of a stairwell on the third floor when I hear raised voices around the corner and skid to a stop.

"You do not appear to comprehend the precariousness," growls a voice with a German accent, "of your situation." So Ernst Hessler must be back from Berlin.

"I've no doubt you'd like to elucidate the subject for me." Nick's voice has lost all its deference in speaking with his boss.

His father, I correct myself.

Holding my breath, I wait for Hessler's fury.

It comes in a blast so harsh I flinch.

"Erstaunlich!"

"Should I ask why exactly you're astonished?"

"The *kleiner Junge* allows the grown man his opinion."

"I think we're both clear I'm not a young child."

"This from the *kleiner Junge* who has been stopped for navigating under the influence more times than I can count."

Nick does not correct Hessler, not his phrasing of English and not that accusation.

I wait, back against the wall, imagining I can feel in the old plaster the vibrations that their rage is transmitting.

"Look, I've made my mistakes. Plenty of them. Really stupid mistakes. But I've been clean for a while now. Past ready to move on. I'm finally figuring out where I need to be headed. I'm giving notice as your driver and personal manservant."

A snort. "I give *you* notice: life does not give second chances. You—how do Americans say—*blew* your first chance. Blew it to hell."

A fist slams, and I squeeze my eyes shut. But it's plaster that crunches, not muscle and bone.

I've heard enough from Hessler and his driver—former driver. *Son.*

Stepping from around the corner, I fire off one round of words—Nick's own, back at him—before I walk away.

"*Authenticity*, Nick? Really? It's *crucial*? I guess that's your rule unless it has to do with your own life. Or your *father's*."

I turn on one heel and head back for the stairs. I'm too mad right now even to remember what I came up here for anyway. Behind me, I hear Hessler's sharp intake of air. Then footsteps—Nick's, probably—running toward me.

"Hadley. *Wait.*"

I round on him just as he reaches for my arm. "Do. Not. Touch. Me."

"If you'd just listen—"

"*Listening* to you was the problem. The one of us who actually *did* walk a rough road growing up learned some lessons the hard way, including not listening to *liars*, Nick."

I'm through the stairwell door, letting it slam behind me, and down the first flight in a flash. Nick flings the door open and calls out again.

"Hadley. Wait!"

But he doesn't follow me down.

That much I'll give him: he knows when he's lost.

∽

Taking refuge back in the room with the stained glass, I stalk several laps around the tables to cool off. Swiping up the photo of Joan DuBarry with her B-25, I sigh.

Once again, I find myself staring at her, wondering what her story really was, why she became important to all three founders of Boundless.

And where she got her moxie.

Suddenly, I'm thinking of Kitzie again, and her health.

It's no cold, a voice in my head tells me. *She knows something she's not saying—or suspects it, at least.*

She's young, I want to shout back. *She'll be fine. We've both lost too much family already. She* has *to be fine.*

"You," I tell the photo of Joannie DuBarry, "had your own battles to fight. I'm so sorry you died so young. So what's your story—your *real* story? And where'd you get all that strength?"

She stares back at me—and past me.

She's not giving up her secrets just yet.

Chapter 45

Joannie

July 19, 1943

Maybe because she's thinking of standing with Dov on the Sea Island beach, thinking how swept away she felt—how much the feeling frightened her in a way she never had been before—and maybe because she's thinking also of Will—sweet, funny, wonderful Will, who deserves unstinting devotion—her bike is swerving left to right on the sidewalk in front of Gray's Drugs.

Can you betray a man's trust even when he's never asked for commitment, or even seemed to expect it?

It's the cover of *Life* magazine that stops her cold and nearly throws her over the handlebars as she stomps on the brake.

Outside the drugstore, Mr. Gray has set up a metal stand of the latest periodicals. The *Saturday Evening Post*, *Collier's*, and *Good Housekeeping* all vie for pedestrians' attention. Three teenage girls cluster around a copy of *Look*. But Joannie only sees one magazine.

On the cover of *Life*, a girl with dimples sits on the wing of a plane. And, yes, she's more girl than woman. Her hair is in two pigtails, in fact, making her appear hardly more than fourteen.

"AIR FORCE PILOT," the headline reads in all caps but small type size, as if to let the reader decide how much to jump at the sight, the juxtaposition of those pigtails with those three little words.

Letting her bike crash to the ground, Joannie moves forward in a daze. Picking up the copy of *Life*, she flips to the article—the inside headline reading "Girl Pilots"—a feature on the US Army Air Force's training of woman aviators at some apparently godforsaken place called Avenger Field, Texas. The lead picture is of a girl with hair streaming, flying a single-engine plane perhaps just a couple of feet off the ground, landing gear still down.

As if, Joan thinks, *the photographer thought he'd better snap something quickly. In case she never got the plane clear of the runway.*

Still, though . . .

The village, the whole world, tilting sideways, Joan staggers away, with the magazine open to a page of young women learning Morse code and wearing flying goggles, the article's author describing the "girls" as they "joyously scramble into the silver airplanes." The tone is condescending at points: the girl pilots are "faster on instruments" and more "smooth and gentle" in certain areas, while the male pilots have a "better memory for details," and one whole page pictures various ways the girl pilots keep their hair out of their eyes while in the cockpit—ribbons or hairnets or braids.

But it's the first time in her life Joan has ever seen the face of another woman who loves the freedom and challenge of flying as she does. It's as if she's walked out of one of the island's dense fogs and into a whole different world. Passing the hardware store still dazzled, she suddenly realizes she's yet to pay the dime for *Life* and has to turn back.

"I read that piece about them girl pilots," Mr. Gray says. "Lord have mercy, what in tarnation will they come up with next, monkeys on the joystick?"

She thanks him for her change and tries to back quickly away.

"Lordy, it's been slow in here these days, everybody trying hard to cut back, buying only what they just got to have to survive. Good for the war effort, but not so good for keeping an old druggist company. Which reminds me to say, Joannie . . ."

Anxious to finish the article, she's frustrated to have to stop and listen. But he is, after all, her neighbor.

"Joannie girl, about what you seen, the periscope last year. I thought sure you'd just imagined it. But you were right. Lord have mercy."

She stops backing toward the door to look at him, the old druggist with the sagging, doleful cheeks of a bloodhound, a moth-eaten bowtie, and old-fashioned ideas—but willing to say he was wrong. That is no small thing.

"I wish I hadn't been right," she tells him quietly.

"Send your daddy next door this evening, how 'bout?"

"Mr. Gray, Pops isn't . . ."

"I know, Joannie, I know. Don't think I don't scoot over a heap of evenings when you're at the Ritz. Sometimes early mornings, too, when you're on your brother's milk run. I know ole Terrence's not remembering much. But he knows mine's a friendly face."

Joan thanks him again, then rushes out.

She knows before she's reached the pier that she will apply to this new program for women aviators, this new Women's Flying Training Detachment. They won't accept her, of course, not with her training on a junkyard biplane. But by applying, she'll at least know that she's offered everything she can to serve her country in this fight against fascism.

Applying will force her mind out of this undertow of emotion that's got her feeling unsteady, in danger of losing her footing for good. Applying will remind her she's not built for standing around waiting to see what life will throw at her next. Applying will make her feel like she's honoring Sam, all his patience in teaching her how to fly.

What she wants to do, even before she's read the whole article, is tear the thing out and mail it to Sam. Instead, she steers her bike with one hand while she grips the magazine to her chest all the way back to the cottage.

Except Pops.

The image of her father slumped at the table brings her to a literal halt, her bike tires crunching on the crushed shell of the shoulder.

Pops.

"I'm serving the war effort already," she makes herself say aloud, in a voice that sounds staged, like the women on those public service posters—if they could speak—as they rivet a pipe, their lipstick and their smiles pluckily in place.

And she *is* serving. By delivering milk to the radar training school and a whole sector of homes so her brother can fly. By working hard at the Ritz, since people still need entertainment and Liberty ship builders need theater seats for sleep. She's serving by participating in every scrap-metal drive, every collection of rubber. By living with less, even though, Lord knows, she and Pops could use more.

As she stumps up the stairs of the front porch, she can hear Marshall's mother, Miz Rose, humming an old hymn, the water in the kitchen sink running. With the toe of her Keds, Joan stops the screened door from slamming, Pops asleep, chin to chest, at the table. Joan treads softly over the wood floor, but Miz Rose turns, holds out one arm.

Joan is still clutching the *Life* magazine to her chest but lets Miz Rose hug her. What does it matter if the article gets crushed? It's not like she could join the program, even if they'd have her. Not with Pops how he is.

Joan closes her eyes against the tide of feelings pulling at her, the flood of affection, the fierce loyalty to Pops, and also that old current of resentment—that men would always be the real actors of life, the adventurers and the heroes, so long as women are stuck caring for the home.

As she and Miz Rose turn toward Joan's father, he blinks awake. Miz Rose is already running a hand over Joan's hair, as if she could smooth down the hurt of whatever's coming.

"His health's good," Miz Rose whispers in her ear. "You're right, hon. But his mind . . . I know it's hard, sugar."

"Well, now," Pops says, eyes bright as he stands. He looks at her, startled. Then holds out his hand.

"Terrence DuBarry, miss. I think we might could have met before."

She squeezes her father's hand with her right, the *Life* magazine still gripped in her left.

Maybe she'll apply to the program. Maybe she won't.

Either way, she can't go.

Chapter 46

Hans

September 1943

I've seen her before, Hans thinks as he piles out last from the truck, the whole group of them having stood up in its back the entire trip from the camp, swaying and knocked about as they hit potholes.

Seen her somewhere before.

But that's not possible, of course. The woman climbing out of her own truck and wrenching hard on a crate to lift it, maybe she only looks familiar from film, some movie star or pinup girl he can't recall the name of.

It's all he has time to think before the man in front of him whirls around, closing both hands around Hans's throat.

Hans tries to cry out, but his air passages have closed shut.

Another man grabs both his feet, lifting him from the ground, while the first holds his throat in a vise. They drag him into a clump of trees and brush, behind the fanned spikes of a bush.

Kicking, writhing, Hans gets out some grunts and wheezes, loud enough that the last couple of men marching away glance over their shoulders. One of them pauses, indecision freezing the man in place.

Time twists and stretches, no longer connected to anything solid, as Hans, out of air, watches the man decide.

Ironic, Hans has time to think, *to have survived all those patrols in the underwater coffin of the U-boat, survived desertion and then posing as a French fisherman, survived stumbling on the battle at Dieppe, then the POW camps of Great Britain, and then, to close out the loop of life, the trip across the Atlantic in an American ship with Axis prisoners on board— loud, undisciplined Italians and dour, angry Germans—with U-boats of the Kriegsmarine trying to sink it. Then the Pullman train car ride down here to Georgia, the most relaxing ride of his life—as a prisoner of war.*

Absurd, this curlicue of fate, yet here he lies, choking to death.

Back on this very coast where we hunted in wolf packs of subs. Here is where I will die at the hands of my own countrymen.

Hans can see broken shards of the palest blue sky up above through a filter of spiked branches, but it's all going dark. He is tired of struggling. He's been tired so long, yet he's kept going. And now time keeps stretching, twisting, thinning like dough pulled from the table.

This was bound to happen, the stink of deserter clinging to him like the smell of dead fish did for so long.

A man can only live around Death for so long, escape its talons so many times, before Death turns on him too.

Hans wishes he could tell his mother goodbye. Maybe taste her *Semmelschmarrn* once more. Perhaps they will tell her only that he died a prisoner of war, not a deserter.

Perhaps she will tell Father Bernhard that Hans, who cared little for pipe organs or reverence or doctrine, had found the priest's English lessons quite helpful. That Hans had liked his sermons, too, even the dangerous ones.

Or, perhaps, *only* the dangerous ones.

But now even the blue shards of sky have gone black. Hans ceases to kick his assailants, or even to move.

The chief engineer of *U-123* ceases to breathe.

Chapter 47
Joannie

Pounding on the glass of the mess hall window, Joan shouts for all she's worth. *"Help!"*

But there may be no one inside this early.

Snatching a rock from the ground, she hurls it at the window—surely shattering glass will get someone's attention. But the stained glass—this one, the lighthouse window—holds firm.

Joan pounds again and continues shouting, even as she sprints back to the milk truck. Leaping into the seat, she throws her full weight on the horn and aims the nose for the three men on the ground in the circle of palmettos. With cries and shouts, the bystanders leap out of her way. Glancing up, the two attackers roll to one side. Inches from the victim, who does not move, Joan slams on the brakes and leaps out.

The German on the ground has quit writhing, his attackers backing into the crowd.

A stream of khaki finally emerges from the hotel. In the chaos of the next several moments, Joan steps back.

Dov is among the officers, but she's fixed on the still form on the ground. Two men grab the two standing Germans, and several drop to their knees around the third.

"Dead?" one of them asks.

"Bloody near it, I'd say." It's a British accent—Dov's voice. "But not entirely."

They drag the nearly dead German up, gasping, red welts at his neck.

Flint stands in front of the prisoner. "You speak English, soldier?"

"A little." It comes out a rasp.

"Name?"

"Hessler. Hans Hessler. *Die Kriegsmarine.*"

"You realize, Hessler, my men don't have time for this, interrupting the few free moments they're given in order to keep you German bastards from your wrestling matches," Flint says.

"A *wrestling match?*" Joan can't help herself from stepping forward. "This Hessler fellow was about to be killed."

An American guard steps forward. "If I may, sir."

"What is it, Delaney?"

"The victim here, he's been tagged by the others as a deserter."

Flint eyes Hans critically. "Deserter, huh? No army smiles on a deserter."

"Desertion *from the Wehrmacht*, sir," Dov reminds him. "I assume we, at least, would smile on that."

"Damn Krauts," Flint mutters. "Remind me why we're keeping any of the bastards alive, Silverberg?"

Not waiting for an answer, Flint sprays out a flurry of orders, then ends by rounding on Joan. "I acknowledge both the delivery of the milk this morning, Miss DuBarry, and the warning, inappropriate as the choice of a milk truck as battering ram may have been."

"It wasn't my first choice, Commander Flint. Or second."

"I trust, given the orders I've just put in place, we won't need the assistance of a local milkmaid again. Your efforts today were, admittedly, helpful. But with all due respect, I hope not to see you again, Miss DuBarry, before my morning coffee."

Dov Silverberg is the last to leave, dipping his head close to Joan's as he passes but not meeting her eye. "It would appear that rather than my keeping a proper eye out for your safety, the tables have been fully turned. The use of a lorry as lifesaving device: well done, you."

He turns back once as he walks away, his gaze moving from her, then north up the beach toward Sea Island, then back to her. One side of his mouth lifts, a smile that's sad and wistful—and maybe, just maybe, hopeful too. So full of things unsaid. Things that might never be said.

He lifts two fingers in a salute, and she returns it with a single nod.

"He has promises to keep," she says aloud, as if somehow that might help.

It does.

But very little.

～

She stops by the lighthouse on her way home, and its white bulk comforts her, as if she can suddenly see the world from the metal-railed top of its tower and let all the little worries of life fall into perspective as just that: small, with the vastness of the ocean rolling as far as the eye can see to the east and the Marshes of Glynn to the west.

As kids, she and Sam came here often to hide in the lighthouse's shadow, drawing warmth and strength from just leaning against it. In their younger years, they hid here from other children in games of hide-and-seek. Later on, after their mother died, they came here together just to sit, the loss too deep for anything but silence and being together.

Overhead, a plane roars as it ascends, its landing gear pulled up late and jerkily: another trainee at the controls and the crank, no doubt.

She pictures Will's first solo flight that ended in the marsh. A miracle he wasn't killed before even being shipped out.

She's not heard from either Sam or Will for quite some time. For Sam, this is less surprising, his missives sporadic but arriving on average about once a month.

Will, on the other hand, writes—or did—at least once a week, long literary letters that make Joannie laugh. Sometimes he describes their rations:

"'Tis an ill cook that can't lick his own fingers" is my quote for the day. I'd bet a barn full of Jerseys our cooks in the mess here hadn't licked so much as a pinky. It's fine, though, since we're hungry enough we'd chew our own shoes.

He says nothing about the missions they're on or the dangers they're facing. Nothing but humor from him, peppered with quotes from, as he puts it, the Other Will.

Me, I'm just the portable Shakespeare, he says of himself. *Portable if you got space for six feet five inches of awkward.*

His letters are frequent, lovable, impossible to ignore—just like Will himself. Even the penmanship slopes large, open and comical.

He rarely speaks of love, but his tone is warm. Intimate, even. Like an old friend who's shared your every skinned knee.

For him not to write means something's gone wrong.

She approaches her cottage slowly, desperately wanting and dreading a letter or telegram.

Marshall's mother, Miz Rose, sits reading in a wicker chair on the front porch of her own cottage. Joan's own mother was like that too: a hard worker who kept her family well loved yet was happy to ignore a few cobwebs in the hall and a few weeds in the vegetable garden and always, *always* spent the lunch hour with a good book. It must've drawn them together as friends, even across the South's color line. That and the fact that with their plots of peas, tomatoes, and beans nearly twining into each other and their houses' thin walls built only a few yards from each other, they very nearly lived under the same roof. It was only thanks to the Hammonds, in fact, that the DuBarrys weren't forced, homeless, off the island when Terrence lost his job a few years ago.

"Joannie, hon," Miz Rose calls, rising from her chair. "I was just over to check on your daddy. You got some mail that looks real official."

Joannie leaps off her bike before it stops and takes the porch stairs two at a time. Her fingers tremble as she lifts the letter with an unfamiliar return address from the kitchen table: Headquarters, US Army Air Forces, Washington, DC.

Turning toward the kitchen window, she clutches the unopened letter to her chest as if she could absorb its contents just through the feel and the smell of paper and ink.

Ripping it open now, she sees the signature first.

Jacqueline Cochran.

A force of nature who grew up dirt poor, married rich, started a cosmetics company, and learned to fly planes to deliver her beauty products, then broke airplane racing records.

Joannie lets herself read several lines up from that.

... So that we may complete your file and issue official instructions to report for the class indicated above.

Which must mean . . .

Joannie pulls in a long breath.

Somehow, it never occurred to her she'd be accepted. Even her age—still twenty when she mailed the application, when the minimum age was twenty-one—was against her. She lets her eyes rise to the letter's first lines to be sure she's right.

Dear Miss DuBarry,

This is to notify you that you are tentatively assigned to the class entering WASP (Women Airforce Service Pilots) training on . . .

Her eyes stop there. Women Airforce Service Pilots. She read they'd merged the two new wartime programs for women pilots and chosen a new name, but seeing it on an envelope she's holding in her own hand feels otherworldly, like she's flown over the clouds and discovered an alternate world.

How is it possible to feel euphoria and heartbreak in the same moment? She's not free to offer her best talents to serve her country in the same way Sam or Will or Dov can. She's just not.

It sounds so incredibly stupid now, but she simply assumed she'd be rejected.

A few feet away in the living room, Pops startles in the overstuffed chair with yellow daisy upholstery, his favorite for years now—since it was Joan's mother's favorite. He raises his head from where it flopped on his chest and lumbers toward his uneaten lunch on the table, then holds out his hand to Joan.

"Terrence DuBarry, ma'am. Can I help you with some milk today? I got some left in the truck."

Joan takes his hand with her right. "It's me, Pops. Your daughter. Let's get some food in you." Rising to her toes, she kisses him on the cheek as she swallows down the lump swelling in her throat.

"My daughter! Of course." He can't quite recall her name, but his eyes fill as he rears back and opens both arms. "My precious daughter." She can give him little else these days but this, so she lets herself be swallowed up by her father's hug.

With her left hand, Joan crumples the letter of acceptance into a ball.

Vaguely, Joan is aware of a figure at the screened door to the front porch: Miz Rose, quietly standing there, ready to help.

Thank you, Joan mouths to her. Because sometimes just another soul witnessing the heartbreak of your world helps. Rose is the kind of person who knows this.

Quietly, too, Rose enters, not letting the screened door slam, and lifts the crumpled ball from the floor.

Rose holds it up: a question.

Joannie nods. What does it matter? She's already given it up.

Rose smooths open the letter. "Well now," she murmurs. "Well now."

257

Chapter 48

Hans

January 1944
Prisoner of war encampment, Camp Stewart, Georgia

About this young woman who saved my life,

Hans writes his family in Bavaria, the German barely legible in his haste,

I do not know much except her name, Joan DuBarry, and that she lives on the island. Although a British officer here named Silverberg who has been kind . . .

Hans pauses. Will the censors black out a Jewish name even for the mention of being an officer or being kind? He has no idea, but it's already penned.

tells me he knows her, so perhaps I will meet her one day. I hope you will write to her, Mother, once the war is over. Perhaps a letter would find its way to her. I would like to thank her someday myself.

He is about to add *you and I know it cannot be much longer, this war.* But there's no use. The Nazi censors would certainly black out any allusion to surrender or defeat.

You write that Father Bernhard has been obliged to travel.

I have worried for him, Hans wants to say. *I've heard rumors of horrible fates for those who've been carted away. The Allied officers here speak of these rumors as if they are fact.*
What he writes, though, is

I pray for his safe journey home.

The horn of the truck that transports them to St. Simons Island is blaring: time to go.

Yes, I am grateful to the American woman. I'm glad you wish to thank her as well.

Your son,

Hans

Chapter 49
Joannie

January 1944
Sweetwater, Texas

Joan feels much like she did the first time she did a barrel roll in the Gee Bee, the disorientation of clouds above and below, no sense of which way Earth might be. Her life shifted course so fast—so irreversibly, it seemed—she's felt these past several days as if she banked into a turn and then began spinning.

Miz Rose had smoothed out the crumpled ball on the floor and read Joan's acceptance letter from the Women Airforce Service Pilots. Then she went to Mr. Gray to come up with a joint plan so Joan could go, the two of them sharing care for Terrence.

"You got skills to offer, child," Miz Rose said.

"And we," said Mr. Gray, "got the home front covered so you can go and feel real steady knowing your daddy's in good hands."

The very day she left home, Mr. Gray moved his half dozen shirts from his house next door into the cottage with Terrence DuBarry.

Miz Rose insists she'll check on Terrence during the day. Neither will take a penny. They both say it's their contribution to the war effort so Joan can go ferry planes.

Mr. Gray did add a final, "What in tarnation will they think of next, girl pilots." But his smile was wide and proud. Joan knows she'll send both neighbors money from her WASP pay and beg them to take it.

Now in Texas, hauling her luggage to the top of the stairs of the Bluebonnet Hotel, she glances back only once, the dusty little town of Sweetwater, Texas, not exactly calling to her. After a few blocks of saloons, a general store, and a couple of clapboard churches, the town appears to dwindle into windswept acres of mesquite trees and cattle.

She feels her throat constrict now. Missing home. *Sam. Pops. The island itself.*

She misses more than that, too, but she won't let herself name anyone else, not even just in her head. Her leaving the island to come do this work is not only serving the war effort but also important, she knows, for the sake of Dov Silverberg's whole community in Golders Green, London, and for sweet, big-hearted Will Dobbins.

She tells herself this every day.

A uniformed doorman, white haired and gentle eyed, steps forward. "Welcome to the Bluebonnet Hotel, miss. Let me call you a bellhop. Little slip of a gal like you could strain herself."

"Thank you. Very kind. But if I don't want to wash out on flight training on day one, I'd better lift my own luggage."

Taking in her dress and heels in a quick sweep down and up, the doorman rears back. "You're one of *those*, are you?"

"Good news or bad?"

"Oh, good, miss. All hands on deck, I say, to stop Hitler from becoming Führer of Texas."

"There's a phrase I've never heard before."

The old man leans forward and lowers his voice. "Though not everyone in Sweetwater's of the same mind about you gals, miss. Them Army Air Force top brass, some of them can be real stubborn—jackasses even, if I may say—about a girl sitting behind the controls of their B-17s."

Joannie leans forward to pat his arm but doesn't lower her voice. "Wait till the jackasses see a girl do *big, lovely loops* in their B-17s."

Lugging her duffel bag under an arm, Joannie passes the elevator and runs as fast as she's able up the three flights of stairs to her room. She's still clanking the key into the lock when a voice behind her calls out.

"Hey! Fifinella!"

It takes Joannie a moment to realize that's meant for her. She has no idea what *Fifinella* means, but there's no one else on the hall.

She turns.

Another young woman stands there, also in a dress and heels, her lipstick a bright, shiny red. "You and me, sister, we look like we're headed to a garden party."

Joannie unlocks the door and nudges it open with one shoulder but doesn't have a chance to respond before the other young woman bounds toward her. "What do you say you throw your things on the bed, then you and me go down to the closest saloon and see how many drinks we can get the boys to buy us?"

"I'm not real sure if I . . ."

"Oh my. What part of the South are *you* from?"

"Georgia. That obvious?"

"And how. Come on. We'll be in zoot suits tomorrow, all in men's forty-four long—thank you, army surplus—with forty-four layers of engine grease till the end of the war, so I figure we stock up now on the looks of longing, you know?"

Joannie balks. "I want to be well rested for tomorrow to—"

"Okay, Georgia. We're all here to risk our lives for democracy. All's I'm saying"—she waits until Joannie drops her bags on the floor, then hooks an arm through her elbow—"is that a free drink and a couple of winks never killed a girl."

In the Sweetwater Saloon, they trade stories of learning to fly and collect a line of drinks they've not ordered on their booth's table. Ohio—her name's Betsy, but they call each other by their home states—smokes two cigarettes and will hardly make eye contact with the officers who swagger up.

Making a short night of it, the women return to their rooms at the Bluebonnet before ten—even Ohio, with her bold red lipstick.

"More bark than bite?" Joannie teases as they unlock their doors.

Ohio sighs. "A whole kennel more bark. Truth is, I got a hometown honey."

"Ah."

"Chompin' at the bit for the altar, my Freddy is. I feel like here's a way I can help the war effort—doing what I like best. But meanwhile, I can't seem to forget about sweet, faithful Freddy. What about you, Georgia? You got somebody back home or . . . over there?"

"Good night!" Joan calls over her shoulder and slides into her room.

～

Joannie is the first to arrive in the lobby the next morning, but not by much.

Ohio arrives last, out of breath, her lipstick fiery red as ever. "We're ready for our transport to the garden party, girls," she announces. The others nod nervously and smooth their skirts. They're all wearing dresses, heels, gloves and nylons—or imitations of them, with brown lines eyebrow penciled up the backs of their calves.

"But how else do you dress," Ohio asks, "for the most important day of your life?"

Hearing the approach of an engine, Joan rushes toward the door. "Our transport!"

She pauses to kiss the doorman on the cheek.

He blushes. "Never did see in all my days so much loveliness headed to barracks."

The doorman throws open the front entrance, but no bus or van idles there for the group of young women.

They stand staring in their high heels and skirts.

Joannie is the first to speak. "Okay, then. Taking a cattle truck in heels it is."

The private who's jumped from behind the wheel of the truck grins at the overdressed herd of them, then winks directly at Joan. "Wait till you broads get a load of the jobs they got planned out for you. My favorite's the one where you're flying whatever scrap model of plane is too old to send overseas, you towing the targets behind, with brand new recruits learning to shoot live ammunition at you. Cattle truck ain't nothing, gorgeous."

It's not the first time Joannie's realized she or any woman here could easily be killed in this job, but it's the first time it's felt this real.

She can't even picture what the private has just described, live ammunition bulleting all around her, from gunners new to the job.

What she says, though, as she hikes up her skirt to leap into the truck bed and bends to help yank the tailgate into place, is "I was hoping target towing would be a part of the job."

Chapter 50

Will

Dear Joannie,

I'll say this for you joining up with the WASP:

a) you are one brave dame, as I already knew, and

b) the Axis powers don't stand the chance of a pig at a barbecue, not with you in a cockpit.

I'd say I'm scared stiff for you, but that wouldn't change a thing of your going, would it?

Dov writes that he'll check on your Pops, in addition to Mr. Gray and Miz Rose. I'm glad for that.

The South Pacific's a mighty big place. I wish I could tell you which islands we're near and what they look like, but the censors would black it out and I'll not let this letter to you show up all marred. Just know if I ever cross paths with your brother over here, I'll say my howdys, and tell him just how much I surely do miss his sister. More than I'd better say.

With love way beyond the boundless sea,

Will

Chapter 51
Joannie

May 1944
Camp Davis, Holly Ridge, North Carolina

Bile rising in her throat, Joannie pounds harder, desperate now, on the cockpit shield of the A-24 and tries the latch again. Stuck. Completely broken.

It's been a battering flight through storms from Wright Field in Ohio to North Carolina's Camp Davis. The A-24, not a tiny plane, felt tossed about like a butterfly in the winds.

I'm riding a tin can in a hurricane, she'd thought.

That was bad enough, the flight itself, one of her first since earning her wings—the recognition she'd survived the grueling weeks of Avenger Field training. But now this: trapped in the cockpit, her right engine pouring black smoke.

She's exhausted and dehydrated, her thinking blurred, her legs shaking with the sheer physical effort. Having flown above ten thousand feet in the unpressurized cockpit, she should've used her oxygen, should've noticed the dizziness—the *graying out*, they call it—before it settled in. She did not let herself drink anything for the whole flight—she had no copilot to take the controls, and even if she had, these smaller planes have no place to relieve oneself except the tubes and bottles the men are able to use.

"Yet another reason," the Camp Davis commander, Major Stephenson, likes to say, "for girls just to go home and knit socks for the troops."

So none of the WASPs here at Camp Davis report dehydration. Or frustration. Or harassment. Pointing out a problem would mean they can't hack it.

Furiously, Joannie beats on her cockpit shield again. She bites down on her lips so she won't yell for help, since her yell might sound like a scream. Something a *girl* might do.

A mechanic lumbers out from the hangar, stops, hands in his pockets, and squints up at the cockpit. Swinging himself onto the wing with effort—his body the heft of a fullback—he slaps at a few mosquitoes and takes his time wiping sweat from behind his neck before unlatching the cockpit's glass canopy from the outside.

"Didn't Avenger Field ever teach you dames how to let yourself out of your own damn plane?"

Joannie's fury fuels her leap from the cockpit, despite her legs nearly buckling under her weight. "For your information, the latch on the inside is broken. I'd have had to shatter the glass and, last I checked, our side of the war is short on dive-bombers as it is."

Now she makes herself take a breath. "And thank you, by the way, for letting me out."

He grunts at her. "Nearly fifty thousand men here at Davis and, what, fifty—a hundred tops—women. A Texan like me don't have to like you dames thinking you're pilots to want to let you out of wherever you got yourself trapped."

"For the record, I didn't *get myself trapped*." She speaks slowly, enunciating the key words. "The *latch* on the *inside* is *broken*. It needs to be fixed."

"Yeah, well, get in line, sister."

"You're telling me they've figured out how to self-seal the gas tank in case it gets shot at thirty thousand feet, but after the pilot lands, it's just *get out if you can, bud?*"

"This one's a trainer. Do I got to spell it out for you?" He motions for her to come with him to the hangar, then shoves a clipboard at her, a Form One fastened there.

Sticky throttle, Joannie writes on the form, giving the specifics of the A-24 she's just flown.

Radio broken—no communication to ground.

Broken latch on the inside of the cockpit, pilot's side.

She circles this and the sticky throttle.

"Like it'll do any damn good," the mechanic mutters under his breath.

"Which would mean . . . what, exactly?"

"You gotta be new here to ask that kind of question, sister."

"You're telling me that serious problems with a sticky throttle, say, or a cockpit not opening from the inside, shouldn't merit immediate attention?"

"*Merit immediate attention?* Where the hell'd you grow up, inside a dictionary?"

She flushes. "Point is, you're telling me safety issues like this aren't fixed right away?"

"You sure as hell didn't hear it from me." Circling his lips, he blows out a long stream of air, then slaps another mosquito on his arm. "Feel free not to quote me, but you may as well know straight off, so you can maybe run home to Daddy."

"Lot of good that'd do the war effort, since Pops doesn't fly airplanes. I do."

"Listen, kid, jalopies with wings are basically what we got here. Not a damn plane on the whole base has got every last thing working right. Us mechanics, we're already putting in what feels like ninety-five-hour weeks. And when there's new parts available, where do you s'pose those parts go?"

"Not here, I assume."

"Not on your life. At best you can expect these damn training planes here to be . . . hell, let's just call it *lacking*."

They're walking now, and the swing of her legs at last, loose and free, after hours working the rudder pedals, helps release most of her fury.

"The plane I got most of my flying hours on wasn't exactly the latest—or safest—thing, a Gee Bee Model A, probably with parts from lawnmower engines. My brother and I worked on it ourselves after its owner cracked up on Sea Island."

"Hell, that model practically killed more pilots than carried them. You actually flew that section of sewer pipe?"

"I did. Me and Sam. My twin."

He scans her up and down like he's reassessing.

She turns to go, her legs still rubbery from the flight, her hearing still dulled by the engines.

"By the way, kid . . ."

She ratchets her neck around, her back too stiff to twist. "Yeah?"

"You say you know a propeller from a rudder?"

"Pretty sure I got that part down."

"I know all you WASP dames had to learn engine repair basics at your Sweetwater training, but I got to say, I'd rather work with one who's got grease under her fingernails regular-like."

Joan holds up her fingers: grease, in fact, under the uneven chipped nails. "I'm a stickler for details on engines, not so much on manicures."

"Now those are some fingers we can work with. You ever want to help out here, us mechanics would welcome the extra hands. That is, assuming you're a broad who knows her bomber engines."

"A broad who knows her bomber engines." Joannie cocks her head at him. "Why don't I think those are words a boy from Texas grows up saying?"

"That ain't the half of it. Listen, I can coach you through what a supercharger does if you can just hold your end of the wrench, you know? By the way, where's that brother of yours?"

"Navy pilot. In the Pacific."

"Jesus." The mechanic's face softens. "Crap news about losses there these days. Sorry. S'pose you already know that."

"I do."

But I'd still rather not hear it said out loud.

Joannie gazes out to the stand of scrub pine. For something to say that's nothing to do with the Pacific, she offers, "I'm Joan, by the way. Joan DuBarry."

"Buck Austin."

"That's a very Texas name, Buck Austin."

"Not as much as my two brothers, Bullet and Boots."

"You're kidding me."

"Swear to God. Mama was supposed to get to name all the girls, and Daddy the boys, but there was only ever the three of us dirt daubers."

Buck Austin has made Joan grin, and even through her fog of exhaustion, she's grateful for that.

Buck lifts his drill like he's making a toast. "Hey, here's to the pilots, even you dames, getting these hunks of steel wherever the hell they need to go."

Goggles clutched in her hand, Joan lifts them in a return toast. She'd like to return the Texan's grin now, but all she can see is Sam in his cockpit, bullets raining down on his wings; Will with his earphones on, watching green blips on a circular screen; and Dov, pouring sweat, urgency in every word, as he teaches yet another classroom of fighter directors how, in a split second, to tell if a bogey is friend or foe and who to shoot down.

"Here's to all of us," she calls back as she walks away, "doing our bit."

Buck gives a loose, friendly salute, and she gives him one back.

What she walks away unable to shake, though, is the image of the Form One she just filled out.

Like it'll do any damn good.

The mechanic's words send a chill across her skin even here in the Carolina heat.

Chapter 52
Hadley

"All that these folks were facing every day," I call into the hotel suite from the porch, where I'm sorting letters. "The kinds of risks they took, the sacrifices they made. I got to tell you, Kitz, I'm feeling soft and selfish out here. Not so much that I can't still do lunch with you at Echo, the best table oceanside, but just saying."

Looking pale again today but uncomplaining, she joins me. "I just replied to Mr. Hessler's daily email checklist, by the way. What's the return-to-sender letter you wanted me to see?"

"It answers at least one question. It's in German. From Hans Hessler's mother, if you can believe it."

"You don't read German."

"Ah, but my best-friend-forever Google Translate does. Took me a bit, but it's a beautiful, wrenching thank-you note for saving her son's life while he was a prisoner of war, addressed to . . . drum roll, please . . . none other than Joan DuBarry. He apparently would've been strangled to death by Nazis from his own prison camp—apparently because some of them were still fanatically devoted to Hitler and he was not—a deserter, even. She somehow intervened. Crazy, right?"

The perfect audience for any dramatic reveal, Kitz claps her hands together. "That explains why at least one of the three families considered Joannie DuBarry a part of their story."

"It doesn't explain why the Dobbins family has been the biggest source of our Joan pictures and letters. Which, I assume, means Will saved them."

"Maybe Will's love for her was undying—not just till her early death parted them, but long after that, even."

"Says the chick who's watched too many Hallmark movies."

"What, you don't think it's possible?"

"I can imagine someone loving *you* that long. The rest of us are probably a whole lot easier to move on from. I mean, look, she dies in her, what, early twenties, and he never finds anyone else in all these decades since?"

Kitz shrugs. "True love. Also, maybe he kept busy. Which reminds me: I finally got around to reading some of those articles you sent that first day, all about the nasty succession drama at Boundless."

"A little late for us to back out now, sister friend."

"Like I could tear you away from your oceanfront view at this point. What I noticed, though, were the references to Boundless's original vision. All about assisting those who might not ordinarily qualify to own their own homes—in Germany, the US, and Great Britain, then expanding to other countries."

"It did sound remarkable, right? Kind of George Bailey in *It's a Wonderful Life* on an international scale."

"No wonder about your phone calls."

"My phone calls?"

"What you told me about the gentle Rabbi Ben versus his brother, King Richard the Terrible. If Benedick Silverberg is part of a group of stockholders and family members pushing for a return to more social-impact real estate investing—"

"Look who knows the lingo."

"Just read the same articles you did. While King Richard is focused only on maximizing profits. Makes sense it would get ugly."

I trot past her, back into the room. "So now I get why our friend the good rabbi sent some old thank-you letters from a bunch of charitable organizations that Boundless partnered with over the years."

Across my bed, I spread the letters with a variety of mastheads. "I wondered yesterday when all this arrived if he was just cleaning out his grandfather Dov's junk drawer, but now, sister dear, the plot thickens: Rabbi Ben is hoping we'll unknowingly—or knowingly—help his side of the succession fight by highlighting what these three founders originally did with Boundless."

Kitz picks up several of the letters. "Lots of these are related to affordable housing globally. But look at these—Aviation Without Borders. And receipts paying for subcontracting pilots with Médecins Sans Frontières."

"Doctors Without Borders."

"Show-off."

"It's the only French I remember."

"But aviation, Hadz? Why would they support that?"

"Will Dobbins was a navy pilot, and we just learned Dov Silverberg was trained as one in Great Britain, though he ended up not flying during the war. Makes sense they'd take an interest, right? So back then, they focused most of their efforts and money on organizations having to do with housing, and then they tossed some token amounts here and there to groups flying medicine or doctors or sick kids where they need to be."

Riffling through the thank-you letters and end-of-year statements, Kitzie cocks her head and lifts one letter from the splay. "Get a load of exactly how much they donated to Aviation Without Borders, and tell me that's token."

I let out a low whistle. "Okay, so even in Lürssen World, that's not token, you're right. Meaning . . ."

"Meaning that it feels like every time we uncover one family secret or dig up something new on these three men and on Boundless, we stumble onto a whole muddy field of more. We still don't understand how the three got so tightly connected."

I look up from the letters to meet my sister's eyes. "I'm beginning to think these families don't understand it themselves. Not the whole crazy picture, at least."

Chapter 53

Joannie

August 1944
McCook Field, Dayton, Ohio

Staggering out of the cockpit and onto the bomber's wing, Joannie turns for her backpack. She left North Carolina ten days ago, not knowing if she'd be gone two days or two weeks. Wearing the thick fur-lined flight suit for high altitudes that the WASPs have nicknamed their Brown Bear, she's already sweating now.

"So much for women needing to travel with a lot of luggage," she says to the photographer on the ground.

Grinning, he snaps several photos of her as she clambers down.

These reporters mean well, she reminds herself, but they flutter like moths around the women pilots, love taking pictures of them with their hair fixed, lipstick recently applied.

So Joannie rounds on him. "You want the real thing, mister? Here's how glamorous a pilot looks after she's flown to ten different bases in as many days. I'm trying to recall the last time I've had a shower or done anything but run fingers through my hair. Nope, can't recall."

He gives her an exaggerated wolf whistle, and she joins him in the laugh.

"Looking good to me," he offers. But something in her face makes him take a step back and add, "Can you tell my readers about your most recent flight?"

"Would they rather hear about the tropical storm near San Antonio or the winds down in San Diego? Or the engine that blew over a cornfield in Kansas? It's something else, watching a whole wing of your plane on fire and looking for a place to land that won't roast a farmer's whole crop."

The reporter opens his mouth to ask something else, then stops, gaze fixed over her left shoulder. Turning, she's startled to see an elderly man standing just behind them, face crinkling as he looks up at the bomber's left engine.

The reporter has raised his camera with its saucer-shaped flash, but the old man shakes his head. "Not today, son. No pictures."

To Joannie's surprise, the reporter doesn't protest, just obediently lowers his camera. Head bowed, he looks, in fact, as if he's about to genuflect.

Joannie holds out her hand to the old man. "Joannie DuBarry of the Women Airforce Service Pilots."

Tottering forward, the man grasps her hand in both of his rough palms. "Oh, I know, missy, I know. I've followed you girls every step of the way, all one thousand or more of you." He raises a gnarled fist. "I've rooted you on. My brother, I assure you, would be with me on this."

Joannie lets him pump her hand until he raises it to his lips, kisses it, and wheels around.

She and the reporter watch the old man limp away.

"Miss DuBarry, let me guess: you're wondering who the hell that was."

"The world's sweetest old man?"

The reporter chuckles. "Could be."

"I'm guessing there's an *and* coming?"

"One hint: *first in flight*."

Her mouth drops open. "Not . . ."

"Orville Wright in the flesh. Apparently a very big fan of yours."

∾

Back at Camp Davis, Joannie eases slowly down between the mess hall table and bench. She's just showered, but the water was frigid, no help for the searing pain in her muscles.

Not that she can say this out loud.

The boys at the next table have channeled their own complaints—their fear too—into thrusts and parries:

I peed so many times in a tube last week, I've near forgot what else to do with my pecker.

Like hell you forgot.

My legs are so sore I'll be crawling to mess come breakfast.

"Weakest is as weakest does," my mama always did say.

Your mama . . .

Sliding in beside Joannie, Marion Hanrahan whispers, "God, I'm beat." But she stops, one leg yet to be swung over the bench. A commander is hailing her from across the mess hall.

"Hanrahan! You're up next. Checking your night-flying skills."

Marion lowers her voice. "I guess it's not enough that I've been training men all day who have a boatload fewer night-flying hours than I do."

Down the table, Mabel Rawlinson speaks up. "Sir, Marion's just in from a flight and hasn't had dinner yet. I still need the night-flight check too. Permission to take her place, sir?"

"Come on then, Rawlinson. Make it snappy."

Marion collapses onto the bench. "You're a peach, Mabel. Remind me to draw you a bubble bath tonight with champagne on the side."

Mabel gathers her tin plate and cup. "Honey, you do that."

A WASP named Suzanne—though they all call her Zizi—yells out, "Remember, Mabel, trust your instruments—"

"Not your senses!" a number of the male pilots and the WASPs call back in unison, lifting their tin cups of coffee to each other and laughing.

It's one of the litanies they share, and to Joan in her exhaustion right now, it feels like a ribbon holding them together, all of them pilots, all of them like Icarus, obsessed with the freedom of flight, daring the gods every day by flying so near the sun.

∼

Joannie and the others are just finishing dinner, the clamor of the mess hall quieted to the dull buzz of mosquitoes and the chirp of crickets. When the siren goes off, all those exhausted bodies sitting slumped on their benches suddenly spring to their feet.

She can smell the low-burning fire before she can see it, and before the fuel tank explodes, sending a ravenous orange-red tongue above the tree line. Joannie is sprinting before she registers who might be in trouble.

A Jeep careens past them, men jumping out before it's come to a halt. They charge into the swamp, hacking through vines, shouting for help as they struggle to reach where the fire is licking the sky.

The stand of scrub pine hides what Joannie knows is a plane.

On a night-flying check.

As she races toward the wreck, three men emerge from the pines, two on either side of a figure whose clothes are blackened, the figure unable to walk alone.

The flight instructor.

From the other side of the stand of pines come harrowing screams.

The flight instructor collapses, sprawls on the ground. *"Get her the hell out!"*

Chapter 54

Will

His hands tremble so violently sometimes these days he has to thrust them in his pockets to still them. Like the captain, he's supposed to be a center of calm, an eye of the storm on the *Enterprise*. He's the one who tells the pilots which of the planes hurtling toward them are the enemy and which aren't. It's on his shoulders if the pilots shoot down their own brothers or let a Zero through that will destroy this whole ship, send three thousand men to the bottom of the Philippine Sea.

Will has aged four decades, it feels to him, in this past year.

He'll be back on duty too early tomorrow, and he should grab every moment of sleep he can. But right now, he wants to close out the letter he's tried to finish for days. It's full of simple, unemotional facts, including the chow that comes from the galley: lots of chipped beef, bean soup, powdered eggs, and beef tough as shoe leather, though he doesn't mention the toughness.

He tells Joan of the poker they play during off hours. Will is good at the game, probably because no one expects subterfuge behind his sweet farm-boy face, blinking with good-natured surprise as he scoops another pile of bills from the table.

"Parting—with one's dough—is such sweet sorrow," he tells them. "My apologies, fellas." His politeness, he knows, and his grin invite the other players to throw cigarette stubs and wet socks at his head.

He wants to write Joan of the terror he feels snake around him when he thinks of the lives he's responsible for.

He wants to ask the truth of her own days, what it's like to be one of a handful of women in these camps of men, if she's frightened or confused flying so many different sorts of planes, each with its different controls and instrument panels.

He wants to ask her if she, too, ever dreams of witnessing a death of a friend. Or has premonitions of one.

Even as he's thinking these dark god-awful thoughts, Will sees the cameraman sprint past—never a good sign, Lord have mercy. Every pilot and crew member knows a cameraman popping up on the flight deck means the conditions are dismal for a good landing, thanks to rough waters or a damaged plane or injured pilot—or just a wavering, unsteady flight path.

It's not Will's shift, but on instinct, he races up to the flight deck, arriving just behind the cameraman—and just in time to see a wobbling Hellcat descending too steeply, the carrier *Enterprise* convulsing in a choppy sea. Cursing, the signalman thrusts up his red paddles, warning the pilot to circle, and the pilot pulls up at the last moment, whooshing over the flight deck so low the crew drops to the deck's timber boards.

On the Hellcat's second attempt, the plane's tailhook misses the first of the several arresting cables that should stop its forward motion, then the second, the craft hurtling toward the end of the carrier's runway. Only the final cable engages the tailhook, and even that one threatens to tear loose and send the Hellcat plunging into the sea.

"Holy damn," the cameraman mutters beside Will. "I was thinking for sure I had another film here the brass'd use to teach trainer pilots what not to do." He wipes his brow, so beaded in sweat he looks like he's just emerged from a shower.

The pilot that leverages himself out of the cockpit is slightly built and pale, with dark circles under his eyes and a gaunt, haunted look. Will's seen that look to a pilot before, and it's a heck of a bad sign, Lord knows. The pilot's seen too much, been through too much, able to climb back into a cockpit again and again only by sheer grit.

"William Shakespeare Dobbins."

Startled near to tripping over his own feet, Will takes a minute to recognize the pilot as Joannie's twin brother.

"Well, Lord have mercy, Sammy DuBarry!"

They take a picture together, the cameraman—elated not to be filming another drowned pilot—snapping it for them. Will hopes to send the picture to Joan after it's developed.

For now, though, he'll mention getting to see Sam but nothing about his gauntness.

Lying is a sin, Will knows. *But is withholding truth—if it's god-awful painful—just a kissing cousin of lying, or is it mercy?*

Big news: Sam landed his Hellcat on the Big E yesterday. What are the durn chances?

Hands shaking worse than ever, Will closes the letter with the words he always includes.

With love that's way beyond the boundless sea,

Will

Chapter 55

Joannie

August 1944
Camp Davis, North Carolina

Weeping, the flight instructor rolls to one side as the screams from the wreck increase in anguish.

Then stop altogether.

Surrounded by North Carolina marsh, the steel skeleton of the plane sits sizzling, doused in the water the fire brigade hoses onto it.

The rescue squad has staggered back from the wreckage, themselves covered in soot.

Into the silence comes a string of obscenities—with a Texas accent. Joannie doesn't need to turn to know it's the mechanic standing near her shoulder.

"*Damn* it." Buck's voice catches as he keeps himself from crying by launching into another barrage of curses, all tangled up with prayers, heart wrenching and hoarse.

She doesn't turn to look at him. She can't.

"You hadn't fixed it yet."

She didn't mean it as an accusation, but he jerks back as if she's stuck a glowing cattle prod into his gut.

"Wasn't next in line of urgent, not when whole engines caught fire this week, not when two tires blew on the runway just today. Hell, that A-24 shouldn't have gone up again yet. Not if anybody checked the damn form for repairs!"

Broken latch, she'd scribbled on the Form One. She hears the words echo now in her own head. *On the inside of the cockpit, pilot's side.*

She'd starred that line. Circled it, even.

Not that anyone bothered to check the form.

To Joannie's left, Marion Hanrahan is hunched, a huddle of the other women pilots holding her up, letting her pour the words out, over and over again.

"It should've been me. I was up next. It should've been me . . ."

The keening, Joannie thinks, *of someone who will never get over what she's just seen.*

None of us ever will.

Buck's stream of words has dried up into agonized quiet, but his silence is worse.

Joannie wants to ask him to start up again, the more roiling the better, the pain and rage his words carried helping somehow. But she finds she can't speak.

Now the fullback heft of the man suddenly leans into Joannie like a little boy huddling against his mother, and she finds she can't hate him for the broken latch.

She needs to blame someone, though. She feels the burn in her chest of hate: For Hitler and the Japanese emperor Hirohito, for every kamikaze pilot, every panzer crew. Hate for the SS and for Himmler and for the U-boats. Hate for every German alive, including every POW. Hate. How good it feels, the burn of it. The kind that feels like it's the only thing keeping you alive.

The kind, too, that will destroy your insides.

Buck leans harder into her, his weight almost crushing.

Dizzy and numb and nauseous, Joannie rests a hand on his back and lets him heave.

~

Buck doesn't quit retching for some time. When he does, his face twists into an expression of such pain, Joannie decides she prefers the stench of vomit and his convulsing back.

She can pick out strands of the conversation from the women pilots behind her.

More than three dozen deaths of a WASP.

Every few days we get word of another.

Don't value our lives.

No different for those poor boys getting sent overseas.

One of them clears her throat and begins slowly, tearfully, quoting the WASP slogan. Linking arms, others join in:

We live in the wind and sand, and our eyes are on the stars.

Joan's hand still on Buck's back, she hesitates to join them.

Straightening and wiping his mouth with the sleeve of his coveralls, he doesn't meet her eye, no swagger left in his voice. "I thank you."

Joan is about to respond, when a shadow falls across their path, the fire still burning through the scrub pines behind them.

"DuBarry!"

Joan and Buck both turn.

It's a corporal she's seen around Camp Davis but doesn't know. She salutes, though weariness and the words of her friends make it hard to lift her arm.

More than three dozen deaths of a WASP.

Every few days we get word of another.

Don't value our lives.

"DuBarry, you're wanted in Major Stephenson's office here pronto, and Colonel Tibbett's office in Alamogordo, New Mexico, day after tomorrow, oh eight hundred hours. Something about the B-29. Publicity for the new plane. You'll leave tomorrow." He stops there, eyes darting to the mechanic. "Strictly confidential."

Apparently, the corporal had forgotten about that last piece of instruction.

Not waiting for her acknowledgment, he pivots away, then turns back. "Possibly not what anyone wants to hear tonight. Can't be helped. The timing's . . . not ideal."

Buck rubs his temples as the corporal stalks away. "Aw, *hell*. This new plane, the B-29. You know about it?"

Joan shakes her head. "Only that it's the biggest of the bombers with longer range."

"Bad habit of catching fire on the runway. Best test pilot in the country just died in one. If Tibbetts wants you to pilot the damn thing, you tell him *hell* no."

"Because the Army Air Force loves it when its pilots, especially its girl pilots, say no."

The mechanic slings an arm over Joan's shoulder as the two stumble back toward the barracks. "'*The timing's not ideal*,' that little corporal said—said it while the smoke's still pouring from the wreck that took a life that shouldn't have been lost. Well, hell. How's that for just the tip of the bull's horn in your gut?"

Chapter 56
Hans

August 1944
St. Simons Island, Georgia

Hans can see the war still on their faces and sometimes in the way their hands shake—at least the men who've seen Death at close range—had a buddy blown up right beside them or seen most of their own unit incinerated. War has left its mark on them: the face muscles more hardened, but also twitching sometimes. The eyes both steelier and constantly darting. The hands sometimes shaking so hard that tying boots is a challenge.

Back at Camp Stewart—where their detachment of POWs rises at 5:30 a.m., roused by their own German officers—a small cracked mirror hangs for the men to use while shaving, but Hans shaves only by feel. He knows Death must have disfigured his face too. He does not want to see.

Today they've finished serving—pork cooked to harness leather again—the Allied officers and stand waiting in five straight lines for their transport back to the camp. Because he loves Goethe and because he's been marked as one of those not loyal to the Führer—rumors also continue to circulate that he was a deserter—Hans has turned slightly away from his unit, eyes fixed on his book.

So he does not see the Englishman approach.

"Entschuldigung, bitte, was lesen Sie da?"

Hans is startled first by the respect in tone, even the form of address, then only after a full beat by the fact that the British officer is speaking German.

Holding up the volume, its binding held together only by threads, Hans says in English, "From the camp. There is the collection of the books—a library, yes?—for us. *Die Leiden des jungen Werther* is this one. *The Sorrows of Young Werther*, as you may know it."

The Brit shifts to English as well. "Well, then. Splendid. We must discuss it."

"You have read this?"

"It's the only book by Goethe I have read, if you must know. Cambridge would be aghast to learn one of its graduates has not read *Faust*. The Shakespeare of Germany, we call him."

"The Goethe of England, we call Shakespeare," Hans returns, and the Englishman laughs.

"Touché."

"There was the man here, American, who had in his name the *Shakespeare*, yes?"

The Englishman's face goes somber. "Indeed. William Shakespeare Dobbins. A smashing good man, yes. A good friend, as well."

"He was not here when I come . . . *came*. But the other men—other prisoners—speak of this man that he was . . . always kind. Always of the humor."

The Englishman nods, though his gaze swings from Hans to focus on the sea, where the setting sun is turning the sky a blazing red. His tone goes as soft as the sky has gone molten.

"Indeed, yes. Always kind. Not a man whose trust one would want to betray. Ever."

Chapter 57

Joannie

August 1944
Alamogordo, New Mexico

"Catching on fire," Joannie repeats back to the colonel. She's trying to focus on his jaw, on the stubble glistening there, not on the memory of Mabel's screams from the blazing wreckage.

"The Superfortress has its . . . quirks, yes. Five crashes in two days, and a fire extinguishing system that fails to put out the fires eighty-five percent of the time."

"Which is why you want two women to fly it?"

"Precisely. That is . . . hell, not when you put it like that. Clearly, I need to line out our dilemma here."

Joan's WASP skirt suit is stiff wool, and she hopes she can keep her face as stiff, the tumult of emotion she's feeling right now pressed flat.

"Five hundred of these new bombers were ordered before the test flights were completed. Blame Hitler if you'd like for the need to blow safety protocol all to hell. For the record, I don't consider your female lives any more dispensable than our male pilots."

She decides against pointing out that when a WASP is killed in service of her country, the US government doesn't pay for the flag or the funeral or even to have the body shipped home. "Have you determined, sir, if the cause could be the magnesium alloy engine components used to save weight?"

His head snaps back. "How the *hell'd* you know that, DuBarry? Not sure the Pentagon brass even do at this point."

It occurs to her now, too late, that she could get the mechanic at Camp Davis in trouble for repeating the rumblings from men who know these engines.

Colonel Tibbets saves her by firing another question. "They tell me, DuBarry, you've got guts in addition to skill. Who taught you to fly?"

"My brother, sir. On a crash-landed heap of an abandoned Gee Bee we—mostly he—rebuilt."

"Taught his sister to fly. Holy Mother of God, I need a cigarette." The colonel skirts to his desk, finds a Marlboro, and lights up. "Between you and me, DuBarry, most of the damn time I wonder what the hell I'm doing allowing women in the cockpits of my bombers. Except for the other moments when I wonder why the hell we don't let girl pilots help us out more with this damn war if they're willing."

The colonel surveys her as he might a plane, wing tip to wing tip. "You must be, what, all of five foot two? How the hell do you reach the rudder pedals?"

Before she can answer, he holds up a hand. "Don't answer that. I don't want to know. The instructors who've worked with you assure me you're as good as the regular pilots—the real ones."

She arches an eyebrow at this, but the colonel doesn't appear to hear the irony in asking a pilot who's not *real* to fly one of his valuable, flammable new bombers.

"DuBarry, I'll level with you, since I'm expecting you to fly a plane that, yeah, has some flaws."

"Like catching on fire before takeoff."

"Like that, yeah." He slows, as if she might have trouble keeping up. "The B-29 Superfortress flies longer range. Its bays hold more bombs.

291

If we want to end the carnage, we *will* put it into service, fully tested or not."

"I understand."

"The *hell* you do." The words come out in a blast, as if she's knocked loose the cap of a fire hydrant. "You have no idea what it's like to send men up in machines that can save hundreds of thousands of lives but also can potentially leave their mothers childless because we didn't have the damn luxury of the damn time we needed to work out the kinks. Those lives are *in my hands*, DuBarry. *On my conscience.*"

This time, she says nothing.

"Meanwhile, thanks to recent reports on the new bomber, I have pilots—former high school quarterbacks, college wrestling champions—letting it be known they'll refuse to fly the B-29."

He squares off at her, fists on his hips. "Obviously, women think emotionally, and men logically."

She opens her mouth, but he's not asking a question.

"So, let's see if you can intuit what I'm logically thinking."

"That if one of those infamous new B-29s flies into a base where your finest pilots are gathered around, what will all those former quarterbacks think when two women pop out of the cockpit?"

"Exactly. Imagine how embarrassed they'll feel if two dizzy broads can handle the thing."

If, Joannie thinks, bristling, *the two dizzy broads don't go down in flames first.*

"I'm assigning you a copilot, DuBarry."

"In place of a crew of ten," she says. Not a challenge—a fact. She's done her research.

"Exactly. It's not math for the pretty, if you know what I mean. Do yourself and your country a favor, DuBarry. The two of you dames read the manual."

"Sir?"

"Boeing tells me it's important to read the damn manual thoroughly on this one. Don't just rely on experience with other planes.

Don't stay on the runway for every last check like usual. The longer you stay on the runway, the greater the chance of fire. Get it up in the air, and fast. Boeing's had the gall to imply some of our pilots who've died in testing didn't read the manual, not thoroughly. Which, hell, could be true. Us pilots tend to be a . . . confident sort."

His eyes narrow, brows drawing together. "Maybe also a characteristic of *girl* pilots? By the way, I know how you females gab. This is strictly classified. I'm speaking with your copilot later today. Dismissed. Wait, something else crucial."

She's already begun turning but now pivots back and waits.

"Wear makeup."

"*Sir?*"

"Also do up your hair—whatever it is dames do. Lots of sex appeal. Just look the part."

"The part of a *pilot*, sir?"

"Ask Jackie Cochran. She'll tell you the importance of this mission: to fly the damn B-29 *perfectly*—and to wear some damn lipstick. The press has got to want to run this story. A final question for you, DuBarry."

"Sir?"

"The truth. Are you frightened of this mission?"

"My brother and several close friends are risking their lives every day for the cause. I want to do my part."

He leans down into her face. "What I asked you, DuBarry, was *Are you frightened of this?*"

"Let's just say, sir, I'll read the manual. Every line."

For all its being the heaviest bomber ever to take to the skies, the wind buffets the Superfortress so suddenly, Joan feels sure she's left her teeth ten thousand feet up, her whole body aching with the strain. The cloud cover is so thick and the day so long, she could easily be convinced she's flying over Tahiti by now, except for the readings on the instruments.

Trust your instruments, Joan can almost hear Zizi call across the mess hall, *not your senses!*

Despite her exhaustion, she loves this freedom, this sailing through clouds. Even with the pressure they're under, even with all that's at stake, she is peculiarly thrilled.

It's what's always made her feel odd, that she's happiest when she's at one with the air currents, the gentle curve of the earth, in watching the cotton-candy-spinning of cumulous clouds and the cauldron-stirring of cumulonimbus all around—the absolute joy of flight.

"Prepare for descent," she says. The truth is, she can barely hear herself speak, the roar of the engines deafening, despite the headsets.

"Preparing for descent," her copilot returns.

Sending the bomber gently down, she can feel the big plane shudder in another crosswind. As they drop below the clouds, Joannie banks left to line up with where the airfield should be.

There, just below, she sees dark blobs, shifting and moving.

"Well now," says Joannie's copilot, Annie, a six-foot-tall brunette who grew up on a farm in Iowa.

"As graceful in the air," the colonel described her, "as she is a klutz on the ground. Damn giraffe at a cocktail party, they say."

In fact, this giraffe is one of the most highly skilled of the WASPs— and fearless. She has more flight hours, and Joan tries not to think about why she herself was chosen as pilot. She tries not to hear the colonel's voice in her head: *Sex appeal. Just look the part.*

Annie peers down at the airfield. "That's more men than we got corn stalks in fall."

Annie's right. Hordes of men, all staring upward, crowd the runways, as if daring the Superfortress to land.

The plane bucks again in the turbulence, and Joan feels her back seize up with the tension.

"As graceful in the air," Joan blurts out now, "as anyone he's ever seen. That's what the colonel said about you." She omits the rest of what the colonel said.

"Well, I'll be a pickle in brine. He said that about me?"

"He did." It's not a lie, only an edit.

Joan's ending this flight with a kind word feels like a tribute to her brother, who never landed a plane without some gift of a few words. Maybe it was to acknowledge the real possibility of cracking up each time, the specter of mortality.

Better to end life with a kindness.

Annie is beaming as she peers at the instrument panel, then down at the field below.

"Ready?" Joan asks.

"To knock their sweet, saggy socks off," comes the reply.

As Annie's fingers run over the instrument panel, she murmurs one of the tunes they sang during training in Sweetwater: *I'm a flying wreck, a-risking my neck, and a helluva pilot too . . .*

Joan lowers the landing gear. The air currents knock the bomber about, but she holds it on course.

Steady now.

The plane's body glides parallel with the runway, then eases down.

Braking is Joannie's least favorite part.

Send me thirty thousand feet in the air, and I'm fine. Just don't make me have to trust brakes and wing flaps on land.

In her head she hears Buck, the only other person at Camp Davis who knew about today's flight.

"Wish to hell I could be there to see you two pop out like two dames from a big cake."

"We won't be wearing showgirl sequins, if that's what you're picturing." She'd kissed him on the cheek. "Thanks for rooting for us."

So now here they are, in the final few inches of descent, wheels almost making contact . . . and down.

Holding her breath, she angles the wing flaps up and waits for the brakes to engage.

They do not.

But then a screech of metal as the brakes make contact. The thrust of the heavy plane protests, the giant silver bird shuddering as it glides to a halt.

"As graceful as they've ever seen!" Annie crows. "You did it, Joan!"

"*We* did it." Joan is too exhausted to say anything more, much less stand.

Unbuckled, Annie pulls her long legs up under her. "Ready for our grand entrance?"

Joan imagines the two of them dressed in showgirl sequins leaping out from the cockpit, and the image, along with the laugh that gurgles up in her chest, lifts her out of her seat. Her legs are shaking so badly she's sure the men gathered below will see.

What if I collapse right there on the runway? Dear God, the colonel will have me tossed into the New Mexican desert.

"Wait!" Annie puts a hand on her arm. "Remember what we promised Jackie Cochran and Colonel Tibbetts we'd do."

Joan rolls her eyes but pauses to apply lipstick.

Headgear and goggles still on, they climb out of the massive plane through the hatch in the nose wheel well and drop from the lower rungs of the ladder to the ground.

My legs. They are absolutely going to give way.

But Joannie musters her strength and stands alongside her copilot. With their helmets, goggles, and flight suits—and from this many feet back—they could easily be mistaken for men, except for the red lipstick, which most of the spectators aren't close enough to notice.

The pilots applaud—though most of them grudgingly, Joannie can see. By now, they would've all heard the stories of the B-29's being too much of a bear to handle well in the air, its penchant for catching fire.

Who could blame them? Joan thinks.

Together, walking out from under the shadow of the B-29, Joan and Annie remove their headgear, waves of hair tumbling out from under the leather.

Going silent, the men stand gaping, the hands that were clapping dropping loose to their sides or freezing in place.

"Like they've just seen two poodles fly a wheelbarrow in," Joan murmurs to her copilot. At least, she thinks she says this out loud, her hearing still dulled nearly to useless by the engines.

In those ticks of silence, Joannie thinks she detects real fear on the faces of several men.

These fellows, it hits her all over again, *not only have to put this flawed hunk of steel in the air; they have to fly it loaded with bombs and a whole crew through storms of antiaircraft guns and swarms of diving German Messerschmitts and Japanese Zeros.*

In the next instant, she wonders if she's done a good thing, being part of this show.

I know your jobs will be harder, she wants to say to the silent, staring crowd of men. *So many thousands of times more terrifying.*

But now one of them starts clapping. Another whoops. Now both sides of the runway erupt in cheers.

"I'm a flying wreck, a-risking my neck . . . ," Annie sings.

"And a helluva pilot too," Joannie finishes. They hug each other as the men, grinning and slapping each other on the back, surge toward them to shake hands.

～

For Joan, the return to Camp Davis was nothing but blur. Even the slaps on the back from her fellow pilots here, the steely glower from Major Stephenson: nothing but blur for a full day or two.

Being back in North Carolina at Camp Davis with its sweltering heat and mosquitoes, even now in mid-September, only feels like a relief because the mission is over—and because there's a new sense of elation among all the pilots, including the WASPs. In the wake of D-day, there'd been good news lately from the European front, if not as much from the Pacific.

Joan is just stretching out of sleep, just thinking she should rise before reveille and write Pops again today, when the door to her bay creaks.

"Hey, Georgia, you awake?"

Eyes still closed, Joan props herself on one elbow. "Mmph" is all she manages.

"Remind me the name of that island of yours. St. something, maybe?" The voice comes from Hazel Lee, one of only two Chinese American WASPs. Hazel can do aileron rolls, loops, and spins in a Hellcat five thousand feet off the ground with the ease of a child doing a somersault. She also keeps her bay mates in stitches with her imitations of the Camp Davis officers who despise the WASP and with her stories, which she tries to make funny but aren't, of farmers and villagers in places she's landed a plane, mistaking her for Japanese and coming after her with pitchforks and bats.

Reluctantly, Joan opens one eye. "St. Simons."

The two bay mates standing with Hazel exchange glances.

"What?" Joan sits all the way up. "What's happened?"

"It's nothing much." Hazel clutches a newspaper to her chest.

"You may as well tell her the truth," one of the bay mates murmurs. "Don't know as I'd call a hurricane nothing much."

Shakily, Joannie stands. "Tell me."

Chapter 58

Hadley

My sister is shaking her head as she scrolls through images on her laptop of St. Simons in 1944. "Like these poor folks needed a hurricane on top of all their worries over the war. Oh my."

Kitz arranges her face in that way she does when she's trying not to appear obvious. "So. Any word from our friendly neighborhood commodore since the drinks and then your finding out he's Hessler's son and now your refusing to take his calls and stiff-arming him every time he tries an approach?"

I don't meet her eye, which she'll understand in Siblingese means to leave the subject the heck alone. "Doesn't really matter what he has to say at this point, does it? I don't trust him."

"Although, Hadz, to be fair, you do always find a reason not to trust a guy."

"This one earned the stiff-arm by lying. Case closed."

Kitz opens her mouth but, at two sharp shakes of my head, only mutters, "I still think you could at least hear him out."

I pretend not to hear.

My email inbox includes a polite message from Will Dobbins, of all people, letting Storied Events know he and his great-niece Cordelia—*the Cordelia, no doubt, whose all-important call Nick took in the midst of our talk on the beach*—will arrive late Friday evening due to a conflict she has. Will Dobbins apologizes for having to check in after the official start time of the reunion.

Composing a coherent email at his age, I think, impressed—although, come to think of it, the message was likely handled by the assistant copied on it. Even with his being impaired by dementia, I'm looking forward to meeting him most at the reunion.

And, come to think of it, my impression of his impaired mental state comes from Richard Silverberg. Speaking of people who've not earned my trust.

Even when Kitz has a rough day physically, she continues working through her to-do list from the hotel suite, and she has now enlisted the help of every high school theater kid in the county to come build World War II sets at the King and Prince. With Kitz weaker and more wobbly, though, and still insisting she's fine, I feel as if I'm functioning like a machine with a blown engine.

It's only now as my sister's head drops to her pillow in sleep that I lean back and breathe. The air smells of salt and something sweet, maybe jasmine. Rising to stand at the balcony rail, I let the sound of the waves, their splashing and sucking and sifting below, wash out the fuzz from my brain for a few moments.

My heart rate is just beginning to drop when a text dings on my phone.

Nick Adams.

Can we talk? Please?

I consider several answers, none of which strike the right tone—distant and noncommittal without being too icy or vengeful—so I send none of them.

Back to sifting through the cache of old photos Ben Silverberg sent, I stop at the baby pictures of Dov Silverberg's children, Beatrice and Edmund. Bea and Eddy, they're called in the captions. Sorting through,

I watch two adorable kids learn to walk and ride ponies and swim and play violin. A smiling group gathers around Eddy at his bar mitzvah.

Under the photos, I find photocopies of mid- and late 1940s documents from a couple of United Nations organizations, the International Refugee Organization and the International Tracing Service, which, I learn from a quick internet search, was the group working to track down children who were orphaned or displaced by the Holocaust.

For the next hour, I go down a rabbit hole, reading about the struggle to locate the families or at least the stories of these children, many of whom were too young to speak when they went into hiding, or children taken in by a neighbor or relative who was then killed or imprisoned themselves. For Eddy, there's a heart-wrenching paper trail of displaced-persons camps and foster homes, ending finally—happily—in adoption by the Silverbergs, cousins of his parents, who'd died. Murdered by the Third Reich. For Bea, there is no official documentation of time in a camp or foster home, but she apparently shares one key category with Eddy: war orphan who joined a loving home.

How much, I wonder, *did these beautiful children know about their horrific origin stories?*

There's Dov with his two kids, his arms around his wife. He's dashing as ever, bits of gray appearing at his temples: the devoted husband and father and community leader.

Dov Silverberg, at least, doesn't seem likely to be the one referred to as *Traitor* on the back of the photo we've posted on our hotel suite mirror.

At the bottom of the stack are two pictures that especially catch my attention, one each of Bea and Eddy as adults, each with their family. Eddy had three children, and I can read their names on the back. Bea appears only to have had one, a little girl. Bea's husband—I assume that's who he is—stands behind her with his hands on her shoulders.

Protectively, I think. Tenderly.

On the back of this picture, someone has scrawled,

Just before our move to C'ton and Mum's passing.

So probably written by Bea's daughter, Deborah and Dov's granddaughter.

My heart hurts for that little girl, losing her mother. I know the gutting of that loss.

From her bed, Kitz stirs. "Wha's up, Hadz?"

"Nothing." My tone sounds unconvincing even to me.

"You are *such* a hopeless liar, Hadley Jacks." Kitz rolls toward me. "Really. What's up?"

"Just thinking about how families come to be."

"And?"

"And get torn apart."

"Like ours," she says. Not pitifully, just a fact.

"Like ours," I agree. I hand the stack of photos and United Nations documents to Kitz, who goes quiet.

"What is it?" I ask.

"Nothing."

"You're an even worse liar than I am."

She stares at the picture of Bea with her little family, snow in the background. A sleek, stylish woman, Beatrice sits wearing fur-trimmed boots and a cherry red, perfectly fitting parka. Her hands rest in her lap, one in a green glove and the other in a red.

The nonmatching gloves strike me as odd, given how fashionable Bea appears, but maybe the photo was taken at Christmas when wearing one red and one green was all the rage in "C'ton," wherever that is, or maybe Bea lost one of each.

"Don't you wonder," Kitz muses aloud, "what it's like to have so many family photos, you can mail a stack off to strangers and not stress if you don't get them back?"

But I'm still staring at the photo.

"They look happy," Kitz says.

"Who?"

She scrunches her face at me. "Aren't we both looking at the same photograph here? Seriously, what's on your mind?"

"It's just a thought I had. Never mind. Probably nothing at all."

Kitzie's gaze lifts to meet mine. "Hadley, there's something else. About that cold of mine."

My heart drops—at her expression, at her tone, at the formal way she's pronouncing my whole name. "That wasn't just a cold?" Deep in my gut, I've known it wasn't true, this flimsy *only a cold* explanation, and also, even more fervently, I've believed in the lie that made everything okay.

"Look, that was what Lindy was calling about last week. Hadz, I didn't want you to worry—especially before I knew for sure. You know how ferocious you are. No off switch to you at all."

I feel as if I'm watching her form words from a great distance.

Maybe, I think, *maybe if I don't actually hear her, whatever she has to say won't be real.*

"Hadz, this was why I wanted to take this job so badly, in case we're looking at big medical bills."

I open my mouth but find I can't speak. Lowering myself to the edge of the bed, I try again. "I think you'd better tell me fast."

"The doctors had to rule out a whole bunch of things that can mimic multiple sclerosis. But now, between the MRI and the analysis of the spinal fluid, my lack of coordination, all my symptoms lately, they're finally in agreement."

"That it's . . ." I can't bring myself to say the words. To me, the disease she just named—about which I know next to nothing—is a death sentence. With a cruel and grueling paralysis first.

My symptoms lately.

I see all over again Kitz collapsing by the pool, her fatigue, her bumping into doorframes, her squinting at pictures and letters.

I should've pushed harder for more tests sooner. I should've put the pieces together myself.

She's rattling off something about prognosis and current treatments for living with multiple sclerosis, but I'm hearing it all through what feels like layers of fleece wrapping my head. I can barely hear, and what I do hear won't process in my brain.

It's my job to see the bad thing coming before it can hurt us. This is my fault.

Guilt has me nearly doubled over as I hunch down on the bed.

Kitz stomps the five strides that bring her directly in front of me, and she places a hand—not gently—on each of my shoulders. "So here's the thing, Hadz. You've always been the strong one while I'm the sweet one. First, it's time I said I find that annoying as hell. I don't want to be known as just sweet, like I've got a candy cane for a spine."

I blink dumbly up at my sister.

"Second, we're *both* going to be the strong one from here on out. You're going to support me in all the exercise to get strength back in my muscles, all the therapy, all the research on all medications they're recommending and why—a number of oral and injectable options that help manage flare-ups. And me, I'm going to be ferociously hopeful."

Rising unsteadily, I put my arms around my sister.

Questions. Fears. I have so many of both. But that's not what she needs from me in this moment.

I try to echo her perky tone, but my voice splinters. "I'm scared, Kitz."

Shaking her head, Kitzie pushes me out of the hug just enough to swat at the tears that are streaming down my cheeks.

"You're going to have to do better than this, Big Sister," she whispers. Crooking her arm around my neck, she pulls my head down to kiss the top of it like I'm four.

"Ferociously . . . ferociously hopeful," I manage, more clearly this time, but the tears keep flooding down my face as my sister wipes them away.

"Don't be scared," she whispers close to my ear. "I've got you."

Chapter 59
Joannie

September 1944
Camp Davis, North Carolina

"There's no point in hiding it from her," one of the bay mates insists to the other, then turns back to Joan. "It's only that the storm hit pretty hard, seems like, on the Georgia coast. Headed toward Jersey now, which is why I'm keeping track. But maybe it just knocked over a few palm trees on your sweet island."

Joan doesn't bother explaining that palms are the last thing to topple, that seeing them bent nearly double in a battering wind, then surviving, is a lesson in life. But the rest of the island . . .

Dov.

If something has happened to Dov Silverberg, the navy would contact his next of kin in London, not Joan, just some woman he danced with and laughed with and at some moments looked as if he were falling in love with.

Guilt stabs at her insides for how quickly her mind flicked to him. Even before her father.

Pops. Dear God, how frightened and confused Pops must've been in the storm.

Like a kick to her gut, she's missing her father—both the man he was before and the man he is now—so much it hurts.

Sliding into her flight suit, she hasn't even finished belting it when a fist knocks once firmly, but then again gently—barely a tap—on the barracks door.

Joan knows by the tentativeness of the knock that bad news is being delivered. A whole world at war means Death is as close stitched to Joan's everyday life as her own shadow.

While she steadies herself on the wall, her bay mates dive for their own clothes.

A moment later, the barracks door flung open, Buck Austin stands there clutching a rectangle of paper, his head down. Texans, she's learned, walk through life with their heads up, chests out. This cannot be good.

"I asked to be the one to bring you this, Joannie." It's the first time he's used her actual name.

It may have nothing to do with the hurricane.

Oh, God, it could be Sam.

Or Will.

Joan reaches for it.

Her bay mates and Buck all watch while she tears open the telegram.

Joan's eyes are less steady than her hands, taking a good three times reading the lines to make sense of the ink that her mind will only allow to be sticks and squiggles, not words. She reads the lines yet again.

Mr. Gray from the drugstore has sent it. This is the first punch she feels—that perhaps she has no family left on the island to tell her this news.

Joan looks up from the telegram. Buck is speaking, his arm around her shoulders. Her brain, though, is a machine out of whack, its gears whirring but disconnected.

"Major says to . . . in his office. Plane to ferry, so flying . . . back home for two days."

She forces her eyes over the words again.

STORM HIT BAD. TREE DOWN. HOUSE &
TERRENCE DIDN'T MAKE IT.
RECTOR SAYS CAN DELAY FUNERAL IF
YOU CAN GET HOME.

Telegrams are especially cruel that way, cutting in their brevity. A letter, even one on flimsy airmail paper, can hold an abundance of words to pad and swaddle the knife points of loss. A telegram just lays it out bare, all its lethal edges to slice and wound.

So much left out.

Oh, God. She'd thought first of Dov's safety, before her own father's.

Pops.

Did he suffer? Was he pinned under some heavy beam and died in horrible pain?

All she can picture is the three of them, Sam, Pops and her, in the top hat, boater hat, and straw hat sitting down to high tea made out of a measly excuse for a meal, the three of them with their pinkies out, making royalty out of poverty.

Pops at the kitchen table alone, waiting up every night for their mom.

Unspeaking, she follows Buck to the door.

One of her bay mates throws her arms around Joan. "We're here for you, Georgia."

HOUSE AND TERRENCE DIDN'T MAKE IT.

Those words clang and grate inside her head. She's grateful for the rhythm of Buck's legs, her own feet having forgotten the skill of walking.

"I'm real sorry," he says, gruffly, "for your loss."

Outside Major Stephenson's office, she stands at attention. For once, she's oddly grateful to be waiting for orders. Her mind is spinning, stuck heavily in the wet sand of that last word, *loss.*

Your loss.

And what about Sam? Somewhere in the Pacific, will he even learn this news for months?

Her gut twists.

Joan doesn't cry in the major's office. For the sake of the other women pilots, she cannot let him see her shed tears that might—to him—show weakness.

Her hand remains steady when she shakes his. Her voice stays calm when she accepts his offer to ride in the ferried plane, then take a bus from there to her home. "Yes, sir."

Buck is waiting with her, concern crumpling his broad forehead.

Broad for holding up a Stetson, she thinks, in that disjointed, jerking way of new grief.

"I never, *never* should have left Pops" is what bursts out instead, before a wave of nausea knocks her sideways.

She staggers alone a few feet into a stand of scrub pine beside the Quonset hut, where she vomits and vomits and vomits onto the roots.

Chapter 60

Hans

September 1944

So much guilt,

Hans's mother has written with painstaking wording,

is what our village goatherd Bernhard says he bears. The bells on the goats, the usual forms of protection, none of this did any good. He fell asleep, he says, as night fell— precisely when he should have been on alert for the wolves. He did not, he says, raise his voice soon enough so the whole village would know.

When at last he did raise his voice, few of us ran to help. You recall how we said to each other we had no problem with wolves here.

Now our goatherd has traveled away. Only now do we under-stand how bereft we are without him, and with so many goats gone missing.

Hans understands what she means him to read: Father Bernhard, racked with guilt, finally spoke out.

And has now disappeared.

Caring nothing for what the prisoners near him might think, Hans sinks to his cot and buries his face in his hands.

Chapter 61

Joannie

September 15, 1944
St. Simons Island, Georgia

I should never, never have left Pops to go fly.

Walking parallel to the surf, she cannot quit hearing those words in each splash of each wave. Joan lets the water wash over her feet and soak the rolled-up cuffs of the flight coveralls she wore on the ferried plane and on the bus. Having packed little more than a hairbrush and a black pencil skirt for the funeral, she's wearing her only option for doing what has to be done.

She's nearing her family's cottage.

Whatever is left of the cottage, that is.

Desperately, she wishes Sam could be here with her for this.

Sam, who'd always been able to make Mama laugh, even on her worst days of confusion, pain, or weariness. Sam, who'd known just how to handle Pops in his grief.

From several yards away, Joan sees what look like parts of London since the Blitz. Chunks of three walls stand snaggletoothed in the near dark, and a moss-clad piece of roof hangs sickly by a thread of siding, like an infection that needs pulling free. Through its middle is the fallen pine that took down the house.

Joan knows walking into the rubble is foolish, but she feels her mother's presence is there, and her father's—back when he helicopter-twirled Sam and her in the front yard until they giggled so hard they couldn't breathe. Sam's presence, too, she feels: Sam across the room, every night asking big philosophical questions of life just as she was nodding off.

"How come kind and gentle people like Mama can get awful sick, and be in so much pain, but a guy like Stalin can wipe out a million or more of his own people and hasn't got so much as a toothache? How's that God running the world fair?"

"Go to sleep, Sammy."

"Why do you reckon it is Marshall's smarter'n you and me both—"

"Go to sleep, Sam."

"But he's got to walk hisself way over to Harrington . . ."

"To sleep, Sam."

"A one-room schoolhouse that can't hardly afford chalk."

"Pops!" She would finally call to the next room. *"Make Sammy be quiet!"*

Looking back, even that ritual feels sacred.

The rubble of the cottage calls to her now, as if the spirit of a once-happy, once-whole family breathes there, arms open, waiting for her to come home.

The tabby steps, made like so much on this island of the lime from burned oyster shells, ash, water, sand, and other shells, hold her weight as she mounts the porch, enough of its wide planks still intact that she can pick her way toward the kitchen. Only part of the staircase remains, leading up to the two tiny bedrooms on either side of the landing.

"I shouldn't," she says out loud.

With the handrail and all the skinny wood pilasters gone, she climbs the stairs by staying close to the wall. A number of the steps give under her weight, and she has to lunge for the next one up.

The last step no longer exists, a gaping hole showing the first floor below. But the landing appears intact. Thanks to the push-ups in WASP training, her arms are strong. She lifts herself halfway up to the landing, then pauses to be sure the boards will hold. Swinging her legs up, she rolls to her back.

A whole section of roof gone, she stares straight up at the sky. Stars blink back at her, scattered sequins of light across velvet black. Pops would have been able to call out the names of the constellations and planets. The startling beauty of them, seen through the wreckage of what once was their house, makes her chest hurt.

How can the natural world both dazzle and also destroy so cruelly?
Why did I leave Pops to go fly?

On all fours, she crawls forward. Her dresser, dropped through a hole in the floor, lies on its side in the living room below, but the rest of the room she shared with Sam appears solid.

Reaching Sam's bed, she sinks slowly, carefully onto the mattress. A fanatic for neatness and precision, he has left the room with nothing on its surfaces, looking as it always did—as if he's merely at the airfield working on his Gee Bee.

Someone releases a choking wail, and it takes Joan a beat to realize it has come from her. The fear sitting daily in her gut has bubbled up and become sound.

On the floor, a hinged brass frame holding two photos lies wedged between a leg of the bed and the edge of a small table. On the right is a photo her mother snapped with her Brownie camera. Sam, Marshall, and Joan must've been around five years old, the three grinning from the front steps of the cottage. Sam sits in the middle, with arms slung across the others' shoulders.

It was just before they began school, Joan recalls—two separate schools. In this picture, they are only three children whose families live side by side in what are hardly more than shacks under palms and live oaks, but within earshot of the surf. They are poor by most standards, but the children don't know this yet. They smirk at the camera as if they plan to take the world by the tail, all three of them. Together.

On the left of the hinged frame, a young couple beams at the camera. The man's smile is less confident, tinged with a kind of wide-eyed fear, as if the two swaddled babies they hold, one each, have leveraged a weight that now hangs over his head.

She runs a finger over the glass.

Pops. I'm so sorry. I was trying to help. I should never have left.

Joan! Joan, where are you?

Twined with her thoughts, it's Pops's voice, calling her to come walk on the beach.

She knows it cannot be real, that it must be echoes in her head. Still, she leaps to her feet.

Joannie!

Her brain bursting with old ghosts and grief, she's scrambling faster than she's thinking. Swinging her feet off the landing toward the first available step a good three feet below, her heart is pounding so fast she's no longer steady.

Pops, forgive me. I was trying to help Sam somehow. I was trying to help the war effort. Maybe, too, I was running away from Dov, because he's engaged and his family needs him and I didn't want to mess everything up . . . oh, Pops, I'm so sorry.

She hears the voice again as she slips, flailing to grab an exposed beam as she falls.

Joan!

She tumbles, her head knocking on a jutting board as she passes, legs crumpling under her as she hits the floor and the rubble that was once her house becomes—just before everything goes dark—a whole cottage again, three children laughing on its front porch and a mother aiming a camera at them.

Chapter 62

Dov

Dov hurtles through rubble and bends over her as, frantically, he checks the pulse at her neck and puts his own cheek next to her nose to feel for breath.

Murmuring, Joan stirs but does not open her eyes. Her pulse, though, is steady, and she has just moved her legs and arms.

"Joan," he whispers. "Dear God, Joan. Are you all right?" He pulls her close, the beat of the waves and his own heart counting out time as she lies there limply against him.

When her eyes blink open, she looks up at him, confusion scudding across her expression like clouds. She lifts one hand, tentatively, to run down the line of his jaw, as if to decide whether he's really here.

"You," she murmurs. For one blessed moment her mind seems to have cleared only that much, a padding of merciful unknowing in which she holds his gaze and a smile flickers.

As she suddenly stiffens in his arms, though, he knows she's remembering where she is, and why. A sob breaks from her as she sits up.

"*Pops. I should never have left him. I should never have gone. I'm so, so sorry, Pops.*"

He does not offer false, flimsy words. So quietly she could choose to hear or not, he murmurs the words of the mourner's kaddish from his own tradition: *May there be abundant peace from heaven . . . help, comfort, refuge, healing, redemption, forgiveness . . .*

Letting her weep into his chest, he sits very still like a wharf piling, anchored deep, so she can hold on as torrent upon torrent of grief and regret crashes over her.

Chapter 63
Will

October 1944
USS Enterprise

He hasn't heard a word from Joannie since early September, but her work as a WASP has her working sixteen-hour days, so he tries not to worry something's happened to her. Joannie's letters flow with warm wishes for his safety and with affection, but not the deep pining for him or passion he still hopes will come.

If she'll have him someday, though, he can love big and long enough for the both of them.

Reaching for paper and a pen, he begins a fresh letter to her.

Dear Joannie,

It was you I thought of first when Admiral Halsey's second in command spotted a periscope today. We spent Lord only knows how many depth charges to disable the durn sub. Periscope turned out to be a mop handle bobbing in the waves. The U.S. Navy's a might sorry match for Joannie DuBarry.

He pauses, a tremor of warmth running through him as he recalls what it's like to hold her hand, to smell her hair, to see her throw back her head when she laughs.

I want to come home to you and never hear or get asked about this war ever again.

He stares at the words. Crumples them up into his fist. He won't worry her with the truth.

Footsteps clanging down the steel corridor are the first sign there's trouble.

I'm not moving this time, Will thinks. *I'm so far past tired my eyelids forgot how to shut. This time, I'm not getting up.*

But the battle siren blares, jolting him from his bunk.

The attack could be coming from the sky, from the sea's surface, from underwater, or from all three at once. The Big E reverberates with the racket of the alarm.

Exhausted men spring from their bunks or from playing poker or writing letters back home and careen through hallways of steel to their stations.

Will's long legs cover the flight deck in just a few bounds. Reaching the combat intelligence center on the carrier's island, he stares at the radar screen's pulsing green dots.

"What the *hell*," he breathes.

It's a phrase he's never uttered before, but it's fitting just now.

Chapter 64
Hadley

Still reeling several days later from Kitzie's news about her health, I feel like I'm going through the motions of life.

Kitzie does seem to feel stronger today—though she'd feign that for my sake regardless. But maybe she's right. Maybe she'll have a milder case with fewer, less serious flares. Maybe it won't progress as brutally as some cases.

Here's what I know for certain: I'll get her to every single specialist in the country.

Thanks to this Boundless reunion, we'll have some padding in our finances for a change. Kitzie's taking this job without my agreement is, I admit, a huge help. There's no treatment I won't pay for so that she'll survive—and flourish.

"Fortuitous," I say, trying to sound as strong as she does. "Fortuitous timing."

"Providential," she corrects me.

We've spent hours reading everything the doctors have sent us, hours discussing treatments, and she's asked me for a break from the constant conversation.

"Let's see," she insists, "how this round of the new medication and exercise goes. Trust me, Hadz, it'll do me good to focus on the reunion details for the homestretch, not more obsessing over whether my quads are stronger or weaker today."

I'm trying to focus—truly I am—but I keep glancing her way every few minutes to see if she's steady on her feet. I'm reading obsessively about the disorder: its symptoms, its treatments, its genetic manifestations in families. It's not inherited, exactly, I've learned, but there are families with multiple occurrences of the disease, so a descendant's likelihood of contracting it is increased.

Catching me staring at her, Kitz assures me I'm driving her batty and deploys me to an office supply store to pick up some of our orders. Biking there, I'm halfway down Ocean Boulevard before realizing I've no idea how I'll get the materials—not heavy but big and bulky—back.

I need to get out in the sun, though, away from my obsessive web searches on MS. Kitzie's right: I have no off switch and need to give her a break. So I pedal on.

Inside the shop, someone has propped our latest round of orders, more than a dozen larger-than-life-size mounted pictures in a semicircle against the copy machines. One image of the long steel corridor of the USS *Enterprise* makes me shudder.

"Did they feel like rats in a tube?" I wonder aloud.

"Did they . . . Who's *they?*" the high school kid behind the counter mutters, like he's hoping he doesn't actually have to wait on the crazy lady who talks to herself in the middle of a print shop. He blinks behind glasses so thick his eyes appear to swim from inside a goldfish bowl.

I'm standing in the shop's center, and I step back to view this latest round of mounted pictures, including a couple of the interior of a German U-boat, several of the various radar training simulation rooms, and various shots of the King and Prince during the war, complete with its gangly radar towers. Two of the families loaned us their grandfathers' navy uniforms, which we'll display, and we'll also have life-size mounted cutouts of all three men during the war.

Kitz and I just discovered the fate of Hans's Kriegsmarine uniform from his letters home, but we're saving that part of the story for one of the later reveals during reunion weekend. We'll bring out new displays each day of the reunion to cover progressing events in these three men's lives and with the war in general, beginning in 1942 with the attack of *U-123* on the SS *Oklahoma*, through 1945 and then the founding of Boundless. Thanks to Rabbi Ben, we have a world of information on the founders' original vision for accessible, affordable housing in communities where people of different backgrounds, nationalities, and faiths form genuine bonds.

Honestly, though, the war years and the early forming of the men's friendship comprise the vast majority of our displays. Ernst Hessler should get the facelift he needs for Boundless just in the peculiar beauty of the men's story.

I'm so lost imagining the world the photos reflect that it takes me a few minutes to realize the music drifting in from the door isn't simply part of this world.

Once I do realize, I stiffen. "'It's Been a Long, Long Time,'" I say without turning around.

"The name of the song, and also it has been, in fact," Nick says. "You haven't texted me back. Haven't answered my calls. Haven't let me explain."

"Nope," I agree. "I haven't." *What more is there to say?*

He lets the song keep playing from his phone as he sets it on the shop's counter. The kid behind the cash register, looking nervously from one to the other of us—and apparently spotting the take-no-prisoners look in my eye—ducks behind a display of school supplies.

"Hadley, about the evening at Fiddlers. It was a really, *really* nice evening. Better than I've had since . . . I couldn't tell you when. When I told you about my childhood . . ."

"Look, Nick, I'm not sure how you knew I was here—"

"Kitzie said—"

"Of course she did."

Whatever he was about to say, he's suddenly distracted by the foam-core boards that are taller than he is. "You were going to cart these amazing and also gargantuan photos back to the hotel on your rental bike?"

"Call an Uber, probably. Look, Nick, Kitz and I are on the final stretch with all the planning. An actual Hellcat—it's an airplane—arrives today. Kitz has about every theater kid in the county helping create the sets she's dreamed up to put people into that world. I don't have time for anything more than a polite working relationship with you—or a curt, icy one, if that's easier on both of us. Or maybe Mr. Hessler—*your father*, I mean—already fired you and you're just hanging out by the pool. In which case there's no need for us to talk at all."

"Hadley, I'd like to explain."

Touching my arm, he watches my face.

His fingers brush lightly on my elbow, and I try not to feel the contact, or to let his touch drain the anger from me.

"Also, Kitzie's sick, and I'm not much in the mood for chitchat today."

"I know. I'm so sorry."

"You know? How . . . ?"

"Kitzie told me. I think maybe she was embarrassed when I saw her have to sit down after just walking across the room. Also, she said I needed to know in case, to quote her, 'Hadley isn't much in the mood for chitchat today.' Again, I'm so sorry about the news. If I can help by researching or driving her to a doctor's appointment or . . ."

I sigh, annoyed that I'm tearing up in front of Nick Adams, who might think I'm weak, and annoyed that even with a potentially life-threatening disease, my sister is being sweet—or maybe it's strong, and maybe it always was—looking out for me.

"Hadley, I need you to know I didn't lie. I should've told you more up front. Like when you and your sister were on bikes that first week and I followed you in the car. But I didn't lie."

"Oh, right. And I built the St. Simons Lighthouse with my own two hands. Also, I'm an expert in radar and saved the free world from fascism."

The high school kid peers up from behind a display, looking more terrified than ever, only to duck back again.

"I'm not . . . look, if you'd quit being so stubborn for half a minute and listen—"

"*Stubborn?* So now the problem is *my* being *stubborn?* Not the fact that you bald-faced *lied?* I may have grown up without much, but I somehow picked up the value of telling—and here's a word you might not have learned at your fancy boarding school—the *truth.* Look, Nick, do me a favor, since you're here, and take all these prints back to the hotel's concierge desk. I'll pick them up there. They're prepaid. I'm riding my bike back. Thanks for the delivery."

"*Hadley.*"

It feels marvelous to storm out the door. Marvelous, even, to catch a glimpse of the high school kid cowering behind the tower of three-ring binders in rainbow colors. I sweep out in a blaze of wounded pride, hop on my bike, and begin the ride back alongside an egret bound for the beach.

I'm almost out of earshot when from behind me, Nick shouts three letters. "EBT!"

I brake but don't turn.

The crushed shell of the road's shoulder crunches under his feet as he jogs toward me.

"Electronic Benefits Transfer."

My head ticks one notch toward him as he goes on. Because I know the term. Lived it.

"The newer version of food stamps. Looks like a debit card. How people needing food assistance buy groceries."

"Okay, you got me to stop. Tell me, how does the son of Ernst Hessler and a product of Phillips Exeter know that?"

"Because I *was*, like I said, raised by a single mom. One," he adds quietly, "with a lot of self-respect. So much she wouldn't take a dime from the older man she got involved with but refused to marry."

"Ernst Hessler."

He's caught up with me now and looks me in the eye. "She cut off all contact with him for years, even when we could hardly make rent."

"The articles about Boundless that referenced you never mentioned your early years."

"Nope, they never do."

Arms still crossed over my chest, I wait for him to go on.

"By the time I was about to start high school, my father finally tracked her down again. Convinced her she owed it to my future to let him at least help me, if not her. Which translated to—overnight, it felt like—suddenly at age fourteen going from second-hand clothes and EBT cards to getting shipped off with button-down shirts and navy blazers, tags still on, to boarding school."

Poor little rich boy, I think, and he pauses, eyes holding mine, as if he guesses my thoughts.

"I didn't fit in, to say the least. Had years of academic catching up to do. Went from riding the T to my after-school and weekend job in Boston to playing lacrosse and water polo."

"And driving a BMW," I contribute. "Two of them. Both totaled. Or so said *Forbes.*"

He nods glumly. "Maybe there are kids in this world who'd have made that transition well. I wasn't one of them."

Poor, poor little rich boy, I want to say.

"I missed my mom, my old friends. I did well in classes—somehow—and crashed in every single other way. Including the literal smashups into other people's mailboxes, cars, café windows. Only reason I didn't kill anyone was the courts at some point took my license away for a year. I was a total high-functioning mess. For years. My mom blamed herself, thinking if she'd stuck to her guns and kept me away from my father . . ."

"And Ernst?"

"Oh, he blamed me."

Here we go, I think. *Poor little rich boy's defense.* But Nick is nodding.

"I'll give him credit for that. In the end, it was on me to figure out who I wanted to be."

This takes me by surprise, and I study his look of remorse: sad, earnest eyes in the tanned face. *Tanned,* I remind myself, *because he's steering his father's Lürssen.* "And the whole yacht-captain-SUV-driver routine?"

"Was no routine. I cleaned up my act a couple of years ago. Paid back the café owner whose window I drove my car into. Tried to make amends wherever I could. Working for my father for the past year was my idea, the last step in my showing remorse, seriousness, hard work. For the record, he pays me the American minimum wage." One side of his mouth quirks up. "No health benefits and blistering performance reviews."

"Not," I agree slowly, "the easiest man to work for."

"And also, I'd earned his disappointment. His father, Hans, was a good man, people say, but never really got out from under the weight of what he saw and did during the war. I wonder if my father's way of making the world around him feel safe was by taking control—of every detail he possibly could—and by making money. All the more reason he couldn't understand an out-of-control, ungrateful son like me."

My arms are still crossed over my chest, but my voice softens. "I wish you'd told me the full story earlier."

"Clearly, I should've."

"Absolutely you should've. Instead of yammering on about authenticity and coming from nothing, all the while you neglected to mention a dad who's an *ultra.*"

At this, he chuckles. "Ah. You remember the term."

"And you probably have a plum job at the family business just sitting there waiting for you."

"Not until I prove myself first, probably starting in the mailroom. Too much ink has been spilled on Bad Boy Nick. I've got plenty more years of penance ahead. Meanwhile, I'm hoping that not working directly for my father—as his driver and designated person who's right there to catch all his unfiltered critique of the world—maybe there's some chance to actually know the man. Maybe have some sort of relationship—assuming he even wants that someday."

Suddenly, he brightens. "I do, though, finally have a sense of where I'm headed, where we're headed as a firm, if Cordelia and Benedick and their side win out. I do believe there are ways to do good in this world like the founders dreamed and still do well for the bottom line. That people across national lines can . . ." He stops there. "I've gone on way too long. What I meant to say was I'm sorry. And that I didn't technically lie, though I did—"

"Give me an incredibly false sense of who you are now," I finish for him. "That's not authenticity, Nick."

"You're right. You're one hundred percent right. I just thought if I told you the whole thing too soon, you'd write me off as the guy the press described, the coke-snorting, sports car–smashing, skirt-chasing spoiled brat blowing his father's money."

"Which, to be fair . . . ," I point out.

"*Was* who I was. But that's why languages have a past tense. For the times when *was* is the key."

"Thanks for the backstory. And the apology." I look away out toward the marsh, then back. "Still. You weren't straightforward with me."

"Fair enough." He rakes a hand back through his hair and, for instant, head back, looks like he will mount a defense but then lets out a breath as his shoulders sag. "Fair enough."

Kissing the tip of my forefinger, I brush it against his cheek, rough with blond stubble. "Thanks for delivering the pictures. Bye, Nick."

Chapter 65

Joannie

October 1944
Camp Davis, North Carolina

She's trying to close her letter to Will with the honest truth. But what is that, exactly? Joannie may be back physically at Camp Davis, but her mind spins all day long on Pops's funeral.

A good man was Terrence DuBarry, and much beloved . . .

The door to her bay creaks open, and she's aware of someone standing still, listening.

Pen poised above her scrap of paper, Joannie stops, aware of the five other women in her bay sleeping soundly, one snoring softly. Her flashlight casts a large enough triangle of light for her to scrawl a line at a time. There's so much more she needs to say to Will, that she owes him.

Will, I need you to know . . .

But her door creaks wider, a petite figure silhouetted in the doorframe.

"Joan?" comes a whisper. "You still awake?"

Rather than answer and risk waking up the others, Joan slips from her cot and pads to the doorway.

"Joan, I had to tell somebody. I know I should wait until morning when they intend to announce it. But I had to."

Joan searches Hazel Lee's usually placid face. One of the smallest of the WASPs and one of the toughest, Hazel proved her strength in early pilot training. While riding with her instructor, he decided to impress her with a loop, but Hazel's seat belt wasn't properly latched, and she fell headfirst out of the open cockpit. Engaging her parachute, she saved herself and walked back to base unscathed, dragging the chute behind her.

Joan makes out Hazel's stare, dazed and distraught, in the silvery glow from the window.

"How can I help, Hazel?"

"You can't. That's just it. We're done."

"Who's done?"

"All of us. Every last one of us. We're not even supposed to be sore about their decision. *Just set down your goggles and step aside, ladies. Go home and darn socks.*"

It takes Joan several beats to gather what she must mean. "Congress, you mean. They've voted."

"General Arnold gave it his best shot. Said how working with us convinced him how valuable women pilots can be. But the fellows coming back from the war will be sent right back overseas as infantrymen on the ground if women take up the pilot spots on the home front."

"So . . . they want to come back and ferry planes."

"Here's what I guarantee we'll be hearing tomorrow: *Thank you for your service, girls. Now say goodbye forever to flying planes—oh, except the paper ones you'll make for the thirteen pretty babies we want you to go home and have.*"

Joan lets all this percolate through her brain, through the grief and fear already pebbled there.

The war still rages on, still a bloodbath.

No! She wants to insist. *This is my way to help bring my brother home.*

I can't go back to the island without Pops or Sam there. I don't want to knit socks for the war effort after I've ferried bombers.

"Congress can't just . . ."

Hazel wraps thin arms around her. "We're done, Joannie. They've disbanded the WASP."

≈

Joan watches as Brunswick comes into focus through the bus window. Across the water she can see St. Simons and knows there's nothing but a collapsed cottage waiting for her. No home. No brother. No mother or father.

Her breath fogging the glass, she uses the cuff of her bomber jacket to wipe it clear.

Bomber jacket. With its Fifinella figure on the left side, its fleece collar that was such a comfort in those high altitudes.

She wears it on top of the matching wool jacket and skirt she chose for that first day in Sweetwater, Texas, that day all her class of WASPs, wearing high heels with eyebrow-penciled lines on their calves imitating nylons, scrambled into a cattle truck to begin training.

This jacket is nothing but a memory scrap of this past year of her life, of a woman, some former Joan, who was allowed to study and work and show courage and be recognized for it. Be valued for something other than nice legs and dark wavy hair.

The bus brakes squeal, and Joannie lifts her chin.

I am coming back home to a home that doesn't exist.

Sam might now be a prisoner of war somewhere in the Pacific.

Will's ship could be under attack at this moment.

I will not feel sorry for myself. I will not.

She hasn't written Dov to tell him she's coming back. He was there to comfort her when she came home for the funeral. He stood close by at the interment in Christ Church Frederica's cemetery, along with a handful of villagers. He walked on the beach with her and let her pour out her grief—her guilt too.

But he'd promised himself to someone else. Not just to Deborah; he'd promised himself just as urgently to their families, their community living through unspeakable horror, even on the free side of the English Channel. She's heard the rumors of cattle cars and camps, the news of ghettos and roundups and massacres, the relatives who disappear, their homes taken over by neighbors who don't respond to questions.

With the world burning, honoring such a promise surely matters.

Amid all the carnage and loss and pain, surely the feelings of one woman who met one man by chance on an island, as world war rages on, surely does not matter at all.

Joan!

The crowd milling around the depot surges forward as another line of luggage tumbles out from the bus's belly. Joan can't see behind the men's fedoras and ladies' turbans, toques, and pillbox hats.

But she knows in her gut whose voice it is, that low tenor. The one so gentle on the notes of "I'll Be Seeing You" as they danced out on Sea Island.

It's not Dov this time, she tells herself. *It's not.*

She's afraid it will be Dov.

She's afraid it won't.

As the crowd thins at the depot's left, a face appears. His cheekbones sharply defined, his black hair swept back from his forehead in a wave, a rogue curl dropping onto his forehead.

He reaches her in a dozen running steps and lifts her in his arms before she can speak.

Burying her face in his neck, she feels the punch of all the loss—her father's death, her brother's silence, her churning guilt, the end of the WASP, and her feelings of utter uselessness now—all that she's held up so long by herself collapses on her again, like her house crushed by the pine.

All she can do is hold on as he circles his arms around her, pulls her in tight and doesn't let go.

Chapter 66

Hadley

I'm still tweaking the reunion weekend schedule on my laptop screen when a text swoops in.

Felicia Hammond's name appears at the top. Something important to show me, she says, and I respond.

> Come to back of hotel, double doors
> open to ocean.

Her reply comes in all caps like a shout.

> YOU WILL NOT BELIEVE WHAT I'VE
> JUST FOUND

Out of breath, Felicia arrives a few moments later at the ocean-facing doors, a shoebox in one hand, just as Nick appears at the doors leading into the hall.

It's clear Nick hasn't given up on talking to me, but he greets Felicia with a nod, then stands to the side, like he'll wait his turn. The room already throbs with emotion, Vera Lyn singing "We'll Meet Again" in the background.

Rushing forward, Felicia holds out the shoebox, then pulls it back. "Hard to know what to show you first. Let me ask you this, Hadley: I heard you ask at Fiddlers that night about the little character on Samantha Mitchell's cane, but did you ever investigate what it could be?"

"About thirty seconds of googling. Came up cold." I don't add that I'd felt jilted by Nick that evening and also fearful for Kitz, then forgot about the little creature and Samantha's odd reticence to explain it. "I tried the words *female cartoon figure WW2*. Nothing like it pulled up."

"May I?" Felicia asks, even as she reaches for my open laptop on one of the tables.

"Sure."

"See what happens when I use those same words and add"—she types as she speaks—"*goggles*."

Goggles, I remember suddenly. *Of course. How did I forget that?*

As Felicia hits Return, my screen fill with images of a blonde gremlin with red boots, red lips, and blue wings, about which I read aloud from one of the captions:

Fifinella. Designed by Disney for a proposed film version of The Gremlins, *former RAF pilot Roald Dahl's first children's story, in 1943.*

But next is the kicker:

Adopted during World War II by Women Airforce Service Pilots as their mascot.

I blink at the screen. Then at Felicia. From behind us, Nick approaches to look at the screen, but I'm too transfixed by the words to notice his reaction.

"Oh my God. So frail, tissue-paper-skinned little Samantha Mitchell must've once been a WASP, too, just like the late Joannie DuBarry."

"Exactly."

"Felicia, have you asked Samantha if she knew Joannie DuBarry before she died?"

Felicia glances back at my laptop screen filled with Fifinellas. "Thought about going straight to her. Here's what's hard. I've known Samantha all my life. So when I confided in her how tough it is some days, being Black in mostly White spaces or a woman in a man's world, why did it never occur to her to mention she flew military aircraft as a woman in the 1940s? Why wouldn't she tell me?"

"No idea. Except that whole generation was like that, right? The Silent Generation. You read about it all the time, people finding out a parent or grandparent was a war hero or saved two dozen children from a death camp and never said a word till the end—or ever. Maybe Samantha's like that about being a WASP. Hard for us even to imagine what they lived through."

At the same moment, we turn from the screen toward each other, and then toward the giant mounted photos. With the early morning light slanting through the stained glass lighthouse and the other windows glowing in a ring around the room, the people in those life-size pictures look as if they might speak.

In one, Will Dobbins plays his mandolin, body sickled to one side like he's transported by the music. In another, apparently taken after the war, since they're both wearing business suits, Will plays his mandolin while Dov plays a violin, their eyes closed in concentration.

In another, shown mostly from the back, Hans Hessler sits beside Dov, both of them bent over a single book. Physics, I guess from what I've learned of them both. Or *I and Thou*, by Martin Buber, a Jewish philosopher both men loved to read and debate. The *PW* stenciled on Hans's back shows, but since he's sitting with a British officer reading, I've dated the photo from the late summer or fall of 1945, after the war ended but before all the prisoners of war could be sent home, and before Dov sailed on the Big E back to England.

Unspeaking, eyes wide, Felicia examines this photo in particular, then moves slowly on to each of the others.

In another cutout, a gangly Will Dobbins stands next to the shorter, slightly built young man I learned is Sam, Joan DuBarry's brother, in a khaki flight suit—life jacket around his neck, goggles slung over one arm—on the flight deck of the USS *Enterprise*, a line of folded-wing Grumman Hellcats and one Mitchell B-25 behind them.

"My sweet Lord," Felicia murmurs, hardly audible over the music. "They look too young to be so far from their homes, much less expected to save the world."

In yet another picture, Will Dobbins and Dov Silverberg, both in uniform, stand in front of the structure I've learned is Lovely Lane Chapel. Will's face radiates joy. Dov has one hand on Will's shoulder, as if congratulating his friend. His face, though, is a stoical blank as he stares straight ahead, the face of a man being . . . *what?* I wonder.

Suddenly, I regret my decision to have this one mounted. Enlarged so much, Dov's face is raw, vulnerable, capturing some sort of a tumult of emotion in the moment.

"All this," Felicia says, turning back to me, "and the backdrops outside under the tent. You've made it all feel so real. What a trip back in time—into these people's stories, Hadley."

"There'll be live big band music, too, both evenings. I hope you can slip in to see it all. Especially now that we know"—I nod my head at the shoebox she still holds—"you've got your own unexpected connection to Sam and Joannie DuBarry."

"Which reminds me." She sets the box down and eases its contents into a fan of newspaper and magazine clippings across the table. Felicia turns her head to address Nick in the corner. "Hadley knows this, since we've traded a couple of surprises lately, but ever since I found this box while clearing out my great-grandparents' attic, I kept these tucked away, thinking they were some sort of damning evidence that my great-grandfather Marshall had been collecting articles about this White woman Joannie—guess I was afraid it was someone he'd been in love with. Even though the articles stop in 1945—makes sense with her death—it just felt . . . odd . . . to know he'd had this other woman in his life before my great-grandmother and so carefully kept the clippings all those years afterwards, like he still treasured that other woman's memory, you know?"

She holds up a full-page feature from a Brunswick newspaper, with a three-column photo of Joannie DuBarry in bomber jacket and slacks, with goggles on top of her head and a broad smile. "Hadley, after you and I talked at Mullet Bay—my family's connection with the DuBarrys—and I read up on Women Airforce Service Pilots and then discovered Samantha's connection, I think my head exploded. Honestly, I never knew much about the WASPs. They did so much."

Nodding, I reach for the ripped photo of Joannie DuBarry on the beach. Handing it to Felicia, I watch her examine it, her eyebrows lifting at the word *Traitor* scrawled on the back.

From the shoebox of clippings her great-grandfather so carefully gathered, she holds up a photograph of Joannie DuBarry, this one in her Santiago blue dress uniform—a fitted navy jacket and pencil skirt—with its brass wings. The accompanying short article is from page eight of a local St. Simons weekly, and it's peppered with typos. It mentions the disbanding of WASP and local girl Joannie DuBarry, recently bereaved after her father's death, returning home after helping, along with other "girl pilots," in the war effort. In the photo, she wears her usual thousand-watt smile, but in the first line of the article, she's quoted as saying she's "devastated."

"What if . . . ," Felicia begins.

"Someone had that headstone in your church's cemetery made for Joannie DuBarry, but she didn't die?" I finish for her.

Felicia and I stare at each other and at the young woman pictured in the article. Vaguely, I'm aware that Nick, standing a few feet away now, wears his inscrutable look—and that, strangely, his expression isn't one of surprise.

I round on him. "Before the Reverend Doctor and I go pay a visit to her neighbor, what is it you know?"

"Nothing," he says and looks away, out toward the sea.

I march around to face him. "Which, once again, is not true."

He flinches, and the corners of his eyes tighten with what might be regret. "Which is not technically true," he agrees. "And, again, I'm sorry for not telling you the whole truth about me from the first. But this time"—he nods toward the shoebox—"it's not my story to tell."

Chapter 67

Samantha Mitchell

June 2022
St. Simons Island

No one understands a damn thing about life before they've reached seven decades—hell, maybe eight.

Samantha believes this fiercely—no less fervently than today as she watches the three young women approach her door.

They will not understand, of course. How can they?

How could she have understood at their age?

Even now, she hasn't completely forgiven herself, not really. Some days, not at all.

Other days, the good ones when an ocean of mercy is swelling around her, she knows she was grieving and scared, her head gone dark in ways her generation didn't know how to name.

There's just so damn much screwup to living, Samantha thinks, watching their faces, distorted by the tiny peephole. *Judging without understanding: that sucks the life clean out of a person till there's nothing left but a fossil.*

But these young women will not know this yet, not fully—not even the Reverend Doctor, for all her fancy clergy training. They won't know not to show horror at the hairpin turns and crashes of other people's lives. Even Felicia's brown eyes will widen at what Samantha has done—and not done. Those nice brows of hers will steeple and maybe never come down again, Samantha suspects.

The other two, the sisters . . . Samantha tries to imagine how they will react, but she can't bear it, the looks she knows she'll see in their eyes. The confusion. The anger.

She's lived this long partly out of a sense of purpose and partly out of a granite strength that allows no one else fully inside. Softening any of that means the whole structure collapses.

Samantha feels the weight of her years as if they were stacked, all one hundred of them, on her shoulders this morning. She's never been one to slump or shuffle, and she's no intention of starting today, but she stumbles now over a throw rug in the hall, a rug her primary doc suggested she get rid of decades ago—old-people tripping hazard, he said. She ignored him.

Stumbling, she thinks, *just like I stumbled through that whole season of life. One stumble after another.*

No, *stumble* is too mild a term for what she did then, and too passive, letting her off the hook.

For *decisions,* then, in those days that no one should be asked to forgive her for.

So Samantha does not answer her door. Not at first.

Don't be a damn coward, she tells herself.

But she knows she's not. Never has been. Fear of things that terrify other people has never been a failing of hers.

Why, then, can't she answer the door?

She can hear them on the other side. Cautiously, Samantha rises to her tiptoes again so she can see out the peephole.

"At her age," suggests the blonde one, Kitzie—the one who moves awful slow for such a young woman—"she's allowed to take naps."

Naps, Samantha fumes. *As if naps are all anyone's good for at my age—when I've seen the whole damn world on fire and walked through it. Hell,* flew *through it.*

"She does have one of those things to punch if she's fallen, right?" Kitzie asks.

The Reverend Doctor nods. "For years, she agreed to check in with my mother every morning just to let her know she was okay, but Mama ended up passing first. Now Samantha checks in with *me* every morning—just to make sure *I'm* up and okay."

All three young women chuckle. Of course they do.

Samantha can't blame them—not much, anyway—for not knowing what they can't possibly know in their twenties: that she, the ancient one, might be most likely to die in the night, her final heartbeats already ticking down, but *they're* in a stage of life, Samantha knows all too well, when one of those sharp turns of a single day's decision can send you over a cliff.

"Samantha also likes being out and about," the Reverend Doctor is saying. "She could just be . . ."

Suddenly, on impulse, in a decision that defies her decades of silence, Samantha is once again her old, reckless self—and the joy of it straightens her shoulders. With a heave, she flings open the door.

All four of them blink at each other a moment.

Lord knows, Samantha has no idea where to begin. With the "White Cliffs of Dover" or "You Belong to Me"? These girls—and they *are girls* when you're eight decades ahead—simply stare.

The Reverend Doctor is the first to speak—thoughtfully, of course. "Is there anything we can help you with, Samantha?"

A beat into Felicia's question, though, Hadley plunges in. "Could we ask just one thing?"

Samantha allows herself a moment to survey Hadley, this young woman wound tight with all the things she wants to know in life, all the things she wants to do. How well Samantha knows that feeling, that way of being in the world.

It's exhausting as hell.

And also, it's vitality itself, like surfing a huge wave every day, that surge of curiosity and energy always lifting you up and up and forward.

Even now, when her body has slowed to a walk, Samantha still feels that swell of all that's left to learn and do. She sees that in Hadley.

In Kitzie, Samantha sees kindness and strength. A remarkable strength, in fact, behind the blue eyes and a body that appears to need propping up against the doorframe.

Is she sick?

Samantha feels her own heart twist in fear—twist so hard she puts a hand to her chest.

Fear. Not an emotion she's used to.

Samantha addresses Felicia first—she owes her neighbor that. "Thank you, dear. I don't need a thing. You're kind to ask." Then she shifts to Hadley. "Forgive me, won't you, if today's not a good time."

Coward, says the voice in her head. *When did you, of all people, get to be a damn coward?*

But I need more time, she wants to shout back at the voice. *I'm not ready yet.*

She nearly laughs aloud at herself. The ludicrousness of a woman a hundred years old needing more time to tell a very old truth.

"Soon" is what she says out loud. "Soon I will answer your questions. I promise." Samantha begins closing the door.

"Fifinella," Hadley blurts, then covers her mouth with one hand. "I'm sorry. I'm being too pushy. I do that sometimes."

Of course, thinks Samantha. *Of course you do.*

And also, don't make me do this. Don't make me see on your faces what I know I'll see. I've borne the guilt and survived. I know the goodness, too, of my life. Don't make me defend that.

All the decisions of a single life—how could anyone else understand? All those chapters, the happy and the utterly harrowing. The guilt and the triumphs, the firsts and the lasts. The secret shame and the public accolades.

She waits until Hadley locks eyes with her, then Samantha lifts her cane. "Fifinella, yes. I did love my time as a WASP. The Mitchell B-25 was my favorite plane to fly."

In the silence that follows, Felicia steps forward, lays a hand on the old woman's shoulder. Samantha suspects she looks her age this morning, festoons of skin at her jaw, crepe paper neck, eyes staring off into space.

Seeing, though, not the *nothing* that young people assume to find in an old person's unfocused gaze, but the *too much* of the past.

"Oh, Samantha," the Reverend Doctor breathes.

Just as Samantha has so often done herself, Hadley leapfrogs over emotion to land on the facts. The young woman stares. Then blurts, "Mitchell. Samantha *Mitchell*. As in the Mitchell B-25. Oh my God, you really are . . ."

Shrugging, Samantha settles her gaze on the three young women. "It was one of my favorites to fly. I chose the name because the plane was so blasted resilient, what I realized I'd have to be, and partly because it was simply a hell of a kick to fly."

Samantha lets them take all this in—*process* it, as people say nowadays.

They've no idea, though, how much more there is still to process.

Or what it was like back during that war, when she and everyone else processed their grief and their guilt and their screwups thirty thousand feet in the air, one engine dead and the world as they knew it at stake.

"Your brother, Samuel," Felicia murmurs. "The first name you chose . . ."

The past slamming up against her like giant frothing breakers now, Samantha grips the doorframe and sticks to the facts. "To honor him, yes. A kinder soul never lived. Unless it was your great-granddaddy."

"Marshall," the Reverend Doctor whispers.

Samantha has never liked whispers.

Yet hasn't she been the one to shroud so much of her life, all these decades, in layers of them? Didn't she once let whispers nearly choke the life out of her?

"Marshall," Samantha says, with a volume from the old vocal cords that does them credit. It's good to say her old friend's name out loud.

And soon, very soon, she will say the rest of it out loud for the people who need to hear it. Despite the fact she decided long ago to cut herself off irrevocably from the past. Despite the fact the past will soon gut her all over again—this time maybe for good.

"For now," she announces, beginning to close the door, "I will add that a headstone was purchased for a young woman who needed to cease to exist but had not died. More than that, I will answer soon. I promise. And I do"—she inhales and pictures the face of a young man she hasn't let herself picture for years—"I do take promises seriously."

Samantha closes the door on them. Not a slam but a firm push, letting them know she's taken down as many of the walls as she's able today. And still, it might be too much.

Leaning against the door and her cane, Samantha feels as if she might sink under the scenes that she's not let herself replay in her mind for decades.

She has not often cried in her life, but she does now, guilt and regret and fear washing over and swelling up until she can't breathe.

Chapter 68

Joannie

December 1944
St. Simons Island, Georgia

Joan has never processed emotions too well—or so Sam often told her. Sam, in fact, took on that job for both of them. But now he's not here. Not even answering letters.

With only a vague kind of faith, Joan sidles into the back at Christ Church Frederica more often than anyone knows but the rector. He nods to her—small, nearly imperceptible bobs of his head—as she slips in during the first hymn and out after the Holy Eucharist. It's not the sermons that help her survive so much as the moments inside that space—polished wooden rafters under the long-armed live oaks, as if she's been swept under the wings of a great, transcendent bird.

Now back in her tiny second-floor apartment that Mr. Gray insisted she use for a time, she can hear the thrum of human life below in the drugstore: the slam of the screened door, the burst of laughter from children, the whir and hum of the ceiling fans or the soda fountain, the ring of the cash register.

A *tink* on her window makes her cross the room and drop her gaze to the street. In past years, its sidewalks would've been lit with holiday lights, circles of red and green on the wet concrete, but since the war—since the torpedoings, at least—the street remains dark, the setting sun just visible between clouds, faintly tinting the village.

A man stands on the sidewalk, wearing a white naval officer's uniform, complete with shiny-brimmed hat. Joannie can't see his face well in the shadows, but she knows this silhouette—better than she'd like to admit.

She hopes he's far enough away that he can't see the disarray of her apartment, the cans of Campbell's tomato soup left empty on the counter, the contents of her suitcase strewn about since he drove her here from the bus station.

She raises the sash. A warm front has blown in, and this December night is unseasonably mild. "Hello, sailor," she calls down to him. "May I help you find someone?"

Smiling, he sweeps off his hat. "As it happens, I believe I've already found her."

Joan stares at him looking up at her, intensity in his eyes. The words seem to swirl in the air between them, as if the sea breeze is keeping them aloft like a streamer.

Careful, she wants to tell him. *Play with numbers, if you like, with calculations, with flight simulations. Don't play at this.*

With no idea how to respond, she cocks her head and waits for him to go on.

"I say, I've come with the mission of rousting a friend who's a bit knackered back into the world."

Bending, she rests her chin on one of her fists. "Does this friend *need* rousting?"

"If the friend were a grumpy old man in dodgy quarters with a proper beard to his knees, perhaps I'd allow him to stay put. I'm afraid in this case, however, the young lady has been featured in any number of periodicals across the land. Her public demands that she reappear."

He's directly under her window now, so she can speak in a normal voice as she gazes down toward the pier and the sea. "They loved the starlet shots, you know, the press did. Loved to catch us in the rare moments we sunbathed behind the barracks in Sweetwater—after a week of sixteen-hour days training. Or they'd snap one of us climbing out of a cockpit looking, the captions would say, all glamorous, when really we'd been on a two-week ferrying circuit without a single decent shower."

"Ah, you're in luck. I've already been persuaded that the women of WASP were magnificent specimens of humanity, a corker of a gift to the war effort, all."

Joan brings her other elbow to rest on the sill. "Then what might I do for you, Lieutenant?"

"You must come out dancing with me—for your own good and mine. The Cloister's opened its terrace again to the officers."

"For my own good. I see. And how for your good, Lieutenant Silverberg?"

Several seconds swim by in the patter of light rain on the pavement and sidewalk, puddles prisming the last of the waning light.

"I jolly well could stand to talk."

∼

From a record player precariously placed by the edge of the pool, Judy Garland croons that new tearjerker of a song "Have Yourself a Merry Little Christmas" as Joan's left hand rests on the muscle just below Dov's right shoulder, her right hand draped lightly in his left. It's proper dance position but feels somehow too intimate tonight. As they move, the skirt of her dress swishes, his thighs brushing past hers, his right hand warm at the small of her back, the light pressure of his fingers sending little electrical jolts through her.

She needs to put words—dull, practical words—between them.

"You mentioned you needed to talk?"

"I shouldn't bother you with it, my own struggles. Not when you've had to bear so much more."

"Or you might do a gal a favor, letting her think she's helping by listening in the midst of this crazy world."

He shakes his head, his eyes on the strip of black, sea and sky melded together, short ribbons of lace appearing across the dark when starlight touches the froth of the waves. "It's about what I do all bloody day, for God's sake, training other men to go out where Zeros aim for their flight decks, subs aim for their hulls, and their own fighter pilots wait for them to say who to shoot. I teach. I do it in the comfort of a former hotel. They go out and take all the risks."

"Dov. Look at me." As he does, she rests her right palm along his cheek. "You're teaching men how to operate in terrifying conditions and potentially save hundreds, even thousands, of lives with their decisions. I'd say that's one of the biggest jobs anyone could do in this war."

His eyes squeeze shut. "I'm not facing any danger, though. I'm not living minute by minute under the kind of pressure they face—the pressure to be right every bloody time, whole planes and whole ships depending on their split-second decisions."

"That's just it, though, isn't it? The top brass have chosen you not from some random drawing of names but because only you can train these men in a way that will save Allied lives—the pilots, the sailors, the foot soldiers. It's your training, *yours*, that saves lives."

"The truth is, I think every single day of insisting they transfer me back to active duty as an aviator."

"Yet they send the best aviators back to train the new pilots, don't they? That's why you're here. If it helps, word on the street is that you're the toughest—and best—of the instructors."

"Every day I think of telling them they have to send me to the Pacific theater, where things . . ."

He drops his forehead to hers in a kind of apology for recalling, too late, where her brother and Will are both stationed.

"Where things are the absolute worst right now," she finishes in a whisper. "The kamikazes intensifying their raids. I do read the news."

As he steps in closer, his cheek presses to hers, his hand moving from the small of her back to rest lightly, very lightly, on the bare skin of her upper back.

His skin is warm and smells of meadows still—*how can he be so far from home and still smell of what she imagines are English meadows and moors and heaths?* His body sways and swings next to hers, the muscles of his back rippling and tensing under her hands.

His head dips, as if he's breathing in the scent of her hair, but he straightens again, tensing. Desire spider steps up her spine.

"I'm worried," she says into his ear. "For Sam and . . ."

Two heartbeats go by with what's left unsaid.

"Also for Will," he fills in for her. Not resentfully. Just a fact they share, like the salt taste of the air. "I worry about them too. The Battle of Leyte was brutal. The fighting at Ormoc Bay. It's been . . . I say, Joan. I'm so sorry. I shouldn't have—"

She leads him from the side of the Cloister's pool to the path that winds to the beach. Leaving their shoes in the sand, they walk in the dark toward the sound of the surf and stop where the moon shows them only the silver outline of scalloped wet where the waves fizzle out and withdraw.

There's something she needs to say, desperately so, but she's not sure what it is. She's afraid if she says this thing, whatever's clawing so hard to get out, she'll have to hear it for the first time at the same moment he does.

They drop to the sand and sit side by side and listen to wave after wave swelling and cresting and crashing. When her head drops to his shoulder, he kisses her forehead. Then, shifting, brushes his lips along the crook of her neck—so lightly that with her eyes closed as they are, his lips might be only the breeze.

Rounding toward him, she lays her palm along his jaw. His thigh moves to rest alongside hers. She shifts into the crescent of him, the breeze cooler now off the water, his long frame a bulwark of warmth.

"You're needed *here*. As an instructor you're saving lives *here*, thousands more than you could flying one single plane."

Dov's dark eyes on hers, he appears to be searching what he can see of her face by the sliver of moon.

"Is it selfish of me," she hears herself add, whispering, "that I want you here too?"

Dov's eyes never leave hers as he leans in.

But she's already shaking her head. "I won't let myself hurt your girl back home in London. Or your family. Or Will."

"God, don't I know." His voice is husky. Deep. Ragged with this same thing that's nearly choking her now. "My girl back home. Who's lost a father in the Blitz already and a brother in a German stalag somewhere. My family, who adores her . . . God, don't I know."

With a jerk, he sits up suddenly, his back bowed over bent knees spread apart. "All this duty. All this doing what other people need us to do. Not just the war but everything else, too, all the family grief we've got to shoulder. You with all your loss. It's too much at once. My friend Will, who's pledged his undying love, who asked me—*me*, of all people—to keep an eye out for you." Dov lifts his head to look at her miserably.

Resting a hand on his back, she leans against him. She means it as comfort, to simply connect. But he rests his left palm on her shoulder, the bare of her upper back. Joannie's breathing staccatos. She will not let herself move.

"Joan. I need you to know . . ."

She places a finger over his lips. "No. I don't think I can bear to hear you say it—whatever it is. Let's talk about how I relished getting grease under my nails when I worked on the engines. Or about the physics classes we had to pass at Avenger Field in Texas—how I zipped through the calculations and thought how you . . ."

"You thought of me, then, in your time away? You never wrote."

She looks out over the ocean. "How could I? How could either of us?"

Gently, he lifts her hair back from her face and whispers into her ear. "Just let me tell you once, perhaps the only time I'll be able to, the truth."

Body coiled tight, she waits.

"That I want to be with you more than anything. More than anyone. *This* is the truth."

A whisper, she thinks. *In case the words carry to London or the South Pacific. The words must only ever be whispered.*

"Yet you're not free to do what you want. I've understood that from the beginning. I won't be the cause of your breaking your promise to people you love, people who need you to keep it. You're a man of integrity. I admire that in you, I do. We should go."

His answer comes slowly, the words pried out. "Will Dobbins too. He's a good man. Splendid, in fact."

"The kindest," she agrees. "The best."

"The bloody best, and he trusts me. Writes to me still. We should go."

Rising, he pulls her up from the sand but does not release her hand. Instead, he lowers his forehead to hers, and they stand like that for a time.

Joan's fingers twine back into his hair, his arms around her waist. Then he lowers his head for a single kiss on one of her shoulders, just a brush of his lips over her skin. And for a moment, he leans back, eyes intense, searching.

Her palms on his chest feel the bass drum of his heart. Her fingers pull at the buttons of his shirt. He kisses the soft skin under her jaw as she lengthens her neck. He's loosened the knot of her dress at the back of her neck when he freezes.

Breathless, they both step back at the same moment. He slides his fingers down her arms, and his hands catch hers. She trembles but keeps her eyes steady on his.

"Joan. What if I didn't keep the promise? What if we thought for once about us and not the agony of a whole bloody world?"

"We should go," she says, the heat of her bare skin where his hands have been suddenly cold in the December sea breeze.

"We should go," he echoes softly.

But neither one of them moves.

Chapter 69
Will

December 24, 1944
USS Enterprise, en route to the Philippines

The outlines of palms wash into a blur of green as Oahu's coastline begins to fade, and Will is not sorry to leave Pearl Harbor, not one shaving of one little bit. Even three years after the raid that brought the United States into this war, the base feels like a battleground of defeat, twisted metal still rising up from the sea like a raised fist.

From the ship's speakers, Judy Garland is singing "Have Yourself a Merry Little Christmas," the mournfulness of its melody and its words washing over the ship. A man at the starboard rail wipes his eyes on his sleeve. Another beside him weeps openly.

Maybe some other Christmas Eve, next year or the next when the world is at peace again and we've muddled through all this awful and ugly, we'll come back here, Joannie—together.

Though maybe that's a mite too presumptuous.

Still, it keeps him sane, thinking of her and their future. Together on the farm in Tennessee, maybe. Or together on St. Simons Island.

Together somewhere, the two of them learning to forget the roar of engines all the blessed day long, the chop of airplane propellers, the screams of the injured men—and women, too, Will reminds himself.

They could settle somewhere in a cottage and shut out the world, him and Joannie. His ears would no longer ring with the shriek of bombs; his hands would learn not to shake. She'd heal from the loss of her Pops and the end of the WASP. Her brother Sam would reappear, with a rip-roaring story to tell from the Battle of Leyte Gulf, maybe. They wouldn't speak of flying or fighter direction or the war ever again. They would be happy and whole.

Will glances through the porthole. Nearly dark. In Oahu, the *Enterprise* had an "(N)" for night operations painted on her hull, of which Will had taken three pictures, one for Joan and one for his mama back home and one for his friend Silverberg. Someday, somewhere safe by a cozy fire, he'd tell them how the *Enterprise* was the only American carrier capable of night operations, something to be right proud of.

Will's not a proud man, he hopes to goodness, but he knows he's doing difficult and classified work.

He knows, too, he'd never been able to succeed without Dov Silverberg's training, tough and exacting. None of the other instructors expected so much or worked their students so blasted hard. None of the others sweated clear through their shirts with the teaching, treating every single split-second decision like it meant life or death—which, it turned out, it did. Every day.

Will rises from his bunk and stretches. If he hurries, he'll have time for a Coke from the gedunk.

He'll have to remember to write Joan about that, the snack bar with the odd name. Sometimes the gedunk offers ice cream, too, in this city of steel carrying nearly three thousand men. They have a post office here on the ship, a dart board, a barbershop, a clinic, and a hangar large enough to hold an eye-popping one hundred planes—near everything you could need, all floating on salt water.

Just no women. No quiet. No peace.

How to explain that to Joannie?

That even in the moments with nothing to do, even when they're bored stiff playing poker, the men live with tension like glowing-hot rails, fearing that any moment sirens might suddenly blare, that as the Japanese navy gets more desperate, the waves of kamikaze attacks are coming faster and harder.

How the heck does a man describe what it does to the mind watching a plane dive straight down into an aircraft carrier's deck, the geyser of flame— taller than any big-city skyscraper—that explodes from the hundred planes in its hangars and the thousands of gallons of fuel below?

How to explain that, someday cuddled close with his wife on the couch, fields of daffodils blooming outside, and her wanting to know if liver loaf sounds nice for dinner?

Bracing himself for another stretch across open sea, with God only knows what might come swarming down from the skies or hissing through the sea, Will raises the Coke he's been handed just now.

"To Joannie," he says, not caring who hears, "the girl I'll love till I die. To Mama back home and my sister, Biscuit. And to Lieutenant Dov Silverberg, the best instructor there is and a mighty good friend."

Several beer bottles and one other Coke rise to toast his.

"To the folks we'll love till we die," someone says.

"Till we die," they echo and drink. Then they sit for several rack-stretched moments in silence.

Chapter 70
Hadley

Reunion weekend, June 2022

Passing one of the pictures Kitz and I chose to have mounted, I feel my stomach twist with the full graphic view, enlarged, of how so many innocents died, how much the world lost.

A niece of Hans Hessler's, in fact, called my cell from Berlin and in flawless unaccented English said, "The family's priest in Bamberg, Father Bernhard, spoke openly about the treatment of the Jews, gays, and others, you see. My grandmother, Hans's mother, learned later, in fact, that more than two thousand priests were imprisoned on what became known as Dachau's Pfarrerblock—the 'priests' barracks,' it means in English. Our own Father Bernhard was among those, Grandmother learned, who was tortured one Good Friday as the Nazi guards' way of observing Easter, if you can imagine."

"Dear God" was all I could manage.

"Indeed, yes."

"Do you know what became of your family's priest? Did he survive?"

"We believe he died there, in Dachau. I hope you will include something of this horror. You may say that one of the Hesslers has requested this, that our family—the new Germany too—wishes to remind all of us of the price of silence in the face of brutality."

Because families with young children are coming, Kitz and I bypassed the more graphic depictions and chose a photo of the exterior of Dachau, which we enlarged and mounted with a long, detailed caption that a parent might steer young children around, or not. Still, it's a disturbing jolt just a few yards away from the interactive fighter director training room that guests can enter and from the actual Hellcat, ignition disabled, whose cockpit guests can climb into.

Next to the soda fountain already serving up root beer floats to arriving attendees, the Hellcat looks more like extravagant playground equipment than a deadly machine. I wonder about our choice in bringing it here. Maybe—it's my hope, at least—if Kitz and I have done our jobs well, we'll honor courage and sacrifice without glorifying war. The impossibility of ever truly creating peace by fighting. Yet the impossibility, too, of letting cruelty go unanswered.

By the time I return to the welcome table in the grand lobby, Kitzie is in her element, energetic and beaming as she turns to the next guest. Since Ernst Hessler's return from Berlin, he's had time to survey every aspect of our work, and *that*, I suspect, is part of Kitzie's beaming.

A man of few words, he marched from each interactive exhibit to photo to backdrop. "Yes," he pronounced at the end. *"Das ist gut. Das ist* sehr *gut."*

Kitz and I were able to translate that well enough just by his face: not smiling, but a satisfaction—good golly, a tenderness even—I'd not seen in him before.

We hand out packets now with the reunion schedule and a map of the various venues, including our displays, tickets for complimentary drinks in Echo and the pool bar, a list of carefully curated local restaurants and shops, a few photos representing our larger mounted collection, and—my personal favorite—complimentary tickets to the World War II Home Front Museum, a short walk from the hotel.

Near the welcome table sits a working toy Jeep large enough for two children to clamber in and pretend to steer. With its boxy metal shape, light-brown paint, and a star on its hood, it looks as if it just rolled off a World War II battlefield but shrank in transit. The parents of grumpy, road-weary darlings gaze at us worshipfully.

I check the list. Most of those expected have checked in, except Rabbi Ben, Richard Silverberg, Will Dobbins, and his niece Cordelia.

Cordelia. The name on Nick Adams's phone when he hurried away from the beach that night. The call that couldn't wait.

As the resort staff scrambles to keep up with the crowd, Nick appears, helping people with their baggage and unfolding walkers and wheelchairs and strollers. He plays the part of a bellhop well.

Not a bad look on him.

Into this gleeful melee of people checking in enters a short, stocky man patting the valets on the shoulders, throwing open his arms with a boisterous, upflung gesture each time he turns to greet the next person.

"Hullo there, Benedick!" a young woman calls.

The newcomer's laugh carries from the porte cochere all the way to where Kitzie and I stand watching at our welcome table.

"Now *there*," Kitzie says, "is the person worth doing this whole shebang for."

"I see you've got your sights set on a new best friend."

"If he'll have me, I'm in. That *has* to be the good rabbi you told me about."

Continuing his greetings, the rabbi scoops yet another toddler from the ground and nuzzles her with his beard. Then he marches to Kitzie and me, arms out.

"Such a party, and it's only just begun!" He thanks us for our work as he shakes our hands so hard my shoulder socket feels rattled.

"Rabbi Silverberg, would you be a guest at every single event we plan?" Kitzie asks.

"Wait until you meet Uncle Will. That man makes me look stand-offish. Ah, here must be the excellent Hadley who conducted so splendid an interview over the phone."

"Your three families—how you all got connected—fascinate me. I hope some of that research ends up making this event more interesting for the guests."

"Well, *of course* it will. Also, I'm rather a fan of the truth. Makes for a bumpier road to travel, I find, but always, *always* more interesting. Speaking of which . . ."

Into this moment walks the very picture of fashion and polish, of elegance meant for display.

The whole lobby, honestly, seems to tense as he crosses toward us, even the little soldiers in pastel polo shirts and hair bows charging into Normandy on their toy Jeep.

As he passes, beige linen suit in perfect creases, he holds out his hand to a number of guests, who don't quite kiss his ring but who treat him with a strange deference.

"The almost-chair of the board," I say to Kitzie. "The challenger to Ernst Hessler's rule."

"Is everyone more quiet all of a sudden," Kitz whispers back, "because of the power he wields at Boundless? Or do they not trust him? Or both?"

Rabbi Ben must have heard us, his eyes shifting our way, but he says nothing.

Richard focuses briefly on various groups that amble by to greet him, but he's clearly searching for a particular face in the crowd, one he can't find.

Looking somehow regal even in his annoyance, he strides closer to our table, pausing only to shake his brother's hand stiffly.

"Well, well, Benedick."

"Hullo, Richard. It's time we caught up, you know. Had a real heart to heart."

"As we shall. Soon." With that, Richard turns his back to his brother.

I expected Richard Silverberg to be elegant. Even his name evokes the glow of sterling by candlelight, and the tone of his voice over the phone suggested chauffeurs and estates and stables with twenty-four stalls.

Very rich people raised by very rich people carry themselves and speak differently, I've noticed, their posture ramrodded—with an air of assumption, maybe, that the best table will always be offered. It's almost as striking, that posture, as how people who've come from struggle on struggle carry themselves with a feisty defiance that dares you, just *dares* you to look away, and you can't.

Me, I've not mastered either of those ways of being in the world.

Richard Silverberg cocks his head as he examines this crowd, this room, the reunion packet. I wonder if he's estimating the cost of all this.

A freakin' bundle, I could tell him. *Thank you, Ernst Hessler and Boundless LLC.*

Chin raised a little too high, he approaches us now.

He's got this haughty thing down, I think.

Kitzie, who, for all her warmth, isn't much for ring kissing—bless her—thrusts out her hand. "Kitzie Jacks, and this is my sister Hadley, whom I believe you spoke with already. We're delighted, Mr. Silverberg, that you could make it."

Richard murmurs something vaguely polite to Kitzie, but his gaze settles on me.

"Welcome," I manage and hold out my hand.

He takes it—that crushing handshake of someone who believes himself clearly in charge. "Hadley. Yes, we chatted. You were quite keen to know all you could." Without dropping his eyes from mine, he somehow assesses the whole length of me. "You look *just* how I pictured."

Feeling thirteen years old, my face a moonscape of acne, my hair a world of frizz, I make myself smile at him. "I was just thinking the same of you. Welcome."

Just as he opens his mouth to respond, Nick jogs back into the lobby from out by the pool, where he just escorted a guest.

Raising one hand to shoulder height like he's clutching a scepter, Richard pivots in place. "Well, bloody hell."

Nick stops in midlope across the lobby, his face full of things I can't read.

Stiffly, Richard thrusts out his hand to Nick across the room—*more a demand that Nick come shake it than a greeting*, it looks like.

"You," Nick says, "have some kind of nerve, given what you've tried to do to Boundless."

"Well said," I hear myself mutter. Not loudly, but enough that Richard apparently catches it.

Shifting his gaze back to me, hand still held out, Richard gathers himself like a big cat on the hunt.

"I wonder, *Hadley*, if you've had the opportunity to meet what we—and the press, I might add—like to call the *royal failure* of the family, decidedly the *very* dark horse for any future leadership position at Boundless, Nick Adams. So very Shakespearean, too, that our three families would have our own genuine *bastard* for comic relief."

Before Kitz can stop me, before I can stop myself, I've stepped from behind the welcome desk. "You will *not* behave like that here. There are children present who don't need a grown man teaching them what a tantrum looks like."

He rounds on me. "By God, have you taken leave of your senses? You, just a hired hack who can be fired with the snap of two fingers? Have you forgotten who *I am*?"

"You," I tell him, "are a seven-hundred-dollar haircut and a seven-thousand-dollar suit—in a color that, quite frankly, washes you out—with nothing inside but a supersized sense of your own entitlement."

Only then do I realize the whole lobby's gone utterly still, listening. Even the children in the Jeep sit wide eyed.

Nobody moves.

Chapter 71

Joannie

Like Marshall himself, the letter is fully transparent—maybe too honest, in fact. And it arrives just before another slap of the truth.

Even with its care to use vague language to elude the censors, the letter's words are vivid, evocative. Joan can see the rolling tanks and embattled French towns, can sense the men's raw courage, their disgust at a fleeing major. The guns feel to Joan as if they're blasting inside her chest.

Marshall always was the best writer of the three of them.

Curled up in a window seat in the little room above Gray's Drugs, Joan can even smell the smoke from exploding artillery shells—though she's also left the bread without butter too long in the toaster oven and it smoked.

She can picture it all—the White major, loudly predicting that the colored troops put under his command in the 761st tank battalion would be cowards, inept and useless, only to witness the valor of the men he maligned. Then the major hopping into a Jeep himself and abandoning the battlefield.

She hugs Marshall's letter to her chest. She's heard nothing from Sam, and Marshall's letter from three days ago is the closest she's come to feeling her brother here with her.

"Thank you," she says aloud, as if maybe a whole ocean and a battered French countryside away, inside a tank, Marshall might hear how grateful she is. How much she wishes they could just lie again, the three of them, on the beach and watch the clouds one more time.

She's holding the hinged-frame picture of Sam and Marshall and her, along with the picture Will sent of himself with Sam on the deck of the *Enterprise*, Sam looking so tired and gaunt, when someone knocks on her door—so lightly she wonders if she's imagined it.

Swinging it wide, she stares at the apparition before her: a slightly built figure in a pilot's khakis and bomber jacket holds on to the doorframe as if he needs support to keep standing.

Before she can speak, before she knows if the apparition is real, she holds up the pictures of the boys she was just thinking about, the brother she has missed like a hole in her own heart.

Who is standing right here.

Sam.

But also not Sam.

This boy's face has lost Sam's gentle innocence, its delicate features too prominent under skin that's sallow, nearly gray.

"Hullo there, Little Sis," he says.

With a cry of joy, she wraps him in her arms.

∼

Together, Sam giving a tug to Joannie's pilot jacket with the Fifinella on its left side, they walk arm in arm down the beach. Neither of them announces that they're walking to the old cottage—its ruins—but they both know.

Neither of them speaks about how Sam must lean on Joan for support as they walk.

You were 4-F! Joan wants to cry out, but keeps it inside for most of their walk.

As Sam stumbles, though, and she keeps him from collapsing into the sand, the agony spills out before she can stop it. "Your heart. You did not have to go."

"I *did* have to."

They walk a few more steps in silence until he speaks again, his voice barely audible over the crash of the waves.

"I'll give you this: maybe most wars are people taking revenge on people they hate—treating weapons of war like really big toys. We tell ourselves it's good versus evil, because we want the excuse to hate and hate hard. This time, though, this time was different. I couldn't sit by and watch any more than you could."

Hooking one arm around her neck like he used to do when they wrestled as kids, he kisses her on the side of the head. "*Little* Sis."

"By two blasted minutes," she says.

In front of the cottage's ruins now, they stand arm in arm. Sam limps toward the front steps, some of them still intact, and she keeps him from falling. They sit together facing the ocean.

"The picture," Joan says. "Of the three of us here."

Eyes out on the sea, Sam smiles. "Just thinking of that."

As the tide rises, the surf splashing and fizzing, Sam glances back toward the tree that demolished their house. "Guess there's no need for you to fix the roof now—there's that mercy."

She tries to laugh but it sticks in her throat. "Us. For *us* to fix the roof now."

She loves the sound of that word on her tongue again: *us*.

He shifts to face her, waiting until she lifts her eyes to him. "Joannie, I'm so sorry you had to do all this on your own, all this loss without me here to help."

"You're here now, though. You're back. We'll get you strong again."

Sam looks away. "I'm not sorry I went. I want you to know that."

She senses some sort of letting go in him, and she wants to shake him, to tell him he cannot, he *cannot* give up. "Marshall will be so glad to see you too. Maybe he'll get shipped home by late spring. You'll be all good by then."

Sam keeps his eyes on the ocean, and she wonders if he's picturing Marshall in the tank that he had to demand the right to use instead of a mop to defend his country.

She puts her arms around him, her breath catching at how thin he's become, how faint the beating is inside his chest. Squeezing her eyes shut, she tries to keep out images of his heart muscle struggling, straining to do its work.

"Half my brain, half my heart," she whispers.

"Except you got the better heart."

Fiercely, she shakes her head. "*You've* always had the better heart. You've always known how to love people and stick by them. I get annoyed with the world and just want to shut people up. If it'd been me in your Hellcat, I might've started dropping the bombs and not been able to stop."

He lifts his face to smile at her. "You know I'll always be sticking by you, right? Every time you fly."

"Don't you dare start talking like that, Samuel DuBarry. Don't talk like you won't—"

But he holds up his hand for her to hush, and for once, she does.

He speaks slowly, drawing shallow breaths between batches of words. "Every time you do something addlebrained and need . . . someone to harass you. Every time you feel all alone. In my own way, from wherever I am, I'll still be doing this." He lifts an arm to scrub his knuckles on top of her head. But even just that exertion depletes him, and he sinks back against her. "Tell Marshall goodbye for me, hear?"

"You'll tell him yourself," she insists. "When he gets back." She says it loudly, defiantly, as if somehow that will bring it to pass.

But she can already feel the life slipping from him, like the tide receding. Unable to speak, she holds him tighter.

"Joannie," he whispers. "What do you reckon it's like, where I'm going?"

You're staying right here with me, she wants to shake him and say. But she knows now it's not true.

And for all her doubts, all her unbelief, she can't help at this moment but see through Sam's eyes. "It's all love," she says, choking on the words. "It's all open arms. It's all welcome."

"Don't forget . . ." He can barely get the words out. She moves her ear close to his mouth. "Don't forget who taught you every single thing you know." He grins at her and wipes at her wet cheek. "Don't forget this either." He has to wait a moment and breathe before forming the next whispered words, one by one. "I am so proud of you."

"It's *you* I'm proud of," Joannie tells him, voice slivered to pieces, and she's no idea if he can still hear. "It's *you.*"

Sam's eyes are looking out over the ocean when his body goes limp against her.

~

Joan didn't leave him. She stayed there, holding him, shouting for Miz Rose to call for help.

Now Miz Rose is here, holding her, as they try to take Sam away.

"The hospital," Joan tries to insist. "He needs the hospital. I should've taken him straight to the . . ."

They nod at her gravely and wrap her in blankets.

"Sam," she tells them. "Wrap him up too. Sam's getting cold too." Miz Rose wraps a blanket around Sam on his stretcher.

"He's my twin," Joannie tells her. "One of us can't be gone without the other."

Miz Rose wraps her arms around Joan.

"He taught me to fly," she tells the faces gathered around. One of the faces is Edo Miller from the funeral home, and she knows what this means, yet her brain has gone numb.

"What," Joan asks, "do you do when half your heart and half your soul don't work anymore?"

"Your country," someone in the crowd of faces says, "is grateful for your brother's service."

"4-F," she tells the face. "He was 4-F. He shouldn't have gone at all."

She doesn't recall how she gets back to the little apartment over Gray's Drugs, except that Mr. Gray and Miz Rose help her climb the steps.

~

When she wakes sometime in the night, she's on the floor. Rising and without putting on a coat, though the temperature is at freezing, she walks from the village north along the beach toward the cottage's remains again. She stays there, wandering around the crumbling walls, until the whip of the serrated winter wind off the ocean cuts into her face, her arms.

The riptide, Joannie thinks. *You always warned me, Sam, about the riptide, that it could pull a person straight out to sea. You just didn't tell me the riptide could be you—your leaving, just half of yourself behind, pulled out to sea and flailing for air.*

She doesn't recall walking back toward the village, but somehow she finds herself there, and someone is leaping from a Jeep, running toward her. Putting his own coat around her, bundling her upstairs. Making her coffee from the remaining grounds of Maxwell House she has left.

"Hypothermia, or very nearly," Dov might be saying, forehead crumpled, but it doesn't matter. He's bundled her in blankets, just like Miz Rose did.

Miz Rose. Who cried with her and held her when Edo Miller took Sam away.

Dov is urging hot tea on her now.

"Joan," he's saying, and maybe explaining how he got word of Sam, but she only half hears.

In answer, Joannie lays her head on his chest. Throbbing, her head feels so heavy, her whole body so cold. He is warm, and he is here. She dozes like this for some time, possibly hours.

When she comes to, he's looking at her with a tenderness that makes her throat ache.

"Should I leave?" he asks.

"Stay," she says, and he does. For how long, she's not sure.

Waking again, she stirs, lifting her head from his shoulder. Dov's eyes are closed, and she admires the thickness of his black lashes.

Eyelashes. The high cheekbones of his face. Something to think about that's not loss.

Glad his eyes aren't open quite yet, that she can't see the intensity of them, she brings her lips to the line of his jaw, the corner of his mouth.

"Joan," Dov manages slowly, woodenly, like a man forcing himself to speak. "Your loss . . ."

She feels the grief shredding her insides like a wild animal trapped and desperate. She feels also the heat of her own skin, as if it might melt off her bones, the ache in her nearly unbearable now.

She finds his mouth and kisses him, hard and long and deeply. She will kiss him to forget. She will kiss him because she wants to, is frantic to—and because her sorrow has swollen so big she knows it will crush her one way or the other. None of it matters anymore.

Sam's gone and Pops's gone, and the memory of a sweet boy across the boundless sea feels so distant right now. Dov is, though, right here, his heart and her own hammering so hard she can feel the throb in her toes.

She's all alone in the world, except for this man who's here with her. This man she loves and isn't supposed to. This man who's brushing the tears from her cheeks with his thumb, smoothing back the hair from her face.

"Joan," Dov whispers again. "I'm so sorry for all your sorrow."

"Kiss me," she hears herself say, "until it doesn't hurt anymore."

"Your grief. Joan, in your grief I can't—"

"Just kiss me, Dov."

He doesn't try to speak again—except for, later, her name. His hands slide from her neck to slip across the curve of her shoulders. His head dips to brush his lips across the skin on her clavicle and out to the edge of her shoulder.

Slipping one of her hands behind his head, she pulls him to her, all of him taut, like a mandolin string tightened to near breaking. Untucking his shirt, her palms flex against his bare back.

He is warm. He is all muscle and comfort. He cares for her more than anything. Anyone.

His curls, she thinks once. *His lovely black curls.*

It's the last clear thought she has for some time.

Chapter 72
Hadley

Thoughts muddled, I need a moment to be alone. To breathe, not in a lobby teeming with people, most of them still staring at me.

Out here under the massive event tent, I feel the sea breeze and hear a steady hum of voices as clusters of the reunion guests circle through the displays.

Nick finds me in a back corner of the tent, where Kitz mounted and hung two enlarged love letters, the first a particularly eloquent one from Sam DuBarry to Marshall Hammond, their lives and their sacrifices woven in with these other stories of loss and silence and courage. The second is from Dov—in his own meticulously neat handwriting and his own passionate voice—that ended up back in the family's possession because, Kitz and I gather, he sent it to the woman he loved, his wife Deborah. Maybe it's the gut-wrenching tone of the letter that's drawn me to it again.

I speak before he can. "That was awful. Richard Silverberg's treatment of you."

He gives a single nod. "Abrasive and ugly is what Richard does best, all with his signature gloss. You, on the other hand, were spectacular."

"Wasn't she, though?" says a voice from behind us.

We turn at the same time to find, of all people, Samantha Mitchell cocking her head at me, her Fifinella-figure cane in one hand and her other arm looped through the Reverend Doctor's.

"We just came in for the final lines, but I must say, Hadley, your delivery was superb."

"I should've kept my mouth shut, not blasted one of the guests at the party."

Samantha pats my arm. "I suspect that man will recover. His type always does, more's the pity."

"I'm so glad you came." I reach for her hand that's not gripping the cane. "Kitz'll be thrilled, as well. And thank you," I say to Felicia, "for delivering the invitation for the reunion to your neighbor here."

The older woman tilts her head up toward the letter on the foam-core board I'd just been rereading before Nick showed up. "Not a bad letter."

I scan it again, hugging my arms over my chest as I do.

So much loss. So far from peace. So far from the White Cliffs of Dover we laughed about hearing again and again, and never getting tired of the words.

Please, I must hear from you today. I've received orders this morning calling me back to L. I hope to return in a few weeks but I can't be sure what my superiors will decide.

This war is bloody brutal and the last thing I want to do right now is leave you in your grief . . . I must know, please, what you're thinking before I go.

Until we speak, I'm sending you love and comfort and peace ever after. For me, the sun will not shine on the other side of this ocean, and it will never go gold again without you.

"Not a bad letter at all," I agree. "It's from Dov Silverberg to the woman who became his wife, Deborah."

"No," she says. "It's not."

The Reverend Doctor and I both stare at her.

Samantha shrugs. "It's from him all right, but not to her—not that we'll publicize this to anyone else, of course. The woman he sent it to, she was in a tangle of grief at the time. She never answered the letter. Didn't even open the door when he knocked—pounded, really, like he'd tear the thing down. Never answered before he went back to London, at least."

Chapter 73

Joannie

April 11, 1945

Starting in her middle, the nausea rises up through her whole body, straight to her fingertips.

She scans this note that she kept, one that an enlisted man brought to her door last February. Earlier that same day in February she'd read but never responded to two other desperate notes from Dov. He'd knocked on the door, then pounded, calling her name, then left his messages at the threshold.

Like the others, this one is full of love and of anguish.

Forgive me, I beg you. I will go to my grave believing I let my own feelings overwhelm a sense of duty, that I took advantage of your grief like the most despicable of cads. Tell me, please, that I may come see you.

This note, like the earlier one, was not signed.

Like a whisper, she thinks, *that can't be heard across the Atlantic or the Pacific. Like a secret no one can know.*

Like he's ashamed of himself. Of me too.

The enlisted man had stood awkwardly shifting his weight.

"Thank you," Joan told him and moved to close the door.

"I was instructed, miss, to wait for a message back."

"There's no message back. Thank you." When the door slammed shut—she doesn't recall swinging it so hard—she leaned her forehead against it.

It hadn't been his apologies or his sense of duty she wanted to hear.

Another wave of nausea rolls over her.

No point in seeing a doctor, Joan thinks.

Not on this small island, where, outside the servicemen stationed here, everyone knows everyone. Her private news would not be either soon—not hers and not private.

The metallic taste in her mouth is strange and unfamiliar, yet she recognizes it somehow . . . same with the tenderness in her breasts, the dizziness, the violent, gut-inside-out retching—all that, too, feels both new and ancient. As if millennia of women before her were gently smoothing her hair, holding her hand.

Tell him. Now that he's coming back from London, you must tell him.

Joan lays a hand across her belly and tries to picture her future.

She cannot. Not even ten minutes from now.

With just one other woman pilot, she flew a B-29 bomber, built for a crew of ten and prone to engine fires, then landed it, smooth as Irish cream. Yet she wasn't as frightened that day as she is now.

Also, that day, a whole flock of pilots turned out to applaud her and her copilot. Whistled and cheered, even.

But here she stands now, alone. No whistles or cheers. Not even an arm over her shoulders.

She's accustomed to flight plans and throttles, to hulking machines that, if she follows her training—reads the manual, by God—and uses her best instincts, she can lift into the air above the seagulls and marsh hens. She knows how to dip and bank and roll and dive.

She does not know how to do this next thing, to plan a future that is no longer just hers.

Or how to tell him the truth when she's not seen him in months. When she has no idea what he'll say.

As Joan feels her way along the wall back to the window, bile still souring her mouth, she stares out at the rain sheeting down on the village.

Tell him. You must tell him, she hears in the deluge.

But telling him has consequences, not just for him and for her. Joan tries to picture the young woman in Golders Green, waiting. Will Dobbins in his combat information center on the USS *Enterprise*, in free moments composing the lines he'll write her tonight, always ending his letters now with the same words:

With love way beyond the boundless sea.

In his last letter, he told her less of the battles the *Enterprise* was facing—which she knows means the conflicts have intensified—and more of his hopes.

It's been three years now since we met, you and me. I've tried hard for your sake not to speak every last wild yap of love I've felt all this time. I may not come home in one big, gangly piece like I left, but if I do, my Joannie, would you do me the honor of marrying me?

My Joannie, he said. That sweet, faithful boy.

Write him. You must tell Will too.

Dear God, tell him what?

Instead, she wraps herself in blankets, watches the spring storm that was brewing all day finally let loose its winds. She wants desperately to tell Sam her troubles, this vortex of death and life.

Sam would know what to do.

Chapter 74

Will

April 11, 1945
USS Enterprise, off the coast of Okinawa

He has not slept in so many hours he's lost count. Someone shoves another coffee at him, and he downs it, never taking his eyes off the radar, a host of green dots throbbing at eighty miles out.

An incoming wave of planes could only mean one thing.

"Thank you kindly," Will mutters to the source of the coffee as he checks the speed and altitude of the approaching wave.

"Hell, you're the only damn man on this ship who still says 'thanks' under pressure." It's a soft voice, the voice of a kid, really, and with a Jersey accent thick enough to dig a fence hole into. The kid had to have lied about his age, that face of his nothing but peach fuzz and pimples.

Will glances up only for that wheat seed of a second. "I'll say 'thank you kindly' again if you bring another two cups. Black. Hay bales of sugar."

He's relayed what he's seen to the captain on the bridge, the gunnery officer, the lookout topside, and the fighter pilots already fourteen thousand feet up.

Scanning the dials and the radar scope, Will sends the new numbers. They all know what this means.

The deck guns are blazing, the Dauntless dive-bombers and Hellcats plunging and rolling and swooping as they meet the oncoming wave of Zeros from the Imperial Japanese Navy, the kamikaze pilots not just prepared but planning to die.

Pacing, Will picks up the phone, then the headset, no time to think of anything else but the facts he must pump back out from this information heart.

Before he can speak, he sees from the windows of the combat information center, high above the flight deck, a Zero break through the air fight above and aim its nose directly down at the *Enterprise* deck.

The deck guns follow it down, but the plane is cometting on its own course.

Only now does Will think about anything other than the sweep of the radar.

He pictures Joannie first, and hopes his mama would understand being second in his thoughts just this once. He pictures the best of his instructors, too, the Englishman Silverberg.

He's repeating aloud the first words of the twenty-third Psalm, *The Lord is my shepherd, I shall not want,* when the Zero's nose pierces the flight deck a few yards away.

The boy from Jersey stands holding two coffees, the kid's eyes saucered at what he's just seen, that jaw that's never been shaved, not a once, dropping open as the *Enterprise* shudders with the impact. Will dives to cover the kid as the windows shatter, shards flying toward them, and the flight deck explodes.

Chapter 75
Joannie

April 21, 1945
St. Simons Island, Georgia

For this hardest of conversations, Joan wears her best dress, a lilac organza—an old one from before the war, the one she wore to the Cloister when she danced with Dov that first time.

The fabric lifts in the sea breeze from the open window as she leans out. Just below on the sidewalk, a Western Union man is asking directions. A telegram, then.

Joan's heart twists in her chest, though it can't be for her this time. It just can't.

Mr. Gray steps out from the drugstore below and points up at the studio window where she sits.

Another telegram for her, after all.

But she has no one else to lose, does she?

If Will is dead, the navy would send news to his parents in Tennessee, not to the girl he wanted to marry who never fully gave him an answer.

If Dov is dead, the Royal Navy would send news to his family in London, not to a lover they know nothing about.

The Western Union man at her door asks only, "Miss Joan DuBarry?" and hands her the telegram without waiting to hear an answer or even meet her eye.

A man can deliver only so much searing news in a day, Joan thinks. *I would run too.*

She feels nothing, not even dread, as she opens the telegram. What is there left to feel?

She scans its few lines, her mind on the conversation ahead with Dov, and she barely comprehends what she reads.

WOUNDED.

She manages to understand that much.

WOUNDED. WILL HEAL. PUN INTENDED. SENDING ME HOME TO TN BY WAY OF SSI. WILL YOU MARRY ME?

Joan's heart stops along with the telegram's last two words.

It would be the answer to this problem—for some person who's not Joan.

Because you can't marry someone you've lied to in the most fundamental of ways, can you? And you can't tell someone the truth who'll be forever destroyed by it.

Can you?

Joan is startled to see that she crumpled the telegram in her fist. She smooths it on her tiny breakfast-room table and smooths her skirt but doesn't bother putting on shoes.

Winding her wristwatch again out of nerves, she walks barefoot north up the beach.

She hasn't seen Dov since he returned yesterday from London.

Barefoot and pregnant, a voice sneers in her head. *That's where skill or intelligence or ambition or a sense of adventure will get a woman—right back to where she should be: barefoot and pregnant.*

But then it's Sam's voice she hears pushing back.

If anyone in this family's likely to do something extraordinary, I'd lay my money on Joannie.

This, more than what she's about to do, makes her want to weep. That Sam thought her capable of doing something useful—extraordinary, even—in this hard, violent world.

Yet for all Sam's vaunted view of her, here she is, in fact, barefoot and pregnant, walking down the beach to meet with a man and tell him a truth that will wreck several lives, regardless of what they decide.

The gulls dip and dive beside her through the soft twilight air, the ocean itself gone gold. It's as if they recognize her as the girl in the plane, the one they've flown with over this very beach.

Can birds sense worry and sorrow? If so, maybe they sense what she's headed for and are coming alongside for support.

It would serve her right if the marsh hen showed up about now, reminding her how dangerous it is to build a nest on watery sod.

There he is up ahead, turned the other way, as if she might come walking toward him from the cottage ruins. His black hair and deep-blue officer's uniform create a dark silhouette against a cloudless blue sky.

It occurs to her briefly to wonder how he convinced his superiors at the Fleet Air Arm of the Royal Navy to let him return, however briefly, to the United States.

Listen, blokes, my love life is a royal wreck. I'd fancy a leave to sort it all through . . .

Definitely *not* what he said. His Majesty's admirals must've agreed he's still needed here.

His shoulders are hunched, a posture she's never seen on him before. Always the athlete, he always keeps his shoulders thrown back, his posture always straight as a wharf piling.

How odd that one such minor thing, his shoulders hunched, could reveal the sharp bend of the road her own life is about to take, before anyone's spoken a word.

He looks, she thinks, *like a man sailing a boat in a storm all by himself.*

He looks so remarkably . . . sad.

She knows.

Before he turns to look at her, wet tracks down his cheeks.

Before she hears him speak.

Before she checks his left hand for a ring that is, in fact, there.

She knows.

Joan thinks of the riptide just a few yards away, how it could pull a person straight out to sea. How the sea would mean oblivion. No more hammering words in her head. No more grief.

She will think about that soon. For now, though, she only holds her head high.

"Congratulations," she says.

Chapter 76

Hans

May 8, 1945

Hans is praying to die. Right here. Right now. He does not want to draw another breath if he has to watch another minute of this film.

He's slumped down so low in his seat, another inch will send him to the floor. Not that he will notice.

Unmoving, he and the other POWs stare, stricken, at the black-and-white images on a screen that feels as if it must be two hundred feet high, Death leaping from the projector, Death leering at them from every frame.

Hans's friend, Lieutenant Silverberg, addresses them, first in English, then German, his tone flat, his Cambridge accent, if anything, more pronounced as he enunciates each word. Every weekday for weeks now, he and Hans have shared a smoke just before the transport arrives to take the POWs back to their camp. They began by discussing Goethe, then their common love for physics and math, then their lives before the war, their families. Even, lately, their dreams and their dreads for the future.

For all his love of physics and math, Hans is surprisingly keen about the workings of the heart. He understands more than the Englishman has told him about himself.

"You see before you footage of what the Allied forces are finding as they liberate camps across Germany and Poland, this one liberated by my own British forces, a camp called Bergen-Belsen." Silverberg glances only once at the screen. His eyes rove instead over the men's faces. "We are under orders to allow . . . to compel, I should say . . . all POWs being held in America to view this footage."

"Eine Lüge!" the man behind Hans bellows. Then in English, "This is the lie. Propaganda!" Shifting back to German, he adds, spittle spewing from chapped lips, *"Ein Jude!"*

"I am," Silverberg responds without emotion, "indeed a Jew."

The man behind Hans spits as if he could reach Silverberg. It lands, instead, on Hans, who's so paralyzed by what he sees on the screen—by what he himself had been a part of—he can't lift his arm to wipe the vileness from his neck.

It's one of the men who tried to strangle Hans during his first week here, a Nazi officer who became during these months in America more vitriolic, more crazed, more loyal than ever to the Führer, who'd died eight days ago—or so the American guards have informed them. Hitler had gone down fighting valiantly, the Nazi officers assured each other, or he escaped in disguise and will reappear soon, triumphant.

"Eine Lüge!" the man shrieks.

"I wish," Hans manages in English as he turns in his seat, "that I could believe these images we see could be the lie. Yes, I wish this."

The camera shifts to a gully mounded in emaciated bodies, then pans a line of what appear to be skeletons propped to standing, which suddenly move. They are human beings, alive—if this can be called life. Hans's voice trembles. "But it is no lie."

The man lunges for Hans's throat, but he cannot hurt a man who wants to die. American guards drag the Nazi officer to his feet.

"You bastard Jerrys," one of the guards says—but he struggles to get the words out, as if his throat has closed shut, as if he might weep—"will damn well . . . watch what the film crews . . . recorded when the troops went into these damn . . . camps."

Hans is almost sorry when they drag the Nazi officer away. At least being knocked unconscious would have been a welcome escape from what he's witnessing on the screen.

Hans's misery has been deepened by a letter from his mother. Word has made its way to Bamberg about the liberation of Dachau. Hans's mother gives few details in the brief letter except to say:

> *I cannot describe to you my sorrow, my son, my shame. All of us. Our shame.*

Even the sound of her words in German strangely fits the emotion: *meine Schande.*

Except, Hans thinks, *perhaps a bit too gentle, this sound. There should also be the sound of something sharper, more wrenching too—a cry of pain.*

> *We wait for news of Father Bernhard, who may have been also at Dachau.*

In his head, Hans hears Father Bernhard's voice celebrating the Mass: *mea culpa, mea culpa, mea maxima culpa.*

The man to Hans's right, a fellow built solid as a panzer, has pulled his knees to his chest and rocks back and forth like a small child. The man to Hans's left stares, eyes glazed, body gone catatonic as if he could bear no more and shut down, his mind gone to gray blur.

No one is allowed to leave until the film is over.

When at last the reel is empty, Hans files past his friend Silverberg without speaking, their glances meeting. Hans has no words in German or English.

Chapter 77

Dov

May 9, 1945

Caught in currents of elation and loss that swirl around him, that keep him unsteady, distracted, sometimes even struggling for air, Dov intends to walk the beach alone just now.

But yesterday's film and the news of what happened last night in the POW encampment make him turn and join the POW—or whatever status he is now—Hessler for a smoke on the strip of beach.

The Allies have declared victory in Europe. Germany has surrendered. The prisoners of war who are deemed trustworthy have been granted increasing freedom, and now they all must wait. The American soldiers must return home—through Operation Magic Carpet, their government calls it—before the POWs will be sent back to their home countries and before exchange instructors like Dov can be sent home. The war in the Pacific rages on.

"Months," Flint announced to the POWs just this morning. "And no complaints from you Jerry bastards if it's taking too long."

Hans Hessler, Dov saw, only shook his head, as if saying he's not likely to complain.

Easing down beside him on the sand, Dov eyes him now. "I heard what happened last night in your camp." He speaks in English but slowly to give Hessler time to translate.

The German nods. "I had the match."

"So I heard, yes. Jolly well burned your military uniform. Started a trend, too, I understand. Rumor has it so many of your fellow POWs joined you in the burning, the guards had to start a bloody bucket brigade."

"Bloody necessary," Hessler says.

"Bloody necessary," Dov agrees. The two men exchange slow, small smiles.

They sit smoking in silence, both of them watching the sunset. Dov pulls off his shoes and socks to feel the grit of the sand and the stab of the shells—to feel something at all in his body that isn't grief. Watching, Hessler also slides off his shoes. He's wearing no socks.

"You are . . ." Hessler searches for the word. "Thinking about something, yes? The fire of Wehrmacht uniforms, perhaps. Or the news of the surrender."

"All of it," Dov tells him. "I'm contemplating bloody all of it."

The German glances at the ring, silver and weighty, on Dov's left hand.

"The young woman Joan DuBarry. You spoke of her. She is not . . . for you?"

Dov does not meet his eye. "She is not for me, no."

"Perhaps I will marry her myself."

The German is kidding, Dov thinks. God, surely he's kidding. Or maybe, come to think of it, maybe not. Hessler's face, young and eager, appears all too earnest.

Dear God.

Disgust churns in Dov's gut. A Jerry who looks like a recruitment poster for the Third Reich wanting to marry Joan.

The hell you will, Dov thinks, but manages to drag on his cigarette rather than speak.

"I do not know her. Except that she saved my life. I have the gratitude to her."

"Hardly reason to marry." If the German hears repugnance in Dov's tone, he ignores it.

"Also, she seems very . . . full of the life."

"Yes." Dov will not, he will *not* let himself be drawn into a future of longing for her like this every day. But right now, *dear God*, how can he not?

"*Congratulations* is how you say in English? She is a fine woman, yes? Your new wife."

Another drag on his cigarette, and then Dov is ready to speak what is true, and also what has to be said. "An excellent woman in every way. Intelligent. Lovely. Faithful. Kind." Dov hears himself say it with conviction, which is the very least Deborah deserves. But she deserves more, so much more from him. And he will learn to give her more, by God. Somehow, he will.

He's dropped his head into his hands before he realizes how that might look in the wake of *congratulations*.

Hans Hessler watches him closely—too closely. But the fellow does not ask the obvious: why Dov is slumped like a shepherd's crook, sorrow and guilt like a cloak that he cannot throw off.

If nothing else, this German knows the meaning of tact. He doesn't ask the question that hovers in the salt air between them.

"Let us speak," Hessler offers after a span of silence, "of books, yes? Or of music, perhaps."

Meeting his eye, Dov sees the understanding that has settled on the German's face. Compassion, perhaps, too.

Dov nods.

"Bach," Hessler offers. "He is my favorite of the German composers. Of yours, of the English, Handel—whom we Germans also claim, of course. Because of our countries' shared Handel, or rather, Händel, I once teach—no, I once learn, *learned*—to play the organ."

Dov lifts his head. "That so?" After several crashes of waves, he finds he can speak if he stares out at the sea. "I do fancy Handel. Though I rather despise the organ. Sorry."

"Then you must hear me play it. You will despise it much the more."

Dov's laugh surprises them both.

Looking at the shock of blond hair, the pale-blue eyes, the POW garb, Dov still feels hate gnawing at his insides at this German, at all Germans, the images of the camps still so fresh in his mind—images that will always feel, Dov suspects, like the burn of acid.

He remembers Flint's scoffing over the POWs: *Mercy of God, my ass.*

For today, in this moment, Dov agrees with Flint. To hell with high-mindedness.

Dov has been shaped by a tradition that honors the sackcloth and ashes of repentance. Now, too, though, he's been shaped by the cinders and slag of cruelty. Unforgivable cruelty.

Dov is in no mood just now to contemplate mercy.

Justice, now there's a word. Better yet, *revenge.* Revenge on the monsters that tortured and brutalized and decimated Dov's people in Europe.

Revulsion. That's as far as Dov can move away from revenge just now. Someday, he knows, he'll need to move on from that, too, or it will eat away at his soul.

He can almost taste ashes on his tongue as he pictures how this must look, a British Jewish physicist sitting beside a German submariner, speaking of love for music—and, together, not speaking of love for a woman.

Ashes.

Dear God, the ashes everywhere in those newsreels covering the death camps.

Ashes, too, from all those German military uniforms burned last night by prisoners consumed with shame. As they should be.

Dov stays where he is, the tips of both men's cigarettes bright throbbing dots, and pictures again last night's bonfire of uniforms glowing garish, bloodred.

The surf surges, washing their feet.

Chapter 78

Joannie

Not showing yet, Joan is still working behind the counter of Gray's Drugs, still living above the drugstore—although her days are numbered, she knows. Mr. Gray treats her with kindness, but his customers will never tolerate a cashier who's gotten herself in the family way with no husband and not a single family member left to her name—not even a boyfriend.

She avoids all contact with Dov, which isn't hard, since he's done the same after his wrenching announcement that day on the beach after he returned from London.

She told him "congratulations," of course. What else was there to say? She told him he'd done the right thing, and she partly believed her own words. Partly still does.

Still, she thinks of the riptide—so often she frightens herself, she who can do barrel rolls in a biplane.

She made no announcements of her own to Dov that day on the beach, and never would.

Even if he has spasms of private pain or regret, he will be a faithful and devoted husband, Joan has no doubt.

But she'll be damned if she'll put herself in the path of having to watch.

The navy is serving lunch on the beach today to all comers, an ongoing celebration of Victory in Europe Day yesterday, the day sparkling, the whole island in bloom, as if nature had suppressed its sunniest, warmest weather and most of its blooms until the declaration of peace in at least part of the globe. Even the pelicans fly as if they're euphoric, diving, Joan thinks, with a gusto she doesn't remember seeing for years.

The situation in the Pacific theater is still dire, the loss of life staggering on both sides, but at last, at long bloody last, the outcome, however it's finally reached, appears only a matter of time—and of more lives that will be lost before it's all over.

Today, three navy men have formed their own tiny brass band and are playing tunes that Frank Sinatra, Ella Fitzgerald, and the Andrews Sisters have made famous.

Joan spots the POW she saw nearly strangled to death that day that seems so long ago, when she was making Sam's milk rounds. To her, they will always be Sam's rounds, even though she's taken them back up since the WASP was disbanded. But with the boys coming home, her services will no longer be needed on the milk run, either, she's been told. Which is just as well—only so much longer before her condition shows.

Today, though, she will focus on the moment, the euphoria in the air. She still cannot imagine the future, but today she will simply watch the driveway to the King and Prince for an arrival.

She smiles at the POW, a stocky blond with piercing blue eyes and a somber expression. He is handsome in that way of the Third Reich's propaganda posters she saw in newsreels—Aryan features that look especially eerie these days. She nods to him but doesn't expect him to recognize her.

Standing behind a rectangular table serving hot dogs, he hands her a plate, holds out his hand, and speaks surprisingly decent English. "My name is Hans Hessler. I do not forget your help." One side of his mouth lifts in a smile. "*Hello* is how I should begin."

Extending her own hand, Joan wonders whether she's greeting a prisoner of war or a free man who's stranded in the victorious country. Either way, she's drawn to the deep sadness in his blue eyes, above a shy smile. "Hello to you. My name—"

"Joan DuBarry here has also served in this war," a voice with a British accent says from behind Joan, though she doesn't turn, "as one of the United States Women Airforce Service Pilots."

Hans nods. "Yes. You speak"—he stops to correct his verb tense—"you spoke to—*of* her, yes? To me. Of her. Often."

Joan can feel Dov go still behind her, but she still refuses to turn and meet his eye.

"Yes," he says quietly. "Yes, you're right. I have been an admirer of Miss DuBarry's abilities for quite some time."

"Hedy Lamarr," the POW offers, apparently oblivious to the awkwardness between Joannie and Dov and warming to the subject. "This I thought to myself when you saved the life—*my* life. Here is the woman who looks like Hedy Lamarr."

"So she does, yes." Dov's voice sounds pained with the admission. "Saved your life, quite unpredictably, by nearly running you over with a lorry, as I recall. Joan, Hans and I have enjoyed several discussions of our favorite authors, our favorite philosophers."

"Our families," Hans adds. "They are different. Very different. Yet also much the same. Family, this is important."

Joan's gaze drops from the hot dog on her plate to Dov's left hand. *Family,* she thinks bitterly. So much she could say. So much he does not know. Will never know.

As if feeling where her gaze has landed, Dov twists the silver band.

Still, she does not look at his face. "Hans, when will you go back to your home country?"

"They tell us it is months, many. I am not in the hurry." His head dips. "This is selfish of me. My family has need for—of—me. Things are hard there. Very hard. But for myself, I am in not the hurry."

Joan waits for him to go on.

"I wonder," he begins again, "if you—"

Joan is focused on the German's question—anything to keep from facing Dov—when a Jeep whips down the driveway of the King and Prince, its brakes applied so suddenly a cloud of shell dust engulfs it. A tall, gangly figure emerges from this cloud, an olive green seabag slung over one shoulder and a grin that appears to embrace the entire shore, filled with people and gulls and pelicans, all turning to see the newcomer.

Joan runs a few strides to him, but Will is faster, covering the yards of crushed shell and sand in seconds and twirling her in a circle.

The moment blurs, her delight to see him, seeing his wince of pain—the lacerations—as she and Dov and radar training school instructors all surge to greet him.

The three-man band breaks into another song, "When Fools Rush In," everyone laughing and slapping Will on the back, until he admits his wounds are still healing.

"Stitched together like an old rag doll," he apologizes. "Like to split my seams if we go too rough."

They circle around as Will tells stories that make them all laugh—though something has made his hands tremble. It's hot enough that Will strips down to his white undershirt, a padding of bandages reaching across his chest and visible beneath the cotton.

Joan sees Dov notice the tremor in Will's hands, too, sees Dov's face contort—with guilt, maybe—telling himself once again he should've been there in battle himself. Or should've kept his distance with Joan.

"The amazing Joannie DuBarry," Will says, taking her hand, spinning her out for a twirl in the sand.

No, she wants to tell him. *No. Listen to me. Here's the truth* . . .

But she's whirling, and the sky overhead is cloudless, a dazzling cobalt, and Will Dobbins has made it home in one piece, even if stitched back together.

Joan forgets for a moment that there is any reason in the world just now to despair. Will spins her out again, her feet corkscrewing into the sand with the turn.

Now she's spiraling back in, stopping just short of Will's chest so she doesn't slam into those scars. He tips her chin up to him. "I've come a mighty long way to ask this official, Joannie DuBarry." He drops to one knee. "Will you marry me?"

"Yes," she hears herself say. "Yes, William Shakespeare Dobbins, I will."

A betrayal if there ever was one, and yet it comes out of her mouth.

A life preserver in the storm of her life. An answer to her condition. If she can only close her eyes long enough and pretend she can lie to this dear, lovely man.

"As soon as possible," she hears herself add.

Whooping, he twirls her around again, then kisses her hard.

"I love you," he says, nearly shouting. "I love you, Joannie DuBarry!"

No whisper, she thinks. *He's said it out loud.*

Will turns to Dov, who's handed a camera to Hans. The prisoner of war snaps pictures.

"You, Silverberg. You did a mighty fine job keeping an eye out for her. I thank you. If you'd do us the additional favor, Joannie and me, and stand up beside me tomorrow in front of the preacher, I'd be much obliged."

Chapter 79

Will

May 10, 1942
Lovely Lane Chapel, St. Simons Island

His lacerations, still healing, were oozing this morning, the bandages already changed twice, but he barely notices now, standing here outside the chapel. Like everything else that has survived this war so far, the chapel stands in need of repair, its shingled roof ravaged by storms and the war years' neglect, its green spire a little askew, the paint of its white clapboard peeling.

A little like me, Will thinks, grinning. *Not a heck of a lot to look at these days but mighty durn grateful to still be upright.* He feels his grin grow until it must truly take over his face.

Will hates that his folks can't be here for the wedding, but he's written to them these past three years about the woman he loves, and his mama and Biscuit are already planning a big shindig in the barn when he takes Joan to meet them once the war's truly done. Will's friend Dov, as steady and brainy a fellow as you could want, is here beside him, both of them all gussied in their navy dress whites, neither one of them saying a word. Which is just what Will wants, his joy bubbling so high he'd rather not speak.

Joannie is late, but all brides likely are. This only gives Will more time to relish this moment, this day.

"She'll be here," Dov says, his hand resting light on Will's shoulder, like Will needs bucking up, which he doesn't. Not one splinter of a tiny piece.

The German fellow Dov brought, the former prisoner, snaps a picture. Will found it odd at first to bring this guy along, but Hans appears to handle the camera well, a skill they need today, and he speaks often of his farm back home. He and Will have discussed cows at length.

Also, Will liked that yesterday over hot dogs, when one of the American officers referred to Hans as "one of you Nazi bastards," Hans shot back without hesitation, "*Bastard*, this is fair, sometimes. *Nazi*, no. Perhaps *German bastard* is most fitting, yes?"

This had made Joannie laugh—another good reason to learn to like the fellow.

"I'm sure she'll be here," Dov says again, looking not at all sure.

"She'll be here," Will insists, and knows that she will.

"It's called Lovely Lane Chapel?"

Dov, bless him, must think Will needs distracting. A kindness from him.

"As storybook of a name as it looks, sure enough."

Dov's eyes flit upward to the spire and over the clapboard. Maybe he's seeing the repairs crying out for a good hammer and brush. Or maybe since Dov was just back in London on Royal Navy business—the sly dog slipped in a wedding to the gal he'd told Will about nearly three years ago—maybe he was thinking how compared to poor, battered London, anything left standing was good.

But now at the same moment, Will and Dov spot a sailboat approaching on the river, a few yards away. It's a tiny old vessel, its hull an oak lacquered to a high gloss, glowing in the light of the evening.

At its stern, manning the rudder is, sure enough, Will's beautiful bride, cheeks windburned, hair wild, a dress, gauzy and light, swirling around her legs as she rises to tie the little boat to the dock on the river. The Hessler fellow snaps a photo as she straightens and turns toward him.

Pale lavender, Will tells himself, because his mama will ask what color the dress was and the pictures will only show it as a pale gray. He'll always remember she wore lavender, gauzy and light, to their wedding. She's the loveliest sight, sure enough, that Will's ever seen, *ever.*

Only my Joannie, he thinks, beaming, *would sail a boat to her own wedding.*

"Me smiling this wide just might split my face clean open like an old melon," he says.

Dov's hand goes to Will's shoulder again. "Splendid, old chap. She looks splendid. She *is* splendid. As are you. As are you both. I wish you the best. All the best. Truly. Truly, I do."

His friend's voice has gone crumbly as an old cookie. Another kindness: a friend who feels so powerfully strong for your sake.

Will can't look away from Joan, but he slaps Dov on the back of his dress whites. Gratitude washes over him in a wave so sudden, so strong, Will is nearly knocked off his feet: for the instruction that saved his own life—hundreds of others too. For the friend who stands beside him. For the union today with this woman he'll love till he dies.

"Beyond the boundless sea," he says, choked up full with all the grateful, before breaking into a run to meet her.

Chapter 80

Hadley

"I couldn't, of course," Samantha says, her Fifinella cane tapping as she walks just ahead of us toward the Friday-evening buffet line.

Following in her wake, Kitz and Felicia and I exchange glances, eyes wide and mouths open with the gazillion more questions we need to ask—on top of the few we've already managed.

Kitz is the first to wade back in. "So the letter we thought was from Dov to Deborah was actually to Joannie . . . that is, to . . . you?"

"The man was eloquent. He wrote a good letter. Not that I could bring myself to answer any of them." Samantha sighs. "And I couldn't marry Will, of course. Not in the end."

Kitz and Felicia and I exchange looks again.

After Samantha closed the door on us a couple of days ago, Kitz and I tried to weave the story together ourselves as we hung photos and finished the last of the sets.

In the midst of the setup, we shook our heads at each other.

"Samantha *is* Joan DuBarry," Kitz kept saying to me. "Can you believe it?"

I can't. And I have my own questions, too, but I'm keeping those to myself for now.

Soon, she'd said. *I will answer your questions. I promise . . . I do take promises seriously.*

"You couldn't marry Will?" I prod—and I hope it comes across gently, though I'd rather go after the truth with a spade.

Samantha smiles at me beatifically, like she's acknowledging the question but isn't compelled to respond, as she reaches the lobster on the buffet line.

All our guests except Will Dobbins successfully checked in for the weekend, and I can't help but wonder if his health kept him home or if he's just running late, as his email said, because of his great-niece's schedule. Kitz and I have allowed ourselves a few minutes off duty to hear more of Samantha's story and grab dinner. At the buffet table, Felicia holds Samantha's plate for her and fetches it back to the table.

Kitz and I nod at each other over the food: fresh melon, lobster thermidor, shrimp scampi, steamed asparagus, grilled brussels sprouts in a balsamic reduction . . . every dish looking and smelling superb.

Oh, and fried Spam for historical accuracy. It smells less superb.

So far, so good. We sit, quite literally, on the edge of our wooden seats under the strings of Edison lights by the sea as we wait for Samantha to settle herself enough to go on.

"You know, I can still see it: the preacher must've wondered what ghost I saw when I walked down the aisle just stoic and calm as you please, then took off like a shot straight back to my little boat. Without a word to a soul." She shakes her white, curly head at the memory. "Poor dear Will. Bless him. He didn't deserve that."

Felicia leans forward. "You couldn't marry him . . . why?"

"Because," I offer softly, "you were pregnant."

Kitz and Felicia both stare at me like I've accused her of a crime.

Sweetness I've never had in abundance; imagination, though . . . *that* I've got. Also, random puzzle pieces have suddenly snapped into place for me. There are only so many reasons a young woman in love with a man—or two—leaves her hometown in a rush and stays gone.

Also, there's the issue of Joan's mother dying relatively young of a wasting disease, and of Deborah and Dov's adopted daughter Bea also dying of a wasting disease. I'm not ready, though, to let any more pieces fall into place yet, even though some of them seem to hover, ready to drop. I'm not ready for the full picture.

Nodding at me, Samantha sighs again. "I wasn't showing yet—not with clothes on. Turns out I didn't have it in me, though, that sort of deceit—to marry a man when I was pregnant with another man's child. Truth is, I didn't have it in me to tell Will the truth either."

Felicia takes her older friend's hand. "How could I have known you my whole life and never known so much about you? Being a WASP. Everything you accomplished. Everything you went through during the war."

Samantha pats her hand. "Getting pregnant out of wedlock—what we called it back then—wasn't exactly something you talked about. Ever. Being a WASP, that belonged to Joannie DuBarry, the girl I used to be. I don't expect you all to understand now what it was like then. But when I ran away from Lovely Lane Chapel, I felt—I *knew*—I had to start all over again. Leave Joannie behind.

"You already know I chose the name Mitchell for one of my favorite planes—because it was so resilient and because it was a thrill to fly. I couldn't say this out loud at the time, but I also thought"—Samantha lowers her voice—"it was quite the looker, the B-25—sexy as hell even, all those glass panes in its nose. Lord, the things you couldn't say back then if you showed up with breasts in the boys' club."

Just taking a gulp of my wine, I spew sauvignon blanc into my hand.

"Back *then*?" Felicia murmurs, and we all laugh again. "But what happened? What on earth did you do after you ran?"

Toying with her shrimp, Samantha looks up at Felicia. "That, my dear, is where your great-grandfather Marshall came in again. Just back from the war, but not done with heroics just yet."

Chapter 81

Joannie

November 20, 1945
Jekyll Island, Georgia

A world of phantoms, that's what Jekyll Island has become: deserted by the richest of the rich, watched over now by only a skeleton crew of caretakers drifting among the ghosts of the past, and all that swaying Spanish moss.

For Joan, it's a place for someone like her—her waistline ever expanding, her mind in shreds—to disappear. A place for outcasts and outlaws.

Jekyll sits to the south of St. Simons—also a world away. Until the war began, it was a winter playground for several of the wealthiest families in America. But when Hitler began rolling across Europe, when it became increasingly apparent there was no telling what this madman might do, the panicked American government thought it best that a terrifying percentage of the nation's gross national product not cavort on a single torpedo-vulnerable island off the coast of Georgia. The families—the Rockefellers, Vanderbilts, Morgans, Goodyears, Cranes, Pulitzers, and Astors, to name a few—abandoned their "cottages" and the private club they'd built and simply paid to keep the homes and grounds from rot and ruin.

Skeleton crew.

A fitting term, Joannie thinks as she dusts a parlor in the Jekyll Island Club. Because everything feels dead here except for the natural world, which teems and thrives like always, the pelicans gliding and diving, the dolphins leaping and splashing as if death camps had never existed and a Final Solution never been planned, as if tanks had never rolled across fields of bodies, as if the world hadn't just lost millions of its bravest and best, its most innocent too.

Joan has shrunk to something of a skeleton herself these days, her arms and legs hardly more than pieces of pale driftwood and looking about as healthy. Her middle, though, has swelled visibly under her dress.

But no one here cares what nice girl from what nice family got herself in the family way and ought to be banished.

The head housekeeper does sometimes pucker her lips, but she's had trouble keeping good workers out here in such a remote place, so she holds her tongue, at least. Joan has learned to avert her eyes from those puckered lips and just continue to the next floor to scrub.

She fled from the chapel without letting herself see the look on anyone's face—not Will and not Dov and not the preacher.

Her eyes did snag for an instant on that German, Hans, holding the camera, but only because he'd stationed himself by the door and she had to bolt past him. His expression, she thought, was one of compassion.

Or maybe that's just what she wanted to see.

She left St. Simons without saying goodbye to anyone. Not even to Mr. Gray, who also deserved an explanation. She left him a thank-you and the next month's rent, even though that left her with only thirty cents to her name. He'd been kind to her always, but she didn't want to know if his kindness extended to harboring a young woman who'd gotten knocked up. Certainly, he couldn't let her keep working at the drugstore behind the counter. Joan wouldn't do that to him. Or to herself. She wouldn't stand and listen to people say that's what comes of letting a woman do a man's job, flying a man's plane.

If she's to be tossed out of the island's village, she'll do the tossing herself, thank you.

Dov.

She won't let herself think about him. Not about what he would say if he knew about the baby. None of that matters now.

No, that's not true. She does lie awake envisioning herself going back to tell him what she didn't that day on the beach when he'd just returned from England.

Except that he'd already made his decision.

Maybe he did at some point love Joan in a way he didn't love the girl back home in London, but he'd made a promise, a promise that scores of other people were counting on in their grief and their own loss. If he doesn't already, he will grow to love this Deborah in a larger way, Joan knows, in a long-journey, side-by-side kind of way that will become the real love, the stubborn love that walks on through the glitter and gloaming of life, a love that keeps showing up.

Who is she, after all, but a small complication in the scope of this terrible war and all its terrible choices?

Some nights she dreams he's searching St. Simons for her, that he's frantic with worry. Some nights she dreams she comes to him after the baby is born, just as he is boarding the ship to England.

Some nights in her dreams, he boards the ship anyway, waves sorrowfully from the deck to her and the child.

In one dream, though, he takes her by the hand and begins running. Both of them running, the baby bouncing on her hip, until they reach East Beach beyond the Coast Guard station. There they live in a little cabana—on what, she has no idea. In dreams, no one needs an income or indoor plumbing. In that one dream, they are happy, so happy.

But she always wakes up. To an ever-swelling belly and a sore back and a mind that refuses to plan for a future, other than waking up the next day to dust another parlor, scrub another floor.

Marshall is the one who finds her.

Marshall, who always listened more than he spoke when they were little, and still appears to have little use for words.

He arrives on Jekyll one day around twilight, soon after Japan has surrendered. He's just back from the war and has sailed her old boat across where the St. Simons Sound meets the Brunswick River and appears in her path just as she finishes cleaning the clubhouse, her dungarees only partially zipped to allow for her belly, blouse ballooning over her waist, hair smelling of floor wax.

Marshall's eyes drop to her middle, but he doesn't look shocked. Rather, he lets her throw her arms around him and hang on, nearly knocking him off his crutches. The two of them laugh when the considerable bump of belly keeps her from hugging him close.

She does not stare down at where his leg was, but he does, lifting the stump that ends just above the knee.

"Well, Joannie. Guess one of us has added some flesh and one of us lost some."

She laughs with him, because what else do you do with an old friend, with so much sorrow, so much life threaded between you?

"You're back," she breathes. "Dear God, you're back."

"Got brought back on the *Enterprise*, if you can believe it. They're using her to bring fellows home."

"Will Dobbins's ship. Sam flew on and off the *Enterprise* a few times. But then, you'd know that."

Marshall nods, eyes filling.

"Sam," she says, voice catching on his name, "said to tell you good-bye. Somehow, it felt like you were there with us at the end."

They reach for each other's hands and hold on for dear life.

"I know. I do know." Crutches swinging, Marshall falls into step beside her. Together, they stroll to the pier where the millionaires' ships used to dock, at the zenith of the Jekyll Island Club's popularity. The palmettos rattle their fronds, soft percussion nearly drowned out by the squawk of the gulls.

"I prefer this," he says, "all the sounds here, to gunfire."

She can see on his face that even this effort to speak has cost him.

He's come here to see her, and that is enough.

"So the Seven Sixty-First Tank Battalion," she says. "I read everything that journalist fellow Trezzvant Anderson wrote about you all. General Patton not on board but desperate for men. Patton persuaded of your valor. You came away with a medal, I think?"

"Traded in a leg for it."

"Is it painful?"

"Not much. Not compared to lots worse loss you and me got to face."

They sit down on the sand.

He jerks his head up toward the clubhouse. "They might think . . ."

"Yeah, they might," Joannie says. "But after they've already thought . . ." She lays a hand on the mountain of her belly, and they both chuckle again.

Dear God, she thinks, *it feels so good to laugh.* "There's freedom, it turns out, in not caring what people think and working a job no one else wants."

He reaches to pat her hand. It's not safe for him to be seen holding a White woman's hand, and she doesn't want him in any more trouble than he may already be in just coming out here to see her. But they both need to hold on to something, to someone.

"I'm getting married," he says at last.

Joannie's jaw drops. It's the last thing she would've expected from him.

But . . . ? she wants to ask. She knows he's asked it himself. She sees on his face that he's struggling enough already, without her asking the obvious thing.

"She's an old friend. A good, gentle soul." He meets Joan's eye now. "Had her own share of loss. Reckon we'll be some kind of comfort to each other. Good, steady companions. Just nothing like . . ." His eyes well up again.

It's Joan's turn now to reach for his hand. "I know." This time again, she holds on for more beats than she should. "I'm so sorry," she whispers. Which feels incredibly rude in response to a marriage announcement, but also feels like it has to be said—three little words to mark all that she doesn't know how to say. *So sorry you have to pretend. So sorry for the hurt and the loss. So sorry for all the ways people don't understand . . .*

He squeezes her hand as they sit together in those ellipses, that silence teeming with words.

"So," she says at last, "you were a hero, Marshall. I'm not surprised."

"That whole battalion. You never saw such a bunch of brave men. Heard you did some good work yourself. You and that crazy love of flying you got from Sam."

"I did get it from him, you're right." They sit again in silence awhile.

"Joan. You can't stay out here, you know. Not all by yourself."

"I'm not all by myself. There's a skeleton crew." That word again. *Skeleton.* She's seen the newsreels of the camp liberations, back before her middle was showing and she could watch from the back of the Ritz, the owner welcoming her.

"You know what I'm meaning. You and . . ." He nods at her belly. "Y'all got to be where folks can help." He waits until she looks him in the face. "You got people who care, you know."

Joan holds up one finger. "Let's see, there's you. Then there's Mr. Gray and your mama. Though neither one of them would likely ever get past my being a big disappointment. So there's really just you." She shakes her head. At this rate, she's liable to start feeling sorry for herself. "I don't want you to worry."

"Too late."

"You suggesting I move in with you and your new wife?" She meant to be funny—facetious, maybe. The thought of what the villagers would say, all that opprobrium, the explosion of it, making the corners of her mouth twitch into a grin.

But Marshall isn't smiling. "If that's what we got to do, yeah."

Joannie's eyes fill now, and she's not one for crying. "You're serious. You would actually do that for me." She leans closer to him. "And for Sam."

They sit like that for a time—who knows how long.

She squeezes his hand. "Means the world that you'd offer. But I'll be just fine."

"What about the baby? Baby's got to be fine, too, you know."

He says that word *baby* like it's real.

Dear God, it is real, Joannie reminds herself. *It is.*

Marshall looks at her almost sternly.

Because, unlike me, he's thinking about a real baby.

Joan pulls a breath from deep in her chest—as deep as she can, at least, around the form of this thing pushing her organs to the nether regions of her body. "I will keep that in mind. The fact you'd even offer is remarkably kind."

"You'll make a plan?"

She sighs. He's not leaving, she knows, until she promises she will. "I'll make a plan."

Marshall scrambles to his feet, holds out a hand to help pull her up—which she actually needs, weighted down as she's become. He does her the service of looking away, out over the sound, as he asks this last thing. "The father? He's rejected . . . ?"

"He doesn't know."

Marshall's eyes swing back to hers. "But surely—"

She shakes her head.

Their eyes meet for several beats.

That's the thing about people you've known since childhood. So much that doesn't need to be said. Here's one person in the world who knows not to argue with her.

Now he shakes his head. "I'm keeping your boat all waxed, until you'd be ready to sail again. I want you to know that. You and the kid. Same with the Gee Bee. I'm not so handy with engines, but I'll keep it painted—always the same red and white—against the sea air."

You keep the boat and the Gee Bee, she wants to tell him. *I for sure won't be needing either.*

But he'd know that was a bad sign, her with no plans to fly or to sail. He'd know that was a white flag of surrender, a life of no interest to her.

So she thinks it. But leaves it unsaid.

He holds out his hand. Embracing her in full view of the clubhouse would be stupidly foolish, and for all his courage, Marshall has never been stupid or foolish. "I expect you to let me know how you're doing on a regular basis, you hear?"

"I hear." She squeezes the hand he gives her. "Thank you for tracking me down."

He grins now. "Thought I was going to have to bring the whole damn tank battalion to find you."

"Oh, I wish you had. Never had an entire tank battalion hot on my trail." They laugh together one last time.

"Don't be a stranger," he tells her as he walks toward the end of the dock, where he's tied up her sailboat. "Remember, I'm keeping up the skiff and the Gee Bee till you're ready to soar, sea or sky."

"Till I'm ready to soar," she echoes.

Because that's all you can say to an old friend who's trying his best to salvage your life from the ash heap, even if you've no intention of saving it yourself.

"Bye, Joannie," he calls and begins untying the boat.

But when she doesn't return the goodbye, he turns—to find her sickled over, hands on her knees. At her feet, the ground has gone wet.

"Oh, God," she whispers. "Oh, God."

Chapter 82
Samantha

They stare at Samantha, and she knows what they see: a little old woman, withered and weak, made stupid and slow and inconsequential by age, no more capable of beauty or childbirth or flying a B-25 to help save the free world than a marsh hen.

She grips her cane harder, like it's a handhold on a cliff.

She does, in fact, feel as if she's hanging on a rock face, a sheer one, and very likely to fall.

She could stop here in the story. But she can't make a break for it and run anymore—not with these brittle old chicken bones that once were very nice legs—but she could stop talking and not have to face this last bit. The part they won't understand.

She's waited too long already, though, and it's clear to her now, painfully so, that one person's story is never only her own.

She takes a deep breath, and they wait, leaning forward, not making a sound. They're wondering where this is headed, her tale. She wishes—*dear God, how she wishes*—she didn't have to say.

She continues speaking again: Chin up. Shoulders back. Precise.

What she's had to be all these years.

"So, what with my water breaking like that, Marshall had to run get the housekeeper, of course. As it was, a Black man nearly delivering a White woman's baby in 1945 . . . it was so far beyond what anybody back then could stomach. I think the housekeeper decided she was just helping deliver kittens and got through it that way without fainting or calling the fires of hell down on me. Got shed of us that same day, Marshall carrying us back on my boat, him and his mama hiding us for a day or two after that."

"Wait," Hadley breaks in—of course she does. "Sorry. Just a couple of days? But—"

Samantha's gaze, though, swings from Hadley's eyes—widened to sand dollars with what she's just heard, and maybe what she thinks she might hear next—up to the young man approaching the table.

Samantha holds out her hand. "*There* you are, Nick. I was wondering when you'd be able to join the story."

Bending to hug her—carefully, as if she might break—which annoys her no end, how people do this, though they mean well. "Have you gotten to the part of the story," he asks, "where you called Boundless to speak with my father about what you'd just discovered— and *who* you'd just discovered, and he decided to pay the original event planners their kill fee—or double that, maybe—then arranged to hire Storied Events to come here instead?" His head tips toward Kitzie and Hadley.

Just lifting her wine again, Hadley sets it down hard. "She *what?*"

"Not yet, Nicholas. Sit down and be patient." Samantha gestures toward the empty seat on the other side of Hadley. "Now, where was I? I know, I'm just now to the part of the story where Hans Hessler comes in again."

"I thought," Hadley says, nearly coming up out of her chair, "the last you saw of Hans Hessler after you saved his life, which Kitz and I learned about from his mother's letter—returned to sender, that never reached you—was when he took those few photos we have of you and Will at the beach, and then from your wedding. The marriage that never happened."

"Ah, but then Hans comes back into the story, you see. This time, to return the favor." Samantha nods at Nick. "Your grandfather."

Young Nick, bless him, tilts his head back, voice soft. "Poor guy. After all he survived, all he went on to do, he probably couldn't have imagined what a royal screwup his grandson would be."

Samantha shakes her head vigorously, white curls bouncing. "Just look at what the reformed royal screwup is doing now, making good use of his energy and education. I've heard what you—while you were doing penance here—and your Uncle Benedick have been planning, along with Cordelia and your Uncle Will: the revitalization of Boundless's heart."

"With *Will?*" Kitzie murmurs to her sister. "We thought he wasn't mentally competent to—"

"Except that information," Hadley murmurs back, "came from Richard Silverberg, so if we consider the source . . ."

Samantha reaches across the table to pat Nick's hand. "If I were six months younger, I'd sprint across the lawn and snag Ernst by the ear. As it is, Nick, do bring him over here, won't you? He needs to hear this story too."

Her little audience sits fidgeting, trying to relax and listen to the band, but they shoot glances at her. As Ernst follows Nick to the table, he extends a hand to Samantha.

"It is my honor to meet you at last, Ms. DuBarry."

"Ms. Mitchell for some decades now," she corrects him. "Although it's probably time I answered to either."

"It was you, I understand, who saved the life of my father. Which makes you a most honored guest."

"You should know that he also saved mine." Samantha shakes his hand and does not let go. Then reaches for Nick's hand with her other. "Ernst, you should know I've chatted with Nick several times on the phone as you and I were making plans, and I must tell you, I like what I've found in Hans's grandson, your son."

Ernst shoots Nick a look. "Indeed."

The way Ernst says it, the indeed *is not quite a question or an exclamation of surprise,* Samantha thinks, *but if I'm being precise, it's not agreement either. Ernst Hessler doesn't know what to make of his own son.*

Samantha levels her gaze at the young man. "*This,* you must remember, is your family legacy. This is who you really are, Nicholas, like your grandfather Hans. The kind of person who's made, if I may say so, a crazy-ass hash of your life—"

Nick's mouth quirks. "Fair enough."

With a jerk on Ernst's hand, she pulls him down lower to face her. "Hans Hessler was a man who believed in second chances."

Ernst gazes down at Nick, and though that stony old face of his doesn't soften except at the eyes, Samantha watches his shoulders relax. "My father raised me to know the shame over what his—*our*—country had done. He raised me to know what he himself did during the war— and what he felt he'd not done quickly enough. He raised me to hear how his village priest practiced the silence at the beginning of the war but not by the end, when it cost him his life. Ms. DuBarry—Ms. *Mitchell*—is correct to remind me. My father believed in second chances."

Slowly, tentatively, as if he's not sure how he'll be received, Ernst Hessler rests a hand on his son's shoulder.

"Hans Hessler," Samantha says, looking past them all toward the sea, "was a man who'd lost all hope at one point. But later held on to hope for someone else in despair. *That* is who he became."

Chapter 83

Joannie

November 22, 1945
St. Simons Island, Georgia

She's still bleeding, her body still sore and torn from the birth, when she limps through the dark, having left the bundle behind, safe and warm.

The bundle.

It's all she lets herself think of it as. She blocks other words from her mind.

Bundle.

The bundle she's left in the care of Marshall and his mother, who will figure out what to do—people far better equipped than she is to do all that needs to be done.

This probably endangers Miz Rose and Marshall, Joan might realize if she stops to let herself think—if anyone here in the Deep South found them with a White baby they're keeping secret . . . but she's not thinking. Not feeling either. Just exhaustion. Cold. And darkness. Darkness she's certain never will end.

Already, she's failed the bundle, having given birth in a parlor of the abandoned Jekyll Island Club, laboring with her eyes fixed on a framed photograph of J. P. Morgan hanging on the club wall so she didn't have to see the housekeeper's lips gathered into a tight pink knot of disapproval.

No one should have to be born like this, Joan thought between pains, *under the watchful eyes of these two: J. P. Morgan, arrogant, and the Jekyll Island housekeeper, appalled.*

She at least should've told the Hammonds she was leaving. Marshall and Miz Rose will be frantic tomorrow. But she can't face the shame, see the looks in the eyes of people she loves as she walks away.

She has to. She won't stay and mess everything up again. Marshall will know what to do, where the bundle should go. She's sobbing as she collapses beside a cluster of palmettos, her blood soaking through her undergarments and skirt.

The bundle knows none of this, though. She left the bundle sleeping, tiny eyes closed against this moment, tiny fingers flexing in its dreams.

Wiping the back of her arm roughly across her eyes, she welcomes the birth's physical hurt, which at least distracts from the ache of her heart, a sword thrusting and turning inside it.

From inside Mr. Gray's cottage, next to where her own once stood, she hears the end of a radio commercial and then the next song, Vera Lynn crooning "I'll Be Seeing You."

"I'll be seeing you," she whispers back toward the Hammonds' cottage, where the bundle sleeps. Joan's voice crumples on the final word.

Vera Lynn sorrows over picturing the one she loves in all the old, familiar places.

The lyrics make Joannie sob more. Because unless you count the floor of the Jekyll Island Club, she and the bundle have no familiar places together.

And never will.

Joannie lifts her hands, the emptiness hitting her all at once, the space between her arms now like a gaping wound.

I can't bear it.

I can't.

Fourteen thousand feet in the air and one engine on fire—that she could do.

But this . . . leaving has gutted her.

And yet somehow her body still moves. How can that be, since she feels flayed alive, nothing but raw flesh?

She must not look back. She mustn't.

"I'll Be Seeing You" is rolling to its final refrain.

Covering her face with her hands, Joannie hears the last chords fade into the night.

Nearly doubled over now with the ache of her body and, far worse, the ripping open of her heart, she turns back only once.

"Goodbye, sweet baby," she whispers, using the word only this once. "May you have a better life than what I could give you. You deserve so much more. May you . . ." But whatever benediction might have followed, she's too racked with sobs to finish.

~

Standing there shivering at the water's edge, she considers how it will feel to walk into those waves and keep walking.

This is her island, her ocean, and it feels as if she'll never know a real home again. A walk into the sea, *her* sea, will hardly feel like anything foreign or frightening.

By the light of the moon, she can see the silvery surf, her bare feet tracking along the wet sand. She watches as her feet leave clear impressions, then the waves lick them away as if they never existed.

As if *she* never existed.

It's that easy. That smooth. To exist and then not.

To be and not to be.

She thinks of Will now, who'd quote Hamlet and wrap her in his long, gangly arms and ask what on earth she is thinking. What on earth she's just done. He'd want to know how on earth he could help.

He'd despise me for doing what I've just done.

Or possibly not.

He might be horrified or bewildered. But possibly he'd have understood that she felt she'd betrayed him—that her despair, the darkness that's rooted into every inch of her brain, has choked out every sliver of light.

But Will is not here.

Will Dobbins has gone back, no doubt, by now to Tennessee. Probably will marry the willowy, rafter-reaching Ruby Sloan and start a family. A real family. Not the imagined one he drew in his head for Joannie and him when he was an ocean and a whole world of horror away. Back when he pictured Joan faithfully waiting for him.

She thinks of Dov, who's gone back to England by now, she feels sure. Who'll be devoted and kind and good to his family, and if he thinks of her ever, won't dwell on Sea Island or the girl from St. Simons he danced with there.

He's done what he needed to do, and now she will do the same.

The dark things in her head twine tighter together, no light at all.

She can't think of the future, and she won't think of the past.

The sea is cold, so very cold, as she wades forward.

The riptide is strong, and that helps. Even powerful swimmers are no match for that, as Sam liked to say.

Sam. Half her heart and half her brain has already died.

This last won't be so hard.

The water is paring knife cold, and that will help too. The temperature is painful only just now, but in a moment, she'll go numb and she'll not let herself fight, and then it will be over.

The bundle is safe, she tells herself as the water reaches her neck.

The bundle, at least, will be safe.

Chapter 84
Samantha

No one speaks for a full minute, the laughter and clinking of glasses from the other tables feeling irreverent.

Like revelers stumbling into a funeral, Samantha thinks. *Fitting, that image. Because death, of course, is what's waiting.*

Samantha sees fear spark in their eyes. They're terrified at what Joannie has done, left undone, and might do.

Why wouldn't they be?

"Which was when"—Samantha nods toward Nick, who's returned to his seat beside Hadley and has gone very still—"your grandfather, and your father, Ernst, showed up just walking down the beach with a flashlight. He'd gotten permission to stay on at the King and Prince doing custodial work until they could ship him and the other former prisoners back home. He was out looking for sea turtles who might be laying their eggs, he told me later—entirely the wrong time of year, of course, but since not a lot of sea turtles lay eggs in Bavaria, we'll forgive his not knowing. Especially since what he *did* find was a young woman in her own private hell."

Rising, Nick comes to kneel beside Samantha. She's been right about him, then—this young Nick does have a quiet kindness to him so like his grandfather's. Ernst stands awkwardly where he is, but even his stony old face has eased into something much more like flesh.

Samantha's hand goes to her chest, because it still hurts. Even after all these years it still hurts desperately, like she can still hear the cries of a baby mixed with the crash of the waves.

Samantha's heart has ceased beating, she's sure. And she sees Hadley reach for her phone like she might dial 9-1-1.

"Samantha," Hadley offers, "if it's too hard to talk about . . ."

The girl poses this softly, and it startles Samantha that she can be soft, in addition to funny and impatient and determined and tough.

Of course she can be, Samantha thinks. *I of all people should know.*

But Samantha ignores the offer—there's no turning back now. "It was a bitterly cold night on that beach. I've wondered sometimes over the years if maybe the burn of the guilt Hans was facing himself—his part in what his country had done, you know—made him more raw to feelings. Like several layers of skin got burned away and he sensed things that others had too much thick hide to feel."

Leaning back, she stares out at the ocean before speaking again. "'Course I had my own burn of guilt from that day on."

She looks past them as if she's seeing other faces out on the shore—and she is. "I did what I did, and I've had to live with it all."

From beside her, Nick whispers, "What was it he said, my grandfather?"

"Wish I could tell you exactly. I think it had to do with his having struggled himself, his having felt unworthy to live, to go home and be happy again someday in Germany. His having considered taking his own life at one point. It was strange: I knew him least well of the three friends, but he was the one who had to hold my secret—which was its own kind of love. He might have been grateful to me, perhaps found me striking—I was a looker, you know. But he wasn't *in* love with me, I don't think. Hans's love for me was just this: he didn't make me feel like a monster for the choices I made, and respected what I'd asked him never to say."

"Including," Hadley asks quietly, "who the father of your child was?"

"He was no fool. He'd seen the look on Dov's face, the way I ran from the chapel. I made him swear he'd never tell Dov about the birth. He argued, but he finally swore to keep my secret as long as I needed him to, which turned out to be a lifetime, it seems."

Kitzie sits forward. "The . . . bundle. Did Marshall and his wife or his mother . . ?"

But Felicia shakes her head. "I'm the only child of the only child of Marshall and Grandmother Felicia's one child. I think I'd know if a little White kid showed up in the family portrait in 1940s Georgia."

"The bundle," Samantha echoes, "deserved a family. That's all I could think, all I could see through all that dark in my head. I could see her with a family. That's all. When Hans talked me out of the water, he swore he'd help me figure it out. Hans and Marshall together, later that night, they swore to me they'd make a plan for the baby—where she'd be safe and loved, they promised. Miz Rose and Marshall took me in for a couple more days.

"Back then, we didn't have names for when darkness takes over your head and you can't think, can't see even one day ahead, can't just buck up and move on. One morning, once I knew there was a plan for . . . for the baby I'd borne, I slipped out, got on a bus headed I didn't even know where, God's honest truth. I think I bought a ticket to Boston, then realized the winters were six months too long, so I got off along the way and never looked back."

Samantha draws another long breath, the tension she feels like knives thrust in her lungs. She has to look over their shoulders, not at their faces, to speak. "Well, now, hell, that's not true. I did look back. Plenty. I prayed for my little girl in her new life. Every day, all through the day. Prayed I'd at least let her have better than what I could've given. Hoped to God I'd make some kind of use of the life Hans Hessler made me take back that night."

A silence follows.

It's the Reverend Doctor who breaks it. "You did, Samantha. You did that."

Without warning, Hadley sits bolt upright. "I saw the receipts of the donations from Boundless to all the aviation charities. You flew for those organizations. Contracted with Doctors Without Borders and all the rest."

Samantha tilts her head. "If you're willing to fly medical personnel and lifesaving drugs into places with nothing but furrowed fields and beaches for runways, often with wars or famines or floods raging, it's remarkable really how many people will put up with a woman pilot."

No one speaks for some time, and Samantha is grateful for that, feeling spent and just wanting to hear the surf whispering now, the shells clacking and chattering softly.

Oddly, it's Kitzie, the quieter one, who takes the next leap. "The bundle."

Or maybe that isn't so odd, Samantha remembers. *Quiet waters like Sam—Marshall too—could run very deep.*

And it's Kitzie who speaks next again. "So Hans and Marshall knew what family ought to be given the bundle—the *baby*. Meaning, then, that it—*she*—was adopted by Dov and Deborah Silverberg as a war orphan."

It's not a question.

"Beatrice. Bea." Kitzie looks for confirmation to Samantha, who nods. "The one child of the two without official United Nations documentation. Also, Bea had her father's cheekbones."

Kitzie reaches for the older woman's hand.

"Bea grew up to marry an American and have a daughter of her own," Samantha says in a voice that sounds, even to her, fragile as spun glass. "They moved to Charleston, South Carolina. Not too far up the coast from where Bea's father, Dov, was stationed during the war."

Hadley is nodding. And looking less shocked at what's probably coming than her sister. Hadley has already put some of these pieces together, Samantha can see from her face. Here is one more piece to be eased into place—and the girl blurts it out loud. "Charleston. As in 'C'ton.' Scrawled on the back of one picture."

"Oh, Samantha," Felicia says, sitting forward. "How wonderful. How difficult too."

Samantha grips her cane so hard now she marvels it doesn't splinter. "I promised myself to follow her life but never reach out, never spoil what they had as a family, you know. Bea died young. Of an autoimmune disorder that there are so many more treatments for now." She does not let her eyes shift to anyone in particular at the table—she can't.

Dear God, she can't breathe.

"It was Deborah," Samantha manages to get out, just barely above a croak, "who let me know when Bea died."

"Deborah!" This bursts from Hadley.

Samantha meets the young woman's gaze and won't let herself look away. "Dov Silverberg wasn't a man to keep secrets from people who trust him. He must've told her as soon as he put the pieces together himself. While I was flying all over the world, ferrying doctors and very sick kids, living in a tent on a savanna or a hut in a jungle or a cabin on the side of a mountain, Deborah was steady and stable. A marvelous woman. She loved those children well. Her whole family, their synagogue—all of London, I'm pretty sure—adored her. Dov and I never spoke again—there wouldn't have been integrity in it for him—but Deborah was the one to track me down and reach out. With Dov's blessing, she said. I never met Bea before she was too ill to understand who I was—and, dear God, where could I even start? After Bea's death, I cut myself off again. Completely. I didn't know what happened to Bea's daughter."

Didn't know, Samantha thinks. *Not* don't *know. Past tense, not present. If they're listening with precision, they'll hear the difference that makes.*

Dear God, they must already hear.

"*Didn't know what happened to Bea's daughter,*" Hadley repeats quietly—Samantha watches her beginning to see a picture where there were just pieces and patches before. "And Bea with symptoms of the disease that include, like MS, not being able to tell red from green. In that photograph in the snow, Bea was so impeccably dressed—but with one red glove and one green. Just like Kitz mixed up the green light with red when we first arrived on St. Simons."

Samantha doesn't know how to answer that, even if she wanted to, and she does not want to.

Looking out into the dark, she lets a dozen waves crest and crash on the shore before she speaks, a voice that's gone flimsy and tremulous—like the old woman they must surely see. "The hard part, you know, is facing how poorly one's own walls protect one in the end."

All of them at the table, unmoving—unblinking, even—wait for her to go on. To explain. To roll out the end of her story.

She lifts her face miserably to look at the two sisters. "I can't possibly hope you'd understand. If I thought I might've helped. If I'd known Bea's daughter would mourn her mama in all the hard ways and run away and cut herself off from her family and have two girls of her own and find all the worst men and get sick herself and try to make it all right in all the wrong ways, that her girls . . . *dear God, if I'd known . . .*"

This last comes out in a low moan, like a creature who's mortally wounded, and Samantha knows that it's true—all the wounds of her insides feel as if they must surely kill her now. And surely that's what she deserves. She doesn't realize how low her head's dropped until her chin brushes her chest.

It's Felicia who rises and wraps Samantha in her arms as the old woman weeps. Felicia, so like her granddaddy Marshall, who needed few words to speak oceans of comfort and truth.

"How beautiful," Felicia whispers, "how splendidly beautiful, that your great-granddaughters would get to know you."

Chapter 85

Samantha

"*Great-granddaughters.*" Hadley echoes what the Reverend Doctor's just said, but the look on her face says the words still make little sense in her head.

Even with Hadley's suspicions, Samantha thinks. *Even with what she must've worked out on her own. Still, it's a shock. How could it not be a shock?*

"But . . ." It's all Hadley can muster.

Wiping her face with a napkin, Samantha takes one more deep breath for this final stretch. "When I saw a news article about Boundless and that one of the founders, dear Will, was approaching a hundred, I thought, *Why not? How many breaths can there be left in this old carcass of mine? What's there to lose at this point? Why not make contact with the head of the firm and find out, from a safe distance, how Bea's family is doing?* Which is when I first talked on the phone with Ernst, and then also Nick here."

Nick's gaze swings to Ernst. "It was my father, to his credit, who put up the funds to find where Katherine, Bea's daughter, the runaway, had disappeared to before she died of an overdose." He ducks his head apologetically at having said that last word out loud, and Samantha likes him still better for that. A man with feelings. "The same private detective tracked down where her two daughters ended up after she died. The family had tried, but never found a single lead. Katherine had changed her name."

Now it's Kitzie's turn. "But . . . generations of our family were alcoholics and meth heads. Our first foster mom said how strung out and pathetic our whole family had been."

"If she was your only source for that information," Felicia asks quietly, "could that have been something she . . . made up?"

Looking dazed, Hadley and Kitzie sit a moment staring at each other, then at Samantha, then back at each other.

Samantha watches them take all this in, the possibility of that one foster mother's shattering lie. The possibility of a different truth—one with its own hurt, but also with its share of beauty.

In all her years, Samantha has so often been startled by the human capacity for lies and destruction—but even more often by the people who can mine goodness and change out of that dust.

When they round the table to hug Samantha—hesitantly at first— these two young women reach for her like they're weighted with so many questions their arms can hardly move. Slowly, they step in tighter. Closer.

The kind of hug you'd give family—when it's been a long, long time.

Then Hadley gives her sister a hug so hard Kitzie gasps.

"You're going to live as long as Great-Grandmother Samantha," Hadley tells her. "That's an order."

Hadley has, Samantha thinks, *a pushiness to her she comes by naturally, bless her. .*

All that stubbornness that can be so off-putting to others, it does have its strengths.

"Got it," Kitzie laughs. "I'll make a note."

There's more Samantha would like to say—too much, in fact— and the live band has stopped playing, its members fumbling with their horns. Then with a "One, two, three" from the band leader, they suddenly begin a new song, all about bluebirds flying over the white cliffs of Dover.

Samantha's hand goes back to her chest again like it hurts. Which it does.

"Oh my," Kitz and Hadley say together, watching their great-grandmother's face. Samantha knows her pale skin must have just turned whiter still.

Two figures inch forward from the far side of the lawn near the bandstand, where several strands of Edison lights merge. A forty-something woman in a business suit walks beside a man—with a wild thatch of white hair jutting up straight from his scalp—who, even lurching forward with a walker, appears remarkably tall.

Samantha is forming the words, though she's no idea anymore if she's making a sound or if it's merely the echoes of the past here in this same spot by the sea. A world of radar and submarines and women in bomber jackets, a world of love and longing, of duty and sacrifice and mess and secrets and beauty. A world not so different, really, from now.

"'Since brass,'" she says, "'nor stone, nor earth, nor boundless sea . . .'"

Chapter 86
Will

Joannie—she'll always be Joannie to him—is quoting the sonnet—*their* sonnet—almost to the final couplet as he moves forward, and he finishes it with her: "'That in black ink, my love may still shine bright.'"

A low choking sound comes from deep in his throat, and Cordy—*bless her kind heart, all the pressures of her job with the firm and still she insists on seeing to him*—springs forward, alarmed. But he pats his great-niece's hand and continues, eyes on one person alone.

They all freeze, watching, as he and Cordy approach.

"Truth to tell," he says, lifting Joan's hand to his cheek, which is now as wet as hers, "a boy from East Tennessee can't often wander into a party and find a girl who'd be a mighty dead ringer for Miss Rita Hayworth."

"Gray's Drugs," she tells him, shaking her head. "Eighty years ago. How does a man remember that sort of detail?"

"I remember you wore a lavender dress last time I saw you."

"Will, don't. Don't take us back to that day."

He presses her hand. "You got my word on that, no getting stuck in the muck of the past. Except for this one thing I got to say, maybe two . . ."

"Will—"

He lets her know with his eyes, the gentle of them, that he's not come for inflicting more hurt. The time for that is long past. "Hear me out now. First, we've had good lives, you and me. We've *done* good in this world. I kept up with you from a distance, you know."

"How did you—? Hans swore—"

"Hans never did say a word, no."

"So Hans wasn't the traitor," a young brunette at the table says—likely to herself—but Joannie, for all her years, hears her and turns.

"*I* was the traitor—that's how I thought of myself all those years. Hans and I were in touch. He once sent a photograph to me he took of the day you came back from the war, Will. I so loathed myself at the time, I wrote on the back, then ripped it in half and sent it back."

A blonde leans in to the brunette. "So she was the one who wrote the word *Traitor*."

Looking tenderly at Joannie, Will shakes his head. "It was Dov that told me."

Her lips form the word once before she manages sound. *"Dov?"*

"Before my old carrier, the *Enterprise*—after they got her up working again—took him back to England early in '46, he went out to the Episcopal burying ground to pay respects to your daddy's grave. Found the headstone with your name on it and saw the death date, November 22—and wondered how that could've happened so soon after we'd all been at Lovely Lane Chapel on May 10 . . ."

He doesn't say the words *wedding* or *jilted*. He won't thrust a knife when he can hold out a hand.

"Dov, he asked around on the island. His not knowing too many folks here once the radar training school was over, he'd mostly kept to himself, not gotten local news much, just what was going on back in Europe. Found out November 22 was the day folks found your shoes there on the beach, and then in the water, just washed up with the tide, was a bomber jacket with that little gremlin on it."

"Fifinella."

"That's the one. The tide'd washed up the jacket, and the pharmacist fellow, Mr. Gray, swore you'd never, *ever* have left it behind, so you had to have taken your own life, sure enough—especially after acting so strange, then disappearing from the island back a few months before. People mourned you hard, Joannie, I want you to know."

This next thing costs him to say it, but Will makes himself add, "Including Dov."

Joan draws a long breath, and Will touches a hand to her elbow in case she needs steadying. He won't let her fall.

"It was the date," Joan tells him, watching his face, "when the strong, fearless Joannie DuBarry I thought I was up and died. How it felt at the time, at least."

"You could have told me, you know. The truth."

"No. No, Will. I couldn't," she says—says it just as stubborn as he remembers. He'd loved that about her—admired it too—even when it nearly did him in.

He kisses the back of her hand. "I was back on the farm making plans for tracking you down, wherever you'd disappeared to, when Dov's letter arrived, telling me how you'd died. It liked to have killed me, Joannie."

"Will, I'm so very—"

"Wasn't your fault you couldn't love me like I did you back then. Another girl might could've batted her pretty eyes and pretended. Not you."

He squeezes her arm. "*Was* your fault, though, for letting me—all of us—suffer like that, us thinking you'd put an end to your own life." This time, he waits for what he needs to hear.

"It was cruel, Will. It was. But all I could think at the time was I had to make it all stop. In fact, I wasn't *thinking* at all. I'm so sorry, *so* sorry for the hurt I caused you."

He brings her hand back to his lips. "It was only years later, maybe the late '60s or so, I stumbled onto a *New York Times* feature on Doctors Without Borders forming in France. And durned if there wasn't a picture of one of their contracted pilots, a Samantha Mitchell. That liked to have killed me all over again, seeing your face back to life. Knowing you didn't want to be found."

"I thought I couldn't—"

"I know. At least I tried to know. I kept up with you since then, from a distance."

"I kept up with you, too, Will. From a distance."

"We've done *good* in this world, you and me," he says again. "That's a mighty rare gift, don't you think? To be able to say, when we're looking down the long coaster ride of life from the final stretch, *we've done good in this world?*"

As she stands now and leans into him, he feels his heart lift and flip like he's twenty.

"Second thing I got to say, and then I'll hush up."

"All right then. I'm listening."

"I said I'd love you till I died." Running a hand through his white thatch of hair and gesturing down his tall, now-crooked frame, he laughs. "I reckon I've sure enough proved my point."

Laughing with him, Joan pulls his head down to her height and uses both her thumbs to brush tears from his cheeks. "You've proved your point, Will, sure enough. You've proved your point."

Tears stream unchecked down her face. "You always did see the best in people. That's just who you were. That's who you still are, Will Dobbins."

From the bandstand, the singer is crooning. It's a song Will remembers well—so well, the heart-wrenching lyrics of a dream of a world where valleys bloom again and shepherds tend sheep and children go to bed safe in their own rooms.

"Everything," Joan says to him, "was at stake. Remember?"

"I do. I sure enough do." They both listen to several more bars of the song. "Love and laughter and peace. *Everything* was at stake."

Her long neck, still graceful for all its crepe paper pleats and wrinkles, swivels around now. She waves a hand toward the table. "Will,

I don't know if you've been introduced to these two young women, Hadley and Kitzie"—she stops there, like she needs more air to sound out this next. "Dov and Deborah's great-granddaughters."

"And yours," one of the young women offers.

"And . . . mine." Joannie nods like she's still awful dazed.

Will feels the smack of the news like a wave in the face, but he lets her lean into him as she says this, lets her gaze lock on his so she'll see him smile. So she sees that he isn't jealous—not anymore—but glad.

Glad for her sake. All that's ever mattered to him.

"Well, Lord have mercy. If this isn't some kind of family reunion, for sure."

"And, Will, this young woman right here, she's my neighbor who grew up on St. Simons Island. She's been assigned back here as clergy, the Reverend Doctor Felicia. Marshall's great-granddaughter."

"Marshall's," he repeats. "Lord have mercy. He was a war hero, you know. Mighty glad to know you all. Awful lot of questions I got to ask, so y'all don't hightail it out of here too fast tonight." He smiles at each of them but turns back to Joan.

She holds tight to his hand as if it's a rope swinging her over the pain of their past. "I'm feeling grateful for them, Will. For all this. For *you.*"

Will gazes out over the ocean as he holds out the crook of his arm for her. "We dreamed of a peace that would last, you recollect? A whole world of kindness and peace."

Behind the words, he's asking a question, one that haunts him all these years later, and Joan will know what he means. She always understood him that way.

She knows like he does that somewhere several oceans away are sunken Hellcats and Dauntless dive-bombers and aircraft carriers, all the trenches and fields and seas where hundreds of thousands have lost their lives in the endless cycle of wars before and since the war he and Joannie survived.

"That was our dream," she agrees, head tilted against his. "Still is. A world of kindness and peace. Something to work toward in our next hundred years."

Will grips his walker with one hand and holds the other out to Joannie. "May I have this dance to our song?"

Clutching her cane in her right and holding Will's hand with her left, Joan steps in closer. She is shorter and more slight than the girl he held all those decades ago, but to him, she hasn't changed. Her eyes still dance when she smiles up at him, the same eyes he watched scan the skies for flying conditions.

Together, they rotate and sway, the walker and cane a part of their dance right here beside the table.

Chapter 87
Hadley

A dance of two time-weathered bodies who've been through so much, they're both sweetly comical and something else I don't even know how to put into words.

"That may be . . . ," I begin.

"The most beautiful thing I've ever seen," Nick finishes. His eyes brim.

Another point in his favor, I think.

"Yes." I'm choked up now and can barely get out the next word. *"Precisely."*

Samantha's word is how I think of it now: *precisely.*

The walker and the cane and these two people who've loved each other in so many ways from so many miles away, through so many of their own and the world's battles, keep swaying to the big band's music.

Nick's glance cuts to me again, and we share a smile, both of us fixed on the couple swaying cheek to cheek and hand in hand, walker and cane.

Kitzie and Felicia and Nick and the great-niece Cordelia and I—even Ernst Hessler, who's found his way back—stay at the table as the two of them keep swaying and holding on to each other, keep gazing out over this island where their stories first crossed. We sit there until the deep darkness falls, and the band keeps playing on.

"Great-grandmother." I try the words in my mouth. "Great. Grandmother." My tongue is clumsy on the sounds—or maybe it's my brain still stiff and awkward with the idea, the whole outrageous idea of family.

Beside me, Nick holds his arm close to mine, palm up—an offer this time I'll take. I put my hand in his, grateful just to hold on to someone as we listen.

And also, his hand is not a bad one to hold, I decide. Maybe—*maybe*—even one I could trust.

With my free hand, I reach for Kitzie's. For the first time in weeks, she glows with growing good health—*please let that be true*—and contentment. We share a look, wide eyed and dazed, that only siblings and very old friends can share—whole conversations we've had and will have in that one look.

"Ferociously hopeful," I whisper.

"*Ferociously* hopeful," she echoes back.

So much to say. So much to ask. I feel numb and bewildered and alive all at once.

But right now, it's enough to sit here listening to the slide of trombones, the strut of the trumpets, the swagger of the sax, and imagine the radar towers that once reached from the sand to the sky, the lives they saved, the loves and the loss this beach has seen, its surf pounding on.

All of us at the table watch, mesmerized by the two people swaying beside us.

"Kindness," Will Dobbins murmurs into Samantha's ear just loud enough I can hear.

"And peace," she murmurs back as Will touches his lips to her forehead.

"Kindness," I echo, "and peace."

AUTHOR'S NOTE

If you've not read my books before, first, *warmest welcome* to you and thank you so much for spending time in these pages.

Second, I always assume most readers are, like me, endlessly curious about where story ideas come from, how they grow, and, in dual-time-line novels and historical fiction, which elements in the story are the historical figures and events and which are the fictional mortar or embellishments. So if you're intrigued by that behind-the-scenes sort of background, you've come to the right place—and also, please feel free to visit my website, www.joyjordanlake.com, where there's lots more info, as well as loads of photos for you or a book club to inspect. Also, please see the "Books and Articles" section of this novel for people and background research articles and books that inspired and informed *Echoes of Us.*

Maybe because I was paying very little attention in high school—always distracted by the next football game or Friday-night pizza—I seem in my adult years to be drawn to the events and struggles and personalities that absolutely startle me. Maybe that's why I so love the quote (which appears in an earlier novel of mine, *A Tangled Mercy*) from President Harry Truman: "The only new thing in this world is the history that you don't know." Writing novels, for me, is not only a passion and a privilege (and cheap therapy); it's also a way to rediscover all that my hardworking public school teachers or university professors might've dutifully mentioned but that fluttered right by me. I love getting to dig up or dust off those remarkable blow-your-socks-off sorts of individuals, movements, and incidents that have gotten buried or overlooked in our era—at least for those of us not paying attention.

For example, as it was to Kitzie and Hadley in this novel, it was news to me that more Americans were killed on the East Coast of the United States by U-boats than those killed in Pearl Harbor. Always intrigued—and sometimes appalled—by the complexity of the human spirit, I was fascinated to read about the actual captain of *U-123*, Reinhard Hardegan. This book's fictional U-boat chief engineer Hans Hessler's struggles with whether or not to desert from the Kriegsmarine are based partly on Hardegan's postwar statements that by at least 1942, he knew his country was headed by a madman—and that he himself therefore was fighting for one. Hardegan did, in fact, attempt to save sailors of enemy ships he'd torpedoed, contacting neutral ships and in some cases offering to pick up survivors in his own boat. So the scene in which *U-123*'s captain does just this, as outlandish as it seems, is based on Hardegan's actual practice, according to a number of survivors.

Regarding the brave merchant marines: although I had an old friend who attended Kings Point Academy and became a US Merchant Marine, I had no idea how much they sacrificed during World War II and, because they were not officially military personnel, how little credit they received. Like the character Will Dobbins in this book, they did, in fact, have to purchase their own uniforms. According to the National WWII Museum, a higher percentage of merchant marines lost their lives between 1939 and 1945 than in any US military branch: 9,521 in total.

If you've not visited St. Simons Island, Georgia, by all means put that on your must-travel list. The lighthouse, mentioned repeatedly in this novel, is lovely, and the view from its top is absolutely worth the climb. The museum at the lighthouse will get you started on your exploration, and you must not miss the related World War II Home Front Museum not far to the north on the island. The Coastal Georgia Historical Society staff in both places are delightful and offer a wealth of knowledge. The King and Prince, serving as the Naval Radar Training School (NRTS) in this novel, returned to its original purpose as a beach resort, and although it has grown considerably since 1945, many of the most charming historical elements remain, including the stained glass in the historic Delegal Room. Visitors to the hotel or its restaurant, Echo, can inspect a number of pictures from its days as the NRTS that hang on the King and Prince walls.

If you've known very little about the Women Airforce Service Pilots (WASP) before now, I'm right there with you. Until the 1970s, the WASPs had, for many of us, been mostly lost to memory, except for brief mentions in history textbooks. Like so many other World War II veterans, many of these women spoke little of their service even to their families until many years later. In 1976, when the US Air Force incorrectly announced that for the first time, women would be trained to fly military aircraft, this feisty group of women rose up as one and pointed out that they had, in fact, been the first. Their records were unsealed for the first time, and in 1977 under President Jimmy Carter, the WASPs finally became recognized as military veterans. In 2009 under President Barack Obama, the WASPs were awarded Congressional Gold Medals. Stories of incredible moxie and sacrifice abound about this group of women, and I've included several of their stories in this novel. Although Joannie DuBarry is a fictional character, a number of other WASP characters are historical, including Hazel Ah Ying Lee, one of two Asian women pilots. As mentioned in this novel, for example, Lee was, in fact, riding in early pilot training with a flight instructor when he decided to impress her with a loop, and because her seat belt wasn't latched properly, she fell headfirst out of the open cockpit. Engaging her parachute, she landed safely and, dragging the chute behind her, walked back to base.

Also included in these pages, Mabel Rawlinson, who volunteered to take her friend Marion Hanrahan's place during night training, did die in a crash and its subsequent fire, probably in part because of a faulty cockpit latch. Sadly, it was also true, as reflected in the novel, that when a WASP was killed in the service of her country, as thirty-eight of them were, the US government didn't provide a flag for the funeral or even to have the body shipped home, since the WASPs were not technically military. Collectively, they flew seventy-seven different types of military aircraft over sixty-six million miles.

Regarding the scenes in which two WASPs are asked to fly the B-29 by Colonel Paul Tibbets, the spirit of the story is accurate—a ploy dreamed up by Tibbets in the face of the new heavy bomber's reputation for catching on fire and killing test pilots. But instead of the fictional characters, the actual two women pilots were the courageous Dora Dougherty and Dorothea Johnson. By all means, read further about this event and their lives.

The WASPs have their own fascinating museum in Sweetwater, Texas, complete with interactive exhibits (I was an epic fail on the flight simulator), informative videos, and even an entire hangar of the actual planes on which the women trained. Not an aviation expert myself, I still found it enthralling. Although, tragically, no Black women were allowed to be WASPs, despite the existence of such superb aviators as Bessie Coleman, the museum includes an exhibit dedicated to notable Black female pilots of the time.

A sidenote about the term WASP: sharp-eyed readers will note the trickiness of grammar with a term like *Women Airforce Service Pilots* that includes a plural—so when to use *WASP* and when *WASPs*. The editors and I did our best to prioritize making the meaning clear for the reader.

The invention of radar and the role of fighter direction was something I'd frankly thought ridiculously little about, other than watching a few Hollywood war movies where radar got featured in a few scenes. (Thank you to my husband for insisting I watch *Das Boot* with him and keep learning more than I'd intended to about U-boats.) The crucial role of fighter directors is featured in superb interactive exhibits at the World War II Home Front Museum, at which my younger daughter Jasmine proved her quick-thinking mettle and I proved I'd have been sent immediately to swabbing the decks.

The character Dov Silverberg, an instructor at the NRTS, is based on an actual British instructor—about whom I learned only that he, like Dov, was sent to St. Simons in exchange for an American—and on comments by Curator Mimi Rogers regarding a fighter direction instructor at the NRTS who wrote heart-wrenching letters about his struggles feeling that he should be out with the men he'd trained on the front lines, taking the same life-and-death risks, rather than teaching in the safety and relative comfort of the King and Prince.

Across the causeway from St. Simons Island, the Ritz Theatre in Brunswick, Georgia, originally built in 1899 as the Grand Opera House, was, as described in the novel, one of the few air-conditioned buildings at the time and—given the severe housing shortage once the town began building Liberty ships—also became a place where workers grabbed a few hours of sleep before relinquishing a seat to the next shift. The Ritz remains in operation today, hosting movie screenings and live performances, including the fabulous Golden Isles Penguin Project performances each summer, dear to the hearts of my own extended family. On the day of this writing, I've just purchased my own tickets to this summer's Penguin Project show. I encourage you to look it up and admire the remarkable people behind it.

The use of Pervitin by the Third Reich as a drug to keep its military personnel fighting, flying, and sailing without the usual need for food and sleep and operating with fewer inhibitions has been well documented, but was still a surprise to me. Please see the "Books and Articles" section for a key source on this subject. Scholars may argue over the prevalence of this drug in the Wehrmacht, but its use at all intrigued me.

I need to admit that Hog Wallow, which the character Will Dobbins cites as the original name of his hometown (and mine) on Signal Mountain, Tennessee, was the name I distinctly recalled from my own very first (possibly grade school) research paper on the history of our area. To be honest, however, I can't find any sources now to back up what I recall from that first, no doubt feeble, scholarly effort, so I invite readers to either assume that gem of a name has been temporarily lost to memory and some reader-hero will email me someday with a precious reference to Hog Wallow, or else we simply all agree to call my memory faulty and just enjoy the name.

For those of you who, like me, are animal lovers, the Marsh Tackies, descendants of horses brought by Spanish colonists and featured in one scene of this novel, are now considered a critically endangered breed, with only a few hundred still in existence. As described in the story, breeds such as Tennessee Walkers brought in to assist with coastal surveillance during World War II proved to be disastrous. The Marsh Tackies—strong, small, and unflappable—once numbered on the Carolina coast in the thousands and served in critical battles during the American Revolution as well as coastal patrol during World War II.

If you've read other novels of mine, you'll know I tend to be drawn to periods in history of tumultuous cultural changes and to people who navigated those changes in remarkable ways—both remarkably horrific and remarkably courageous. As Hadley observes in this novel, "I can't help but wonder if any of us see the drama of our own stories as they unfold: the unlikely beginnings, the crises and triumphs and sorrows, however small or stage worthy."

Please note that while I'm decidedly not a historian but a storyteller, I always hope that if readers are surprised or intrigued by obscure bits of history in novels, they will dive deep down a rabbit hole, reading actual historians' accounts of the people and events. Book club members so often take up this challenge (amazing what the combo of wine, research, and friendship will do!), and we novelists love and applaud you.

This storyteller-with-history-to-share case holds true with, for example, the challenges represented in Marshall, who in one scene holds up the Double V for victory abroad in the war and at home with civil rights for Americans of color, or in another scene has to watch Nazi officers allowed by Geneva Convention rules to eat in a restaurant in which he himself as a Black American in the 1940s could not dine. For an article on the subject, see Matthew Taub's "'Are We Not American Soldiers?' When the U.S. Military Treated German POWs Better Than Black Troops" in *Time*. Whether or not a restaurant on St. Simons as described in the novel existed in the 1940s, the stark difference between how American citizens of color were treated relative to German POWs was painfully real. Regarding Marshall's service with the 761st Tank Battalion, this was an actual unit of men who proved their bravery under fire, even in the face of the doubts of some top military leaders of the day. Please see several book titles in the "Books and Articles" section on the heroes of the 761st.

If you're a fan of the Wright brothers, you'll be thrilled to know that Orville Wright was, as he appears in the novel, a big proponent of the WASP program in particular and women aviators in general.

As to those POWs in American camps, more than four hundred thousand German, more than fifty thousand Italian, and approximately five thousand Japanese prisoners were, in fact, brought over from Great Britain and housed in camps throughout the United States. Enlisted men were required to work, though they were paid a set rate for their labor, and some German POWs did, in fact, serve meals to the officers at the radar training school housed at the King and Prince. In these POW camps on American soil, there were documented cases of Nazi prisoners harassing and even killing other German prisoners who were not loyal to Hitler. Beginning in 1945, as the Allied forces began liberating death camps and exposing the horrors they found there, POWs in the United States were required to watch footage of these camps. Like Hans Hessler, some POWs reacted by burning their uniforms, while others refused to believe the films represented the truth. See a fascinating article from the *Washington Post*, Michael Farquhar's "Enemies Among Us: German POWs in America."

If you know little or nothing, as I did, about the aircraft carrier *Enterprise*, nicknamed the Big E, it's decidedly worth some rabbit-holing. I've represented only the smallest sliver of it in this novel, but I chose it not only because it was in the right part of the globe at the points I needed it to be for the plot but also because I found myself intrigued by its story and imagining the lives of the three thousand men who served on it and more who landed on its decks.

Again, thank you so very much for joining me in this story.

BOOKS AND ARTICLES

From these authors and their work, I learned enough to spark my imagination, and I hope the readers of this novel will, as well: David L. Boslaugh's *Radar and the Fighter Directors*; Robert Buderi's *The Invention That Changed the World: How a Small Group of Radar Pioneers Won the Second World War and Launched a Technical Revolution*; Tracy Campbell's *The Year of Peril: America in 1942*; Alistair Cooke's *The American Home Front: 1941–1942*; Jingle Davis's *Island Time: An Illustrated History of St. Simons Island, Georgia*; Matthew F. Delmont's *Half American: The Epic Story of African Americans Fighting World War II at Home and Abroad*; Michael Farquhar's "Enemies Among Us: German POWs in America," *Washington Post*, September 9, 1997; Michael Gillen's *Merchant Marine Survivors of World War II: Oral Histories of Cargo Carrying Under Fire*; Kareem Abdul-Jabbar and Anthony Walton's *Brothers in Arms: The Epic Story of the 761st Tank Battalion, WWII's Forgotten Heroes*; Patricia Morris's *St. Simons Island* (Images of America series); Norman Ohler's *Blitzed: Drugs in the Third Reich*; P. O'Connell Pearson's *Fly Girls: The Daring American Women Pilots Who Helped Win WWII*; editor and compilers Thora Olsen Kimsey and Sonja Olsen Kinard's *Memories from the Marshes of Glynn: World War II*; Bert A. Shields's *Air Pilot Training*; and Matthew Taub's "'Are We Not American Soldiers?' When the U.S. Military Treated German POWs Better Than Black Troops," *Time*, July 28, 2020.

ACKNOWLEDGMENTS

I always look forward to the chance to thank in print many of those who've contributed time, humor, wisdom, companionship, sangria, chocolate, and so much more to the process of writing a book, but I also dread knowing I can't possibly name every last person who's been life-giving during the course of a book's writing, so let me start by saying a general, heartfelt, gut-deep thank-you.

I often start my books by falling in love with a place, then learning more about its history, peculiarities, and little-known people or events as a story idea begins to take root. In this case, though, a love for St. Simons Island is something I was born into—going back, in fact, to my great-grandparents. As I mention in this book's dedication, my late father, Adiel Moncrief Jordan, loved St. Simons Island more than any-where on Earth—and he'd traveled quite a bit. Part of his attachment to the place was its natural beauty and its multilayered, often tragic history, but part of it also was his finding a kindred spirit in his oldest first cousin, Gwen Moncrief Mayberry. I'm so grateful for reconnec-tions in recent years with that side of the family, many of whom grew up on the island: the Moncriefs, Mayberrys, Shedds, Jacksons, Whites, Mayberry-Whites, and Boricks. Through my own parents, not only my brother David and I but also our spouses and kids have built many the drip-castle village and precious memory on those beaches: the Jordans, Jordan-Lakes, and Jackson-Jordans.

Archivists are so often the unsung heroes of any historical writer's research, and this book was no exception. Archivist Jared Galloway was of great assistance at the National Naval Aviation Museum in Pensacola, Florida. Ann Haub, the collections director at the National WASP WWII Museum in Sweetwater, Texas, was so generous with her time and stories, including those about her own mother, who was a mechanic with the WASP. Thank you also to others on staff there, including Justin Hesterly, digital archivist and social media manager, and Connor Aycock, archivist, for the help and hospitality. What a labor of love the WASP Museum is!

On St. Simons Island at the Coastal Georgia Historical Society, Curator Mimi Rogers was incredibly kind to sit down with me and answer a million questions with patience and enthusiasm. At the World War II Home Front Museum on the island, Julya Lizarralde, the museum's then-director, graciously met with me even though the museum itself was officially closed for installation of a new interactive exhibit. Volunteer docent at the Home Front Museum, Paula Galland, was the most bubbly and passionate of any museum docent I've ever met—and, as it happens, turned out to be one of my cousin Mimi Mayberry-White's best friends. Thank you also to members of the St. Simons African American Coalition, who helped answer questions and who are doing marvelous work preserving Black history on the island.

Betsy Christie and fellow writer Suzanne Robertson courageously volunteered to rush-read an early version of this story, and they provided truly invaluable feedback—as well as the gift of ongoing deep friendship. My longtime writer friend Milton Brasher-Cunningham provided not only a timely bottle of Writer's Tears whiskey and the inspiration of his own work but also the nickname of one character, Will's sister Biscuit, a name worth a story all to herself. Ginger Brasher-Cunningham continues to inspire me with her artistry and power with the spoken word, and with a loyalty and infectious laughter that has spanned decades now. Susan Bahner Lancaster, a dear friend since age five, continues to be a source of incredible joy, authenticity, and great goodness, even when one or both of us have been living through grief. Elizabeth Rogers awes me with culinary creativity that not only inspires the imagination but also creates an unmatched community of welcome. She is also the savvy mixologist behind this story's mocktail Detection (recipe on my website). Robbie Pinter's flowers and deeply centered spirituality feed the soul. Liz Waggener continues to provide not only unflagging friendship but also retreats where guests bond, rest, and heal—and where books are written on the porch.

Gloria White-Hammond, medical doctor and African Methodist Episcopal minister, continues to be a model of courage and kindness to me and is one of several clergywoman friends and family members who provided the inspiration for the Reverend Doctor Felicia Hammond in this book. Jay Beard provided invaluable insight as I struggled to paint the beauty and pain of the relationship between Sam and Marshall in this novel that could not, in the 1940s, be fully named. The way in which Marshall later sits "in those ellipses, that silence" is thanks to Jay. Scott Royal has given his words as treasured gifts before in my family's life and gave them again in responding to an early copy of this novel with his own immense compassion and heart—and literary instincts that far surpass mine.

Social work professional (and also my niece) Olivia Jackson-Jordan graciously answered a number of questions about her field, including about foster kids. Benita Walker is, to use one of Dov's British phrases, an absolute brick, a friend of feistiness and faithfulness.

To my Companions group, the Discovery class, and the Race and Faith group of BUMC, Gal. 3.28, Beach Mamas friends, you all are a beautiful source of learning, challenge, kindness, and support— what a rare and precious gift. Janet Byers and Sherrie Cavin connect and empower everyone around them, including me. Judith Bone and Angela Deane are sister-friends in valuing peace. Mandy Austin and Lisa Beavers are such sources of insight, whether on books or the human condition. Gigi Johns and Dana Orange are rocks of strength and goodness. Michael Thomas, salesman extraordinaire, takes the prize for disseminating more copies of my books than any other single person and is a tower of kindness. Kelly Shushok is one of my favorite sources of hilarity as well as compassion in every journey. No idea what I'd do without any of you, but it wouldn't be pretty.

I'm grateful for fellow Blue Sky Book Chat authors Thelma Adams, Barbara Davis, Paulette Kennedy, Christine Nolfi, Marilyn Rothstein, Patricia Sands, and Susan Walters, as well as the generous—and fun—writers of the Historical Novel Society Midsouth and the Society of Children's Book Writers and Illustrators. So many other writer friends provided perspective, laughter, and inspiration along the way, including Dana Carpenter, Jodi Daynard, Camille DiMaio, J.T. Ellison, Jane Healey, Patti Callahan Henry, Bren McClain, Lisa Patton, Rochelle Weinstein, Barbara Claypole White, Sam Woodruff, and many others. Ariel Lawhon, who shared with me many of our early how-the-heck-does-this-industry-work days, continues to earn my admiration for her gorgeous books. WriterFest impresarios Ami McConnell and Sara Wigal not only are authors themselves and leaders of one of the best conferences for creatives around but also have become kindred spirits. Thank you to friend and brilliant Author Genie Kerry Schafer and to talented Belmont student intern Kendall Miller for help with newsletters, social media, and promotion. Laura Kantarowski and Mike Bates continue to be two of the savviest readers and the best of humans.

When writers say it takes a village to create a book, they're not kidding. Elisabeth Weed and Nicole Cunningham at The Book Group (TBG) have, as always, been such sources of insight, guidance, early reading, and encouragement—the absolute Dream Agents if there ever were any. Thank you for not giving up on me. Thank you, too, to DJ Kim at TBG, always a delight to deal with.

I'm so very grateful to get to partner with Danielle Marshall, editorial director of Lake Union, who somehow manages to do all the things, even four days postsurgery. She continues to be a remarkable champion for her writers, and I continue to feel so privileged to create books together with her and the rest of the crackerjack Lake Union team. Thank you to copyeditor Anna Barnes, proofreader Jenna Justice, and cover designer Kathleen Lynch of Black Kat Design. Developmental editor Jodi Warshaw is one of those industry professionals who knows how to call out the best in a writer with not only insight and honest critique but also warmth and encouragement. I am in awe of her gifts.

As always, I'm grateful to Rae Ann Parker, RJ Witherow, Elyse Adler, Hannah Peterson, and all the magnificent folks at Parnassus Books who host book launch parties and who make the book biz feel like a bunch of kindred spirits linking hands and dancing in the meadow (which, okay, it's not always). Thank you for being a crucial hub of Nashville culture and the best indie bookseller in the United States.

While my mother, Diane Jordan, is a very different person from the character Samantha Mitchell, I learn every week from my mom never to underestimate the intelligence, emotional strength, spiritual wisdom, and joy for living of those who've seen many decades.

As always, my husband, Todd Lake, has been my eager fellow adventurer, beloved head research assistant par excellence, and on this book, live-in German studies consultant. I continue to be thankful—and a little startled—every day that two such utterly different people could actually be so often in sync now (who would've guessed?) and, go figure, more intrigued by each other than ever, thirty-five years down a long and winding and not-always-easy road.

My young adult kids and their spouses continue to teach me so much, not only in their own respective areas of expertise (how cool to be at a stage of life when your kids know so much that you don't!) but also about being ferociously loving, forgiving, inclusive, and faithful. I am so unspeakably grateful to you. The way each of you—Jasmine Jordan-Lake, Justin and Mally Jordan-Lake, and Julia and Shelby Jordan-Lake—combines, in your own way, compassion and creativity with activism and humor and love inspires me every single day. Thank you for making this world—and our family—a better, brighter, more loving place. I'm so grateful, too, to my brother and his marvelous family for all the trails hiked, the meals shared, the waves ridden, the theology discussed, and the adventures yet to come: David, Beth, Olivia, Catherine, Jory, and Chris.

I'm enormously grateful to the authors of the books listed in the "Books and Articles" section. Any mistakes with historical facts or nuances in this novel are not because of the writers from whom I learned or the archivists I interviewed but are either creative license (see Author's Note) or my fault alone.

And finally, thank you so very much to *you* for reading. Please feel free to check out my website, www.joyjordanlake.com, to read more behind-the-scenes stories on any of my books or to be in touch. I'm so very grateful for your time and interest. Here's to you, and to building a world of kindness and peace.

ESPECIALLY FOR BOOK CLUBS

1. Hadley Jacks makes fun of her own store of World War II knowledge ("more rust than substance") and is startled to learn that more people were killed by U-boats on the East Coast of the United States during the war than at Pearl Harbor. What bits of history in this novel were new to you?

2. Sibling relationships feature prominently in *Echoes of Us*, both the bond between twins (Joannie and Sam) and between sisters (Hadley and Kitzie). At one point, Sam "squeezes [Joan's] shoulder, a brotherly grip that's part comfort, part pinch, as if he wants her to remember his unique role as tormentor, protector, and friend, as only a brother can be." At another point, Hadley is annoyed with Kitz for pretending to ignore her and fumes: "sisters don't miss a flicker of an eyelash on each other." If you have a sibling, talk about that bond—or perhaps the lack of one—and what might have resonated with you from the story regarding brothers and sisters.

3. Have you read, researched, or watched documentaries or movies that feature WWII submarines; aircraft carriers; or planes, including the Women Airforce Service Pilots (WASP); and the development of radar? If you'd

volunteered for or been drafted for the Second World War, where—if at all—would you have wanted to serve?

4. A number of characters in the novel feel betrayed—sometimes in small decisions, such as Hadley and Kitz always needing to agree on a job before taking it, and on being straightforward with one another—and sometimes in larger, life-altering ways. Who do you view as the biggest traitors, and who do you feel compassion for?

5. Have you ever visited St. Simons Island, Jekyll Island, or Sea Island, Georgia? Talk about your experience of the natural terrain and the history there. One scene in *Echoes of Us* mentions the new historical marker and the spot at St. Simons's Dunbar Creek, Igbo Landing, where in 1803 a group of captured West African people who were shackled to one another walked into the water and drowned rather than submit to being enslaved. The island's history also includes a significant eighteenth-century battle between the Spanish and English (later named the "Battle of Bloody Marsh"). If you're a history buff, what did you already know about the Golden Isles of Georgia, and what would you like to research more?

6. *Echoes of Us* explores a range of ways in which people experience love, from familial devotion to ferociously devoted friendship to romantic attraction and passion. Were you frustrated or furious with any of the characters' decisions—and when did you find yourself sympathetic or heartbroken?

7. Which characters did you find yourself rooting hardest for, and why?

8. Several characters in the novel, particularly Joannie and Sam, engage in conversations about whether or not

war can be justified—and if so, when. At one point, Sam comments, "I'll give you this: maybe most wars are people taking revenge on people they hate—treating weapons of war like really big toys. We tell ourselves it's good versus evil, because we want the excuse to hate and hate hard. This time, though, this time was different. I couldn't sit by and watch any more than you could." Are there wars in your country's history you view as tragically necessary versus ones you view as utterly unjustified? Where do the First and Second World Wars or other military conflicts fit on that spectrum for you? When is pacifism—the view that violence only ever breeds violence, and one must stand boldly for peace— the most honorable position?

9. Marshall Hammond serves his country first by building Liberty ships, then only later (having been rejected for a number of combat roles because of his race) in the 761st tank battalion. Were you aware of the story of the 761st and its bravery? And if you're only just now looking it up, what strikes you about the story?

10. How much did you know about the Women Airforce Service Pilots (WASP) before reading this novel? And if *Echoes of Us* nudged you to do more reading about these remarkable women, what have you learned?

11. Were you aware that several hundred thousand prisoners of war were brought to the United States during World War II? Did you, like Hadley, find it startling that these enlisted POWs would have served meals to Allied officers? If you're curious to learn more, you can find online instances in which some POWs maintained correspondences with their American employers long after the war ended.

12. What reveals in the story did you suspect were coming, and what took you by surprise? Who was your favorite character in the novel, and why?

For more book club resources, including photographs and recipes, please visit joyjordanlake.com.

ABOUT THE AUTHOR

Joy Jordan-Lake is the #1 Amazon bestselling author of thirteen books, including *A Bend of Light*; *Under a Gilded Moon*, a 2023 North Carolina Reads selection; *A Tangled Mercy*, an Editors' Choice recipient from the Historical Novel Society; *Blue Hole Back Home*, winner of the Christy Award for Best First Novel; and three children's books.

Raised in the foothills of the southern Appalachians, Joy spent many a summer vacation on St. Simons Island, Georgia, a place of heartbreaking and surprising history. She holds two master's degrees and a PhD in English and has taught literature and writing at several universities. Now living outside Nashville, she is startled to find only the ten-pound rescue pup still living at home full time, the kids launching to college, getting married, and building careers of their own. She and her husband console themselves with hiking to waterfalls and traveling to story-worthy settings.

Joy loves to connect with readers. You can visit her at www.joyjordanlake.com.